TWELFTH NIGHT

TWELFTH NIGHT

MICHAEL LLEWELLYN

Kensington Books

http://www.kensingtonbooks.com

KENSINGTON BOOKS are published by

Kensington Publishing Corp.
850 Third Avenue
New York, NY 10022

Library of Congress Card Catalog Number: 96-077847
ISBN 1-57566-082-2

First Printing: February, 1997
10 9 8 7 6 5 4 3 2 1

Printed in the United States of America

For
Delores, Jeanine, and Teresa . . .
Survivors All.

ACKNOWLEDGMENTS

I am deeply indebted to the superb staff of the Historic New Orleans Collection, especially Jessica Travis and Pamela Arceneaux. I'm also grateful to Courtney Ann Sarpy, French Consulate, New Orleans, and Kimberly Hanger, Louisiana State Museums, the U.S. mint.

On a personal note, many thanks to JoAnn Ambrosino, Linda Sampson Burd, Bethany Ewald Bultman, Marylou Christovich, Billy Edwards, Amy Garvey, Shelley Holl, John E. Jacks, George Dureau, John Ryan, Henri Schindler, Richard Sexton, Blair and Mark Sollmeyer, Anne Strachan, Robert Strader, my agents Jim and Liz Trupin and my editor Paul Dinas.

Special thanks to Douglas A. Mendini for mining that extra bit of gold.

INTRODUCTION

The year is 1857, New Orleans' Golden Era when cotton and rice, sugar, and slavery buoyed the exotic city to rare wealth as America's fourth metropolis. It is half a century since Napolean ceded Louisiana to the young United States, yet relations between French Creoles and Americans remain strained. Downriver lies the *carré de la ville*, last bastion of the old Creole families, while upriver is the Garden District of the American *nouveau riche*. The neutral ground is Canal Street.

These two widely disparate cultures share neither language nor religion, customs nor cuisine. The xenophobic Catholic Creoles dismiss *les Américains* as greedy bourgeoise boors while the industrious Protestant Americans find the Creoles impossibly aloof and decadent, obsessed with opera, theater, balls, and dueling. Business dealings frequently wrest a crossing of paths, but diehards on both sides of Canal resist social commingling.

Those attempting to bridge the schism often flirted with disaster. This is the story of two such pilgrims meeting on Twelfth Night and confronting their fragile fate on Ash Wednesday. Their destiny, unfolding against the tawdry glamour and raw violence of Mardi Gras, is as heady as carnival itself.

PART ONE

⬚

The Lords of Misrule

Give thyself, but give thyself not away.
This is the lesson of the long strange road of love.
—D. H. Lawrence

CHAPTER 1

Inside the carriage, a malacca cane rapped the roof so fiercely the startled horse struggled to rear. The driver sawed the reins hard left, wresting saccadic control as the hansom lurched and listed through a sea of mud that was the Rue Dauphine. Rain sheeted across the banquettes and exploded in streams from gallery gutters overhead, rendered rudderless by gusting wind. The coachman grimaced at a second rap. A third. Then a voice boomed from below.

"*Mon Dieu*, Hippolyte! Use the whip on that animal or I'll use it on you! You're rattling our teeth down here!"

As Hippolyte shouted back, pleading desperately, he braced for the inevitable reaction. "But the streets are slick as glass, Michie Hilaire! The horse keeps losing his footing. He—"

Hilaire Blancard's cane slammed into the roof again, and Hippolyte reluctantly reached for the whip. Hearing it sing above his head, the terrified horse panicked, this time successfully rearing and very nearly hurling Justine to the floor of the carriage. Blancard was furious, growing rage fueled by a bellyful of whiskey. Justine started to address her husband, thought better of it and remained still.

Blancard seized the handle of the door and pushed. It gaped scarcely a seam before a rain-laden blast sealed it shut. Blancard seethed and tried again, retreating when water blasted inside, splashing perfectly varnished boots. Nothing angered him more than lost control. Hippolyte brought the horse back under control and steered it onto the Rue Orléans. The *Théâtre d'Orléans* was only a block away.

"We're not far now, Hilaire," Justine ventured, cautiously. "I've never seen you so eager to get to the opera."

"Well, I am," Blancard grumbled. He seemed to study the cane. "I can't believe the weather is so damned uncooperative."

She started to suggest that surely the inclement weather would prompt the conductor to hold the curtain, but instead concentrated on the malacca cane, now tightly gripped in her husband's fist. She studied it from the corner of her eye, observing every detail from the feathery weight of the rattan to the cruel, graceful curls of filigreed gold. How heavy such a light stick could weigh, especially when wielded with force.

Justine looked away from the cane and tugged the velvet cloak more tightly around her, diverting herself with irrelevant thought as she often did. The cape was one of Madame Clovis' finest creations, and she prayed the rain didn't ruin it.

"We'll be inside soon enough," she offered.

Though not as soon as she wished. Justine was just as anxious to flee the hansom but for vastly disparate reasons. For her, the opera had always been a grand escape, a majestic flight swollen by the magic of Auber's *La Muette de Portici* or Halévy's *La Juive*. Without fail the triumph of some romantic baritone buoyed by the orchestra or the melancholy wail of a wronged soprano summoned Justine into a world far within herself, one of pure freedom no one could touch. Certainly not her husband. How she yearned for it!

As for Hilaire's eagerness? Well, the infamous *Salle d'Orléans* was just next door.

Alas, their flight was not to be so quick. The rains had forced absolutely everyone to take conveyances that November night. The mud-slicked cobblestones before the *Théâtre d'Orléans* were chaos as carriages of all kinds jostled for position, beleaguered coachmen battling to secure the driest point of disembarkation. Top hats glistened and the whites and reds of satin-lined capes flashed as gentlemen leapt free of landaus, barouches, and hansoms, even a few hackneys, drawing cosseted ladies from the womblike warmth of tufted leather interiors. All then proceeded to make the mad dash to a canopy hastily erected that afternoon when threatening skies eventually made good on their promise.

Hippolyte finally jockeyed the carriage to the front of the line, and the Blancards joined the throng funneling toward the opera house. Grateful to escape the drunken anger smoldering inside the carriage, Justine breathed deeply of the cool autumnal air, ribs crushed against too tight stays as she strained to fill her lungs with air. She grew briefly heady and steadied herself on Hilaire's arm just before they were swept up in the wave of fervent opera-goers.

Such exuberance was contagious. The diehard members of the Creole *crème de la crème* still dominated the local social strata despite fierce competition from those impossible upstarts, *les Américains*. For half a century, since a cash-starved Napoleon sold *La Louisiane* to the young United States to finance his dreams of empire, the haughty Creoles had dug in and refused to be dislodged by the newcomers. Indeed, why should they yield anything simply because the French tricolor had been replaced by a strange flag in the *Place d'Armes?* The Creoles were fortunate, they reminded one another, to be *sorti de la cuisse de Jupiter,* cut from the thigh of Jupiter, and therefore from a better, more genteel cloth. As such they could scarcely be bothered by those *gens du commun* living across the Rue Canal.

Born a Fonteneau, one of *La Nouvelle-Orléans'* first families, Justine knew all of them, at least all who mattered. Her husband's family enjoyed nowhere near so fine a pedigree, but they had been allowed access to the Creole inner sanctum after his marriage to Justine. It was quietly understood, but never discussed of course, that Marin Fonteneau had found the ideal way to replenish the depleted family coffers by marrying the angelic Justine to wealthy Hilaire Blancard. When families passed mutual muster, arranged marriages were the rule among the Creoles, not the exception, and the bride had no say in the matter. Nor was love a part of the sacred bargain. Justine was barely sixteen when she took her vows in the venerable St. Louis Cathedral, without hesitation and certainly without question. True, the Blancards were scarcely a generation from shopkeepers, but . . . well, allowances must be made in such trying times with so much pressure from the Americans uptown.

Justine's face wore a fixed smile as they moved to the dress circle, to seats occupied by the Fonteneaus since the *Théâtre d'Orléans* opened in 1813. From there she nodded politely and smiled to old acquaintances (never anything so bourgeois as a wave!) and waited for the curtain to rise. Tradition restricted the real visiting to intermission.

She loved these seats in the heart of the sweeping horseshoe, always felt like an empress surveying her glamourous court. Dress circle was divided into tidy little compartments, each containing four seats. Immediately behind were two rows of single seats, at the end of which were loges. Justine's eye frequently strayed there, specifically to the *loges grilles,* curtained boxes whose occupants were a mystery. Behind, pregnant ladies took discreet refuge, as did families in mourning. But so did gentlemen escorting women of questionable virtue. Below, on the *par-*

quet, were the nonsubscribers where, unfortunately, full dress was not obligatory. Granted gentlemen were required to wear white gloves and jackets, but their choice of boots and trousers was often far less appropriate. Their ladies, if indeed they brought them, dressed with even less care. Justine found it an amusing if sometimes rambunctious crowd.

What intrigued her most, however, and should have been of no concern to any proper Creole lady, was the uppermost tier reserved for the *gens de coleur libre.* Always among these free Negroes was a young woman or two who not only competed favorably but outshone even the most ravishing white beauties in the dress circle below. They too flaunted elegant silks, satins, and jewels dazzling brilliantly beneath the glow of chandeliers. They were as spoiled and pampered as the Creole ladies and just as eagerly displayed by proud fathers, brothers, and husbands. And on rare occasions, Justine thought uneasily, they looked just as fair, from a candlelit distance anyway. She recalled overheard tales about such women, men as well, who went to France or up North where they passed for white among people less skilled at recognizing the signs. The whole matter was utterly distasteful to her, yet Justine couldn't help wondering how white these Negroes would appear if they were under her close scrutiny. For years she had played a secret game, to be on the alert for such women and make the comparison herself. She had no idea why. She once thought of telling Christophe about her fascination, but feared even he could not be trusted with such an intimate and indiscreet admission.

Christophe, she thought, glancing at the empty seats behind her. Where *was* he?

As her eyes fanned across the rows of elegantly dressed colored people, she was caught by a familiar face and smile. There was Toinette Clovis, her dressmaker, wife of the tailor Bernard, both of whom did work for the Blancards, indeed all the Creoles of substance. Dear Toinette whose gold-rimmed eyeglasses were always at odds with her chic clothes, a luxury she could indulge because of her profession and her access to *Le Folette* and the *Journal des Demoiselles,* Paris publications dictating the *dernier cri* in fashion. There was much whispered criticism because she occasionally outdressed the white ladies, but Justine quietly admired her. Whenever she visited the fancy little shop in the Rue Royale, called simply *La Mode,* she was tempted to linger, and not just because of the delicious fabrics and gossip about what the new Empress Eugénie was wearing.

There was something about Toinette's manner that caught and held her, a genuine warmth that welcomed, not merely patronized. She had encountered this in precious few people, dear Christophe among them, and it was not altogether comforting. Although she had not, she felt that she could tell Toinette anything, even those deepest secrets she dared not share with Christophe, and the fact that Toinette was colored disturbed her not at all. She wondered why her face flushed hot when Toinette caught her eye and smiled sweetly. It was as if the woman knew something, could see through the elegant, reserved facade she so carefully cultivated. At that moment, it so unnerved her that she nodded brusquely and looked away.

Silver flashed as Hilaire took a heavy swig from a flask before tucking it back inside his jacket. He was oblivious to her, to everyone around him as he drank again. Justine propped her elbow on the arm of the chair and studied him. It was difficult to believe this was the same man she had married twelve years ago. True, vestiges of his good looks remained and, at fifty-one, he still cut a handsome figure, especially now in full-dress coat and white kid gloves, jet black hair only slightly invaded by gray temples. But the once chiseled features were turning coarse and jowly, and Hilaire's fine nose was more often than not a rosy bulb, the dark eyes glazed and listless. His short, naturally blocky body had thickened even more, and he always bore a slightly feverish aura. Yet Justine didn't know this man any more than she had known him on her wedding night.

She didn't want to think about it.

Justine turned away, seeking instead the magic of the restless crowd. There were the Pradels with their enormous brood and the De Longuevals with little Pierre who was almost lost to the fever last year. The unpleasant memory was vanquished when she spied Camille La Sére, breathtaking in lush rose satin, as always cut in extreme décolleté to display a bosom some wags said was a trifle too celebrated. Camille was a childhood friend, one Justine secretly admired for her rebelliousness. Camille was always eager to tweak society's nose a bit and because her distinguished husband was one of the city's most admired philanthropists, she actually got away with it. And there was Hélène Fleury, almost as radiant as her daughter, Marie, a symphony in white lace, delicate pearls her only jewelry, who was being formally presented to society tonight. The Creoles scorned cotillions as common, preferring their girls to debut here instead. The Americans, in turn, criticized the practice as cheap and public. (Why, what should have been an intimate affair was being shared with free Negroes only a tier away!) Their voices scarcely counted among the old French families, however. Justine returned Marie's exuberant young smile and remembered her own such night. It seemed a century ago.

Eyes were on her too, eager for a look at one of their own too often absent. At 28, Justine remained one of the legendary New Orleans beauties but not without considerable effort. Even if she so desired, she was the sort of woman who could never go unnoticed. What the casual observer or even friends didn't know of course was that Justine's kind of beauty could be as onerous as homeliness, a bizarre burden that required great skill to merely endure, much less survive. Justine knew only too well that her beauty had been bought and sold at an exorbitant and fearsome price. Just how long she could keep her part of the bargain was elusive at best.

The thick ebony tresses piled high atop her head contrasted sharply with a porcelain skin zealously guarded from the tropical Louisiana sun since childhood. An oval face tapered to a strong chin and boasted wide-set black eyes that sparkled and danced almost defiantly. If one looked closely, however (and few could get beyond such outrageous perfection), those eyes bore a scintilla of ineffable sadness. When it came to artifice, Justine was *non pareil.*

Unlike most married Creole matrons, she never believed the security of a husband allowed her to grow plump. She tempered her indulgence in the fabled Creole cuisine with its rich, waist-destroying sauces and pastries, and with the exception of an occasional glass of wine, she never touched spirits. She never appeared in public without a meticulously executed toilette and therefore dazzled as ever. Tonight she was especially stunning in lilac watered silk that bared her arms and swept low over ample cleavage emphasized by an extravagant diamond necklace. A white, half-blown rose was pinned above her left ear and although it couldn't have been possible, the flower seemed to reflect the lavender hues of the gown. The only *outré* touch were the earrings, so oversized they resembled miniature chandeliers. They scarcely seemed appropriate on a lady whose trademark had always been elegant restraint, but if anyone could get away with such boldness it was Madame Blancard.

As she often did here, Justine closed her eyes and concentrated on the sounds of the crowd, a rich, deep cacophony occasionally pierced by a tuning violin or unidentifiable reed instrument. When she opened her eyes again, her vision was always a little blurred but she did not hasten to clear it. To the contrary, she embraced the foggy pulse of feather fans, the blistered glitter of bejewelled women, and the flash of gentlemen's starched white collars and cuffs. Focusing at last she saw the sparkle of candles and masses of glossy black hair, swept high into weighty but graceful chignons or in carefully orchestrated swirls down bare backs. Wrapping all in an aromatic cocoon was the scent of hundreds of butterfly ginger, China and tea roses, swamp orchids and late gardenias, rising *en masse* from those same gleaming coiffures. Justine closed her eyes and breathed deeply, growing heady from the scent and the moment.

Except for a lone seat here or there, the opera house was now filled to capacity, and there was a near palpable excitement as the crowd waited for the conductor. He appeared at last, bowing to anxious applause before taking his place on the dais and slowly lifting his baton. Justine's heart fluttered as the lights dimmed, and the real world vanished as the maestro began working his magic. The curtains rose, the footlights glowed and Justine was an enrapt prisoner of *Le Prophète*, instantly seduced by the three Anabaptists exhorting the people to be rebaptized. Meyerbeer's opera had always held an inexplicable fascination for her, appealing to a deep inner yearning for rebirth, for freedom from something she did not yet realize held her prisoner.

Justine was utterly captivated, forgetting everything, except concern for the missing Christophe Arnaud.

When the long first act finally ended with a blaze of house lights, Hilaire faced an empty chair and a dilemma. Throughout the performance, while Justine had been enrapt, Hilaire had fidgeted badly, drained his flask and been even less attentive than usual. His disdain for opera and preference for spending time on less lofty pursuits was no secret to his wife, or anyone else for that matter. He was far from alone in these circles. A good many other gentlemen discreetly disappeared during the first intermission and sought amusement elsewhere, returning as if by magic when the opera ended. Often they repaired to nearby gambling houses and billiard halls or perhaps a café or cabaret with less refined entertainments. And, of course, the most famous of the quadroon ballrooms was adjacent to the opera house itself.

When Justine's friend failed to appear, however, none of those options were available to Hilaire. He didn't dare risk scandal by leaving his wife alone. As it was, tongues wagged often enough about how much more often Justine was on Christophe's arm than her husband's, just as they gossiped over where Hilaire spent his time away from home. There were the usual rumors of course, tales of wild wagers at the bear and bull fights, of scandalous orgies at Lake Ponchartrain conducted by the notorious *voodouienne* Marie Laveau, of drunken debauchery in the bordellos of the Swamp where he indulged perversions so unspeakable even men spoke of them in whispers. Hilaire was not always discreet about where he left his coach, and since the French *carré de la ville* was only a few square blocks in size . . . well, *mon ami*, it wasn't difficult to conjecture.

Of course such talk must be carefully kept from the ears of Madame Blancard at all costs, but this was not always easy. If there was one thing the Creoles loved more than *soirées* and a strong cup of coffee, it was gossip! It spread unchecked and with a vengeance, as persistent and meddlesome as that lone mosquito determinedly finding his way beneath the gauzy *baire*.

It was impossible not to speculate about the Blancards. Why was such a lovely young thing as Madame Blancard so often left alone in the house in the Rue Dauphine? Why were there still no children after twelve years of marriage? And what exactly was the nature of her relationship with Christophe Arnaud? Certainly they had grown up together and the Arnaud family was one of the oldest, most respected in the city, but to spend so much time alone? *Mon dieu!* Why, he was seen going and coming at the Blancard residence almost as often as Monsieur Blancard who had apparently given his blessing to this bizarre arrangement. Surely, gasped the most desperate gossips, it could not be some sort of unthinkable *ménage à trois!*

And as for Christophe, why had he suddenly given up squiring the marriageable Creole *demoiselles* to devote himself to Justine? It all seemed so . . . unnatural.

"Bon soir, mes amis!"

Christophe burst into the small box with great flair and beamed a bit drunkenly. His black hair was a mass of damp curls, eyes as always wicked with mischief. His sharp face flowed smoothly into a jutting chin, and full lips lurked with a quicksilver smile beneath a thin moustache. The man was far from handsome, but he was so irresistibly charming that everyone thought him so. Especially Justine, who just then had never been so grateful to see anyone.

"Forgive me for being so late," he cried breathlessly. "It's absolutely disgraceful!"

Greatly relieved, Justine smiled and offered her hand for a kiss, aware that everyone's eyes were on them. She waited anxiously for the usual drama to be played out. All three players knew their lines well, and tonight they were delivered with unusual speed.

"I've some sudden personal business to attend to, Monsieur Arnaud," Hilaire began, not concealing his impatience.

"Oui, monsieur?" Christophe said, full lips fixed in a hard line as though he was hearing the most dreadful of news. He was a little drunk but charmingly so. "May I somehow be of service?"

"Might I impose upon you to see my wife home?"

"Never an imposition, Monsieur Blancard," Christophe replied with an exaggerated bow. "In fact, it will give me delirious pleasure."

"Humph!" Hilaire grunted, scowling at such obviously feigned politesse.

Justine was unnerved. You're overplaying, Chris, she thought. Such emoting belongs onstage, not here in the boxes. When he smiled at her, she shot him a warning glare, but, to her horror, he impishly stuck out his tongue before continuing his performance.

"With Madame Blancard's kind permission, of course."

"Of course," she echoed. She thought she would go mad if Hilaire didn't leave the box at once. Then, quickly, "Good night, Hilaire."

"*Bon soir,* madame," Hilaire said, leaning to brush her cheek with a dutiful kiss. Then, with a hasty bow to Christophe, "Monsieur Arnaud."

The heat of her husband's hasty kiss still glowed on her cheek when Justine reprimanded her good friend. She waved her fan to mask her annoyance from prying eyes, not to mention ears in the boxes flanking both sides. That Adéle Boisquet was sweet enough but she repeated *everything* she heard!

"Christophe!" she hissed. "You were outrageous! You know nothing must interrupt Hilaire's little charade."

"A charade, is it?" Christophe said, settling into the chair left warm by Hilaire. He gave her an adoring look, hazel eyes sparkling unnaturally from too much whiskey. His smile was as beguiling and irresistible as always. "Since when is it a charade?"

Justine took a deep breath, wishing her stays weren't so tight. She made a mental note to tell Marie Tonton not to lace her so fiercely. The devil with the girl's insistence that it pleased Michie Hilaire to see such a small waist on the madame!

"Sometimes the games become too much," she sighed wearily.

The hazel eyes widened. "What games, Justine?"

The ebony eyebrows arched high on her forehead. Her tone dropped menacingly, not unlike the feel of the air when a tropical storm hovered offshore, poised to hurtle in from the Gulf. Christophe was decidedly uneased, more so when he heard Justine's next question.

"How drunk are you, Chris?"

He thought for a moment, as though he must actually weigh the question. "Just enough . . . I think," he replied slowly.

"Too drunk for us to talk about the *Salle d'Orléans?*"

The unthinkable question shocked him sober and he sat bolt upright. "Justine!" he gasped, incredulous. Now it was his turn to worry what might be seen or overheard. "Are you mad?! You're not even supposed to know about such places!" He lowered his voice still more. "Much less mention them. And at the opera on opening night!"

"Perhaps I'm not as naive as you think," Justine dismissed coolly. "It's right next door, isn't it?"

Christophe was stunned again. This was totally unlike her, and yet perhaps it was more revelatory than ever. Their deep friendship involved a great deal of mutual sharing and no end of confidences, but always with restraint and careful navigation within only the most proper realms. They never hinted at anything remotely indiscreet, much less bawdy or, heaven forbid, carnal! Although Christophe was one of the most sentient of men, he never imagined Justine knew anything about the *Salle d'Orléans*. His amazement was such that he didn't realize his mouth was hanging open until Justine gently shut it with the tip of her closed fan.

As he tried to collect his thoughts, forcing the vague alcoholic haze to retreat, Christophe recognized this as another in a series of changes involving Justine. The first and subtlest had materialized when she and Hilaire returned after two years from a European wedding trip. On the surface nothing seemed different. At eighteen, Justine was more ravishing than ever, but Christophe noticed a nervousness beneath the serene surface, an attitude toward Hilaire that bordered on obeisance. Christophe was almost certain she did not love her husband since that dear emotion rarely entered the coldly arranged Creole marriage. In any case, she could not be questioned about something so intimate. Nor could he question Hilaire when Justine tearfully announced she had been forbidden to spend further time alone with him. She was, Hilaire had reminded her, a married woman, no longer a childhood friend without obligation. Her obligations were, he firmly informed her, to him and him alone. Of course, she and Christophe were thrown together at parties, dinners, and salons and they constantly saw each other at Mass, at the opera, the theater, and Mardi Gras balls, but nothing was ever the same between them.

Then, gradually but steadily, Justine began to withdraw from society. Her public appearances were at first occasional, then infrequent, and finally rare. She took long trips with Hilaire, to Paris, to Vienna and Venice, to New York, and even islands in the Caribbean. When she returned, Marie Tonton's response to callers was always the same. Madame Blancard was suffering from mal de mer or a touch of fever caught in some exotic port of call. Madame Blancard regrets that fatigue will keep her from attending this ball or that *revillon*. Frustrated by her reclusiveness and pleasant but chilly politeness on those rare occasions when she ventured from home, people eventually stopped calling altogether. Their tongues were often unforgiving, viperish on some occasions.

Indeed, who did Madame Blancard think she was?

Hilaire, by contrast, seemed to be everywhere at once. When not in his banking offices in the Rue Chartres, he was a familiar face in the gambling halls, the cafés and cabarets along the Rue Royale and, of course, at the quadroon balls. The Creoles began wondering why the ever-convivial Hilaire Blancard had wed Justine in the first place. After all, was the marriage not intended to yield heirs that would advance him up the social ladder? There were endless theories of course and not a few outrageous rumors, but it was all too bewildering to consider further. Yet everyone agreed on one thing: how sad that Justine had no family other than her sweet but hopelessly flighty Tante Nanine to steer her back on course. As far as everyone knew, Nanine Fonteneau was just as reclusive as her niece, giving rise to natural speculation that it was a family trait.

Christophe had therefore been astonished when he received a letter just last fall asking him to call on the house in the Rue Dauphine. Hilaire was not at home, but Justine explained, with no elaboration, that her husband no longer objected to their friendship. What's more, she intended to resume a social life, albeit limited, and since business often made Hilaire unavailable, perhaps he would concede to be her escort.

Christophe asked no questions, delighted by this unexpected turn of events, frankly eager to surrender his laurels as the most footloose bachelor in the *carré de la ville* and spend his time with a less demanding woman. Or so he thought. The Justine he saw, however, was not the one he had known all his life, and it had to do with much more than the mere passage of time. It was as though they needed to become reacquainted all over again. Time and again she shocked him with an unsolicited revelation suggesting something smoldered behind the elusively fragile exterior that ever so often, such as tonight, relinquished a spark that startled Christophe. He was dead certain he was the only one who ever saw it and wasn't at all sure it didn't frighten him a little. Tonight, for example, in the midst of the opera house, it had reared up on its hind legs and stared him boldly in the face. What's worse, not only was Justine being shockingly frank, she was being wildly erratic in her behavior. One moment she was the perfectly proper Creole lady concerned over appearances, and the next she was questioning him about the most indelicate subjects imaginable. He shrank from her, shaking his head to further clear the alcoholic cobwebs.

"Even if it were right next door," he hissed, "you know very well it's not an appropriate subject for discussion. Not here of all places."

Defiant, emboldened, maddening. "Where then?"

He was horrified. "Justine!"

"Very well," she conceded. She had gone too far and, fortunately for Christophe, she finally realized it. "After the opera, we'll go to one of those smart new cafés in the Rue Chartres and have café au lait. No more liquor for you tonight. I want some sober answers. And don't worry about shocking me, *mon ami.*" She adjusted the roses in her hair and discreetly smelled her fingertips. Then, oblivious to Adéle or anyone else who might be watching, she tickled his nose so he could smell them too. "I'm not so fragile as this."

"But—"

"Shhhhh. The lights are going down. Oh, dear! I forgot to catch you up on the plot!"

The opera's second act dragged interminably for Christophe. He knew he had to respect Justine's wishes that he not drink any more, but the evening's bizarre events made him desperate for a bourbon. And more than a little leery of a cross-examination about the quadroon balls. He needn't have worried. During the second intermission, Justine agreed to some fresh air and was delighted that the rain had finally stopped. She even had a delicate sip of the steaming gumbo Christophe bought from the ancient Negresses outside the opera house. By the time the final lights rose after act three and the company took their bows, Justine had obviously undergone a change of heart. She made no mention of either the *Salle d'Orléans* or café au lait as they followed the crowds outside. Instead she insisted on going straight home.

This was scarcely the first time she had behaved so oddly. Time and again, a beleaguered Christophe had seen her on the verge of blurting some intimate revelation or questioning him about something unspeakable when she would fall inexplicably silent or, worse, abruptly change the subject. It had grown increasingly maddening, so much so that Christophe confronted her on the ride home.

He took her hand and held it gently as the coach rocked down the muddy Rue Bourbon. "My dear Justine, you are my dearest friend in all the world, but we cannot continue under these circumstances."

"What do you mean?" she asked, a trace of alarm ringing in her voice. He took a deep breath and squeezed her hand. "As you said yourself, *cher,* sometimes the games become too much."

"Did I say that?" she asked absently. She pulled her hand away and tugged the white roses from her hair. Freed, the delicate blossoms shattered and snowed petals in her lap. She toyed with them as the coach slogged noisily through the mud.

"You know very well you did," he said, anger rising. Had she any idea how infuriating she could be? "You can't go on pretending nothing is wrong when you know very well it is."

She whirled to face him. "What do you mean by that?" Her vehemence was startling as she struggled under the weight of a moment perilous with presentiment.

"I mean that you say something one minute and say something else the next. You disapprove of an action and then turn around and embrace it. You ask questions and then before I can answer, you change the subject. You can be a walking contradiction, Justine."

"I'm . . . I'm sorry," she said, slipping her small gloved hand back into his. "Sometimes, especially when it's late at night and I'm alone, I can't seem to separate what's real from what's . . . oh, Christophe! Dear, dear Christophe! You have no idea how close to the truth you've just come."

"What truth?" he asked slowly. Dare he be encouraged that he would learn something at last?

"When you say I can't go on pretending that nothing is wrong." She took a deep breath, cursing Marie Tonton yet again as the stays cut into her rib cage. "When I know very well it is." She took another deep breath. "Wrong. Terribly wrong. At least I think so."

"Think so?"

She shrugged. "As I said before, sometimes I can't differentiate between . . . things, or understand how they have come to be. If certain things are as they should be."

"What things?" Christophe pressed. "And what is it that's so terribly wrong?" When Justine only looked at him helplessly, his heart was wounded for her. "Is it something I can help you with, *ma chérie?*"

She shook her head, suddenly terribly weary. As she had feared, she wished she'd never begun the discussion. "It's nothing anyone can help me with, Christophe. Not now. Not ever."

He was utterly exasperated. He yanked off his top hat and ran fingers through his wild black hair. "I just don't understand, Justine. Simply open your mouth and say the words."

"If I could have done that," she promised, "I would have done so, long ago. When Hilaire and I first returned from Europe. But I was so weak then that . . . well, things have only gotten worse. I thought when Hilaire agreed to let me see you that I would be able to talk to you, to tell you what it's been like these past years. But . . ."

"But?" he urged, almost frantic.

"But I find that I cannot."

Her voice bore such tragic finality that it shocked him into stillness. They rode in silence until the coach drew up before her house, No. 1107 in the Rue Dauphine. She reached for the door as a sign that nothing more was to be said, but Christophe would not be put off so easily. He grabbed her tight and looked hard into her eyes. Then he gambled wildly.

"Is it because Blancard goes to the *Salle d'Orléans*, Justine?" When she stared in horror, he pressed his advantage. "Is it his infidelities with those quadroon women driving you mad?"

It was a random arrow but it found the target.

The terror rising on Justine's face sent a chill to the depths of his heart. Only once had Christophe seen such a look, when he was fifteen years old and hunting with his brothers at an uncle's plantation on the Cane River. It was the time he shot his first and last deer, and to this day he carried the heinous memory of those great liquid eyes before the soft, downy head exploded in crimson. He was seeing that self-same look now in Justine's eyes and on a face as pale as the shattered white roses.

Her lower lip trembled, face pitifully contorted. Christophe didn't know beauty could be so hideously transformed and he shrank from it. And the voice as well, emanating from a hidden place deep within her and fouling the air inside the carriage with a terrible finality. When she spoke it was from a soul that had survived unspeakable rigors.

"I wish he'd find one and leave me forever!" Justine cried. "I wish he'd left me in the hotel that awful night in Paris! I wish . . . !"

Justine's hand flew to her lips, stemming a flow of words she feared would burst from a carefully constructed dam, the damage irretrievably lost.

For the first time Christophe realized the woman was ill, that she was tormented by an unspeakable malady not of her body's making. It had been forced upon her and had spawned some sort of terrible aureole threatening to crush her from without to within.

He gently took the gloved hand from her lips and brushed it with his own. A small cry escaped Justine, and then, somehow, she was in his arms, tears staining his crisp white shirt bosom. He had never held her like this before, but not even a concupiscent breath attended the moment. It was nothing more than one human being reaching out to another in a desperate effort to bridge some terrible gap of sorrow and pain.

But then, just as swiftly as shem had surrendered to his embrace, Justine withdrew, and when she spoke her tone was unmistakably minatory.

"You must never let him know what I've told you, Christophe. Never!"

"But you have told me nothing!" he insisted.

"To the contrary," she said, nodding at the door. "I have told you far too much."

Defeated by the gesture of dismissal, Christophe swept the door open and stepped quickly from the coach. He assisted Justine as she positioned a satin slipper delicately on the carriage block before alighting on the rain-streaked banquette. Justine ducked as water dripped from the broad galleries overhead, hurrying up the two steps to the sheltered doorway where she turned to say good-night.

"Justine!" Christophe pleaded. "Won't you please invite me in? We must talk!"

She shook her head. "The very walls of this house have ears," she said. "Were I to tell you anything at all, it would certainly not be here. Especially with Marie Tonton hovering about."

"But I cannot leave you like this," he protested. "So unhappy, so . . ."

"But you must," she insisted. She leaned down so he could brush her cheek with a kiss, enveloping him in a cloud of roses. When he was close enough she whispered in his ear. "If he learned I've told you this much, he would destroy me."

Christophe was too stunned to speak. He stood rooted to the banquette until the door closed behind Justine and the gaslights on the lower floor were extinguished. He backed toward the carriage, then, like Justine, sought escape from the dripping gallery above. From atop the coach, a puzzled L'Eveillé watched his master inch backward up the street, almost to the corner of the Rue de Ursulines. Christophe scrutinized the Blancard house, as though he might solve the mysteries within by studying it from without.

Easily the tallest house on the block, its gray facade towered three stories above the banquette. It would have loomed like a fortress were it not embraced by the froth of iron galleries on the upper floors and graced by a wide fanlight swelling above a finely carved door. Above all, on the deeply pitched slate roof, dormer windows peered toward lake and river, flushed gold like alligator eyes lurking above inky swamp waters. Christophe shivered, but not from the omnipresent damp.

He watched the glow of a kerosene lamp moving from room to room on the upper floors. When it remained stationery, he retraced his steps and peered down the carriageway. As he'd expected, Blancard's coach was not there. At the end of the narrow passageway was only an empty courtyard with its faint swell of banana fronds shimmering beneath a half-risen moon. The stars had made a belated debut too, and Christophe found himself reflecting on them until an unwelcome wet gust reminded him he was cold. He hurried back to the coach, glancing up at the bemused driver.

"That same bar on the waterfront, L'Eveillé," he said. "Get yourself some coffee. It may be a long night."

"Don't you worry, Michie Christophe," the Negro said. "They don't call me Wide Awake for nothing."

"Wide Awake indeed," Christophe muttered to himself. Then, "I wish I were dead drunk."

As the coach lurched toward the river, Christophe tried to leave the night's unpleasant memories behind along with the Blancard home. What had begun as a raucous evening slumming with friends on the waterfront had ended badly with Justine's bizarre behavior at the opera. What he needed now was pure *divertissement*, and not merely through whiskey. He hoped he could find those amusing *Yanquis* he had met in that disreputable cabaret on the Rue de la Levée. He wanted to bury himself in witty conversation, to laugh and be gay, to forget those terrible, disturbing moments with the enigmatic Justine.

It was the only relief, albeit fleeting, from witnessing the descent into madness of a cherished old friend.

CHAPTER 2

ilaire Blancard invariably felt a rush of erotic exhilaration when he entered the vestibule of the *Salle d'Orléans*. The raw sensuality masked behind elaborate ritual and feigned gentility always stirred him, sometimes even necessitating a discreet rearrangement of clothing. Especially when he was a trifle drunk as he was tonight.

From the street, the building was undistinguished to the point of ugliness. Its wide, sullen facade was bereft of any ornamentation and hugged the banquettes along the Rue d'Orléans as though dug in by its heels, fearful of being dislodged at any moment. (Indeed there were many, white ladies at their forefront, who damned it as evil and would've relished razing it to the cobblestones!) But rarely have appearances been so deceiving. White gentlemen ascending its grand staircase were transported into a dreamlike world of grace and passion created solely to stroke and sate the ultimate in sensual fantasies. To set them on these flights of fancy they need only take their pick from a glittering array of café au lait women world-renowned for their beauty and elegance.

And their price.

This was home to the infamous *Bals du Cordon Bleu* where the quadroons, those exotic women who were three quarters white, one quarter Negro, made connections with Creole protectors. *Plaçage*, it was called, this peculiar arrangement between a white gentleman and a free woman of color. Sexual liaisons between white men and Negro slave women, forced or otherwise, had been fact from the earliest days of *La Louisiane*, and free people of color had existed almost that long. In time, a society comprised exclusively of the *gens de coleur libres* took root and flourished, hovering precariously between the worlds of black and white. Shunning pure Negroes and most mulattoes, they kept carefully to themselves, a mostly ambitious, lawful people who prospered with impressive frequency. While many men often became merchants and planters, the less well connected women sought survival through an entirely different avenue. They became mistresses of wealthy white men with terms of the arrangement contractually delineated.

A most peculiar New Orleans tradition had been born.

By far the most glamorous ballroom in the city, the *Salle d'Orléans* had been open since 1818, and nothing quite like it existed anywhere else in the world. Visiting New Orleans thirty years ago, His Highness Bernhard, Duke of Saxe-Weimar Eisensach, had been taken, as were most distinguished tourists, to see the celebrated quadroons. Overwhelmed by these sultry exotics, he waxed poetic on their rapturous charms. He extolled them as "the most beautiful women on earth" and wrote that "many of them have as fair a complexion as many of the haughty Creole females." He duly noted that the quadroons were mischievously fond of scheduling their balls to conflict with special white occasions. At such times, the white gentlemen had scant difficulty deciding which to attend, and the duke confessed to finding the quadroon balls "more entertaining than those of a more decorous nature" where, as the duke delicately put it, many young Creole ladies were abandoned "to make tapestry." (Of course no white woman would dream of setting foot in the place, and men of color, except musicians, were explicitly denied entry.) A celebrated English traveler had recently spoken of the quadroons in even more glowing terms. "They resembled," said he, "the higher orders of women among the high-class Hindoos; lovely countenances, full dark, liquid eyes, lips of coral, teeth of pearl, sylphlike figures; their beautifully rounded limbs, exquisite gait, and ease of manner might furnish models for a Venus or Hebe!"

Venus was precisely what sent Hilaire's blood coursing as he left behind the gleaming vestibule with its labyrinth of private card rooms and climbed the staircase to the ballroom itself. There all restraint vanished as sumptuousness was embraced with staggering fervor. The walls were paneled in expensive woods and covered with fine, colorful paintings. Here and there were niches containing marble statuary, most of it female figures *en deshabille* or completely nude.

The ceiling swelled to a dizzying height, punctured by a glittering array of crystal chandeliers reflected in what was called the finest dance floor in America. Made of triple-thickness cypress laid atop a layer of quarter-sawed oak, it had been polished by slaves to the sheen of a great mirror. Those watching the graceful glide of the dancers were rewarded with a gleaming double image. The glamorous spectacle grew even more dizzying when one breathed deeply of air permeated with the heady amalgam of flowers, sweet *parfums* and, underneath it all, the muskiness of sweat. Despite the chill outside, the room was uncomfortably warm. It was also packed.

As Hilaire threaded his way past the Negro orchestra and found space in a corner, he pulled a linen handkerchief from his waistcoat and dabbed his damp forehead. He nodded politely as a brace of dusky beauties swept by, squinting to inspect them more closely before they vanished into the crowd. He was admiring the splendidly seductive sway of their hoops when he was walloped so hard on the back he nearly dropped his wine glass.

"Blancard, you old dog! It's good to see you again!" Hilaire turned to the pudgy face of Henri Meilleure, an old friend and one of the city's most prominent cotton brokers. His cherubic cheeks were flushed from both whiskey and a childish excitement as he threw an arm around Hilaire's shoulders and grinned. Then a memory clouded his merriment. "Oh. Sorry about Josette. Childbirth was it?"

"Yes," Hilaire answered. But there was scant emotion in his voice at the mention of the young mistress lost just the month before. He shrugged and smiled. *"Eh, bien.* Here I am."

Meilleure leaned close, eager to impose his high spirits. When he spoke, his tone implied the sharing of a great confidence. "To be frank, Blancard, I hear the best solution is to find a replacement as soon as possible."

Hilaire nodded and sipped his wine. "My thoughts exactly."

"Not unlike falling off a horse I suppose." Meilleure nudged him in the ribs. "Just get right back in the saddle, eh, *mon ami?"*

Both men roared with laughter, abruptly distracted when a pretty girl, skin the color of pecans, passed close enough to send a message with her perfume. She was a vision in crimson satin, abundant cleavage prominent beneath a necklace of paste rubies. Red plumes danced in gleaming black hair unbound and spilling over bare shoulders. At her wrist flashed a small bouquet of scarlet poinsettias.

"White women just can't wear that color, eh, Blancard?"

Hilaire only half-heard, thoughts clearly elsewhere. *"Mon dieu!* One deep breath and she'll loose a tit!" He laughed again, thoroughly pleased with his joke.

Meilleure nodded approvingly, then joined his friend in scanning the immense room. He couldn't remember when it had last been so packed. "Quite a crowd here tonight, eh?"

"I just arrived," Hilaire complained. "I almost had to sit through the second act of that wretched opera about baptism or some such nonsense."

Meilleure nodded sympathetically. "Thank God my wife doesn't put me through that torture any longer." He swilled his whiskey and took Hilaire's arm as he navigated toward the nearest bar. "I've been here since the doors opened. Quite a lot of new faces tonight, but that's not the reason for this crush of people. Of course you've heard about the one called Chaillot. Her name has been on everyone's lips all evening. Tonight will be her first appearance."

"Chaillot?" Hilaire's eyebrows rose. "An odd name. Pretty."

"Her mother is Colette Baptiste."

Meilleure paused to await his friend's reaction. The *demimonde* of the quadroons and those who patronized them was small, nearly incestuous. Recognition surfaced on Hilaire's face when he heard the name of the fabled quadroon. Colette Baptiste's was the sort of beauty and grace that polished the image of the *Bals du Cordon Bleu*, a woman so breathtaking she could have charmed kings, so fair she could have passed with little difficulty. At least outside the South.

Meilleure continued, "She was with Simon Guedry for years, remember?"

"Then how could the child be so extraordinary? Guedry was ugly as a toad." Meilleure shrugged. "Though I concede he was a damned shrewd businessman. Rich as Croesus!"

"I've always believed the money was why he never married," said Meilleure. "He was so homely he never believed anyone could love him for himself. Still, I always wondered why Colette chose him."

"You and everyone else," Hilaire said.

"In any case, I'm told this girl is spectacular. Perhaps she is strictly her mother's child. It's possible."

"Indeed," Hilaire said. He considered, then, "So this Chaillot is an octoroon?"

Meilleure nodded. "I hear she's about as white as these gals can get." He winked and passed his tongue slowly over his lips. Hilaire found the gesture repulsive and looked away, but his fat friend plucked at his sleeve. "She's supposed to appear around midnight. Rumor says the orchestra is even going to strike up a fanfare when she arrives."

"I've never heard of such a thing," Hilaire said dismissively.

"Times are changing, *mon ami.*"

What Meilleure said was true, and if the balls were declining in popularity, as everyone said, perhaps the management would resort to such gimmickry. He had even heard the *Salle d'Orléans* might soon permit the *ombligata*, an Angolan dance popular in less refined ballrooms because it brought the gyrating couple navel to navel! He pulled a gold watch from his pocket and examined it, annoyed when he remembered it was a birthday gift from Justine.

"Midnight, eh?" Blancard sighed. "I don't know if I'll last that late."

"You know what they say," Meilleure said, nudging him in the ribs. "Anything worth having is worth waiting for."

"We'll see," Hilaire said, draining his wine glass as they approached the bar. "Get me a whiskey, will you?"

They were not the only men discussing the mysterious Chaillot. The entire ballroom was abuzz with anticipation of this girl just recently arrived from an uncle's upriver plantation. Such women had been groomed all their lives for this moment, the magical evening when they would make their first appearance at the ball for consideration by the wealthy white gentlemen. Devotees of the ball likened it to a cotillion with dusky debutantes presented to their unique society while *maman* kept a hawklike watch from the balcony. They considered the arrangement a rare opportunity for girls to find financial security in a world where options were few and obstacles many. After all, went the argument, the men signed contracts guaranteeing subsistence for the girl and any children born of the union. For boys that usually meant an education in France. As for the girls . . . well, if they were pretty enough they usually followed in their mother's footsteps and the cycle was unbroken.

Critics of the practice damned it as veiled prostitution or dismissed it as little more than a glorified slave auction where, although free, modern-day *hetaerae* were legally bound to their "protectors."

Then there was the attitude of the quadroons themselves.

Colette Baptiste ordered her friends from the small bedroom and closed the door. Alone at last with her daughter, she concentrated on inspecting her jewel, the singular finest achievement of her life. Chaillot was frozen at the vanity, studying her face in the mirror. One image was enough, Colette thought. Two took the breath away.

Entering the reflection, Colette leaned down to press their cheeks together. At thirty-three, she remained stunning. Her skin, the color of honey and supple as silk, was still remarkably smooth, the heralded face unlined. With the exception of full lips and almond eyes, her Ibibio features had been mostly vanquished, leached away by the infusion of white blood.

In her octoroon daughter, the transformation was even more startling. Chaillot's skin was porcelain with the faintest flush of gold swimming beneath. The lips were still voluptuous but thinner, the nostrils narrower than Colette's. But it was the lanceolate eyes that were her greatest triumph. Like her mother's, they were thickly lashed and bore the same striking, upward slant, but the similarity ended with color. Colette's were hazel, but Chaillot's eyes were a pale, supernal blue, disturbing in their eerie translucence. Few faced them without being moved.

The hair was thick and coal black, glossy now after a careful washing, and coiffed high atop her head. The chignon was heavy, and she tilted her head from side to side to test its weight, smiling at her mother's watchful reflection. Colette turned up the wick of the oil lamp, exhilarated that it seemed any light flattered her daughter. She did not fare badly, either.

"You are the most beautiful *maman* in the world," Chaillot sighed.

"Ah, but I am nothing compared to you, *ma petit*," Colette insisted, although she cherished the sweet words. She was still vain enough to care about her looks, well knew she could still turn heads, but tonight her vanity needed to take a back seat. Tonight belonged to Chaillot, and her mother intended to do everything in her power to ensure that nothing interfered.

"Stand up, *cher*," she said. "Let me take another look at you."

"But *maman*," Chaillot giggled. "You and Suzanne and Nicole have done nothing but look at me and fuss over me and poke and prod me for hours." She shuddered, remembering the time Michie Simon took her on a short cut through the St. Louis Hotel where she witnessed a human auction in progress under the great dome. She had never forgotten it. "Now I know what a slave feels like," she said with a nervous giggle.

It was meant to be a joke, although one of questionable taste, but it disturbed Colette. The hazel eyes clouded and she spoke sharply.

"Never laugh about such things, Chaillot. You must never forget your great-grandmother was a slave or how she got her freedom. After all, it's how we ensure our own."

"*Oui, maman*," Chaillot said, suddenly humble. Wanting the moment to pass, she brightened and said, "Well, I tell you Nicole was driving me mad! She fussed over me like a mother hen."

"Nonsense. She and Suzanne love you, that's all. And like me they know once you accept the challenge of the *Salle d'Orléans,* nothing must ever be left to chance. *Nothing!*" Her voice was stern, unyielding. "Remember that. Always."

Chaillot nodded before rising obediently, stirring the air with the fra-

grance of rosewater and a gentle rustle of silk as she moved to the center of the boudoir and poised for yet another inspection. Colette had chosen Chaillot's dress with infinite care, swearing Madame Clovis to secrecy from the first fitting to the last just yesterday morning. While Toinette Clovis secretly disapproved of the quadroon balls, considered them grossly debasing, she held her tongue. As she confided to her husband, Madame Baptiste was, alas, paying far too generously to be criticized.

As a result, the gown was one of her masterpieces. It hugged Chaillot's waist like a dream, flaring like the petals of a giant tulip. The scalloped hem was gathered with small, delicate bows and puffed sleeves were positioned low from the creamy shoulders. The neckline was cut in modest décolleté, an old-fashioned cameo nestling atop a hint of cleavage that promised an abundance more.

And it was white. Pure, virginal, unsullied white.

"The others will be wearing bright colors," Colette had said. "They are not for you. You need no such vulgar . . . advertising." Now she couldn't resist a glorious smile of approval. "I am very, very pleased, my daughter!"

"*Merci, maman,*" Chaillot said, executing a perfect curtsy.

Chaillot returned to the dressing table where a bouquet of gardenias reposed in water, a good-luck present from Suzanne. She plucked the largest and tucked it behind her left ear. Colette frowned. She had allowed Chaillot just the barest tinge of rouge on those glowing cheeks, but when the girl pinned the flower above her ear, it struck a discordant note.

"*Mais non!*" Colette insisted, moving swiftly to tug the gardenia from her daughter's hair and toss it to the floor. The unexpected ferocity of the gesture unnerved Chaillot and she stared after the flower, shrinking from her mother's harsh tone. "I tell you all the others will be wearing flowers! You're not like them! You don't need any *accoutrement!*" She touched a fingertip to Chaillot's dainty chin and lifted it until their eyes locked. Softer now, "You are perfection all by yourself."

"But *maman!*" Chaillot protested. "I should wear something in my hair, *non?*" She sought the gardenias, retreating quickly when she found her corset prevented reaching beyond her knees. "Ah! Suddenly I feel like I'm going to faint."

"Nonsense!" Colette snapped. "We've been practicing for weeks. Remember what I told you. It's an entirely different way of breathing. O maybe I should say of *not* breathing!"

Chaillot's head reeled. There seemed to be so much to remember tonight! How to walk pigeon-toed so that her hoops swayed like bell

How to lean the back *just so* against a gentleman's hand during the dance. How to keep her heavily lashed eyes downcast until just the right moment when she would look up and unleash their full power on some unsuspecting gentleman. It was all too much!

She watched as her mother took her hand, squeezing as though she could infuse her legendary surfeit of self-confidence into Chaillot's young body and quell the girl's all too natural fears. There was a far-away look in Colette's eyes, and when she spoke her voice was distant, as though trapped in some long-lost amber of youth.

"I know just what it feels like, *ma petit,*" she said firmly. "I well re-member that first moment when my *maman* steered me along this very same course. Butterflies in your stomach. A fever on your brow. The need for another trip to the privy." She squeezed her daughter's hands. "Hands like ice. Don't worry. It will all evaporate once you enter the ballroom. I promise."

"Really?"

Colette squeezed again. *"Absolument!* And shall I tell you something else that will happen?"

In a small voice, *"Oui, maman."*

Colette took a deep breath and spoke with heartfelt conviction, re-vealing what she had so long prayed for.

"Every woman in that room will be eclipsed. Do you understand me, girl? *Eclipsed!"* Her voice deepened, reverberating in the close confines of the small boudoir. For Chaillot it was at the same time frightening and thrilling. "You don't know how I've dreamed of this moment, planned for it. Waited until you began to ripen so I could whisk you off to your uncle's plantation where you could bloom without scrutiny. And do you know why? *Why?* Because I knew when you were born that you were going to be greater than myself. Greater even than Colette Baptiste who is still talked about as the greatest of them all!"

"Maman!" Chaillot whispered.

She was alarmed by the strength in her mother's grip, the dark pas-sion in her voice. She had never seen her like this. Granted Colette had raised her strictly, but that sternness had been tempered by a genuine gentleness assuring Chaillot she was deeply loved and treasured. But this! This was something unfamiliar, this menacing tone altering her mother's features and rendering her hard and frantic. Chaillot shrank from it, from this sudden stranger where a familiar face and warmth had existed just moments ago.

Colette was deaf to her daughter's frightened whisper. "The dream fell into my lap when I met Monsieur Guedry. Tell me, Chaillot. Have

you ever wondered why I chose him when I could have had any protector I wanted? Anyone!" Colette paused but sought no response. "It's quite simple really. You see, through him I could produce the most beautiful daughter imaginable."

"*Maman . . .*"

"We're like moths, you and I. All of us colored *demimondaines*. Moths with orbits confined to the ballrooms and those little cottages lining the Rue Rampart, fluttering in the shadowy world between black and white, not slaves but never truly free. We're moths, Chaillot, delicate and fine as we circle that fatal flame and, whether or not we wish to admit it, equally doomed."

She studied her daughter's superb blue eyes as though searching for something and, satisfied that she found it, continued.

"Just as the white ladies pray that their fiancés and husbands won't seek us out, we pray that we'll choose a gentleman who will keep us for life, who won't tire of us or abandon us when he marries. Few are that lucky. But for those who are, the years still pass and the flame comes closer and closer, terrifying proof that our beauty is fading. And always, always the fear that he will go back to the balls and find someone younger, prettier." She shot the bed a fearful look, facing the enemy. "Or more imaginative in the boudoir."

She squeezed Chaillot's hands tighter still.

"We have no choice, *ma chére!* That's why we must act while we are at our absolute *apogée!*"

"*Maman!* You're hurting me!"

Colette's head snapped, and she gasped as though waking from a dream. She seemed to see her daughter for the first time and softened her grip before kissing Chaillot's delicate hands. "Forgive me, my angel!" With that she flew from the room, calling for Senegal to fetch the coachman.

"I . . . I'll try, *maman*," Chaillot whispered to herself.

She nudged the fallen gardenia with the toe of her satin slipper. Already the pale petals were rusting, bruised from being hurled so brutally to the floor. For some reason her mother's last words hung in the air like the cold breath of the yellow river wrapping them both as they climbed into the coach.

"*Forgive me, my angel.*"

The *Salle d'Orléans* was still densely crowded when the Baptiste cabriolet drew up before it, hood pulled forward as far as possible to conceal the passengers. Word of their identity swept the floor of the ballroom almost before Colette and Chaillot had alit, and not all of the dancers were pleased. The youngest women, especially those with the misfortune of making their first appearance that night, were less than enthusiastic about the arrival of Chaillot Baptiste. Ladies were not abandoned in mid-dance, but a great many were rather firmly whirled from the dance floor as the crowd pressed toward the top of the staircase. Every man there wanted the first look, prompting some to bound down the stairs and rush through the vestibule for an earlier glance. Some gentlemen in the midst of card games fled their tables to see what the commotion was all about. The vestibule was a mob scene.

Colette kissed her daughter's cheek a final time. Both were silent now. There was no need for more words, for further advice. What loomed beyond that carriage was the product of years of meticulous training, and all that needed to be said had been said many times before.

Colette leaned into the light, grateful that the rains had stopped, and took the Negro doorman's hand before slipping gracefully from the carriage. She had chosen a black velvet cape that made her skin glow fairer than ever. She drew plentiful nods of approval, some from older gentlemen remembering her first and last days in the ballroom. Not a few would have approached her for an arrangement, but she had let it be known she was no longer interested in such things. Guedry's death had left her amply provided for, and her return to the *Salle d'Orléans* was strictly on her daughter's behalf.

While everyone waited, Colette whispered something to the doorman and stepped aside while he returned to the carriage. He gripped the hood and with a single powerful shove, pushed it back to reveal Chaillot, alone beneath the golden glow of gaslights, pale face a half-risen moon all but concealed by the hood of her cloak. She stood slowly, took the doorman's hand and descended from the carriage. Three white gentlemen stepped forward to offer their arms but Chaillot demurred, provocatively, before taking her mother's arm. Colette beamed. She had taught her daughter well.

Chaillot kept her hood almost closed as Colette steered her through the crush of eager men jostling for a better view of this rare octoroon. A slave attendant approached for the cloak, but Colette waved her away.

Not yet. Not yet.

It seemed an eternity to Chaillot before they reached the stairs and another eon before they began the ascent. A drunk tried to pull her cloak open, his efforts rewarded by a fist to the jaw that sent him sprawling. Pandemonium erupted as other fights were triggered, but Chaillot gave them no notice. She focused only on ascending the staircase, one by one, step by step, until she saw the last rise and knew she had arrived. Only then did she open the cloak and let it fall away, caring nothing if it fell to the floor. Several gentleman rushed to catch it, humbled by a gesture truly worthy of a queen.

A collective gasp arose from the eager crowd as she stood before them in all her splendor, a vision in pure white. Light seemed to radiate from her, a golden aureole that was all but blinding. No one had made an entrance like this since Colette Baptiste herself.

There was not a single gentleman who did not stare and, as Colette had promised her daughter, all other women were eclipsed. Earrings danced furiously as heads jerked toward her, and fans paused in midswish. There was an ugly moment of almost palpable jealousy before the quadroon sisterhood reunited and the women rushed, like a singular wave, to embrace the new arrival. Chaillot Baptiste had arrived!

Hilaire Blancard was transfixed. From clear across the enormous ballroom, he could see nothing but this dazzling voluptuary. He started toward her but his feet wouldn't move and he listed crazily, a heliotrope aching for the sun. He felt clumsy and cursed himself for having drunk too much. He had no choice but to watch helplessly as the first of countless gentlemen whirled Chaillot around the dance floor, Meilleure prominent among them. Using all his fortitude, Blancard willed himself to think straight, forced himself to formulate a plan that would gain him access to the girl. Slowly, steadily it came at last, bringing a smile to his red face. He turned toward the nearest mirror and inspected his image, straightening his cravat and wiping the sweat from his brow. That done he set out on his mission, which was to locate Colette Baptiste.

Protocol at the quadroon balls dictated that once a gentleman selected a girl, he asked her mother for permission to call on her. Chaillot's appearance had caused such turmoil that tradition had been momentarily forgotten in the mass stampede to seek a dance with the young beauty. Blancard knew Madame Baptiste would soon be besieged by the same men asking permission to court her daughter. That was one line he intended to head.

He found Colette alone on the balcony, a cloaked figure sipping a glass of wine as she studied the garden of St. Antoine and the triple spires of the Cathedral beyond. He wondered why she had fled the ballroom, why she was not reveling in every moment of her daughter's obvious triumph, but when she turned to see who had joined her he understood. Her face was streaked with tears of joy; she had sought refuge to enjoy her moment of triumph alone. When she saw him she fumbled in her reticule for a handkerchief. His was extended in a trice.

"Please allow me, Madame Baptiste," he said, summoning his most genteel voice, "if I am not intruding."

"You know who I am?" she said, dabbing at the tears of pride.

"Your fame is legendary, madame," he said. "As is your beauty."

"Indeed!" Colette laughed hoarsely and made a wry face. "Are you here to court me or my daughter, sir?"

Blancard's face reddened still deeper as he considered her remark. "Well, I . . ." His embarrassment triggered another laugh before Colette patted his arm sympathetically.

"My apologies for upsetting you, sir. I was making a joke." While he again fumbled for words, she hastily added, "Now please tell me who you are. I am at a distinct disadvantage."

"Hilaire Blancard," he managed. When she returned his handkerchief, it carried her exotic scent, and he fought the urge to sniff it. "And I wish to speak to you about Mademoiselle Baptiste."

"Blancard," she repeated. Her brow furrowed as she sipped her wine. Then, "Ah, yes! The Bank of Louisiana Blancards, monsieur?" He nodded. "And planters on the Cane River?"

He nodded again. "The same." She smiled, altogether disarming. How Blancard wished he had met her years ago. Perhaps he could have wooed her away from that toad Guedry. "I assure you, with your daughter's approval of course, that I can provide amply for her. And yourself as well."

The smile vanished as abruptly as it arose. This was business. "Don't waste time wooing me, Monsieur Blancard. My future is well taken care of, but as for Chaillot . . . well, the Blancard fortunes are certainly well known in New Orleans."

"*Merci*, madame." He bowed lightly, suddenly wishing for another whiskey. No. He'd best keep a clear head around this clever woman. Her skills with money were reputedly as considerable as her skills in the boudoir.

"Save your gratitude for the time being, monsieur. I'm not at all certain you can afford it. We both know my daughter is a rare pearl many consider priceless, and while I admit your fortune has a decided cachet . . ."

"Madame," he said firmly, "I assure you I can provide for her as well as any man present."

Blancard could scarcely contain his resentment. How I hate these negotiations, he thought. How I loathe treating these *sang-melées* as if they were delicate ladies, as though they were *equals!* I, Hilaire Blancard, who deal daily with the most ruthless financial wizards of the city! It is unconscionable that I should be reduced to groveling with this smug black bitch flaunting her power as obviously as her perfume! This was the one facet of *plaçage* he truly despised.

"And to be perfectly frank," Colette continued, delicately twisting the knife, "you are not a young man."

Blancard was further galled but wisely swallowed his outrage. The friendly interchange was now more than a negotiation for a mistress. It had quickly escalated to a calculated duel, one he was determined to win. He had something to prove and he would show the grand Colette Baptiste that she was not holding all the cards.

"So much the better," he said, thinking swiftly. "If something happens to me, Chaillot will still be young and free to do as she chooses with a great deal of money. I'm quite certain you can appreciate the advantages of such a situation, Madame Baptiste." When she merely stared, he said, "But perhaps I am too frank."

Colette was equally swift. "For what we have to discuss, monsieur, frankness is the only avenue."

She smiled again and laid her hand lightly on his forearm. Her mere touch aroused him, evaporating every ill thought of her as she became, at that moment, not a hard-nosed business competitor but a highly desirable woman. How strange, he thought. How could one body radiate so much heat in this cold? That damned Guedry! What a lucky devil he was!

"You want to call on her as soon as possible, I assume."

"*C'est vrai*. Tomorrow perhaps?"

"You are eager." Colette turned away, looking at the Cathedral again, thinking idly that it wouldn't be long before the bells chimed midnight. She took another sip of wine and said, "But then I would be disappointed if you were not eager, monsieur. Come tomorrow at two in the afternoon. I live in the Rue St. Louis. No. 907. Look for a large fig tree."

"I will not be late, Madame Baptiste."

"Somehow I didn't think so, monsieur. *Bon soir*."

She gave Blancard a final smile before acknowledging the gentlemen gesturing wildly over his shoulder, all frantic to discuss Chaillot. She sighed, wearied already by the spoils of her daughter's victory. It would be a long night indeed.

For Chaillot it was just beginning.

Nothing her mother promised or predicted could have prepared her for what happened that strange November night. Yes, she danced and coquetted and, yes, she listened to endless flattery from a string of mostly silly young white men, each of whom was certain she would succumb to their particular charms. And, yes, she found the older gentlemen genteel and more cultivated, more realistic in what they expected her to believe, but for now they too fell by the wayside. As yet there was no one she found irresistible.

Oh, certainly the handsome politician with the wild blond sideburns had a certain appeal and there was the dashing sugar planter who assured her he would, except during harvest, visit her every other week. And what of the cotton broker with the outrageous talk—and too much wine on his breath—of fabulous jewels and trips to Paris, "Where we could pass as man and wife, *ma chérie!* Imagine that!" Imagine, indeed! Chaillot thought angrily. Passing for white may or may not have been what she wanted most in the world, but how dare he presume it? She had been amused by the Americans with their halting French and that older gentleman, the silk merchant? Didn't he waltz divinely? Oh, what was his name? For that matter what were *any* of their names? Chaillot made no attempt to remember, any or all of them. For that matter she hardly recalled their faces.

What dominated Chaillot that night, however, came from within, not without. It was not the endless and quite fabulous promises of glorious destiny that possessed her, rather how she reacted to them. It was an extraordinary and not altogether comfortable surprise, a far greater one than Colette expected when she subjected her daughter to that bizarre baptism by fire.

Chaillot had secretly wanted to hate the entire evening, partly because the phenomenon frightened her and partly because a hidden shred of her soul fought against a concept drummed into her since birth. *Plaçage.* The very word sent a shiver to her spine. It seemed wicked and unnatural, this liaison between black and white. After all, marriage between the races was forbidden in *La Louisiane,* indeed in all the southern states. Miscegenation was a whispered, ugly word, and despite the fact that she, and her mother and grandmother before her, all had white fathers, she wasn't altogether certain the idea wasn't just as ugly.

"It is your only choice!" her mother swore time and again. "And it can be beautiful and fulfilling. Look what it has done for me, for you. Already you are pampered and indulged, educated. It has worked for the Baptiste women for three generations. You will be the *ne plus ultra.* You represent its highest degree of refinement."

Chaillot wasn't sure what that meant either, but she had begun to have doubts, serious doubts. Yes, her parents had been happy. In all her sixteen years, Chaillot had never seen anything but deep affection between her mother and Michie Simon. And her father doted on her, bought her pretty things, took her on trips, sometimes with *maman,* sometimes with his good friend Marius. Marius always amused her, always had a silly story or riddle to make her laugh until her sides hurt and her eyes ran with tears of mirth. Those memories were the best, but there were other memories too, warning her something was wrong with the happy little home in the Rue St. Louis. Sometimes they were strong enough to make her cry. One in particular.

Across the street from the Baptiste house lived a free man of color Martin Dumas and his family. Monsieur Dumas was a successful shopkeeper with a gentle wife, Marie, and a daughter Chaillot's age, a sweet little copper-skinned girl named Babette. The girls had passed each other in the street and studied each other with the sweet curiosity of the very young until they found themselves in the same class at convent school, where they became fast friends. But that friendship was never permitted beyond the walls of the schoolyard, a bitter lesson Chaillot learned when they walked home together. Babette's mother was waiting in the front yard when she saw the children skipping along the banquette, hand in hand, giggling helplessly. Marie Dumas's face was a mask of disapproval and when Babette was within calling distance, she was ordered into the house.

"But *maman!*" Babette cried, corkscrew curls bouncing wildly as she danced along the wooden sidewalk. "This is my new friend Chaillot. Isn't that a pretty name? She lives just across the street. In that house with the blue—"

"You heard me, Babette!" her mother reiterated sternly. "In the house! Now!"

Not a single word was said to Chaillot, left alone on the banquette with nothing more than the lingering warmth of Babette's hand to remind her she had won and lost her first friend in a single day. Chaillot burst into tears and fled inside where Colette tried to explain away what had happened. Oh, that stiff-necked Dumas family, she had said, smoothing Chaillot's straight black hair and holding her head against her bosom. They're friends with no one. They believe they are cut from a cloth as divine as the Holy Father himself. Pay them no mind, *ma petit.* They are not deserving of such tears. Nonsense! You have other friends. Who? Why, myself and Michie Simon of course. And Michie Marius and Michie Narcisse and Tante Nicole and Tante Suzanne. They are the best friends in the world. Friends your own age? Pah! We are all you need.

Chaillot was satisfied until the very next day when Babette spat the truth in front of all their classmates. "Your mother is a bad woman!" she said. "She lives with a white man and she isn't married. Do you know what that makes you, Chaillot?"

Chaillot had no idea, and none of the other girls seemed to know either, but owing to the jeers of derision she was sure it was a terrible thing. Once again she arrived home with tears in her eyes, as well as a scuffed knee earned when one of the older girls pushed her onto the shell walk. This time Simon Guedry was present and when an infuriated Colette announced she would speak to the nuns, he, taking Chaillot in his arms, quietly but firmly declared that she would receive her lessons at home from then on. He would arrange it the next day. Of course, as always, what he said went unquestioned.

So Chaillot's childhood had been a lonely retreat from the rest of the world. Like a Creole bride, she was permitted no voice regarding her destiny. Her friends were all adults, and she dutifully emulated their manners and their ways. She was a grown-up in miniature, a little woman with big blue eyes masquerading in a child's clothes, and if she had not been smothered by so much love, she would have been the most miserable child on earth. The countless dolls, a kitten, trips to the circus, and picnics on Lake Ponchartrain, however, did not ameliorate an ache in her little heart. She was a bright child and knew all too well what was lacking.

When she asked Colette if there weren't others like herself, other light-skinned children she might have as friends, Colette insisted she was better off keeping to herself. Chaillot seized the only opportunity open to children like herself and created an imaginary playmate to replace the real ones she was not permitted. This was Combas, an ugly girl who was alternately black and white and whom Chaillot secretly loved to torment. Had her mother and father known what she did to this pretend playmate, they would have been horrified. Especially if they had known they were responsible for her creation.

Chaillot had overheard enough whispered conversation among her mother and her "tantes" to know all was not perfect in the world of the colored *demimondaine*. Suzanne and Nicole had formed white connections of their own, but none had approached the success of Colette's liaison. Suzanne's first lover was an alcoholic who required constant attention and endless patience to tolerate his wildly fluctuating moods. After he died in a duel, Suzanne had reluctantly taken a second lover. He cared far more for the gambling tables than her company, and when he severed the union after a year she bitterly swore she would never again set foot in the *Salle d'Orléans*. Like many jilted quadroon women, she operated her cottage as a boarding house and proudly turned a modest but steady profit.

Nicole had been even less fortunate. She had fallen in love with her protector, a sweet-tempered young physician who seemed to return her feelings. She had miscarried his child and when she learned, a week later, that Dr. Montagne planned to marry, she attempted suicide. Small wonder, Colette remarked, when the poor girl had learned of the marriage from an announcement in the newspaper! Three years had passed and she managed to work only occasionally as a seamstress and sometime cleaning girl for Toinette Clovis. Had Suzanne not provided her with a tiny room, rent-free—well, the alternatives were not to be considered. The brothels in the Rue Gallatin or, worse, in the notorious Swamp were littered with misfortunate quadroon women sought by white men little better off. They sold a moment of sweaty, grunting passion for a few coins or, all too often for the price of a desperately needed whiskey.

Chaillot's attitude toward the white men in these highly charged emotional dramas was ambivalent in the extreme. She loved her father dearly, but as best she could determine, he was unlike most white gentlemen, a wild card in a deck hopelessly stacked against the quadroon women. *Plaçage*, with all its tantalizing promises of security, of elegant late night suppers with the finest champagne, of fabulous jewelry and Paris gowns, of a deliciously pampered world within that little cottage on the Rue Rampart still could be devastatingly painful and destructive. It might be snatched away in a heartbeat, at the whim of the white master, and leave the woman decimated.

So what was this great surprise that so overwhelmed Chaillot, sending the blood coursing through her veins as she was waltzed endlessly around that glamourous ballroom? What was it that held her transfixed, that clouded her sensibilities and made her want to surrender to one of the white men promising her the moon while perhaps secretly withholding the stars?

Chaillot loved it.

She had taken to the evening as naturally as those ragged Resurrection ferns took to gutters and chimneys, miraculously sprouting high above the city and flourishing with neither soil nor care. And she shared their capacity to appear out of nowhere and seem effortlessly at home.

Chaillot secretly despised herself for it, as much as she had despised poor little Combas. Yet her incorporeal confederate had taught her an invaluable lesson she didn't yet recognize.

Like Justine Blancard, she had cultivated artifice as effortlessly as charm.

CHAPTER 3

Morning was a gleaming topaz. Last night's rainstorm had swept off the Gulf and polished the air to ethereal perfection. Its bequest was a dawn so brilliant it hurt the eyes. Once Marie Tonton stalked into Justine's room and threw open the shutters, it burnished the pale netting of the mosquito *baires* to pure gold.

Startled awake by the brightness, Justine ignored the woman and turned away, squinting against the light. The sun splayed on the worn oriental carpet and streamed across the painting of a haughty Fonteneau ancestor above the mantel before slowly penetrating the prisms dangling from a bedside lamp. The crystal facets caught and shattered the sunlight, staining the room with brilliant rubies and sapphires and blinding white diamonds. For a moment, the room shimmered as though Justine were inside a kaleidoscope, but the enchantment evaporated when a high-flying cloud soared across the face of the sun.

She felt much better equipped to face the momentary dullness and sat up, plumping the pillows and settling against them. She was alone as usual. Hilaire had slept in the adjacent bedroom for years, coming to her bed only when he wanted more than sleep. She grimaced and reached for the mosquito netting, making it shiver just as the dazzling sunlight reappeared. She had enjoyed such refulgent dawns many times, but this particular morning it failed to buoy her spirits as usual. Certainly Marie Tonton was no help, humming off-key as always when she returned with a tray of steaming coffee and fresh croissants. Justine nodded "*Bonjour*" as the servant tied back the *mosquitaire* and positioned the tray on her lap. While Marie Tonton watched, Justine dropped a spoonful of sugar in the inky coffee and stirred. She sipped, found the coffee too hot, and set the cup aside. With Marie Tonton's cold gaze wearing her down, Justine began their inevitably unpleasant morning ritual.

"Is Monsieur Blancard up yet?"

Marie Tonton shrugged, gaunt black face a study in African inscrutability. When she replied, it was in the usual emotionless monotone, thick lips set in an odd curve. Justine often wondered if it was a sneer but the woman was so homely she couldn't tell.

"I don't know, madame."

Since Marie Tonton knew everything that happened in that house, her response was more than annoying. "If the master didn't come home last night, girl, why don't you just say so?"

"That's not what you asked me, madame." Another shrug. The lips shifted slightly. Certain the slave was mocking her, Justine couldn't dismiss her fast enough.

"That's all then. Leave me alone."

"Oui, madame."

Marie Tonton curtsied and was gone. Her manner infuriated Justine because it invariably bordered on insolence. Though the slave always did what she was told, she acted with an insolence that made Justine want to wring her neck. Part of it was because she was Coromantee, a tribe known for arrogance and stubbornness. Hilaire of course adored the woman. She had belonged to his family long before he married Justine and could do no wrong in his eyes. If she hadn't been so thin and ugly, Justine might have wondered if anything untoward flourished between them, but she knew, courtesy of Marie Tonton herself, that Hilaire preferred his colored women much lighter. And certainly younger!

She sipped the coffee, retreated from its heat a second time, and set the cup aside. She studied the portrait again, so annoyed by her ancestor's fey smirk that she was tempted to hurl the coffee cup at his face. She even scowled at the shards of sunlight hurting her eyes and closed the gallery shutters sharply. Yet as she paced the room in her nightgown, she knew none of those things were the source of the morning's torment. It wasn't even the reality that her husband was shopping for a new mistress. In truth Justine greeted that news with some relief since it meant Hilaire would concentrate his attentions elsewhere, both inside the boudoir and out. She had secretly mourned the death of Josette, because the loss of that convenient playground for Hilaire's peculiar and malevolent games meant he would again visit them upon Justine.

Of course Justine knew about Josette. She knew plenty, things that would've horrified dear Christophe and the rest of polite Creole society, all thanks to Marie Tonton. The spiteful wench made certain the *maitresse* knew everything she considered harmful and degrading. A genius in duplicity and collusion with the other servants, whom she ruled with an iron hand, she skillfully delivered ill tidings with a perverse relish that sickened Justine.

Just yesterday morning, when she heard of her master's latest planned infidelity, Marie Tonton could hardly wait to enlighten the madame. Her vehicle this time was Agathe the cook. Justine wondered how long Marie Tonton lurked in the kitchen, waiting for her mistress' footsteps on the flagstones before announcing the news in a tone anything but *sotto voce*.

"Michie Hilaire going to the quadroon balls again, Agathe," she had said. There was a pause before she drove in the nail. "Tonight."

Justine had frozen in the middle of the courtyard, shaking with impotent fury before fleeing back into the house. What could she do? Confront the slave? Marie Tonton would deny it, swear the mistress had misunderstood. Tell her husband Marie Tonton was spinning dangerous tales? Hilaire would merely scowl and reprimand Justine, ordering her yet again to ignore slave gossip. Their childish infatuation with it was inevitable, he would insist, and who cared what they said anyway? Surely the mistress of such a fine house had something better to do with her time.

Tell him the truth? Impossible! Justine could never broach such a volatile subject. Even the most vague allusion to Hilaire's infidelity would trigger an outrage too intense to bear, and it certainly wouldn't be directed at Marie Tonton.

Justine recoiled from the mere notion and stopped pacing. A light chill propelled her to look for a peignoir, but as she approached the towering mahogany armoire its mirrored face caught a flash of color on her pale arm. She froze at the sight of her own image. Hand trembling, she inspected the purple blossom on her wrist, one she had carefully concealed at last night's opera with her gloves. The bruise was the ugly legacy of a savage seizure by her husband, a cruel reef in a sea of otherwise unsullied flesh.

He rarely marked her, and never where it could not be concealed.

Justine absently massaged the bruise, frowning at the surrounding splash of yellowish skin where older marks were vanishing. She frowned and drew on the dimity dressing gown, remembering the imagined transgression that had earned her this latest badge of belligerence. She closed her eyes, conjuring the moment when Blancard had seized her wrist and twisted until she crumpled to the floor.

Justine had long ago learned not to scream, although the man was free to vent his fury as loudly as he chose. He cared nothing for what the servants thought, and as for what curious neighbors might hear, hadn't a man the right to discipline his slaves? When he released her, she had staggered weakly to the dressing table and her jewelry box. It was the pearl earrings he objected to. They looked cheap, he said, and reflected badly on him; she should wear instead the ones he bought her in Paris. Justine didn't dare explain that the simple pearl earrings had been in her family for generations, that they were far more tasteful than the *nouveau riche* diamonds he had chosen. Indeed the best she could hope for was that her wildly trembling hands could affix the glittering monstrosities to her ears before her husband struck again.

It was always some triviality that provoked his outbursts, something innocently said or done that brought Hilaire's wrath upon her head. His rage was as mercurial and unpredictable as the summer thunderstorms that swept without warning from the Gulf. And just as destructive.

She was barely sixteen when Hilaire Blancard won her hand, promising her ill and widowed father Marin Fonteneau that his daughter and only child would never want for anything. Fonteneau knew only too well that the family fortunes were at an irreversible low ebb and saw the marriage as his daughter's best hope for security. Justine acceded to her father's wishes without question, secretly thrilled that he had chosen someone as handsome as he was rich. She had been doubtful at first since the only bankers she had ever met were stern, serious sorts, but this affable gentleman with the curly black hair and dancing eyes had an effervescent manner that bordered on the dashing. Like her father, indeed like all of *La Nouvelle-Orléans,* Justine was charmed by Hilaire Blancard. She never dreamed she was marrying not one man, but two.

She had approached her wedding night with the terror typical of a convent-bred Creole girl. She knew nothing of carnal relations except what the pious sisters had whispered sternly about procreation and had no notion what to expect. Had she been the most skilled courtesan on earth, however, she would have been unnerved by what unfolded.

Following an enormous wedding reception, with Blancard generously supplying hundreds of guests with the finest champagne, Justine was escorted to the groom's home by her Tante Nanine, down from Baton Rouge to fill the role traditionally filled by the bride's mother. Assisted by a female servant specially trained in the needs of new brides, the giddy Nanine helped Justine change into a luxurious embroidered nightgown and negligee sewn especially for the wedding night. Her hair was unbound from its high chignon and brushed by the servant girl until it crackled. When it was tied back with scarlet ribbons, she was told to get into bed and wait.

Left alone, Justine nestled against the huge pillows and pondered her fate. She imagined all sorts of madness as she stared at the massive mahogany bed with its half tester hovering protectively overhead. She thought it was sweet of Hilaire to choose a bridal tester of her favorite pale blue silk, gathered in the center with gilded shells and ornamented with plump cherubs pursuing one another with bows and arrows. And it seemed he had remembered how she loved *dentelle valiencienne* for he had selected that creamy lace for the tester's trim. Such thoughtfulness had made Justine smile and feel a surge of something for this man she had married, this man she did not know. Perhaps, she thought eagerly, it was the beginnings of love.

Such thoughts, coupled with exhaustion from the long day's excitement, eventually carried her off to sleep. She was awakened by a crash when the door slammed open sometime after midnight. Blancard was silhouetted in the doorway, a cloaked specter wielding a malacca cane. Roused from a deep sleep, she nevertheless knew at once that the man was drunk.

"*Voilà!*" he shouted, pointing the cane at the bed and its bewildered occupant. "So the virginal maid awaits the bridegroom in her chambers, does she?"

The coarse words disturbed Justine, both in content and delivery. Sensing danger, she slowly drew the sheet to her throat. Even the slight motion caught Blancard's eye.

"What's this I see? Modesty from the maiden?" He lurched forward, caught the cane on the corner of the rug and nearly pitched headlong onto the floor. He steadied himself against a bedpost and leered at his cowering bride. His lips were contorted into a hideous smile, eradicating every shred of handsomeness from his face.

"Why, the bridal chamber is no place for modesty, Madame Blancard!"

With that, he hurled the cane across the room with such force it cracked and splintered against the marble fireplace. The gold ram's head was knocked free, rolling somewhere beneath the bed. Justine could not have known that he tasted her terror, was actually aroused by its deliciousness. Nor could she have fathomed how he had planned his strategy with calculated perversity. Knowing ignorance was her greatest weakness he played it like a riverboat gambler holding all the cards. Justine was convent-bred and without a mother, fashioned by the nuns into a creature designed for complaisance. She was a lump of clay trained to submit to any mold thrust upon it, and Blancard intended to sculpt the most submissive entity imaginable.

While Justine watched with mounting horror, Blancard seized the negligee and rent it with one ferocious pull. It tore neatly down the middle, exposing the immodest nightgown and her half-bared breasts.

"Monsieur Blancard!" Justine cried, shocked, mortified. "What . . . ?"

The protest died as his hand shot out again. She was dragged across the bed as the nightgown was yanked hard, again and again. The muslin was sturdier stuff and did not yield so easily, cutting painfully into her neck and shoulders. Justine flailed arms and legs and struggled to fend him off as he tore at her with both hands.

His hands! Huge and powerful, they seemed everywhere at once, shredding the rest of the nightgown until Justine was naked. She wanted to scream but Blancard's mouth closed over hers, his tongue choking her into silence while he took monstrous liberties with her bare flesh. Beneath his frenzied clutches, her breasts were crushed until the nipples throbbed with pain. Somehow his mouth found them too, but when Justine tried to cry out she could summon only a guttural moan. His hands traveled lower still. She locked her ankles in a frantic effort to hold her thighs together and pounded his chest, but this too was folly against Blancard's superior strength, multiplied by drunken lust.

Justine felt herself hurtling toward an abyss, inhabited only by Blancard's hands and the burn of his ravenous mouth. She thought matters could not get worse but that hope was decimated when he rolled atop her and forced her thighs apart with his knee. There was a frenzied fumbling as he tore open his trousers and then a searing pain as he drove his hard flesh, with one ferocious lunge, into her very quick. Justine's lips parted in a silent scream while he moved above her, a groaning, sweating madman straining for release. Long before he attained it, Justine drifted into merciful oblivion. As memory faded, she looked beyond Hilaire's twisted, anguished face and saw the cherubs in the blue *ciel-de-lit*, smirking, mocking, maddening. Then she saw and felt nothing.

It was only the beginning. Creole tradition strictly decreed that newlyweds not leave their bedroom for five days and receive no visitors for two weeks. Those two weeks were an unspeakable time of relentless ravishing for Justine, broken only when the seemingly oblivious servant brought food or when Blancard drank himself into another stupor.

The heinous memory conjured and completed, Justine struggled to be free of it again, summoning all her strength as she willed it to vanish. Slowly those swarming, shadow-dusted sunmotes retreated, melting into shreds of images that, in turn, in time, also dissolved. She shuddered with the passing of each memory: Hilaire's terrible grin . . . that palpitating monstrosity he unleashed again and again against her battered, yielding flesh . . . the bloody linens and torn nightgown . . . her skin like bruised magnolia petals . . . the overwhelming stench of raw concupiscence and stale whiskey. And that terrible pronouncement Hilaire unleashed the last night of her sequestered hell.

"Just think, Justine. Tomorrow we sail for Europe where there will be no one to interrupt our pleasure." He kissed her and stroked her cheek with shocking tenderness. "How fortunate we are to have found each other, *ma chérie!* And need no one else!"

For Justine it was tantamount to being sentenced to hell.

"Mon dieu!" she wailed. "Help me!"

She slipped quickly from the chaise longue, terrified by a heart that thrummed alarmingly as she knelt at the bedside *prie-dieu* and hastily crossed herself. Her tightly clasped hands were cold as the marble top where they rested as she begged God for deliverance. In what had become a daily ritual Justine recounted all that had happened at the hands of her husband, pleaded to be heard, and even dared ask God if He might have forgotten her. Fear of such divine deafness was even more disturbing than her enslavement to Blancard, a fear that deepened as she drifted toward an unthinkable apostasy.

Prayer, even novenas to her dear blessed Virgin, no longer strengthened her, no longer assured her that she was heard, watched, and loved. She felt only desolation as the flame of a lone votive candle danced high on a beatific face now battered by tears.

Justine had no idea how long she knelt, knees numb, lips moving silently as she recited prayers that had become monotonous and meaningless until the clacking of her mother's rosary beads was undermined by another, more insistent sound. She cocked her ear toward the Cathedral, frowning at a steady tolling of bells buoyed louder by a strong wind from the river. The Angelus, she thought weakly. How could it possibly be noon?

Everyone in the bustling *Café de Aguila* was absorbed in dominoes this Sunday afternoon, hunched over small tables, sipping coffee and hot chocolate and contemplating their moves. The two exceptions were in a corner looking into crowded Jackson Square. Christophe propped his chin on one hand and fought laughter as he pitied his companion's pained expression.

Duncan Saunders leaned across the table, oval face ashen. The strong chin was perhaps emphasized too much this day, lending him a harsh, ascetic look, draining attention from a pleasantly generous mouth and soft hazel eyes. Thick sandy hair was still unruly despite a thorough brushing, and his cheeks bore the telltale nicks of shaving with a shaky hand. He felt much older than his twenty-seven years and, on this particular morning, looked it. The loud toll of the nearby cathedral bells did nothing to improve his headache.

"I don't know how you Creoles do it," he lamented, running fingers through his curly hair. "I watched you drink last night. Why isn't your head splitting like mine?"

"It's all a matter of pacing oneself," Christophe advised. He tasted his steaming café au lait and smiled. "You *Yanquis* simply never learned how to enjoy life."

Duncan sipped his coffee with tremulous hands and considered the remark. He was just recently arrived in New Orleans, a Virginian come to visit his brother uptown, and he had been repeatedly warned about the arrogance and haughtiness of the xenophobic French Creoles. Although Louisiana had been an American state for forty-five years, New Orleans remained two largely disparate cities, split by more than the Rue Canal, sharing neither language nor religion, customs nor cuisine.

And certainly not neighborhoods. When the Creoles firmly denied them residential entry into their venerable *carré de la ville*, the Americans built homes upriver and dubbed the area the Garden District. The Catholic Creoles dismissed the unwelcome newcomers as crude, greedy boors and considered the word *Américain* a disgraceful term. The hard-working Protestant Yankees found the "Cray-owls" impossibly sybaritic, obsessed with opera, theater, balls, and dueling. Business dealings increasingly forced a crossing of paths, and limited socializing naturally followed, but when the Americans achieved a majority and seized control of the city, the old, smoldering hatreds were stoked. The younger Creoles were far more tolerant than their elders, but serene coexistence was far from a reality.

Yet last night, on his first foray into the French sector, Duncan had encountered Christophe Arnaud, a fine gentleman who single-handedly debunked every unpleasant thing he'd heard about Creoles. Not only was Arnaud amusing and extravagantly polite, he spoke fluent English and seemed hellbent on showing Duncan and his brother Randolph a good time. Since his offhand comment about pleasure was the closest the man had come to being anything less than hospitable, Duncan dismissed it. Besides, he decided, it was probably the truth.

"Perhaps," he conceded with a wry grin.

"*Mais, oui!*" Christophe insisted. "Take your brother for instance," he offered. "Last night he told me he works straight through the day. Fine for November I suppose, but most of the year it's simply unthinkable.

Too hot! Much too hot! That's why we Creoles take long midday breaks. And *siestas, mon ami*. And dine late, when it's cooler. These are the answers for working and living in the tropics."

"My brother is a great success," Duncan said proudly. "One of the most successful cotton brokers in the city."

"I've no doubt he is," Christophe said. "I've a few American friends and the Saunders name is often bandied about. Your brother is, with all due respect, one of those *Yanquis* who . . . how does that saying go? Ah, yes. 'He worships the almighty dollar'!"

"Randolph simply wants to provide well for us," Duncan said coolly.

Christophe hastily apologized. "Please believe I meant no offense, monsieur. It's just that we Creoles don't look at things so seriously." He gripped his striped lapels, pulling them apart so Duncan was dazzled by a sea of gold brocade. "We simply believe no job is worth having if it means a gentleman must take off his jacket."

"Speaking of work," Duncan ventured, "I don't recall your livelihood."

Christophe laughed, twirling the ends of his long black moustache. "I'm afraid there's quite a bit you don't recall of last night, monsieur. You see, you paid much closer attention to the whiskey than to my conversation." He winked, again trying not to laugh. "An admirable choice I might add."

"Please don't, Christophe," Duncan pleaded. "It hurts too much to laugh!" He rubbed his temples. "I vaguely remember you teaching me a word in French. About your profession or something."

"Ah, yes!" Christophe replied patiently. "The word is *fainéant*." He repeated the word and dismissed it with a shrug so grandly insouciant that Duncan conceded a pained chuckle. In response to his raised eyebrows, Christophe answered, "How do you say in English . . . oh! I have it! 'Idler.' "

"You say it almost proudly."

"And why not?" Christophe demanded with mock gravity. "It is something I have carefully cultivated, something I seek to elevate to an ever higher plateau. A civilized perfection of sorts. Something I . . ."

"Could not do without independent means," Duncan finished with another chuckle.

"*Exactement!*" Christophe was pleased with the amiable jibe. "And you, my *Yanqui* friend. What is your profession?"

"I'm a poet," Duncan replied, a bit defensively. "At least I *purport* to be," he added, softening the hard edge in his voice.

"Published? No? *Eh, bien!* But you too have independent means, *oui*? Oh! I am being too frank again."

"Perhaps."

"But I thought you Americans liked to talk about money," Christophe insisted.

"Some Americans, perhaps. But not Virginians." Duncan winked. "You Creoles have a great deal to learn about us as well."

"Then I relish the lesson!" Christophe grinned.

Duncan nodded. "But you were right about something else. My brother is very generous."

"Mmmm. Poetry. It is a difficult vocation, I suspect. As difficult as choosing the right cravat or finding the ideal woman."

Duncan was astonished. "I hardly consider those vocations."

"Oh, but they can be," Christophe insisted mischievously. He was unexpectedly uneasy when Justine came to mind. Then, brightening, "Color is coming back to your cheeks, my boy. Are you feeling better I hope?"

"A little I think."

"*Bon!* Come then. Let's take a stroll. It's a glorious day, and the *carré de la ville* is especially colorful on Sundays."

Duncan drained his coffee and stood, feeling much steadier than before. Whatever was contained in the strong Creole coffee was definitely rejuvenating. Even his headache was gone. He felt good enough to joke a bit and even attempted some French.

"As one *fainéant* to another, Monsieur Arnaud, I think that is an excellent idea."

Christophe bowed and offered his arm, steering his new friend down the banquette, through the iron gates of Jackson Square. They made a strange couple, the stocky, wild-haired American in his dark frock coat and the immaculately groomed Creole in striped jacket, brilliant gold waistcoat, top hat jauntily cocked to one side. After a few noisy steps, Duncan nodded at the sword-cane jangling at Christophe's side.

"Have you ever used that thing?"

Christophe flashed an avuncular smile. "*Bien sûr, mon ami.* Many times. You see, for us Creoles honor hangs in the air like this splendid November chill." Christophe stroked the wide hilt of the *colchemarde*, noting with satisfaction how it tapered abruptly to a wicked rapier blade. "Of course dueling has been illegal since Bienville's time, but the law was always ignored." He nudged Duncan in the side. "You will find that has become something of a hallowed tradition in Louisiana, ignoring the law, I mean. That was the case back in '48 when new state legislation disenfranchised duelists. It was repealed, but dueling remains illegal and is supposed to be heavily fined. But no one attempts to collect.

"Really?"

Christophe nodded. "Predawn gatherings under the oaks at the old Allard plantation are still common enough. If you want to see one, I'm sure it can be arranged."

"Thank you, no," Duncan replied, thoroughly bewildered and not a little repulsed. How could the man discuss fatal encounters with such nonchalance? The civilized Creoles were a contradictory lot indeed.

"A cockfight then!" Christophe continued, undeterred. "There's a cockpit just down the Rue Chartres here. No? Very well. Then may I suggest a bull and bear encounter?" Christophe's enthusiasm was building. "What's that? You don't believe me?"

"What I don't believe," Duncan said as they entered the iron gates of Jackson Square, "is that I am in New Orleans and not ancient Rome. Duels. Cockfights. Animal matches. Gambling houses. Bordellos. And what were you telling me last night? Those dance halls where all the women are colored. My God, man! In Virginia, people would be absolutely horrified."

Christophe beamed. "Then we must go to the Cathedral at once!"

"What for?"

"To thank God we are not in Virginia of course!" Duncan smiled when Christophe threw an arm around his shoulders and gestured expansively. "Come along now, *mon ami*. I will show you the sights." At the center of the Square he stopped. "This is the very heart of the *carré de la ville*, what you Americans call the French Quarter. It was our old *Place d'Armes* until five years ago when the city fathers renamed it Jackson Square for the former president." He pointed with his chin. "This formal French garden and his statue were dedicated just this year. It's one of the few equestrian statues with the horse balanced completely on the hind legs. I rather like it."

"Impressive indeed," Duncan nodded. "Especially the horse's energy. Why, it's barely contained!"

Christophe was pleased. He stared at the statue a long moment, then chuckled. "You remember Jackson was the general who saved us from the British in '15. It's so typical of New Orleans that the battle was fought *after* the peace agreements were signed, but no matter. Hmmmm, yes. I believe everything here is new or has just been rebuilt."

Towering over all was the city's most famous landmark, the triple-spired St. Louis Cathedral. Christophe opined that the gray Spanish Gothic structure seemed to brood between the City Hall and Court House, each boasting gleaming new mansard roofs. Flanking both sides of the Square were the Pontalba Buildings, commissioned by Micaela Almonaster y Roxas, the Baroness Pontalba. Handsome three-story brick apartments, they were graced with exquisite iron galleries rather boldly laced with the baronness's initials. Christophe dismissed the initials as vulgar but unsurprising.

"What do you expect from a woman who rented a furnished apartment to Jenny Lind during her New Orleans engagement and then promptly auctioned everything that 'belonged' to the celebrated Madame Lind?!"

"A shrewd businesswoman," Duncan said.

"Vulgar," Christophe sniffed.

Duncan was admiring the Pontalba Buildings' impressive expanse when Christophe urged him toward the colonnade where they might lean comfortably and watch the Square's kaleidoscope of humanity.

A few feet away stood a gathering of young dandies, spiritedly arguing the merits of last night's performance of Meyerbeer's *Les Huguenots, colchemardes* clanking as they playfully jostled each other. Nearby City Guards, themselves armed with menacing cutlasses, seemed oblivious to any potential trouble, far more concerned with keeping an eye on the female pedestrians. Christophe tipped his hat and muttered in French to a number of promenading Creole families, several with daughters stationed firmly between vigilant parents. The natural sway of one especially comely girl's dimity skirts issued an innocent invitation that was never to be acknowledged, much less answered. The eye of every young man locked on his peers as well as her, waiting, watching for the slightest impropriety—especially from the American stranger.

Sensing danger and recalling Christophe's remark about the Creoles' perpetually hovering honor, Duncan looked away, following instead the progress of a statuesque mulatress sweeping through the Square like a queen, a basket of oranges balanced effortlessly atop her head. Wrapped in tight skirts, her hips also swayed provocatively, but there was scarcely a penalty for looking one's fill there.

The startling pair approaching from the opposite direction, trailed by their colored *domestiques,* posed yet another matter of propriety, and Duncan's eyebrows rose as they grew nearer. Christophe had seen the women coming and waited for a reaction. He was not disappointed. Dressed at the height of French fashion, these women wore elegant taffeta dresses and wide-brimmed bonnets atop carefully coiffed hair. The one in rose twirled a lacy parasol in small gloved hands, casting intricate shadows in her wake. Her companion, in buttercup yellow, dropped her eyes but smiled discreetly at Duncan when she passed. He flushed so furiously Christophe almost burst out laughing. For an instant the women huddled, the one in yellow giving Duncan a long parting look before continuing on. The young dandies huddled too, lusty laughter following the women as they exited the Square. Never a vain man, Duncan's male pride was nonetheless stoked, and he preened under Christophe's amused gaze.

"And who might those ladies be?"

"Those are not ladies, *mon ami*. You have just seen two of our most famous *sang-melées.*"

"Translation please?"

"Women of mixed blood. One is a quadroon. The one on the left is an octoroon."

"Sometimes I don't know whether you're speaking English or French," Duncan lamented.

Christophe nodded, patient as ever. "I explained about them last night."

"Ah!" Duncan said. "The balls . . . ?" Christophe nodded. "But they look white!"

"Act your age, boy. Café au lait, at least." He reconsidered. "Well, the one in yellow has perhaps a surfeit of cream."

Duncan was mystified. "Slave women in Virginia wouldn't dare dress like that. If they did, they'd never go out in public."

"You keep forgetting these women are not slaves, Duncan. They're free to dress as they like, if they can afford it. Such was not always the case, though. Under the Spaniards, fancy clothing for women of color was actually banned in New Orleans. But the *Tignon* Law was forgotten long ago."

"The what?" More and more Duncan felt as if he were in a foreign country. The sensation intensified when Christophe explained the actions of Governor Don Estevan de Miró in 1786.

"In those days high-born Creole ladies wore dull, untailored fashions and were being publicly shamed by the flamboyant fashions of the quadroon women. As they do today, the women of color had a penchant for silks and satins, for plumes and jewels, and happily flaunted their booty in the streets. And booty it was since everyone knew they would all be wearing the *tignon* were they not the mistress of some wealthy white gentleman."

"*Tignon?*"

"A head kerchief, like the one worn by that mulatress with the oranges." Duncan nodded, fascinated. While he listened, his eyes trailed the beauteous mixed-bloods, now engaged in conversation with their maid.

"The quadroons' defiance brought the Creole ladies' wrath upon their heads, quite literally actually, and upon their sisters of color as well. Under considerable pressure, Miró's *Bando de buen gobierno* accused the quadroon women of pursuing a life dedicated to libertinism and threatened them with exile. He even restricted their headwear to the *tignon* and banned the adornment of plumes or jewels in public." He chuckled, noting where Duncan's attention was focused. "But the plan backfired."

"Oh?" Duncan asked vaguely.

"By all accounts, these women were more beautiful than ever, even with adornment restricted to simple frocks and a handkerchief atop their heads."

"Obviously times have changed," Duncan said.

"Thanks to you *Yanquis*, the law rather disappeared. So you see, not all the American influences have been bad!" He took Duncan's arm again as they strolled on. "Come along. This spectacle begins to fatigue me."

As they passed through the gates facing the river, Duncan stepped over two drunken Choctaws, nakedness ill-concealed beneath a filthy shared blanket. The City Guards were oblivious to the spectacle, as were a pair of nuns looking discreetly away. Duncan's attention was diverted by an Arab with a dancing monkey and a Greek ice cream vendor exotic in a tasseled fez. He chuckled.

"I take it back, Christophe. Your city is more like Carthage than Rome."

Christophe nodded his approval. "As you say, my friend. With perhaps a *soupçon* of Babylon thrown in." Then with a naughty wink. "Maybe even some Sodom and Gomorrah as well!"

From there they strolled the levee, no less boisterous because of the Sabbath, where Duncan's mind reeled from sheer spectacle. His night arrival and his excitement upon seeing his brother had inhibited his first impressions of a port stretching over two miles, its waters in a state of unceasing turmoil from the *va-et-vient* of river traffic. New Orleans was America's fourth largest *entrepôt* and the undisputed Queen City of the South. Her enviable position near the mouth of the Mississippi had spawned soaring fortunes. She shipped more cotton than any port on earth, along with tobacco, flour, hooppoles, staves, and furs from upriver and, from her own empire, sugar, rice, and the ubiquitous cotton. From England her groaning levee received woolen goods, farming tools, and crude machinery, while France thrilled the city's fashionable elite with silks and satins and exquisite furniture and liquors. The Caribbean slaked New Orleans' endless thirst for rich coffees and spiced her fabled food with cinnamon, ginger and cloves.

The waterfront roiled feverishly, sweating and heaving all of a piece as hundreds of slaves rolled hogsheads and hefted monstrous bales of cotton, unloading cargo from the Gulf only to reload it for shipment up-river, scarcely resting before they reversed the process. Linking this most glittering nova in the river galaxy with the remaining universe was a bewildering array of watercraft from blunt-nosed European trading brigs to New England coasting craft and heavy Indiamen from Mexico and the Caribbean. Duncan was dazzled by a magnificent clippership making for the Gulf, eye wandering to her billowing moonrakers and stargazers and, at the very top, an angel's footstool.

But Christophe's attention was snared by something else. "Ah, yes! There, they are my favorites, those gorgeous ladies!" He jabbed his sword-cane at the chaos of fretwork stretching as far as the eye could see. "*Regardez, monsieur!* The steamboats!"

Graceful prows muzzled together like nuzzling puppies, docked two and three deep due to insufficient wharfage, the glamorous steamboats were unquestionably the *ne plus ultra* of vessels. A forest of fluted masts bloomed like lotuses against an azure sky, some idle, others spewing black smoke. Banners draped across elegant fretwork bows read like a riverine geography lesson. FOR BATON ROUGE. FOR NATCHEZ, VICKSBURG & PORT GIBSON. FOR MEMPHIS & ST. LOUIS. FOR CAIRO. FOR CINCINNATI.

The great Mississippi River, thought Duncan, oddly, deeply moved. It was New Orleans' *raison d'etre*, which, when it wasn't buoying the city to fabulous wealth, could devastate with monstrous whims. For now a complex system of levees held it at bay, but there always lurked the possibility of a *crevasse*, that dreaded breach that could inundate the helplessly flat delta. When the river rose highest in the spring, it was often the city fathers' surreptitious duty to dynamite the levee somewhere up-river and divert potential fatal flows elsewhere. It was just one more reminder that Jean-Baptiste LeMoyne, Sieur de Bienville, had founded his colony where nature dictated none belonged.

Duncan marveled at this serpent constricting the city in its watery coils. How easy for the beast to flex those great aquatic muscles, reminding all who was most powerful. His poet's mind bowed to the distant whisper.

"You're here only through my benevolence. You were mine before. I can take you back at any moment. Remember that. Always remember that."

"Remember that," Duncan muttered.

"Remember what?" Christophe asked, puzzled by his friend's mumbling.

"I was just remembering that you told me much of the city was below sea level," he hastily replied.

"That it is. We'd all wash away if it weren't for these levees. You can hardly see them beneath such hubbub. I'll bring you back when it's busier during the week."

"It's busy enough for me today," Duncan conceded.

"You have seen enough, *mon ami? Oui?* Then we shall visit Labarre the watchmaker in the Pontalba Building just over there. I saw something charming in his window last week. Then we'll drop by *Valencia* for something to drink. They have the purest Majorca in the city."

"*C'est . . . bon,*" Duncan said slowly. "Is that correct?"

CHAPTER 4

H ilaire had pulled every string available, called in every favor owed, to get the little cottage in the Rue Rampart ready in time. Typical in design of those favored by Creole gentlemen for stashing a mistress, it was a shotgun house, so-called because an *enfilade* could pass from front to rear without hitting anything. Except, the saying went, a cuckholding mistress and her unlucky paramour.

It had been sadly dilapidated, but repairs had not been the only bulwark to progress. It had belonged to Lucinde Rousteau, an ancient mulatress who resisted all pressure to sell. Hilaire's connections had solved the problem by having her evicted. The rights of the *gens de coleur* were protected only so far, and never far enough when the white man's cupidity sought to impugn them. Especially when the man was Hilaire Blancard and he was anxious to set up housekeeping with his new mistress.

When Hippolyte drew the carriage up before the house, excitement rose high in Blancard's blood when he saw lights glowing dimly through the thick grove of banana trees. He scrambled out of the coach and grunted at Hippolyte.

"Don't wait, old man."

It was New Year's Eve, and Blancard had every intention of staying well into 1857. He could almost hear his heartbeat as he hurried toward the inviting glow, feet crunching on the shell walk.

"New Year's Eve," he muttered. "An auspicious date indeed."

The door opened before he knocked, and what he saw fevered his blood. Chaillot awaited him in the dress her mother and "tantes" had agonized over for weeks. Anticipating that Blancard would be formally dressed for a New Year's ball, the women had decided on a formal gown for Chaillot. Madame Clovis' elegant skills had been put to the test as she created something Hilaire would remember all his life.

To emphasize Chaillot's pale skin, the *modiste* had fashioned a rose watered-silk fantasy cut low over the bosom and showered with creamy chantilly lace. Chaillot's hair tumbled freely to her shoulders, a cloud of ebony. Her slender throat and wrists sparkled with jewelry Hilaire had sent weekly to the house in the Rue St. Louis where he had conceded to Colette's outrageous demands on her daughter's behalf. Once the agreement was made and the contracts signed, Hilaire Blancard, albeit at a phenomenal price, had acquired for himself the most sought-after *sang-melée* in the city, and he could not wait to shower her with presents. The house and the jewelry were just the beginning.

"*Bon soir*, monsieur," Chaillot said, cheeks flushing as she lowered her eyes and dropped a graceful curtsy. "Welcome home."

Home. It was as if he'd never heard the word. While he watched enrapt, still unable to comprehend his fortune at possessing this treasure, Chaillot dutifully hung his cloak and tucked his cane into a stand by the door. She gestured toward the row of glittering decanters, filled with what she knew were his favorite wines and whiskies.

"A drink, monsieur? Or would you like to see the house first? I so hope you like the furnishings I've chosen. I . . . Michie Hilaire! What are you doing?!"

As Colette had predicted, Blancard had unashamedly fallen to his knees at the first sight of her. Chaillot was thoroughly abashed by the spectacle and struggled to keep her knees from trembling while she stroked the gentleman's temples.

"You are pleased with me, Michie Hilaire?"

She was carefully humble but her mother's word resounded in her head: "*Eclipsed!*"

"You are . . . divine, *ma chérie!*" he gasped. He grabbed her hands and pressed them to his lips. "Absolutely divine!"

Blancard remained on his knees for another moment, gazing up at her as though he were a mere mortal and she a goddess looming with Olympian inaccessibility. But, he thought as he got to his feet, she was hardly inaccessible. She was his, bought and paid for, with as much finality as a house slave purchased under the great dome at the Hotel St. Louis.

He towered over her, leaning close to inhale her scent, an erotic combination of gardenia, musk, and something uniquely hers. Again Blancard felt his blood coursing at the girl's ripe pungency. He was already erect.

"Come here," he breathed, voice low and slightly choked. "Come here, *mon petit ange.*"

Chaillot arched her head backward as Blancard's lips came down to meet hers. She hadn't expected the sudden whiskey taste of his tongue, but she accepted it as she knew she must. Pleasing the man was all— was everything—and she complacently surrendered as she was swept into his arms and carried to the bedroom.

Blancard was aching to unwrap this dear and costly package, but he forced himself to use restraint. There could be, he reminded himself, only one first time. He took no notice of anything in the small boudoir but the towering *ciel-de-lit* and gleaming mahogany armoire with double mirrored doors. As he perched Chaillot on the edge of the bed and undressed her with care, he smiled at the reflection in those mirrors. Had she, he wondered hotly, intentionally placed the armoire just so?

"Such perfection," he marveled. *"Magnifique!"*

The silk and lace yielded easily, whispering over Chaillot's shoulders, baring the straps of her chemise. These too were pushed aside, and Blancard caught his breath as more pale flesh was exposed to him. He reveled in the splendid heft of her young breasts, creamy mounds with roseate nipples inviting the heat of his mouth. Chaillot moaned when he drank deep, awakening her flesh in ways her mother had not explained. While Blancard hungrily nuzzled Chaillot's breasts, a hand found her bare ankle and began the journey north, toward those mysterious headwaters between her thighs. When his progress was impeded by a corset, layers of petticoats, pantaloons and drawers, Chaillot remembered her mother's warnings and moved quickly.

"Un moment, monsieur," she whispered.

Blancard lay back and watched as the girl divested herself of clothing with remarkable speed. Her hands made short work of the dozens of tiny buttons, and the flowered dressing screen was soon piled high with clothing. Chaillot stood before him, naked now, and waiting. She quite simply stole his breath away.

"Mon dieu!"

With her help, mercifully countering his inept fumbling, Blancard's clothes joined hers atop the screen. Naked, the two fell backward onto the bed where he was consumed by a sea of pale, virginal flesh. His hand discovered those headwaters at last, and Chaillot shivered as his fingers stroked her pubic down.

"Mon dieu!" Again and again, *"Mon dieu!"*

Despite a chill in the room, Blancard's body erupted with sweat as he moved above her, anxious, hungry. Sensing his urgency, Chaillot too moved swiftly, deliciously shocking when her small hand found the puissant flesh and steered him home. Chaillot moaned, throwing back her head and baring her teeth as their flesh merged, spawning a pain both exquisite and swift. Blancard gasped, then groaned as he found port too quickly.

"Ahhh . . . !"

Chaillot clung tight, holding him as he feverishly rode out the storm. She was bewildered by the whimpering that followed, as though the man were bemoaning an irretrievable loss. She could not fathom what it might be, it all being so new to her. The only certainty was that the pain and the moment had passed, and she was glad for both because she knew then, as she had feared, that she would never love Hilaire Blancard.

Blancard had not been hungry when he arrived, but the idyllic interlude with Chaillot had left him ravenous. Acting on his instructions, Chaillot had purchased a cook just two days ago, a woman named Catin, and she instructed her to prepare a light supper. While they waited, Chaillot floated about in a lilac peignoir with, at Blancard's request, nothing underneath. She fetched his robe, lit his cheroot, and poured champagne in an effort to make herself even more beguiling.

"Will you have a look at the house now, michie? I'm most anxious for you to see it?"

"Of course," he conceded.

Chaillot led him from room to room, proudly pointing out an elegant *escritoire* and a marble-topped table with a new argant lamp, exquisite lace curtains, and a dining room with the table already set with the contents of a sumptuous mahogany china cabinet.

She had not, it seemed, overlooked even the tiniest detail, especially the one that poor Josette was so prone to transgress: She never forgot to rise with Blancard and never sat while he stood.

"You have done a splendid job, *ma chérie*," he said. "I am most pleased."

Blancard suddenly wanted to take her in his arms again, but without a trace of passion. As he held her tight, stroking her thick black hair and whispering nonsense, the sound of an opening door prompted a desperate whisper from Chaillot.

"Will you be having supper now, michie?" Chaillot asked, taking care to stand behind him.

Blancard understood when he saw the wide-eyed Catin struggling with a heavy tray. "Not here," he said. When the cook gave him a look of utter bewilderment, he said, "Put it down. There. Now leave us alone." He kissed the top of Chaillot's head and said, "We'll have supper in bed, *mon petite ange.* But without our clothes!"

Some time later, all appetites sated, Chaillot curled up in his arms and slept. Blancard was still awake, watching the child-woman nestled sweetly against him, breath stirring the hair of his chest. "The breath of angels," he murmured, toying with a wild lock of Chaillot's hair. He knew he should sleep, yet he couldn't take his eyes off her long enough to close them.

He drank the swell of her breasts as she breathed, and the wiry fleece between her thighs, but he was also fascinated by the grace of her long neck, the smooth peaks of her shoulders, the elegant curve of her spine reflected in the mirrored armoire. Chaillot moaned softly, as though teased by a bad dream and snuggled closer. Again he was drawn to the mirrored image of her back, mesmerized by the expanse of exposed flesh, pale and vulnerable.

Blancard frowned as the naked flesh shimmered and blurred. An alien image coalesced, faint pink stria appearing on Chaillot's back, spreading and sharpening until Blancard could no longer focus on them. The pale streaks darkened, glowing crimson until there was no mistaking the vibrating image.

He closed his eyes in recognition, opening them quickly when a terrible tableau was wrested from memory. A naked body fluttered in his mind, merging reluctantly with a face. It was that girl, so long ago, at Mimosa, his uncle's sugar plantation on the Cane River. . . . What was her name? Medioza! Yes, Medioza! The very first slave he had whipped, the one who had awakened in him what should have remained forever buried in the dark of his soul.

Nonc Michel had thrust the whip into his small hand. He had been twelve years old and remembered thinking how heavy the whip felt, how it smelled of leather and bore peculiar mahogany stains the color of dried blood.

"She tried to run away!" boomed his uncle. "She must be punished, an example made. Go in the house, Marie."

Another's voice, feminine soft, not the girl but Blancard's mother, entreating her brother. "But he's only a boy, Michel."

"Look, there! If he's old enough to hold the whip like that, he's old enough to use it."

There was an awful tearing sound as Nonc Michel ripped open the back of the slave's shift. The worn cotton gave easily, exposing a smooth black back, free of marks. Hilaire shook terribly as he raised the whip and he remembered his uncle's steadying hand as he guided that first blow. The whip snaked through the air, cracked once and came down on that dark flesh with a sickening, fleshy thud. There was no sound from the girl, no whimper, no pleas for mercy. Medioza simply looked over her shoulder at the chubby little white boy staring with eyes that simultaneously threatened and asked forgiveness.

Then Hilaire looked away.

The second blow was easier, the third easier still. Hilaire was poised to strike a fourth when his uncle clapped him proudly on the back and congratulated his performance as he took the whip away. Hilaire fled behind the barn where he leaned against the rough wooden wall, heart pounding, breath in wild spasms as he shook hard with the most alien sensation he'd ever encountered. He felt exhilarated, exhausted, but most of all frightened as he touched the peculiar hardness between his legs and felt a hot, wet, and exquisitely raw explosion.

He had borne this confusing revelation deep in his youthful soul for weeks, until the next time he visited his uncle's plantation, where he secretly prayed another whip would be put in his hand. Michel Blancard, however, was a man who eschewed beating slaves except for the most extreme transgressions, and that meant an agonizing wait for Hilaire. Not until he was fourteen did another such opportunity arise. The slave that time was Cossa, a powerfully built man of thirty-two, accused of masterminding plans for mass *marronage* and newly retrieved from the swamps with runaway disciples. Cossa had been stripped naked and strung up by his heels. When Hilaire picked up the whip that time, the anticipated arousal rushed on a powerful wave that weakened his knees. This time the slave cried out with the first lash, but his pleas for mercy merely fueled young Hilaire's bloodlust. He beat Cossa so fiercely that the body spun wildly out of control. When the lashes struck the luckless man's genitals, Nonc Michel ordered Hilaire to halt. But not until the whip was forcibly wrested from the boy did the lashes cease. This time Hilaire did not retreat behind the barn. He stayed until the punishment was finished, savoring every ugly moment until the man, now unconscious, was cut down and carried away to the Negro quarters. Not until Hilaire was alone in bed that night did he relive the incident, his erotic excitement mounting steadily. The feel of the whip's hard leather handle metamorphosed into that of his young sex as he quickly—too quickly—found relief, but it was hardly Cossa's naked image dancing in his mind. It was Medioza.

Blancard sighed and looked away from Chaillot as other perverse reveries haunted him. That first time with the whip, that accidental discovery via the slaves Medioza and Cossa, had terrified him, coupled as it was with a bewildering hormonal taunt and pure ignorance. Some Creole fathers, his among them, were as remiss as their wives in explaining sexual realities to their offspring, abandoning little Hilaire to deep self-torment and guilt. He was alternately exhilarated and shamefully repulsed by the key to ecstasy he had found. What caused those alien tingles of pleasure in his adolescent body, roused him to such explosive heights and then plunged him into a pool of remorse when it was over? He wondered if he was the only one to experience such feelings.

Liberation began his sixteenth summer when the family escaped the heat and stench of the city, and the omnipresent threat of yellowjack, for Mimosa. He was both surprised and grateful when Nonc Michel took him aside and enlightened him to the mysteries of sex, explaining that his father, "finds such matters distasteful." The rather graphic education concluded with an offer for Hilaire to disport himself with a number of plantation slave girls and a warning about the prostitutes in the *carré de la ville.*

"Bordellos are plentiful, Hilaire," his uncle had said, "but you must be prudent. Never patronize those in the Rue Gallatin. It's too dangerous for grown men, much less a boy. Again, when you're ready, I can suggest a house in the Rue Burgundy that's safe, clean, and reasonable. Promise you'll ask, eh?"

"Bien sûr," Hilaire had eagerly replied. It was the beginning of a series of lies that would mount in magnitude and grave consequence over the years.

The discussion erased much of Hilaire's guilt, but there still loomed a great, disturbing mystery. Although Nonc Michel encouraged questions, even at sixteen, Hilaire's instincts steered him from the core of his anxieties. He knew there was a reason why there had been no mention of sexual pleasure derived from pain, of the ecstasy of power, of the secret, exquisite joys delivered by a whistling whip. Hilaire remained troubled, but he was armed with enough tools to find an easily available balm for his particular torment.

Upon returning to New Orleans, he wasted no time. Instincts came into play again, warning him against frequenting any place where his uncle was known. His proclivities were much too special for that. Since prostitution flourished in the *carré de la ville,* he had no difficulty finding a place back of town where they questioned nothing, not even his age. Hilaire learned quickly that anything could be had for the right price.

His liberation was completed with a prostitute old enough to be his mother. Named Bricktop for her crown of blazing red hair, the seasoned whore had been in the life since she was thirteen, and there was scant little she hadn't seen or done. She sized up the short, stocky youth with the black, piercing eyes and immediately recognized Hilaire as a first-timer. Only one thing set him apart from the others—he was eerily calm.

As she led him down the hall, to the last of a string of sparsely furnished warrens, Bricktop felt those eyes burning into her. She felt no danger but nonetheless kept up her guard as she undressed. She sat Hilaire on the edge of the narrow bed and tossed off her robe, treating him to his first look at a naked woman. He was aroused in seconds, young sex impatient against the confines of his snug-fitting breeches. Although Bricktop believed him a virgin, she nevertheless checked him for disease, as a matter of routine. As she opened his trousers and inspected his genitals, Hilaire pushed her away.

"What are you doing?" he snapped.

The whore laughed but she was surprised by the show of temper. "Just checking you for disease, honey," she answered. "If I didn't know better I'd think this was your first time."

"Certainly not," Hilaire lied.

Once he understood, he submitted to the inspection, studying her long red hair while she satisfied herself that he was clean. That done, she lay back on the bed and opened her thighs for his perusal. She gave him a gap-toothed smile and motioned him over. Any other first-timer would have immediately stripped naked, climbed aboard, and gone about his business, but Hilaire remained clothed, stroking her flanks. He seemed to be looking for something. When he squeezed her fleshy thighs, gently and then harder, Bricktop read him like a familiar book.

"You want a little roughhouse, kid?" He quickly nodded, displaying a confidence unnerving in one so young. She smiled. "I admire a man who knows what he wants and asks for it. 'Course it's gonna cost you fifty cents extra."

"Doesn't matter," he said.

"Then what's your pleasure?"

"I'm . . . not sure yet."

When the whore heard that first inflection of doubt in his voice, she answered for him. Start him off easy, she thought, and then see what happens. She rolled onto her stomach, exposing her buttocks. Hilaire gasped when he saw they already bore a number of ripening bruises. The telltale intake of his breath was all Bricktop needed to be certain she was on the right track.

"You know what, honey? I could use a good spanking."

It was as though the perverse genie had been unleashed from his lamp. Bricktop had barely spoken the words when her derriere felt the first of a series of gentle spanks. They increased, slowly but steadily, until her backside glowed hot and red. Bricktop was no stranger to this particular fetish. Indeed, she had several regular customers, most of whom preferred getting rather than giving such pleasure. With them it was mostly playful, but for this peculiar young man, it was quite serious. When the pain escalated, Bricktop decided to rein him in, but Hilaire groaned and stopped of his own accord. When she rolled over, she was hardly surprised that he had added his stains to those on the soiled bed linen.

"Good boy," she said. Bricktop watched, puzzled, as he hastily righted his clothing, tossed some coins on the bed and bolted the room. "Hey . . . !" But when she counted the money and discovered a generous tip, she smiled. "He'll be back."

She was right. Hilaire returned many times, always asking for Bricktop by name. The scenario varied slightly as Hilaire, through the whore's tutelage, discovered new passions and refined old ones. By the time he finished his bordello education, his preferences were distinct. His pleasure lay in not administering blows or leaving marks, rather through complete control, either via sheer force or restraints. When Bricktop gave him velvet cords and showed him how to secure her wrists and ankles to the corners of the bed, he felt that his journey was over. That first time she put herself completely at his disposal, unable to move without his permission, his excitement was near overwhelming. He stood for a long time in the corner of the room, simply looking at her, naked and utterly vulnerable, mind thundering with all the possibilities. He found he could excite Bricktop and himself to extraordinary limits, discovering that his own pleasure was sometimes in direct proportion to hers. Most often though, he merely ravished her, paying no heed to her needs or desires and abandoning her like so much rubbish when he was finished.

When he was twenty-one, Blancard's encounters with Bricktop ended abruptly when he learned she had been thrown out of the *bagnio* for beating a man to death with a club. He should have been appalled but found the scenario oddly titillating. Unlike the rest of Bricktop's clientele, who considered themselves lucky to have escaped her wrath, he had no desire to flee her potentially malignant charms. Certainly he'd never wanted to take his game to such extremes, but he was curious to know the particulars of the murder—from her. He didn't ask himself why he wanted to find Bricktop—he was afraid of his own motives.

He almost caught up with her once, when he dared venture into the hellhole that was the Rue Gallatin. For a few dollars, a madam resembling a battle-scarred bulldog revealed that Bricktop was up to her old tricks; this time her victim was a man known only as Long Charley because of his seven-foot height. The poor soul had been dispatched with a weapon custom-made to Bricktop's specifications, a silver-handled knife with five-inch blades at both ends. The knife, explained the woman, allowed her to slash in all directions. She added that when Bricktop was finished, Long Charley's body looked like an alligator had feasted on it.

That ended Blancard's fascination with Bricktop, but he still prowled the bordellos seeking women who could accommodate his peculiarities. In the beginning, he told the whores what he wanted and they only pretended to resist when he used force or drew out the velvet restraints he always brought for such occasions. But he soon learned that his satisfaction soared a hundredfold when the resistance was real, and he hungered desperately for such encounters.

He paid handsomely when matters went haywire. . . .

Blancard sighed and stroked the nape of Chaillot's neck. She stirred and turned toward him, looking up with the hypnotic lanceolate eyes, smiling sleepily before resting her head on his chest. A dark malefic smile grew on Blancard's face as he touched her bare shoulders. Lightly, ever so lightly. The conjured lashmarks evaporated, vanquished by the brush of a kiss before he finally closed his eyes.

"Soon, *mon petit*," he whispered. As he drifted toward much-needed sleep, he confirmed to himself that the arrangement with Justine had been a mere prelude. This Chaillot, she was to be his grand concerto.

"Soon."

Duncan didn't know which unnerved him more, the behavior of the crowd or the event drawing them out on this cold Sunday afternoon. The makeshift arena was a filthy warehouse in the Rue de la Levée, filled with the smoke of dozens of torches and the dirty heat of unwashed bodies. In the center was a cage some thirty feet square, about twelve feet high. It was the combat set to unfold within that cage which attracted the crowd of several hundred people, the vast majority drunk and unruly. Duncan wished they hadn't left behind the convivial warmth of *La Sirène*, a fashionable new saloon in the Rue Chartres that had become their favorite. Not for the first time, he asked Christophe if he thought this was safe.

"My dear Duncan," Christophe replied indulgently. "Have we not become the best of friends these past six weeks?"

"We must have," Duncan answered. "Because I've let you expose me to things I never dreamed I'd want to experience."

"Then you should know me well enough to understand I would never subject myself to the slightest unnecessary peril." He clapped Duncan on the back. "And since you are with me . . . well, *mon ami*. Draw your own conclusions."

"But I can't believe I've consented to this," Duncan moaned. "A bull and bear match!"

"*La Nouvelle-Orléans* is like a fine diamond," Christophe explained. "Such jewels are many-faceted, and if you are to fully appreciate them you must see them in every possible light. This is only one."

"Humph! I'm beginning to think the city is more like a diamond in the rough," Duncan said.

"Nonsense. The excitement at these entertainments is extraordinary. And quite contagious. You'll see." Like everyone else, he turned toward a flurry of activity across the arena. A peculiar hush fell over the crowd, one punctuated by the sound of ferocious snorting and the pawing of earth. "Ah! It would seem at least one contestant is anxious to begin."

As Duncan watched from the stands, a caged bull was rolled into view and unceremoniously prodded until he fled into the larger cage. He quickly set about circling his new confines at a good clip. Duncan was looking for his ursine opponent when the crowd from general admission suddenly rushed the cage and proceeded to climb it from all sides, covering it like flies on an unattended glass of sugar water. He was about to complain to Christophe that he couldn't see when a second eruption, this one from the stands, attacked those on the cage with stones, boards, and bricks brought especially for the occasion. Christophe's only response to this barbarity was to crane his neck so he might see better. Duncan was fascinated by such nonchalance and soon found himself jostling for a better look too. After being soundly battered, the first group protested noisily but retreated, moving farther back as a second cage was wheeled in, this one containing a pacing black bear. While the bull stared with mounting curiosity, the two cages clanked together, and when a door in the bear's cage was removed their separate pens merged.

A hush fell as the beasts warily investigated one another. The bear remained stationary while the bull continued pacing, albeit at a much slower clip and at a safe distance from the other animal.

"The first lunge is always interesting," Christophe opined, twirling his moustache as he often did when excited. His black eyes glistened from a combination of enthusiasm and whiskey. "And I meant what I told you at that club earlier. It is quite possible for men of letters, such as ourselves, to find this sport most diverting. I personally believe it eminently more civilized than the boxing matches so popular up North. Two men beating one another to a bloody pulp?" He snorted. "Now *that's* barbaric!"

Duncan started to ask if it were not true that Louisianians were fond of staging fights between male slaves, with heavy wagers resting on the outcome, but he forgot the question when the crowd suddenly surged forward. He was surprised to find that he, like everyone else, had leapt to his feet as the bull lowered his head and charged.

"My God! Look at that!"

Caught unaware, unsure what to expect from a beast he'd never seen, the confused bear was scooped by the bull's horns and tossed into the air. He landed in a dusty heap and had barely shaken himself off when his horned nemesis charged again. He reared onto his hind legs, flailing his great hairy paws helplessly as the bull's shaggy head caught him in the belly and sent him down a second time. This time, despite angry jeers from the crowd, he did not get up. Since there was no blood, it was apparent that the wind had been knocked out of the animal, and when the bull went to investigate, he stirred something very much alive. With a ferocious snarl, the bear clamped his jaws on the bull's snout. The bull shook his great head furiously in a desperate effort to dislodge the pain in his nose, but the bear held fast. Around and around the cage they went, snarling and snorting and working the rowdy mob to a fever pitch as blood spewed from the bull's nose and stained the dirt floor. Duncan was mesmerized, on his feet, shouting madly and puncturing the smoky air with an upthrust fist.

Christophe watched with satisfaction. He knew his friend would be caught up in the fever of the moment; he'd seen the same thing on the faces of *Yanquis* visiting the quadroon balls for the first time, and especially among those seeing their first Mardi Gras. Before attending they might dismiss them as vulgar, but after a glimpse of the opulent balls they could talk of nothing else.

Thought of the balls reminded Christophe of Justine. He had seen and heard nothing of her since that night at the opera. His letters had gone unanswered and his calls at the house in the Rue Dauphine were met with icy rebuffs from Marie Tonton.

"She's seeing nobody," the servant said, nostrils flaring in an ugly sneer. When Christophe's dark eyebrows rose in doubt, she added, "I got my orders, Monsieur Arnaud."

"Is she ill?" he pressed. Marie Tonton merely shook her head and remained stationed between the white man and the stairs to the upper floors. He was tempted to push her aside and see for himself, but fears for Justine's safety held him in check. Her words that night still haunted him.

"If he learned I've told you this much, he would destroy me!"

"Then see that she gets my card," Christophe ordered through clenched teeth. He loathed the slave almost as much as Justine did.

Marie Tonton shrugged, taking the card as though it disgusted her. "It'll just gather dust like all the rest in that salver over there." Christophe followed her pointing finger to the stack of engraved calling cards on the silver tray. "Guess one more don't matter." She tossed Christophe's card onto the salver and waited for his reaction. He refused to give her the satisfaction of showing anger or even annoyance at her insolence. Instead he bowed with mock *politesse.*

"Merci, dear Marie Tonton. Always a great pleasure to see you!"

He turned, cloak flaring grandly as he exited, leaving Marie Tonton behind to puzzle the strange ways of white people.

Ah, Justine. What am I to do about you?

Christophe was startled back to reality by a tumultuous roar from the crowd and Duncan's hand frantically gripping his arm. "Look, Christophe!" he shouted again and again. "Look!"

The bear had finally sought a better grip. That was his undoing. The instant he relaxed his jaws, the bull dislodged him and threw him underfoot. The bear roared as he was trampled again and again in a hailstorm of hooves, a furry blur fighting for escape. There was none.

"My God!" Duncan muttered.

The bull twisted his mighty head to the left and back again. The tip of one horn gleamed dully under the torchlight before plunging into the bear's furry hide. A loud, pitiful howl penetrated the arena, quickly drowned by an equally terrible roar from the stands. Blood gushed from the bear's side, fueling the frenzy of the spectators and eliciting ever-louder cries. The crowd undulated as one bloodthirsty body, shouting, screaming, jostling for a better look at the carnage. The floor of the arena ran crimson, and for Duncan the air grew heavy, thick, unbreathable. The smell of bestial death made his nostrils flare with disgust. Suddenly he had had enough, had to get outside into the cold air. He said nothing to Christophe, only shot him a desperate parting look before fighting his way through the enraged crowd. Christophe followed as quickly as he could, fully expecting Duncan to vomit the excellent lunch they'd just shared.

Instead he found his friend leaning against a stack of cotton bales, head tilted back as he drank the Mississippi's cool breath. Fog swarmed off the brown river, washing the city in quicksilver.

"Was it too much for you?" Christophe asked, concerned.

Duncan nodded. "But not for the reasons you might think."

"Oh?"

"I have no aversion to blood, but cruelty disturbs me. Even when it's as natural as what happens between two beasts, it is anathema to me."

Puzzled, fingers busily twirling the moustache, Christophe asked, "Then why did you come?"

Duncan shrugged. "I don't know, Christophe. A poet's eternal quest for the truth, the meaning of life if you will. Probably just perverse curiosity. Call it anything you like. In any case, it's satisfied and I won't need to do it again."

"I'm sorry I brought you," Christophe said.

"Oh, don't be sorry, my friend. I'm not." He smiled and put his arm around Christophe as they strolled the waterfront. "It's nothing more than the poor tormented soul of a poet."

Christophe was relieved. The friendship that had ripened between them meant a great deal. There was something about this affable, refreshingly naif American that he found most appealing. Christophe's circle of friends was mostly like himself, footloose and insouciant, never considering anything more serious than which restaurant had the most cachet or how many gentlemen paid calls to Marie Fleury at the opera. There was also in Duncan a gentle warmth that made him want to share confidences, doubtless because his only real confidante was sequestered. He longed to tell Duncan about Justine, to share his private grief over the loss of an old friendship recently restored only to be snatched away again.

"That reminds me. You've never talked much about your poetry, never offered to let me read anything. At the risk of being presumptuous, might I have that honor?"

"I'm afraid you would find it boring and probably a bit pretentious," Duncan said.

"I'd like to be the judge of that," Christophe said. Then, with a self-deprecating laugh, "Besides, I'm something of an authority on pretension."

"Nonsense," Duncan laughed. Then, "Christophe, may I be frank about something?"

"*Bien sûr, mon ami.*"

"Well, these past few weeks have been most exciting. I never dreamed when I agreed to come visit my brother that I would meet someone like yourself, someone who would make the city so fascinating. Especially not a Creole. You have been wonderful."

"It has been my great pleasure," Christophe insisted. "Ah! But *La Nouvelle-Orléans* fascinates all by herself. She needs no poor ambassadors like me."

"You are the finest ambassador I could hope for," Duncan said. "Although I don't know why you keep secrets from me."

Christophe was stunned, whirling so quickly to face the accusation that his *colchemarde* slapped against Duncan's knee. "Secrets? *Mon ami*, you wound me deeply! How can you insinuate such a thing, even in jest? Why, men have met under the Allard Oaks for far less!"

"I am not joking," Duncan insisted, serious tone unwavering. "We have talked of many things, but always, when one in particular arises, you tempt me and then retreat."

The back of Christophe's neck burned. He knew what was coming, knew there was only one allusion Duncan could possibly be making, and he was relieved that the matter was about to be brought into the open.

"The woman called Justine Blancard," Duncan said simply.

"Ah..."

"She has some sort of hold over you, and I cannot help be intrigued. From that first time you mentioned her at the watchmaker's shop, when you spoke of her fascination with the Byzantine, I have wanted to know more about her. Time and again, at the cockfight, the opera, the day we took the train to Lake Ponchartrain, the night at the theater, you mentioned her. A moment you shared, something amusing she said, how beautiful she was at this ball or that premiere. You have spoken of others of course. How many duels your friend Etienne Dumont has won. Your father who fought along General Jackson in the Battle of New Orleans. Scandalous tales about your dotty Tante Josephine. You may not realize it, Christophe, but this Blancard woman permeates your conversation." He shook his head. "And it is my guess that she permeates your blood as well."

"Duncan, I..."

"Granted there is much I don't understand about your Creole customs, and perhaps it is now *I* who am being presumptuous, but since she obviously disturbs you so deeply, I cannot understand why we cannot discuss her. Are you in love with her? Is she some sort of exalted saint who...?"

"I no longer know who she is," Christophe said, interrupting uneasily. "And you are not being presumptuous at all. You are merely being a concerned friend and I thank you for it."

Momentary silence descended on them as they fell in step together.

Christophe's mind raced. Where to begin? How much to tell? Did he dare confess what he feared was behind Justine's bizarre behavior? Only one thing was certain—Justine was not to be discussed here, publicly, on the docks. For what Christophe had to say, he needed the warmth and comfort of familiar things about him.

"Come home with me, Duncan. We will have brandy and talk." His voice trailed off, so low that Duncan strained to hear. "Of mysterious things that should have been discussed long ago."

Within the hour, Duncan was sitting with his long legs crossed at the ankle, feet aimed toward a crackling fire as Christophe paced and talked uneasily, carefully, of Justine. Although Christophe denied it, Duncan couldn't help believing the man was in love with her, whether he knew it himself or not. His face was too flushed, his emotion too deep for this to be some ordinary friendship.

"We were born just two weeks apart and have been friends since childhood," Christophe explained. "The Arnauds and Fonteneaus are among the oldest families in the city. We have always been close, always shared holidays, were always together during the *saison de visites* from November to Easter. Of course when we reached a certain age, custom dictated that we could no longer enjoy the freedoms and lack of inhibition that was the birthright of youth. We were both taken aside and told we had different roles to play in life. At the time it didn't seem to matter because our thoughts, our desires were indeed turning elsewhere. Well, mine anyway. Of course, ladies don't have them.

"Not long afterward, Justine married Hilaire Blancard and assumed the duties of a proper Creole married lady. Or so I suppose."

"Suppose?"

"Very soon after the wedding, Blancard took her to Europe for two years. When she returned, only I noticed a difference. To all outward appearances, she was the same, perhaps even more beautiful, but in the eyes, yes, in the eyes I saw something terrifying."

He wandered to an *escritoire* where an ornate mahogany humidor reposed. He extracted a cheroot, lit it, and blew a stream of bluish gray smoke toward the ceiling. He propped a foot on the fire fender and drew on the cigar again, and again, making Duncan wonder if he would ever continue the story. Finally he explained about Blancard's bizarre edict that his wife spend no time alone with Christophe or, for that matter, any man. And about how Blancard abruptly changed his mind a year ago and how he had subsequently squired Justine more often than her husband. And finally, about their strange parting the night of the opera.

"She said she had already told me too much, that Blancard would hurt . . . no, *destroy* her if he knew what she had told me."

"And what was that?"

"Nothing!" Christophe spat. "That is what is so maddening, my friend. She has told me nothing. Oh, there was some hysteria about something terrible that happened in a hotel in Paris and her shocking wish that Blancard would take a mistress and leave her alone forever."

"What's so shocking about that?" Duncan asked. "I'm sure plenty of wives are bored with their husbands . . ."

"You still don't understand honor among Creoles, monsieur. No matter how much evidence to the contrary, even if she saw the two together, a Creole woman would never acknowledge that her husband had a mistress of color. Much less speak the words. Not even to a female confidante. To another man? Absolutely unthinkable!"

"So you want to know why Justine broke that taboo, eh?"

"Exactly. I want to know why she thinks Blancard would destroy her. I'll admit their marriage is hardly ideal, but he provides well for her. She wants for nothing. And as for his mistress, well, who doesn't have one among that old man's circles?"

"I would say your clue is what happened in Paris," Duncan offered.

"But even if I wanted to ask her face to face, it would be impossible. Since that night at the opera, the night I met you and Randolph, she has refused to see me or respond to my letters."

"Another edict from Blancard?"

"I don't know," Christophe said, clearly frustrated. "I could get nothing out of that nigger bitch. She is as scheming as Blancard."

"Why do you think he's scheming?"

"How strange," Christophe said. He went to the tall windows and studied the reflected cloud of cigar smoke mirroring the fog outside. "I've never voiced that opinion before. I'm not even certain I believed it until now. Oh, I've always disliked the man, always secretly considered him a vulgar *parvenu*. Damn!"

Christophe's face contorted suddenly, twisting his features as though in pain. The dark eyes narrowed with rage, and color rose high in his cheeks like a sudden fever.

"That bastard could never have married Justine if her father hadn't been so ill, so destitute, too proud to ask someone for help before selling his daughter into this bondage of a marriage!" He retreated from the window and again sought the warmth of the fire. "Yes, Duncan. I think Blancard is scheming, perhaps even evil. And I think something evil is going on in that house, something involving Marie Tonton and perhaps the other servants as well. Something that holds my poor Justine a prisoner in her own home."

"But what on earth could it be?"

Christophe took another tug at his cheroot and shook his head sadly. "I haven't a clue, *mon ami*. Not a clue."

CHAPTER 5

Badly jarred by Edgar Allen Poe's too vivid descriptions of plague and pestilence, Justine closed the book and traced the title with her fingertips. *The Masque of the Red Death.* She put the book away.

She could endure no more. It conjured too much horror from three summers ago when fever had swarmed wildly from the swamp and strangled New Orleans for four agonizing months. The air had been leaden and unmoving, stirred only by the boom of cannon and smoke from burning tar barrels as the city fathers, American and Creole alike, sought frantically to purify the toxic air. The malodor of death straddled the town like putrid valkyries, ravenous for more corpses, hunger unsated until the death toll bloated beyond eight thousand! It had been surpassed only by the Epidemic of '32–33, which took Justine's mother and sister along with 10,430 other souls.

"How you would have loved it, Mr. Poe!" she whispered.

Justine shuddered. Mere memory of the plague had resurrected that unforgettable stench of death, and the crackling fire in her bedroom felt suddenly stifling. She sought the cool air of the gallery, breathing deep of the night air she could not consider unhealthy as she moved into a fresh cloud of gardenias and jasmine. She rested her hands on the cast iron railing, grateful for its chill. A heavy riverine fog was slowly smothering the *carré de la ville,* transforming the streets and banquettes into an undulating silver carpet beneath the hissing gaslights. Justine watched the rooftops disappear one by one until only the spires of the Cathedral pierced the curtain like great black *colchemardes.*

Watching those spires, the tallest capped with a cross, Justine felt a peculiar yearning in her breat. Her long dead mother Adéle still tugged at her heart, and as she stared into the swirling fog, images slowly coalesced, mercurial memories that had eluded her until now.

It began as her happiest, clearest recollection, a family outing at Lake Ponchartrain. She and her sister Céleste, older by two years, were dressed in Sunday finery, lacy white dresses that prompted her mother to call them her angels. Justine distinctly remembered her mother had worn apple green taffeta that Sunday, black hair all but concealed beneath a straw leghorn with green and pink ribbons. As she held her mother's hand, Adéle's lace parasol danced above their heads, so tantalizing Justine that she had asked to play with it.

"Only for a moment, *ma petit ange*," her mother had said. "The sun is very strong today."

More than twenty years later, Justine could feel the ivory handle of the sunshade as she danced along the lakeshore that day. There were no clouds in a sky boundless with blue, beating a steady wind that white-capped the lake. Justine was drawn by the hypnotic lapping of the waves and pranced closer to the shore, pretending she was a ballerina. Indeed, she held an audience captive with her graceful antics and a pure prettiness startling in a five-year-old child. Not everyone was so fascinated, however. Her father watched with neither admiration nor amusement. Marin Fonteneau was waiting for the inevitable, wishing it, and it came when Justine's tiny satin slippers slipped from grass to mud and sent her sprawling.

The parasol sang far over the water where a gust of wind lifted it high. Tears burned Justine's eyes when she saw the ugly mud stains on her skirt and a streak of red where she skinned her knee. She remembered fleeing from the lake to her mother's outstretched arms, but more vividly than that she recalled her father's hoarse command that they leave at once. Céleste's meek murmur of disappointment that the much-anticipated picnic had ended was hushed with a ferocious glare from *papa*. All climbed into the carriage where her father spoke only once before they rode back to the city in a silence so heavy it throbbed in Justine's head.

"For the love of God, Adéle!" he said through clenched teeth, knuckles ashen as he flicked the whip and frightened the drowsy horse to life. "Can't you do something with those brats? They are an embarrassment to *la tout famille!*"

Adéle of course said nothing.

But the worst was yet to come, and as it materialized for Justine, she felt a chill that did not come from the fog cloaking the city. When they reached home, she and Céleste were bathed and sent to bed without dinner. As they lay in bed, waiting for a sleep much too early to come, they heard muffled noises from their parents' room next door. Justine understood now that they were familiar sounds, noises that often caused her and her sister to put pillows over their heads or cuddle together in fear of something they instinctively knew was bad. Justine also recalled that on the mornings after such nights, *maman* would be sick, would often stay in her bed for some days. She always had headaches, and sometime she appeared in veils, although they had long since ceased to be fashionable in Creole circles. And sometimes when her mother lifted the veil so her daughters could kiss her good-night . . .

"*Mon dieu!*" Justine gasped. The remembered purple blemishes bloomed so violently through the tormented memory that she nearly pitched from the gallery. "How could I not have known until now?"

Sanity fluttered and paled as she grasped at last what had happened between her mother and father, the source of the cries and bruises and the carefully executed charade demanded of all family members. She had obliterated it so fiercely it now threatened to crush her senseless. Aside from her family, the faces of old friends waltzed wildly through her thoughts. How much was concealed behind those lovely, smiling facades?

Was it possible that Frederic Pradel abased his wife Julie? Did Mathilde de Longueval ever succumb to gentle Patrice's humiliations? And could the devoted Jacques le Sére ever have brushed Camille's flesh with anything but the gentlest caress? Did all women share it, this terrible, secret duty? Was it, this *thing*, their lot in life to be accepted without question? Were they—*was she?*—doomed to bear this as Christ bore the cross through the suffocating streets to Golgotha?

Dear God, please! Help me!

The ache in Justine's breast deepened, demanding a few more bewildering moments to fully manifest. When it did, Justine responded to an overwhelming urge to make confession. She had no clear idea what she would tell Father Gregoire, but she was certain about what she would *ask* the old priest. As she hurried downstairs and hastily threw a cape over her shoulders, she pondered what lured her into the chilly fog. Slipping into the night, she hoped this summons was somehow divine, that it was nothing less than the hand of God guiding her through dangerous streets. For this was hardly the time for a woman to be about the city alone.

Startled by the echo of her heels on the wooden banquettes, Justine scurried on tiptoes. Like the fog, she floated wraithlike through the streets and alleyways, silent, mercurial, unstoppable. She drew the hood of the merino cloak closer around her face as she turned left into the Rue

Orléans, relieved when she saw the rear of the stony Cathedral soaring behind the garden of St. Anthoine. Those spires beckoned to her, and she knew now that she was a pilgrim seeking sanctuary. She rushed through the cathedral alley, heart pounding when she discerned sudden movement against the shadowy walls of the Court House. Fear turned to revulsion when she saw a man and woman coupling in the cold fog. The man had wrapped his cloak around them both, but low moans left nothing to Justine's imagination. She was scandalized. Copulating in public and practically under the eyes of the Madonna! She hurried on, not pausing to catch her breath until she was secure in the glow of the candlelit sanctuary.

She had less than an hour before the sacristan would begin putting out the lights. Confession was uppermost in her mind, but devotion directed her to the altar of the Virgin Mary where she whispered a hasty rosary, beads flying through trembling fingers. That done, she hurried to the confessional which she knew was occupied at this hour by Father Gregoire.

"Forgive me father for I have sinned . . ."

At first, Justine babbled the standard admissions, but eventually she found her mouth moving of its own accord. She was as astonished as the elderly priest to hear the hideous secrets of her marriage poison the air between them, as well as the truth about an equally monstrous father. The more she revealed, the greater the torrent became. The mental dam was breaking, propelled by the torment of twelve years with Blancard and the hideous recollection of what had been interred in her soul longer than that. All was delivered with a frankness both found shocking.

"My father . . . hideous . . . to my mother . . . with my sister . . . and with me!"

Father Gregoire listened solemnly to her tearful revelations, cheeks blazing when Justine described the more sordid details. Her hysterical description of endless humiliation, of verbal ravishing and abasement shocked him, but they were things he both heard and did not hear.

"And then my husband . . . violent . . . evil . . ." The unnerving tale continued, spiraling down to an ever-deeper level of depravity. "His cane, Father . . . his malacca cane . . . thrust . . ."

"Please, my child . . ."

Justine's voice strained to intolerable tautness and broke as she ranted on, of bondage and unspeakable degradation at the hands of Hilaire. The priest was stunned into silence, actually praying that this hysterical woman's diatribe would cease. But Justine would not be stopped.

"Father, what can be the purpose in continuing a life so dreadful, so *horrible*, that one prefers death?"

Still Father Gregoire said nothing. He was stirred to respond only when Justine confessed to praying to catch the fever when she nursed during the Great Epidemic, asking God to take her life along with the thousands of others. He interrupted just long enough to remind her that suicide was a mortal sin, but quickly retreated when she railed anew against other invectives and perversions suffered under Hilaire Blancard, her words a perverse catechism. They continued until, utterly spent, Justine fell still enough to hear the priest's labored breathing.

What the woman had confessed was deeply repugnant, yet none of it stirred Father Gregoire to deviate from what Rome dictated, and when she heard his pronouncement, Justine ached with an indescribable loss.

"Love for a father is a blessed thing. Just as marriage is a sacred union, my child . . ."

"But Father, my husband is cruel . . ."

". . . your vows holy . . ."

". . . degrades me . . ."

". . . and not to be questioned."

"And he ravishes me, Father! *Hurts* me! Why must I endure this suffering?" Pause. A desperate heartbeat. "I don't believe this is God's intention! Forgive me, Father, but I can't!" Her face streamed tears, pain so swollen in her throat she feared she would choke. She mustered all her strength and fairly screamed her final, desperate plea.

"Father, I am begging you! For the love of God, help me!"

She felt the next words before they were uttered, and they fell on her like so much leaden weight, the doomed prisoner sentenced for a crime he did not commit.

"My child, your duty is to stay with your husband."

In her soul, Justine had known it would be his response. She wondered why she had bothered, why she had nurtured the remote possibility that Father Gregoire would grant her a means of escape. Yet how was it possible that the Church sanctioned a life that was a living hell? This was not—*could not*—be the God that she knew.

Justine shook her head in defeat, blood turning cold, flooding her veins with ice. The walls of the confessional began shrinking, floor rising, ceiling sinking, as it grew suddenly claustrophobic. Her breath strangled somewhere deep in her throat, and she felt she would die if she remained there another instant. In flight, the hem of her cape caught on the confessional door and hurled her to the cold floor, so hard that pain shattered both knees. Sprawling derelict, she sought the benign faces of the saints, faces that now mocked her. Even the face of the Madonna seemed to turn away, dark and dead, nothing now but lifeless plaster. She looked at the crucified Christ, terrified of what she might see or feel. His eyes were closed, seeing nothing, least of all the frantic woman prone on the floor of the cathedral.

"Non," she whispered. *"Non!"*

Christ could not see her, nor she Him. With this divine blindness there no longer existed the concept of good and evil, of doing for others, of suffering for redemption. *Of submission!* Christ had abandoned her to continue to this personal Golgotha alone. But slowly she was recognizing her life for what it was, one of unnecessary pain and suffering, and because of that revelation, she refused to continue the journey. Apostasy, the absolute unthinkable, was on her brow like a fever. Still, those long years of careful indoctrination forced her to make the sign of the cross again and again as she struggled to her feet and retreated from the sanctuary.

"Non!"

Justine trembled terribly, heart burning as she felt her soul consumed in flames. Hundreds of candles flickered, hissing and blazing skyward, reaching beyond the great ceiling of the cathedral and into heaven itself. Justine knew what was burning and she shrank in abject terror. This is not the God who loves me! This is not the Christ who died for my sins! Those eternal Catholic teachings spurned, those years with the nuns a lie, the advice of a priest, the sacred word of God *questioned?* It couldn't be! *It couldn't be!*

Then, slowly, "Yes!"

Justine's fears had metamorphosed into doubt and finally a rage that drove her from the church as surely as Christ drove the moneychangers from the temple. Fury had shaken her beliefs to the core, and as she rushed from the Cathedral, she knew it was a symbolic flight as well. For a moment, she couldn't move. The square had vanished beneath a mantle of fog, and the streetlamps, eerie nimbi like eyes lurking in the gloom, should have terrified her. She took a deep breath, and as the cold air filled her lungs, she oddly felt no fear. Her feet moved of their own accord, and as she walked home, her stride was firm and sure. She felt like the carved figurehead on the prow of a ship, cloak parting the fog and cleaving a smooth wake as she embarked on a voyage that had begun with a single step back at the cathedral.

Justine's heart leapt. It was clear now, the direction of this journey to redemption. Christ's eyes had never been closed. He had been watching her all along and just now—with that sweet pain in her breast—revealed that He would help. He had forced her into the final reaches of earthly hell to make her question her faith, which in turn had made her question herself and her destiny. Her victory was the strength to escape and she wept as she felt it coursing wildly through her soul. It was pure and irrevocable, for God's Son had put it there. How and when it would manifest itself was unknown, but no matter. Justine had only to wait.

"*Mon Dieu!*" she wept. "*Merci! Merci!*"

That miraculous moment still glowed in Justine's mind as she rose wearily from her bedside *prie-dieu* the next morning. Knees ached from long hours spent with her face bent beside the smoking votive candle, and her lips were numb from constant motion. Her temples throbbed as well, and she sought relief by closing her eyes against the plump cushions of the velvet chaise longue. It had long been her custom to pray often and hard, and this intense communiqué with God had lasted most of the morning. But she didn't mind sacrificing a little physical pain for the spiritual serenity yielded in return.

Aside from attempts to assimilate last night's events, trying to determine how to best direct her newfound strength, Justine had sought guidance regarding the pale envelope tucked into her skirt pocket, one she had retrieved from the trash early that morning. But when Marie Tonton burst in later with the terrible news about Jacques La Sére, she had forgotten the envelope and prayed hard for his soul. Poor Jacques was the husband of her childhood friend Camille Gaillard and, according to the slave's wild ravings, was the latest statistic in a crime wave that had held New Orleans in thrall for years. One of the city's most prominent, beneficent citizens, La Sére had been beaten to death by wooden cudgels left at the murder scene, trademarks of the notorious Live Oak Boys. He had been one of the few daring enough to condemn those murderous hoodlums and such courage had cost him his life. The loss hit Justine hard as it brought the city's omnipresent dangers terribly close to home.

"I don't know which is more perilous," Justine lamented, momentarily forgetting about the envelope. "Inside this house or out."

Her concerns were not exaggerated. New Orleans at the dawn of 1857 was threatened by more than the whims of the great river and growing rumblings of secession from the Union. The legendary refinement of her salons and parlors was imperiled by another city in the nearby swamps, desperately poor and wracked with crime.

Until the Creoles lost control in 1836, New Orleans cited with pride the honesty and integrity of her city fathers. Those scrupulous gentlemen were displaced by American politicians, most schooled in greedy partisanship and chicanery, who set a course of greedy self-destruction.

Demoralization worked its evil magic into every branch of municipal government, including the police department. Since policemen owed their appointments, and allegiances to corrupt politicians, one could expect little else.

Naturally a powerful underworld grew fat with robbery and assault as commonplace as flooding but, unfortunately, not as seasonal. The local correspondent for the New York *Tribune* wrote "murders here are an everyday occurrence," while the New Orleans *Delta* reported that "a thousand murders might be committed in New Orleans, but unless the murderers could be found on the spot, our authorities would make no effort to have them punished!" The rival *True Delta* screamed the city was under a "reign of terror," while the conservative *L'Abeille* lamented, "it is most true that our city has been infested by a band of desperadoes who have shed innocent blood and spread terror and consternation among certain classes." That was a thinly veiled reference to the Live Oak Boys, but there were other, even more mercenary gangs who had made the last Mardi Gras so dangerous that the city fathers hoped it would die a natural death this year. European visitors probing beyond the city's dazzling social life were horrified. One French traveler wrote home about a proportion of crime to the population that was, by European standards, truly astonishing.

There was one crime, however, which remained unthinkable, except of course among those denizens of the most destitute *faubourgs* where poverty and ignorance conspired against them. In the tiny, cramped houses of the Irish Channel, in the tawdry taverns of Gallatin Street, and in the bordellos of that most infamous haunt of all, the Swamp around Girod Street, women were beaten with frequency and alarming ferocity. Such behavior was virtually unknown among the upper reaches of Creole society, as the notion of a gentleman raising a hand to a lady was anathema.

Slaves could be beaten, of course, and although the vast majority of slaveowners treated their property well, there were undeniably cruel individuals who punished with unnecessary frequency. Still others took a demented pleasure in such practices, notably one Delphine Lalaurie, whose evil escapades were unsurpassed among the city's annals of raw perversion. Madame Lalaurie had been a prominent, celebrated Creole whose charitable works were legendary, who wore a genteel mask concealing a perfidious sensualist. A fire set by one of her desperate slaves had revealed the terrible secrets of the gracious mansion in the Rue Royale, had exposed her starved, shackled, and brutalized chattel to all the world. An outraged citizenry had been ransacking the townhouse when Madame Lalaurie escaped in a runaway carriage, and she remained the subject of gossip and much speculation twenty-two years later. The city would have been horrified to learn there was an heir to her fiendish mantle, another *doppleganger* proffering a dangerously duplicitous facade.

Hilaire Blancard.

Yes, what went on behind the heavy *portieres* of the mansions in the *carré de la ville* was sometimes as frighteningly violent as the worst street corner in the Rue Gallatin. Perhaps worse.

Justine opened her eyes and saw the face of the Madonna on the *prie-dieu,* and without warning she was flooded by the most heinous of her memories with Blancard.

Her lifelong wish to see Vatican City had come true, but at a terrible price. The majesty of the basilica was merely an opulent haze, the agony of the pietà something she sorely felt as, through eyes riddled with pain, she saw the sensually contorted marble melt into nothing. She strolled the sands of the elegant Venetian Lido on legs so weak they almost refused support. She saw the magnificent spires and glorious rose window of Notre Dame, but when she contemplated the massive stone bulk of the cathedral, she felt her heart was being slowly crushed to death beneath it.

What was happening to her?

She simply had no answers and, worse, no chance to find any. Alone in Europe with Blancard, Justine was totally ignorant, oblivious to the possibility that her life might not be the norm. She had had no mother to explain connubial duties, in the boudoir or otherwise, and even if she had, few Creole women would dare tell their daughters anything more than that they must submit.

Submit!

That was the word Justine heard bandied about more often than any other, in shreds of conversation between married women, which ended abruptly when she walked into the room. She had never associated submission with pain—such a thing was beyond her ken—but it was inevitable with this man whose eyes blazed like coals when he took her with such force. She had come to know that look all too intimately, more often than not accompanied by the raw stench of whiskey, and she had come to accept it as part of her marriage vows.

Submit!

If only, she thought, helplessly unmoored. If only someone had told her this was what to expect, if only she had been prepared, then perhaps she would have been able to better endure the humiliating ordeal. She chided herself for such thoughts, remembering the lessons drummed into her by the good sisters, of love and devotion and especially of humility and selflessness. After all, for the most part Blancard was sweet and gentle, indulging her outrageously when they were in public. Luxurious hotels, sumptuous dinners, glorious clothes—nothing was too good for Madame Hilaire Blancard. And the gifts! She dared not mention some opulent bauble in a store window lest Blancard rush in and buy it. Nor did she dare suggest something might be a trifle vulgar. At even the slightest criticism, his face would cloud and Justine would know that night in the boudoir would be especially turbulent.

Submit!

Justine believed she had no other choice, and so she capitulated with as much grace and silence as she could muster. And she prayed for strength to endure what each night might bring.

It all came crashing down that bitter night in Paris, their last night in Europe before leaving for Le Havre and home.

They had attended the ballet. Blancard had drunk too much wine, aggression revealing itself in little bursts at the theatre. A nasty remark about the climactic *pas de deux*. Bitter complaints about the rain. A grip on Justine's wrist so ferocious she almost cried out as they descended the grand staircase. And the insults heaped upon her in the hackney ride back to the hotel.

"I paid a fortune for a new gown just yesterday and you wear instead these rags from home!" he snarled. "This is Paris, Justine! France! Not *La Nouvelle-Orléans!*"

"I . . . I chose this dress because I thought you liked it," she ventured softly.

"Then you made the wrong decision, didn't you?" he grunted.

The verbal assault continued into the hotel, interrupted only when he donned a serene facade to stroll through the stately lobby, nodding politely to everyone of importance. Once they reached their room he exploded again. Never, not in all the days of their hellish marriage, had his attack been so thorough, so exquisitely scathing and geared to hurt. Even in his drunkenness, Justine marveled at how he could calculate the pain so skillfully. Nothing escaped his vicious tongue as she retreated to a corner of the room and stared at hands clasped in her lap. Blancard paced as he ranted, fists opening and closing in maddening rhythm. He had never struck Justine, but for her the omnipresent possibility lurked like a hurricane poised in the Gulf, awaiting the right moment to roar ashore and lay waste. She glanced at those fists as he passed her again and again, recoiling with a shudder that made her head snap in small jerks.

"Perhaps it's because you had no mother to school you in the fine points of dressing properly. You could be the most elegant woman in

Paris if you chose. If you chose!" He stomped to the corner, leaned into her face and shouted, blasting her with the sour tang of wine. "Unless you have forgotten, you are no longer the daughter of some pitiful, destitute shopkeeper! You are Madame Hilaire Blancard! That is supposed to *mean* something, supposed to elevate you above ordinary women, put you on a plane reserved for very few. It means you comport yourself with grace and decorum, that you set styles, not follow them!"

Blancard's fist crashed atop the delicate rosewood table beside Justine, toppling a vase of flowers and her book of poetry to the floor. When she leaned, unthinking, to retrieve it, he stepped on the hem of her dress. A shove came from nowhere, hurling her to the carpet. There was a terrible ripping sound as the dress tore at the waist, separating bodice from skirt. Blancard seized the tear and with a single forceful tug, tore it apart. He waved it in the air like a trophy, face black with rage, eyes narrowed. The veins in his neck were a violet spiderweb.

"You are never to appear in public without looking like a queen! Do you understand me, woman?"

Blancard glowered at the small disheveled figure cowering at his feet. The flowers in her hair had come askew when she tumbled, and they too became fodder for the man's fury. He seized them and tossed them into the blazing fire. Justine's precious book of poetry, a wedding gift from her Tante Nanine, followed. A little gasp escaped her lips before she could stop it, and she began to weep. A smile tempered Blancard's contorted features, but it vanished as abruptly as it had appeared, shards of light dispersed by a prism. Justine looked at him, eyes brimming with pain, face streaked with tears. He drank her agony like fine champagne and pronounced it superb.

In a very small voice, quavering badly, "Why . . . why did you choose me, Hilaire?"

His eyes narrowed. "Don't you know even yet?" He shook his head, regarding her as something disgusting he would avoid in the street. "What a pathetic little fool!"

"I'm . . . I'm sorry I disappoint you," Justine managed weakly.

She tried to rise, but her husband's boot was planted on the torn skirts. She tugged futilely while Blancard watched, a cat toying with its prey. Her eyes pleaded, clouded with tears, the corners of her pretty mouth down-turned and quivering. When Blancard seized her beneath the arms, the familiar odor of raw concupiscence overwhelmed her, terrifying as always, and she whimpered as she was dragged roughly to the bed.

"Please . . . don't . . ."

Her protest was scarcely audible, but had it chimed as loud as the bells of Notre Dame outside the man would not have heard. The dress, this beautiful gown of delicate white satin and lace that had dazzled everyone at the ballet but her husband, was the innocent target, the vent for his mounting sexual rage. The room was a snowstorm as it was ripped apart, seams yielding to brute force and shredding like paper. He tore at her corset like a madman skinning an animal, stays digging into Justine's side as the garment was wrenched, just partly unlaced, from her body. She was half slung, half hurled against the headboard where, always embarrassed by her nakedness, she struggled to cover herself. Her pitiful efforts merely fueled Blancard's fury.

"This is one night I am going to see you exactly as I want!"

What happened next was a bizarre blur in Justine's mind. She was paralyzed with fear and disbelief as her husband seized the red velvet ropes draping the portieres and ripped them away. She merely stared as her wrists were seized, one by one, and bound with a skill Blancard had perfected in the bordellos. Justine barely comprehended what he had done before another rope was wrested from the portieres and her ankles were likewise secured. Only when her limbs were bound and stretched to the bed's four posters did she grasp the enormity of her husband's madness. She opened her mouth to scream, but his raised fist murdered the sound.

"Don't!" he glowered.

Blancard didn't need to speak the consequences; they were clearly readable in the bitter convolutions of his face. The unspoken threat rumbled down the corridors of Justine's mind, reverberating, chilling her to the very marrow.

Or I will kill you!

While Justine lay helpless and hideously exposed, Blancard stripped away his clothes and paraded triumphantly before his naked victim. Seeing his monstrous arousal, Justine looked quickly away. It was terrible to her, but he would not permit her such indulgence. He had decided she would participate more fully in this night's scenario than ever before.

At first Justine tried not to respond, not to struggle against the restraints, but as Blancard's mouth burned her flesh, involuntary reaction was forced. Knees jerked, elbows twisted, and she bit her lip to keep from screaming. Frightening her as much was a mysterious numbness glowing at that most exquisite confluence of limbs, flowing like restless tides throughout her body. She didn't dare consider the possibility that pleasure teased beneath the man's insistent touch. It was not, could not be true! Submission! That's all it was! Submission!

Blancard moved against his bride's body with purpose, hands searing hotter still as he explored ever further. Down, down to her very quick, probing her roughly and triggering a gasp of . . . what? Shock? Rapture? Terror? She no longer knew.

He played the game expertly, tormenting her until she glistened with sweat, until her mouth was dry and she verged on begging for, of all things, water. Only then did Blancard decide what would make her humiliation complete. He abandoned her body and knelt, naked, by her head. Justine looked away in disgust, her rejection an exquisite thrill for Blancard. He grabbed her hard by the hair and turned her face toward his loins. There was no doubt what he wanted. The notion was so abhorrent that Justine could not breathe, and for a few desperate moments she gasped like a fish out of water. Her breasts swelled as her lungs finally filled with air and, mustering the remainder of her strength, Justine spit in Blancard's face.

"God*damn* you!" he roared. Enraged, he rocked the bed hard against the wall. Justine, tethered as she was, had no choice but to rock with him. It was a sickening motion she sought to quell by staring at the trail left by her spittle on Blancard's cheek. She felt certain he would strike her, but instead he retreated. Never, she thought, can I anticipate this monster.

"Tell me, *mon cher*," he said, as he stretched out beside her and rubbed his swollen sex against her thigh. "Have you ever wondered why I've never marked you?" She shook her head "No? *Eh, bien.* I assure you it's not out of deference to your delicacy. Nor is it that I don't like to be reminded of my naughty handiwork."

Justine abandoned hope as he straddled her thigh and inched his heavy body inexorably forward. She thought her leg would break beneath his weight but she did not cry out in pain. Instead she looked at him; she had never really seen his nakedness before, always turning discreetly away, but now she saw it clearly, and him as well. To her surprise, she discovered a bittersweet beauty, a near corporeal aura radiating doom. She saw a man compelled to pursue some sort of hideous destiny not of his choosing. And, unbelievably, her heart went out to Blancard as he closed that final gap with one deliberate, ferocious stroke. He entered her, hard, fast, a man with an urgent mission.

"Surely I will die!" she cried. A thousand suns exploded at her temples, glowing with such intensity she didn't know whether her eyes were open or shut. "I will die!"

"No!" roared Blancard. "I will not permit it!"

Justine bit her tongue as he crushed her head against his shoulder, burying her beneath his great fleshy bulk. She moaned with every vicious lunge and recoiled at the metallic taste filling her mouth. Blood—

her own blood. There was numbing pain as the man drove against her, again and again until he foundered, near frantic until he regained course and, through her agony, finally found release.

As he withdrew with anguishing slowness, he studied his prize. Humbled, wretched, Justine lay before him naked, booty offered a barbarian king. He smiled and reached for the velvet cords.

"You must understand, *ma pauvre petit,* that I prefer leaving my mark inside, where no one can see it. But you and you alone know it's there. Always!"

Justine fainted.

Her next clear recollection was the sway of the coach as it made the westward trek toward the sea and home. Someone sat beside her, holding her gloved hand, but his face was blurred as though glimpsed through a rain-blistered window glass. Slowly it focused and when she identified her husband, she saw that he was smiling.

"Feeling better, *ma bébé?*"

"I . . ."

"Good," he said. "You've been running a little fever, but the doctor says you'll be fine. We should be in Le Havre in about an hour. And after that we'll be aboardship and bound for home." He squeezed her hand. "Won't it be good to see *La Nouvelle-Orléans* after these two long years?"

"Ye . . . yes," she managed. "*La Nouvelle-Orléans.*"

"It's been a wonderful trip, hasn't it, Justine?" When she only stared, he said, "So many amazing sights, so many memories. *Eh, bien.* All good things must come to an end, I suppose."

"I suppose."

Justine only half-listened as her husband prattled on, something about the Leaning Tower of Pisa, the food in their Madrid hotel, the odd windmills and quaint canals in Amsterdam. Nothing seemed real, not him, not the jouncing coach, certainly not the trip. The only thing that smacked remotely of reality were his words as he leaned so close she smelled the generous splash of sandalwood on his neck.

"When we return home, of course, you will tell everyone what a wonderful time we had, won't you, *mon cher?*"

"Of course," she replied automatically.

"And you know what will happen if you don't, eh?" The smile was as radiant as ever. "Eh?" he urged.

"Yes, Hilaire," she answered weakly. "I know."

Justine opened her eyes again and sat up. Mercifully, the headache was gone. She dropped a hand lazily to her side, remembering the envelope when it brushed against her hand. It was strangely heavy balanced on her palm, and she felt as though she were weighing her destiny. Indeed, if she yielded to the temptation to respond, considering the possible dangers adherent, she was doing precisely that.

She opened it again and studied Héléne Fleury's pitiful scrawl. The woman was lovely and effortlessly managed one of the grandest townhouses in the *carré de la ville*, but she could barely write her name legibly! A Twelfth Night Ball was being held at the Fleury home in the Rue Royale. Justine knew why she had received the invitation by accident. For years, Marie Tonton was under strict orders to give Blancard every piece of correspondence that came to the house. The first time it happened, when Justine wondered aloud about a missing party invitation, her husband reminded her that he would decide what functions they would attend. Of course the issue was never again raised.

Justine tapped the envelope against the tip of one finger, realizing that January 6 was less than a week away. This was her answer then. It was no coincidence that the invitation had arrived immediately after her flight from the cathedral. This was what would move her back into the world. Why, except for mass, she hadn't been out in public since the opera in November. There had been no social intercourse, nothing more than polite nods in the streets, a faint, drawn smile here and there. And poor, dear Christophe. She hadn't responded to his letters or received him when he came calling. What must he think?

Justine regretted her behavior toward Christophe, and Camille as well, especially now. She missed them. And she missed Toinette Clovis, not simply for her fine dresses but for that gentle countenance that invariably warmed Justine's heart. For once, none of this was Blancard's doing. He wasn't to blame for keeping her prisoner in her own home. In fact she had seen precious little of the man, enrapt as he was with his new mistress. Justine cherished the solitude but knew she was merely in the eye of a hurricane. Although Blancard had a new plaything for now, who could say when he would set it aside long enough to turn his full, ferocious attention on his wife?

And what would she do when he did?

He had long ago ordered that she live in his shadow, and she had willingly accepted his dictate, loathe to do anything that would draw attention to herself. The less he noticed of her, the better, but now, this strange morning tempered with her own resurrection and the death of a friend, she dared pursue a course she knew would rile him. It was as simple as making a decision without permission. Ordinarily Justine would never have dared accepting an invitation without first clearing it with Blancard, but someone else was guiding her hand as she perched at the *escritoire* and penned a reply to Héléne Fleury.

"Yes," she announced, quill scratching noisily against paper, "I would love to attend the ball."

Justine finished the note with a flourish and yanked the bell pull, summoning Marie Tonton. Despite Jacque La Sére's death, she couldn't control her ebullience and didn't mind that the servant took her time climbing the stairs, wretched humming growing louder with each step. Nor did Justine care that Blancard would know her plans as soon as Marie Tonton could report them. The sooner the better, she decided, shocking herself with the thought.

By the time Marie Tonton appeared, Justine was behind the flowered screen, struggling into her corset. "Get the new navy merino and lace me up!" she called. "And hurry!"

Curious, Marie Tonton rummaged through the armoire until she found the right wool dress. She draped it on the bed and went to assist with the tedious laces. "Isn't the *maitresse* going to mass a little early?"

"Who said I'm going to mass?" Justine said airily.

Marie Tonton was immediately on the alert. For almost two months, Madame Blancard had virtually ignored her, giving her only the most rudimentary orders and making it clear that she wished to be alone with her precious books. Neither mood nor behavior were normal for her mistress, nor the color in her pale cheeks. Marie Tonton had expected her to be graver than ever when she brought, with secret relish, news of Monsieur La Sére's death.

"You're in good spirits this morning," she ventured, finishing the laces and dropping the smart wool dress over Justine's head.

"Mmmm," Justine sighed, maddeningly evasive. She said nothing as Marie Tonton secured the row of pearl buttons down the back of the dress. She slipped into her gray wool cape and paused before the mirrored armoire, nodding approval of her appearance.

Marie Tonton scanned the room, sharp eyes seeking something awry, a clue to Justine's giddiness. She saw the open invitation and a sealed envelope in Justine's pale blue stationery beside it. She frowned, wondering how anything could have escaped her hawk eyes.

"Your good mood wouldn't have nothing to do with those envelopes, would it?"

"Why, Marie Tonton!" Justine fairly chirped, smoothing her dark skirts and adjusting the matching plumed bonnet a final time. "How obvious can you be? I believe you're losing your touch."

As usual, the sullen mulatress drew upon arrogance when she was confused. "I don't know what you mean, Madame Blancard," she snapped.

"Then figuring it out should give you something to do all day, shouldn't it?" Before Marie Tonton could respond, Justine added, "Aside from reporting my every move to Monsieur Blancard, of course." She snatched her sealed reply to Héléne Fleury from the dressing table and flounced triumphantly downstairs, lacing her farewell with as much sarcasm as she could muster,

"*Bonjour!*"

Justine hurried down the steps and into the Rue Dauphine, still smiling until she saw the dark notices fluttering from every visible lamp post. Black-bordered posters announced the death of Jacques La Sére and included the time and place of his funeral. Of course Creole ladies did not attend such events, but Justine reminded herself to pay a call on Camille within the week. The sooner the better.

Forgive me, Camille, she thought, but I cannot see you just now. I have only so much newfound strength and no knowledge of how long it might last. Today I must set my sails on a different course.

Part Two

Twelfth Night

Souffrons, mais souffrons sur le cimes.
If suffer we must, let's suffer on the heights.
—Victor Hugo

CHAPTER 6

The sight of Hippolyte bearing a letter brought a smile to Christophe's face. "It's from Justine!" he cried. He tore open the envelope and eagerly read the message, beaming at the old coachman. "She wants me to accompany her to the Fleury ball." He clapped poor Hippolyte on the back with such enthusiasm he almost pushed him through the front door. "Tell her I said yes, man!"

"*Oui, monsieur.*"

"And hurry!" Christophe closed the door and hurried to the parlor. "*Maman!*"

"You needn't shout, *mon fil.*" Amélie Arnaud had heard her son's excitement all the way from the hall. She did not look up from her crocheting, gnarled fingers working with astonishing ease as she shot the needle deftly through the linen. At sixty-six she was an old lady, but her face still bore traces of youth, especially the mischievous dark eyes she had bequeathed to her son, along with a pointed chin.

"A Twelfth Night ball, eh?"

Snuggled against a tufted silk *méridienne* accommodating her wide skirts, high-necked brown merino dress trimmed with alençon lace at throat and cuffs, yellowed cameo above her left breast, needlework in hand, she was the perfect picture of a New Orleans lady of leisure. Her hair was parted in the middle and pulled into a severe knot at the nape of her neck. It remained black as ever, but Christophe knew she sometimes darkened gray temples with coffee. Gold-rimmed glasses sharpened her eyesight, but Amélie's hearing was as keen as ever.

"I don't know why you waste time with that woman, Christophe," she snorted. "It's bad enough that she's married, and but doesn't it bother you that her friendship fluctuates like the tides?" She countered his argument before he could present it. "I don't care if you were childhood friends. Childhood things are best put behind you." She snorted again. "Look at me when I am speaking to you, boy!"

Christophe had been drawn to the tall windows where a gentle winter rain misted the panes and the Arnaud courtyard beyond. He turned obediently, unaffected by her demands. He had heard the arguments before.

"Justine and I have something special, *maman.* Your generation wouldn't understand it."

"I understand only that she came from one of the strangest families I ever knew," retorted Amélie. Her spectacles had come to rest on the tip of her nose. She shoved them back into place with a practiced hand, not missing a stitch. "Her mother was a Moulin, you may recall. The Moulin women were always beautiful but much too fragile if you ask me."

Christophe bit his tongue to keep from reminding her that no one had asked her anything. He prayed she didn't launch into one of her all-too frequent diatribes on the bloodlines of the older Creole families. Christophe swore she could recite the more grandiose family trees with as much ease as a rosary. He retreated politely and perched on a stool at her feet.

"*Oui, maman.*"

"They were peculiar enough but, oh, those Fonteneaus!" She made a face and jerked her chin as she often did when trying to make a point. "I tell you Marin Fonteneau was one of the oddest creatures God ever put on this earth. Arranging a marriage is one thing, but . . . well I've always thought Justine's problems could be laid squarely at the doorstep of that man."

"Justine is, like you say, *maman,* a little fragile sometimes. She enjoys her solitude."

"Too much if you ask me," his mother observed. He bit his tongue again. "She retreats into that house a little too often and you know it. She demands too much from a friend."

"She demands nothing I'm unwilling to give," Christophe insisted. That wasn't altogether true, but his devotion to Justine was deep and unconditional. If it was one-sided, he didn't mind. "In any case, she's asked me to take her to the ball, and I'm accepting."

"And why is Hilaire Blancard not escorting his wife to the Fleurys' ball?" Amélie asked. Again the spectacles slid down to the end of her nose and she studied her son closely. "Eh?"

"Perhaps he has another engagement."

"And what could be more important than the first social event of the Mardi Gras?" she pressed.

"*Cher maman*," he said evenly, "with all due respect, you don't want me to answer that. Or do you?"

"I'm an old woman, Christophe," she said with a sly smile. "I was almost forty when I bore you. I've seen plenty in my long life, and precious little shocks me, even in these difficult times."

"As you say, *maman*."

He turned toward the French doors again, absorbed by the garden, enjoying the pattern of raindrops on the fish pond. He cringed at the sound of his mother's loud sigh, a signal that she was not finished with the discussion. He wished he had not mentioned Justine's note, but it was too late. His mother had been especially critical of the Blancards ever since the opening night of the opera, and she had apparently chosen this moment to tell her son exactly why.

"It's not her I worry about so much, Christophe," she said, her tone softer. "It's you. No matter how old you get you'll always be my little boy, and I don't like seeing my child hurt. Oh, I don't think Justine can help herself. I don't really think she's selfish or cruel, just peculiar. But whatever it is, she plunges you into those terrible fits of melancholy and it breaks my heart. I never thought I'd have anything good to say about *Yanquis,* but thank heavens for Duncan Saunders. If you hadn't had him to divert you these past weeks . . . well, I just don't know."

"He's become a good friend, *maman*," Christophe said, warming to the subject. "I want you and papa to get to know him better."

"I perhaps, but not your poor father. He still spends his time at the *Café Amelioration,* with those other ancient Creoles, dreaming of impossible revolutions, of throwing out the Americans and restoring the French to power. But I must concede that your Monsieur Saunders is a fine gentleman." Madame Arnaud set aside her needlework, a sure sign conversation was turning grave. "Which is more than I can say about Hilaire Blancard."

"*Maman,* do we really need to . . . ?"

"Hush now. I've wanted to speak of this for some time. Your father would die of course, so what I am about to say is in strictest confidence. Promise me, Christophe!"

"*Oui, maman*," he replied, suddenly uneasy.

His mother was showing him a new face today, one both serious and menacing. The fire crackled as it devoured an acorn. Was it Christophe's imagination or were the flames trying to compensate for a sudden chill in the parlor?

"There are things about him, about all the Blancard men, that are suspect, disreputable. Believe me, plenty of tongues wagged when that marriage was announced, but of course you were too young then to concern yourself with such serious matters. And believe me they were quite serious."

"What are you talking about?"

She took a deep breath and continued. "You may recall the Blancards come from the Cane River. Hilaire was the first one to come here, to seek his fortune in the city. I always thought it was as if he were waiting up there, biding his time until the moment was right." Christophe's eyes narrowed. "There's that colony of free mulatto planters up there, you know. Quite civilized I've been told. Almost respectable. They've always intermarried, of course."

Christophe felt his skin crawl. Was it possible she was going to suggest . . . ? No!

His mother's voice cut through the warmth of the room like an icy scimitar. "It's much easier to hide the issue of miscegenation up there, far from city eyes."

"*Maman!*" Christophe was genuinely shocked.

"I'm not saying that Monsieur Blancard has a touch of the tar brush, but there have always been rumors."

"*Non!*"

"I met Blancard's Uncle Michel once. He was extremely dark, but of course he's a planter and they can always blame the sun." She shrugged and studied her hands as though seeing them for the first time. "Skin color is scarcely the only criteria, of course. Frankly I consider it the trait of least concern. I would be far more concerned about—"

"This is absurd!" Christophe interrupted. "Hilaire Blancard could not possibly have a trace of café au lait. He's an officer with the Bank of Louisiana. He's married to a white woman. Such marriages are forbidden by law. It's inconceivable that . . ."

"Hopefully you are speaking not from naivete but loyalty to Justine, *ma chéri*. In any case, we both know rules are only made to be broken. Our unwieldy legal system is full of cracks through which miscegenations slip all the time. "Why do you think all other Creole papas refused when Hilaire Blancard wanted to call on their daughters?"

He swallowed hard. "I . . . I didn't know."

"Certainly you didn't. Some things are far above idle gossip, my boy. Some crucial things are discussed only behind closed parlor doors by a concerned few. It's one thing to suggest a gentleman cherishes his brandy too much or to imply that he has not one but two mistress. But to even hint that someone has a touch of Negro blood in their veins, especially when that blood is supposed to be as pure as ours . . . well, it's absolutely unthinkable. There are claims, you see, that his great-grandmother was a *sang-melée*. If those claims can be verified or not I do not know."

Christophe's throat went absolutely dry. His words were so strangled that Madame Arnaud asked him to repeat himself. "Do you . . . think it's true?"

"What I think is of no consequence, *ma fil*. Marin Fonteneau was the only one who mattered and obviously he didn't think so." She shrugged. "Or simply didn't care."

"*Maman!*"

Amélie's dark eyes narrowed. "Things like that are almost always exposed if those involved stay in *La Nouvelle-Orléans*. If they flee to Paris or hide up North, that's one thing, but here . . . well, you know as well as I. You've seen what happens. You know the terrible consequences." She took his hand and held it gently, as if she could cushion the next blow. "Some say what Marin Fonteneau did was tantamount to selling his daughter into slavery."

"*Mon dieu!*"

He tried to withdraw but her hand gripped with surprising strength. "I don't say these things to hurt you, Christophe. I say them out of love. The Fonteneaus and the Blancards are people with dark, dangerous secrets, and we are ill-advised to explore them further. They are, to be frank, people best shunned."

"You're not suggesting I give up my friendship with Justine!" The hand held him fast.

"Of course not. I'm merely saying that there's something wrong in that marriage. Terribly wrong. I see it in that poor girl's eyes. I can't be more specific, but it's there all right. I only ask that you be aware of it and not get hurt when . . . well, if something dreadful happens." The hand relaxed at last, leaving Christophe to rise unsteadily and prop his foot against the fender.

"Why do you think something dire will happen, *maman?*"

"I think it already has, my son. Many times. Just look at how Justine has been dangled in and out of public like a puppet."

"You make it sound like someone's controlling the strings," he said uncomfortably.

"*Exactement!* Blancard's treatment of his wife seems directly related to his satisfaction with his colored mistresses!"

Now she had gone too far. "*Maman!* You shock me!"

"Nonsense!" she fairly spat. "I firmly believe our world would be a much better place if people were more often shocked and didn't shy from the truth. It would mean we women didn't have the unenviable career of treading a high wire like performers at the circus. Did you really think we don't know about such things? Oh, certainly most of us deny the existence of those beautiful quadroons even when we see them strolling the Esplanade or at the dressmakers. Why, René Moreau has sired seven children by his colored woman and they look exactly like him. But what do you think his wife Claudelle would say if she saw one on the street? She would *say* nothing because she would *see* nothing, my dear. Do you understand me, Christophe? Nothing! Why? Because they do not exist for her if she does not acknowledge them and her precious husband, therefore, remains as loyal as ever." She was shaking not with rage but with righteous annoyance. "Maybe Justine has been staying home because Hilaire Blancard has been all too flagrant with this new mistress. He's flaunted her in the Blancard carriage, and I don't mean the closed coach either! They were seen at the lake just yesterday." She shook her head, appalled by her next words. "I heard he even rode in the colored section of the train, no doubt so they could be together. *Mon dieu*, has the man no shame?"

"I've heard enough," Christophe said.

Indeed he had. Little of what she had revealed about Blancard was news. He had even caught a glimpse of the couple himself. He was returning from visiting friends on the Bayou Ste. Jean when he passed the Blancard carriage. From a distance he wondered if the woman beside Hilaire could be Justine. She was certainly white enough and beautiful too, but upon closer inspection Christophe realized his mistake. He was so awestruck at Blancard's audacity that he barely remembered to turn his head discreetly away. But Christophe was daily out and about in the gossip-riddled *carré de la ville*. Since the pain in her hip had grown during the last two years, his mother rarely ventured from home. How could she possibly know such things?

"There are few secrets in the Creole quarters, *ma cher!*" she smiled, reading his mind as she often did. "Very few indeed." She reached for her needlework as a signal the conversation was ending. "If you don't know that by now, it's high time you did."

Madame Arnaud was right. The heart of the *carré de la ville* pulsed at the rear of its mansions and cottages, that labyrinth of fence and forest where property lines conjoined, where rumors spread with the frenzy of yellowjack. The slave grapevine had taken root there and flourished from the Rue Rampart to the river, from the Rue Canal to the Esplanade, nourished by washerwomen and ladies' maids, cooks and gardeners, and countless other slaves. When a white lady enjoyed coffee and gossip with a friend a few blocks away, both a description of the quality of the pralines and the number she consumed often reached her household before she returned herself!

Even now, Marie Tonton was busily spreading word of Justine's mysterious behavior, of her visit to the cathedral last night as well as her decision to venture out this morning. Marie Tonton couldn't read, but she soon learned the contents of the envelope brought by Madame Fleury's maidservant the day before Christmas. She didn't know her own mistress' reply, but she was unerringly shrewd when it came to putting the pieces together, and when she badgered Hippolyte into telling her he had delivered a message to Monsieur Arnaud it wasn't difficult to solve the puzzle. Madame Blancard had decided to attend the Fleurys' Twelfth Night ball without consulting Michie Hilaire. That, thought Marie Tonton, was something he needed to know and soon. She did not need to be reminded that the man had threatened to take the whip to her if he was not informed of his wife's every move. She prayed he would come home tonight since she didn't dare seek him out at Chaillot's house.

While she brooded, her mistress was off on another errand. Since she had risked Hilaire's wrath once, Justine decided she might as well do it a second time by purchasing a new dress without his permission. This second bold decision affixed a smile on her face that lasted all the way to Toinette Clovis' shop in the Rue Royale.

"Ah!" cried Toinette when she saw Justine bustling down the banquette. This was a customer she always enjoyed serving personally. She waved and opened the door. "Madame Blancard! How good to see you."

Justine returned the dazzling smile and laughed. "You may regret those kind words when I tell you why I'm here."

"To buy a dress, *non?*" Toinette asked, pretending to be guessing.

"For Twelfth Night!" Justine said. "Madame Fleury's ball."

The implication was clear. She wanted something special and she needed it immediately. But if she expected to see Toinette's composure flag, she was mistaken. The woman calmly ushered her into the shop and asked for details.

"I know it's impossible to make a ball gown in two days, but perhaps there is something you can rework to my satisfaction."

"You need worry about nothing, madame," she smiled. "I've been known to work miracles within these walls!"

Toinette knew Justine better than she thought and had always cared for her more than any of her customers. She didn't know why this particular Creole lady should have special appeal, but it was undeniable.

She had once told her husband Bernard that Justine reminded her of the wounded sandpiper they'd seen one day at the lake. Toinette was suspicious of Justine's excessive effervescence and carefully made a verbal venture.

"I'll do my best of course," she insisted. Then, continuing as lightly as possible, and with a new smile, "Why, I've never seen you so excited, madame."

"*C'est vrai!*" Justine confirmed. "But I don't know why, Madame Clovis. Oh, I love carnival as much as anyone and I'm always glad to see it return, but this particular ball seems especially important." She sat and adjusted her skirts more comfortably. "I can hardly wait!"

"Are you and Monsieur Blancard expecting special guests perhaps?" Toinette ventured.

"No," sang Justine. "I'm just looking forward to being among friends again. I've been nowhere since the opening of the opera. I saw you there that night."

"I remember," said the dressmaker as she disappeared behind the curtain dividing the shop from the workroom. Her two seamstresses, Soona and Nicole, looked up as she bustled about the room, inspecting this dress and that, finally choosing one in Soona's lap. "This one!" She snapped her fingers, demanding the half-finished ball gown.

"But it's for Madame Dupre!" Soona cried.

"Hush, girl! That woman has never once picked up a dress on time. We can fashion another one before she knows this one went out the door!"

Soona and Nicole were eager participants in the conspiracy. Neither was fond of the overbearing Madame Dupre who always found fault with their exquisite work.

Toinette scooped up the dress and carried it in for Justine's perusal, insisting she try it on at once. "This is one of your favorite colors, *n'est-ce pas*, madame?"

"Indeed it is," Justine said, fingering the scarlet watered silk. "And I adore the full flounces." She had guessed correctly that the gown was being made for someone else, but asked no questions. "It will be no hardship on you to have it for me by Wednesday afternoon?"

"Of course not," Toinette insisted. Then she threw her hands skyward in mock dismay. "But as for my poor assistants, eh, who can say?" Justine smiled at the giggles outside the dressing room curtain. She knew Soona and Nicole were devoted to their employer.

When she was dressed again, Justine took Toinette's hand as she so often did. She knew exactly why she did it. The woman's touch never failed to give her a feeling of warmth, of caring. What she did not know was why, any more than why she felt Toinette knew something about her no one else did, why she had seemed to look right into Justine's soul that night at the opera.

One thing she knew without question was that the Clovis family seemed to be absolutely bursting with love. It radiated from them like rooftop steam after the rains. In her soul, Justine knew there could be nothing but utter devotion between Toinette and her husband Bernard, a devotion eagerly, willingly extended to their three children. She had seen them in the streets, at the cathedral and at the opera, always well scrubbed and perfectly behaved, a genuine reflection of the perfection flourishing in their home.

Now more than ever, there was no question that Bernard Clovis would never humiliate his wife, never criticize her friends, never abase her for accidentally waking him in the middle of the night. And most assuredly he would never raise a hand to her. Justine had always been moved by their happiness, and now she envied it. It bothered her that she would covet anything belonging to a person of color, yet she was inevitably attracted to the petite, pecan-hued woman with the dancing dimples and ready smile.

"It's always good to see you, Toinette."

"And you as well, Madame Blancard."

The women studied each other for a few long moments, each wishing to say something more, neither knowing exactly how to proceed, bound as they were by a convoluted code of behavior confusing even to those who practiced it. Deep friendships between white women and free women of color were hardly uncommon, but they had to be carefully nurtured. Understandable, when the law required that no woman of color, free or slave, could sit in the presence of a white woman unless first given permission, and could be whipped by that same woman whenever she so desired, for any infraction, real or conjured. Friends naturally ignored the rules, but their reality gnawed the flesh of their relationship like a cancer.

The limited rights and privileges of the *gens de coleur libre* were perched precariously upon the whims of the white man, just as New Orleans depended upon Negroes for its very survival. An entire civilization had been built by one race subjugating another, a perverse concept now threatening to consume itself from within. Friendships between black and white were not easy, even when both women were free.

Toinette saw pain in this lovely woman's eyes, saw an ache that yearned for a balm she was powerless to supply. Justine wanted to talk not to a priest but to a woman, *this* woman, about what happened between her and Blancard and what had brought her to *La Mode* today. But she did not. Confidences had always been difficult for her and impossible once Blancard took control of her life. In the end, all she could do was squeeze Toinette's hands and thank her for being so accommodating.

"I'll pay extra, of course," she promised.

"As you wish," Toinette said, ushering her to the door. She watched Justine pause in the doorway, one boot in the shop, the other on the wooden banquette. She looked caught, a butterfly snared helplessly in a gauzy net. Toinette's heart bled for this strange white woman.

"Will there be something else, Madame Blancard?"

"Yes!" Justine blurted. Her face illuminated for a heartbeat then paled again. There was nothing she could say, not now. Perhaps not ever. "No," she said finally. "I was mistaken."

With that the butterfly took wing and sailed into the cold morning air, gloved hands tucked into a fur muff for additional warmth. Toinette could only close the door and shake her head helplessly. Long as I've known that woman, she thought, there's been a war waging inside her. I wonder which side will ever win.

Like Amélie Arnaud, Toinette knew something was wrong in the Blancard house and secretly hated Hilaire Blancard. She hated all white men with mistresses of color, hated all men, black, white, or colored, free or slave, who believed women were put on this earth with no privilege other than to serve them. She despised Hilaire Blancard for other reasons, namely for tossing Toinette's good friend, the old mulatress Lucinde Rousteau, out on the street like so much trash so he could install his mistress in Lucinde's little home. She wondered what emotions she would stir in Justine's heart if she knew about poor Lucinde, if righteous outrage would trigger what she had locked away in her soul. And, oh Lord, thought Toinette. What would Justine Blancard think if she learned the fate of her husband's last mistress? Josette was a perfect example of everything she despised about *plaçage*.

"They're exquisite, Michie Hilaire!" Chaillot tossed her head so the huge diamond earrings danced and sparkled like fireflies beneath the glow of the argant lamps.

"Do you really like them, *ma petit?*"

"*Mais oui!* You've been so generous these last three days, but you've never given me anything this extravagant!"

"Then we'll have to remedy that, won't we, my dear?" Blancard said, opening his arms wide so Chaillot might rush between them. Since such baubles brought such delicious dividends, he decided he'd have to raid Justine's jewelry box more often. Those earrings certainly sparkled with more radiance on Chaillot's ears, no doubt because she appreciated them more. "And now, my sweet, I must go home."

"Oh, must you?" Chaillot purred, slipping into the new role she played with remarkable ease, one in which she was utterly convincing. She plucked a fresh rose from the bouquet he had just brought and tucked it in his lapel. "Take this to remember me by."

"I promise," he said, lifting his lapel so he could sniff the fragrant boutonniere. When he leaned down, Chaillot obediently stood on tiptoes, offering her lips for a farewell kiss. She loathed such moments, but kept the truth from him with a vigilant ferocity. Absolutely nothing in her plans could be left to chance. "And now I must be gone before you bewitch me into oblivion." He couldn't resist kissing her again and tapping the earrings to make them dance. "I love you so!"

"And I you, *ma cheri!*" she cried. "Now *adieu!*"

The door of the little cottage felt inexplicably heavy as Chaillot shut it against the winter chill. She shivered, not from the blast of night air funneling into the room but from Blancard's touch. It made her skin crawl, but that was only part of her disgust. She was revulsed by the man's lovemaking, especially when that gross bulk of pale flesh crushed her against the mattress. Then his frantic, desperate thrusts and pitiful whimpering afterward . . . well, it was almost more than she could endure. If she had not affixed her mind to what all his wretched grunts and groans would award her, she could never have succeeded in this masterful masquerade.

"Ugh," she snorted, returning to the bedroom where she tossed the gaudy diamonds into a forest of perfume bottles atop the dresser. "I can still smell his cigar and that dreadful cologne. I must get him some patchouli!"

Chaillot sprayed the room liberally with her own perfume, hoping to drive away the memories of those three days in hell. She realized with horror that much of his smell lingered on her body. She called for Iris, the new maidservant Hilaire had brought as a surprise just yesterday. She was the same age as Chaillot and came scurrying into the room eager to please her new mistress. Blancard had made it clear that Mademoiselle Baptiste was to want for nothing.

"Fill the tub," she ordered. "I need a good long soak to wash off the odor of that man."

"*Oui, mademoiselle,*" Iris said with a brief curtsy. She was surprised by Chaillot's disparaging tone. From all she had seen and overheard, the two seemed more like lovebirds, but she was new in the household and had much to learn.

"And lay out my new dress. The gray wool with maroon trim. I want to visit *maman*. I haven't seen her in days."

"*Oui, mademoiselle.*"

Still in her lacy pink peignoir, another gift from Blancard, Chaillot stretched out on the bed to wait for her bath, displeased when she again inhaled the man's scent. It seemed to be everywhere. She called after Iris who was bustling toward the kitchen to fetch hot water. "And change these linens!"

"*Oui, mademoiselle!*"

Chaillot left the bed and tossed cedar chip into the fire, nostrils flaring at the welcome scent. She sat in a crude pine rocking chair in the corner and settled into a rush seat worn smooth by four generations of Baptiste women. It was the only piece of furniture left by her great-grandmother Chocola, and Colette had insisted on installing it in the newly refurbished house. She got no argument from Chaillot who had nothing but fondness for this old chair.

How many times she had been rocked to sleep here nestled against Chocola's great breasts. Her *grandmere* Megdelon and *maman* had rocked her too, but it was the memories of her great-grandmother that she most cherished. She closed her eyes, very nearly conjuring the sight and sound of the old coal-black woman who crooned to her in the strange Ibibio tongue. As she started the familiar rock back and forth, it lulled her toward happier, more innocent times, but such memories could not hold her mind. Thoughts of Hilaire Blancard intruded abruptly and the ghost of her dear great-*grandmere* fluttered into oblivion.

"Oh, *maman!*" she sighed, glancing around the small well-appointed room with gleaming new furniture, at the armoire swollen with new gowns, at the expensive sparkle of perfume bottles and diamonds. "What shall I do with all this?" She sighed again, dreadfully weary.

"And what, oh what, shall I do with Michie Hilaire?"

The combination of warm water and the toasty heat of the fireplace almost lulled Chaillot to sleep, but the shock of the outdoors sobered her quickly as she bustled to her mother's house in the Rue St. Louis. It was only a few blocks, but a mounting winter storm made the trip seem much longer. The sudden, unexpected chill had sent everyone scurrying inside, and the Rue Rampart was almost deserted. Chaillot quickened her steps, carelessly stepping in front of a carriage making a sharp turn from the Rue Ste. Phillipe. She screamed as the horse reared, steam blasting from its nostrils as it struggled for footing. The Negro driver, thinking Chaillot white, tipped his hat and apologized for what was clearly her fault. She knew his reaction would have been altogether different had he known she was colored too. Such things only made her firmer in her resolve regarding Hilaire Blancard. She tugged the hood of her cloak higher across her face and rushed toward the Rue St. Louis, grateful for the golden glow in the windows of her old house halfway down the block. As she drew nearer, she squinted, trying to separate silhouette from shadow beneath the huge fig tree. Was it possible? Had he come back? Her step quickened again, this time to a near run.

"Xanadu? Is that you?"

The horse whinnied as always when he heard Chaillot's voice. She pressed her face to his neck and stroked him as she had a hundred times, then hurried up the short walk to the house. She found them in the parlor, both mellow after a good deal of Madeira.

"Michie Marius!"

"Chaillot!" he cried. *"Mon petit chou!"*

Chaillot squealed as Marius Gautier leapt to his feet and threw his arms wide. She hugged him tight. There were few people in the world she loved more than this tall, white gentleman with the golden hair and pale hazel eyes. As always *soigné,* he wore a flawlessly cut frock coat of deep blue velvet and gold brocade waistcoat with matching silk stock. Long legs were encased in wool trousers of the finest dove gray and his feet were shoved into gleaming black boots. He never failed to dazzle Chaillot, and not for the first time did she notice the powerful physique lurking beneath the fine clothes.

"Oh, Michie Marius! It has been too long since I've seen you. Much too long! Can it possibly be three years?!"

"Sweet little Chaillot!" he smiled, holding her tight and smiling at Colette who beamed over her daughter's shoulder, drawing deep pleasure from seeing those she loved together. "But you're not so little any more. I didn't think it was possible, but, yes! By God, you're more beautiful than ever! The most beautiful woman in all *La Nouvelle-Orléans!"*

"Please don't, Marius!" Colette laughed. "No doubt her head is filled to overflowing with compliments." She offered her cheek for Chaillot's kiss and added, "I was telling Michie Marius that you have a protector."

"That's not news," Gautier laughed. "I may be recently returned from Paris but I know all about it. The bistros and cabarets are filled with talk of the daughter of the legendary Colette Baptiste and how she made her debut at the *Salle d'Orléans.* And snagged no less than Hilaire Blancard, eh?" He winked at Colette. "You made an excellent choice, Chaillot. The man's fortunes are well known."

As is his temperament, thought Colette. *Eh, bien!* Who knew what was truth and what was rumor? Tales about the behavior of white protectors always vacillated wildly, especially when they were known to have a fondness for drink.

Chaillot shrugged her cloak into Senegal's waiting hands and gathered her heavy skirts beneath her as she sat at Gautier's feet. "I suppose." She rubbed her cheek affectionately against his knee. Most men would have dueled for that privilege, but Marius took it in stride. "I'd much rather have *you* for a protector."

"Chaillot!" Colette gasped. She and Gautier exchanged bemused looks. "What a thing to say!"

"Oh, he knows I've always been in love with him, don't you, michie?"

"And I you," he conceded. "Like the daughter I never had."

Chaillot bristled at the platonic dismissal. Those endless four days with the insatiable Blancard had clarified carnal matters in her mind. In the two years since she'd seen this man, she had matured into a young woman with desires and a mind of her own. She might be contracted to another white man, but it did not preclude her flirting with one she'd known from childhood.

"I'll bet you never envisioned a sister like me," she teased rubbing his thigh with a gloved hand. Colette leaned over and smacked it away.

"Behave yourself!"

"*Maman!*"

"You're not amusing, mademoiselle!" Colette snapped. Chaillot was puzzled by the harsh edge in her mother's voice.

"I was only playing," she said.

"With someone like you, it's never a game," Colette warned. Her face was drawn, eyes deeply cautionary as she spoke to Gautier. "She doesn't realize she's no longer a little girl talking to that ridiculous Combas. That one night at the ball changed her into a woman with powers she never dreamed of." Then, to her daughter, "You must wield those powers carefully, Chaillot. They are not to be trifled with. For those who are careless or abusive with such an extraordinary gift, beauty can be like the the sword of Damocles."

Colette trembled inside when Chaillot giggled and tossed off her cavalier response. The face Chaillot showed tonight was the one her mother had always feared and dreaded most. It was all too common among the girls who, deep down, didn't want to go to the quadroon balls.

"Michie Marius wasn't offended, were you?" Chaillot implored.

For someone so voluptuous, Gautier considered, she could be bewilderingly, irresistibly childlike. He had no doubt that she would make some man's life alternately exquisite and miserable, depending merely upon her whims. Such women like that could be deeply dangerous. So could such men.

"Of course not," he promised. While Colette sniffed, he pulled Chaillot into his lap and stroked her long hair. Careless and unbound, it reached almost to her waist and gleamed dark blue in the firelight. "Any man would be honored by your touch."

Chaillot giggled and snuggled against Gautier's chest, inhaling the clean scent of vetiver mingled with leather and tobacco.

Colette protested again, but her good humor had returned. "I'm telling you, Marius. Her head is already swollen. Every day she has sent me notes telling me what new thing he has brought her. Three days with Blancard and already she could masquerade as the Queen of Sheba!" She smiled adoringly. "I couldn't be more proud of my daughter. She has made a superb match. Chaillot! Why did you pull such a face?"

Chaillot was about to burst. Just as her mother had waited endlessly for the night when she would present her daughter at the *Bals du Cordon Bleu*, Chaillot had longed for this moment, her first with her mother after she had chosen her protector and the first time in her life she would ignore her mother's wishes. She loved her mother dearly, but she had inherited her shrewdness along with her beauty. The days with Hilaire Blancard had proven that Chaillot wanted a life of her own, and it would not, as *maman* so fervently prayed, include him!

"I hate Hilaire Blancard!" she fairly spat.

Only a brief lull elapsed before her mother responded. "I see."

Colette fussed with her lace cuffs and smoothed her skirts unnecessarily. Her face was an unreadable mask. Chaillot had expected her to leap from the chair, to grab her by the shoulders and shake her until her head rattled, demanding to know why she would even think such a thing. She would scream that Blancard's wealth was there for the taking, that he could give her things the others could only promise. Why, what he threw away at the gambling tables was a year's income for most men!

Instead, Colette was a portrait of composure, calm, unruffled, her repose maddeningly *dégagé*. Chaillot tumbled headlong into the trap. "I . . . I thought you'd be angry, *maman*."

Colette shrugged. "The man was your choice, *ma chére*, not mine. And he is therefore your problem."

Chaillot looked to Gautier for support but found only a benign smile on his pale face. She took a deep breath and continued. "I'm going to find a way to leave him," she announced. "I'll sell the house and go to New York. I'll have plenty of money and I intend to become an actress. I . . . *maman*, why are you shaking your head like that?"

"Because it is impossible."

Now, thought Chaillot. Now it comes, the eruption from that dozing volcano. Now come the tears and the accusations and the blame. She was wrong again.

"Why?"

"Because you only think you have those options," Colette announced smoothly.

"What do you mean?"

"Girl, you know very well what I mean."

Colette rose and stoked the fire herself, preferring not to call Senegal. For what she had to say, she wanted no one else present. Except dear Marius. She seated herself, smoothing her skirts again and sipping her wine.

"The only ones to end such liaisons are men. They created the system to suit them, so naturally they control it. The most you can do is wait until the man tires of you or until he dies."

"Then I'll make him tire of me!" Chaillot shot back.

Colette's laughter filled the room. She sipped more wine, considered the cut-glass crystal in her hand and lofted it high so that it caught the sparkle of the chandelier. "Beautiful, is it not? Michie Simon gave it to me. Part of a set from Paris. The finest crystal in the world. I know how easily you have grown accustomed to such exquisite things, Chaillot, and I will remind you they do not come without a price."

"Don't change the subject!" Chaillot insisted. She slid from Gautier's lap and paced the room, skirts rustling loudly in the weighty silence. "If I cannot make Monsieur Blancard tire of me, then perhaps I'll arrange for him to die!"

Now *she* had struck a nerve. Two could play this game, she thought. I am, after all, my mother's daughter.

"*Eh, maman?*"

"You're talking nonsense, girl!"

"Am I?"

"Tell her, Marius. She seems to have forgotten who she is tonight." Colette struggled to maintain her composure, but anyone looking closely enough saw the volcano was seething.

"Very well," he sighed unhappily, wishing he were neither hearing all this nor required to recite such unpleasant facts. "I think your mother means a woman of color, even a free one, can be imprisoned for merely laying hands on a white man."

Chaillot was unmoved. "Since I was a child you've told me things are not always as they seem, *maman*. You of all people know how to manipulate the rules, along with the men who make them."

"Nonsense!"

But Chaillot was unswayed, warming now to the battle. Suddenly Colette was seeing herself in this warring naif, and it alternately thrilled and terrified her.

"Michie Marius was right, *maman*. You *are* a legend! I've heard the stories!" The sapphire eyes pierced her mother like deadly rapiers. "I know about the broken hearts, the suicide, the invitation to live in Paris. I even know about the duel."

Gautier stared at Colette, astonished by her composure.

"What duel?" she asked.

"The one you provoked to get rid of Monsieur Bernard Lestain. The man you arranged to have killed by my father!"

"Oh."

Colette's fragile voice cracked like thin ice. She did not bother to ask how Chaillot knew, nor did she deny the accusation. Feeling at once old and relieved, she prepared the revelations Chaillot sought. The girl wants a taste of my peccadillos, thought Colette. Instead I shall glut her. It was time for her daughter to grow up.

"So be it." Colette stood slowly, full lips drawing into a thin line. She stood behind the chair where Gautier lounged uneasily and rested a hand on his shoulder. "Before you flee for a life up North, dearest daughter, you need to know the facts about your life here." The man's hand immediately covered hers and she nodded. "It's time, Marius. Perhaps it was time long ago."

"All of it, *mon cher?*"

"All!"

The reply was swift and decisive. Like Colette, he felt old yet welcomed the end to a lifetime of masquerading. It was as if they had, all of them, been at a *bal masque* destined to go on forever. Perhaps in their hearts they knew a time would come to unmask and lay their souls bare, but for them there had been no Ash Wednesday, no cathedral chimes to remind them carnival had drawn to a close. It was up to one of them to end the deceit.

Of course it would be Colette. After all, it was she who, in the beginning, assembled all the maskers and made them dance.

"As you say," Gautier sighed.

Chaillot retreated toward the fire, wild with what she might learn from them. Until then she had not fully understood fear of the unknown. Now that she faced it, she wished she were back home, huddled beneath the downy counterpane, shutters drawn, lights extinguished. She wished she were anywhere but here.

"I won't deny I had a hand in Monsieur Lestain's death," Colette began. "He was a cruel man, Chaillot. Once he had bought and paid for me, he thought that entitled him to treat me like the lowest of slaves. He never beat me, but he invited his friends to this very house and put me on display like a blooded thoroughbred."

"Sweet Jesus, Colette," Gautier moaned. "Please don't—"

"I must, Marius. Chaillot wants the truth, and she shall have it. One does not respond to a daughter's accusation of murder without stating the facts, *n'est-ces pas?*"

"If you insist," he said tiredly.

"But it is not I who insists," Colette reminded him, gently but firmly. "It is my daughter who insists!"

"Go on, *maman,*" Chaillot whispered.

"Oh, I shall," Colette said sharply. "Nothing can stop me now." She moved from Gautier and rubbed her hands together before the fire. "Monsieur Lestain, for the amusement of his friends, forced me to perform things before an audience that few people do in private."

"*Non!*" Chaillot gasped.

"Certain things that are not allowed in some bordellos. And not just with him, my darling daughter." She leaned close into Chaillot's face and fairly spat the terrible truth. "*With anyone he chose!*"

Chaillot whimpered. Gautier looked away.

"Very well," Colette said. "I will say no more of my humiliations. To be frank I am not certain I have the strength to tell you what still gives me nightmares, all these years later." Chaillot winced, a glaze of sweat breaking on her forehead that was not spawned by the fire. She was horrified.

"I was so beaten down that I took the greatest risk of all and began an affair with another man. I knew Lestain would kill me if he learned the truth, but to be frank I didn't care if I lived or died."

"Oh, *maman!*" Chaillot cried. "I had no idea!"

"But it's time you did, Chaillot. You must remember that all the glamourous trappings, the genteel facades and courtly manners, such pretty labels as courtesan and *demimondaine,* beneath it all, we quadroons from the *Salle de Orléans* are little more than prostitutes. Better off than that trash in the Rue Gallatin but whore sisters to those wretched women nonetheless. Therefore we are all too often treated as such. To our men we are nothing more than beautiful, skillfully bred animals, niggers masquerading behind white masks." Colette swallowed, then expelled centuries of injustice in a long single breath.

"But niggers nonetheless."

In a small but steady voice, "I have always known that, *maman.*"

"*C'est bon,*" Colette sighed. "That makes things easier." She held out her glass for Gautier to refill. The Madeira was rich and warmed her throat. She managed a wan smile. "Lestain also took me to the bull and bear matches. That's where I met Simon Guedry." Chaillot thought it strange that she didn't refer to the man as her father. Colette smiled at the memory. "It was the beginning of my . . . liberation. It took a year of dangerous clandestine meetings for us to devise our plan. Luckily, Lestain loved his bourbon as much as he loved making my life miserable."

"I've never known such a base soul," said Gautier.

Chaillot was surprised at the venom in his voice. Marius Gautier had always been a gentle soul, rarely given to displays of temper, aggressive only when someone's weakness was being exploited. She still remembered a childhood trip to Carrollton when he stopped a man from beating his son on the train. She had been frightened by the deep red discoloring of Gautier's face and the fierce, voice issuing from his throat when he confronted the man. No doubt Lestain was a genuine monster to elicit such condemnation.

"When I learned Guedry was a superb swordsman," Colette continued, "the rest was easy. Forgive me if I smile at the memory, Chaillot, but it was my hair that caused the duel. And forgive me, Marius, for laughing at the inane impetuosity of men, but it was the sheen of moonlight on my hair that inspired the argument that left Lestain dead under the Dueling Oaks." She shuddered at the memory.

"That fateful night set me on the journey that has led here, to the three of us sitting before the fire."

Chaillot slipped silently to the floor and rested her head in her mother's lap. "Dear *maman!*"

"Believe me," Colette said, stroking the raven tresses splayed across her skirts. "In all those eighteen years since Lestain's death, not a day has gone by that I have not thought of him. It. The duel that was of my doing. You hear of people of whom it's said they must live with their sins. I understand that only too well." She took another deep breath and looked at Gautier. He waited with a heart as leaden as her own, wondering if he could endure the rest of her story. He knew it was time too, and yet . . .

But Colette's strength ebbed and she reached for her wine. With that single gesture Gautier knew that not all the terrible truth would be told. At least not tonight.

CHAPTER 7

"You know, Randolph. There's something hypnotic about this city, something about it that goes down like warm honey."

"Indeed?"

"Oh, yes." Duncan took a draw on his cheroot and exhaled a long stream of bluish smoke. "The rich, fecund smell of the river. That ghostly moss and lacy grillwork. The *voudou* drums and that wild African dancing in Congo Square. That terrible swamp unleashing snakes and alligators at front doors of houses with French furniture. The whole city is an exotic anomaly, much more Caribbean than American."

Outside the tall windows, a grove of wind-serrated banana trees shuddered in the November dusk. At their feet, huge elephant ears nodded guard amidst a dense bracken. From the great gnarled oaks, curtains of Spanish moss lifted and parted all of a piece when stirred by the wind, and just outside an explosion of pink camellias nudged the window. Duncan remembered being disappointed to learn the delicate flowers had no scent. Not so with the gardenias in a nearby vase, wrapping him in a cloud of their showy, mesmerizing scent and making him heady.

"And these Creoles! Have they ever learned how to enjoy life! Did you know there are four operas a week at the *Théâtre d'Orléans?* Four! Two *grand* and two *comique!* There's certainly nothing like that back in Richmond!"

"But they're all in French," Randolph reminded him pointedly.

Duncan ignored him. Nothing could dampen his good spirits.

"Christophe insists that the only nights to go are Tuesday and Saturday, and of course full dress is *de rigeur.*"

"I see," Randolph said. He chose to ignore his brother's new and annoying habit of sprinkling his conversations with French.

"It's all a little unnerving. That is to say, the longer I stay here, the more remote are my memories of home. Is it just me or is New Orleans capable of erasing one's memory?"

"You're not alone," Randolph conceded with a smile. Like his brother, he cherished these moments together. He had endured a bear of a day with wildly fluctuating cotton prices and had been looking forward to a quiet drink with Duncan. "Some people call this the land of dreams. Now you're beginning to understand why."

"Dreams, eh? Well, they're right. If I could ever stop gallivanting long enough to pick up a quill, I might be able to translate some of this magic into poetry."

"Simply commit to paper what you just described," Randolph encouraged.

Duncan unleashed another trail of smoke. "I've been a true *fainéant*, big brother. You've been very indulgent with me."

"And why not?" Randolph asked, again uneased by the use of French. "Indulging you stirs the only memories of home I wish to recall."

It was a joke but it carried a ring of truth. As long as Duncan could remember, his older brother had babied him, catered to his whims, doted in a way more appropriate for new parents. It was Randolph's way of compensating for an absentee father and a mother far more concerned with dressmakers and dinner menus than raising children.

John Carter Saunders divided his time between running Tarleton, his Tidewater Virginia plantation, and the banking houses upriver in Richmond. His primary goals had always been to maximize the tobacco production at Tarleton and elevate his standing among the local gentry. The former he achieved through long hours in the saddle; the latter was accomplished through his marriage to Anne Langford. Anne was as socially ambitious as her husband, and the two of them embarked on a selfish voyage that should never have included children on the passenger list.

While care of Randolph was relegated to Cora, Anne's equally cold nanny, the mistress of Tarleton devoted herself to holding open houses which had no place for children. Gentlemen and ladies slept separately on mattresses spread on the shiny floors. The men indulged in boat races on the James, foxhunts and bouts of drinking while the women enjoyed gossip and harpsichord music. Both feasted and danced until the wee hours.

When Duncan was born, Randolph was seven years old. Instead of being jealous, Randolph embraced the new arrival, and devoted himself to the child. Everyone except their parents took note of the unusual bond between the brothers. Unlike Randolph, Duncan didn't know such an abundance of love should have come from mother and father and was soon trailing his brother like a faithful puppy. Randolph was always there to wash and bandage a scraped knee, repair his kites and welcome him into his bed during thunderstorms when the boy was little more than trembling limbs and big hazel eyes.

For Duncan the idyllic relationship continued until Randolph was seventeen, when a third party entered the brothers' exclusive world. Molly Lewis was the daughter of a neighboring planter and a frequent visitor to Tarleton. She was plain but had an enviable appetite for life and a quick wit that amused some and shocked others. Randolph was desperately smitten. His attentions were returned in full, and for the first time he preferred spending his time with someone other than his brother.

While a saddened, confused Duncan drifted rudderless in the background, Randolph was dispatched to the University of Virginia. He continued his courtship of Molly, his horse burning up the road between Charlottesville and Annabelle, the Lewis plantation. He knew Molly had other suitors. After all, Annabelle was one of the grandest plantations on the James and, as an only child, Molly stood to inherit everything. Randolph knew she loved him and was understandably devastated to learn she was engaged to a fellow student.

Injury compounded the insult when he was informed by none other than her fiancé, Edwin Hill. A swaggering boastful youth, Hill was roundly despised by his classmates, Randolph among them. Randolph's response was to get riproaring drunk and give his rival a most ungentlemanly thrashing. Those two deeds earned him immediate expulsion from the hallowed college and, to his utter shock, praise and long-overdue respect from his father. What he had so desperately desired all his life had fallen into his lap with a calculated act of revenge, but it had come too late. Many said the elder Saunders was equally outraged by George Lewis' choice of a son-in-law, although his disappointment came not from his son's unhappiness but from an old dream of merging Tarleton and Annabelle into the largest plantation on the James.

With his father's considerable influence, Randolph quietly entered William & Mary College in Williamsburg where complete devotion to his studies saw him graduate at the top of his class. He returned to Tarleton where his father assumed he would follow in his footsteps. But

Randolph's bitterness was too profound, and he stayed only long enough to announce that he was leaving for Wilmington in North Carolina.

Longing to reunite with his brother, Duncan promised to join him when he finished college, but their father forbade it. Furious with Randolph, whom he promptly excised from his will, the elder Saunders was determined to have an heir take over Tarleton. When Duncan evinced no aptitude for the complicated machinations of a vast tobacco plantation, his father grew embittered and eventually reverted to the aloofness and indifference Duncan had always known. His mother, in the meantime, found more diversion in daily doses of laudanum than maintaining a social whirl. Neither noticed their son's frequent absences. Neither knew nor cared that he found his only happiness galloping over the hills to some distant creekbottom where he daydreamed in the sun and wrote poetry. Friends and neighbors praised the Saunders' only dutiful son, but the truth was Duncan stayed only because he pitied his parents.

Randolph's letters continued, pleading for Duncan to join him, postmarks changing from Wilmington to Charleston to Savannah, and finally to New Orleans. His descriptions of that exotic city whetted Duncan's wanderlust more than ever. While Duncan agonized over leaving Tarleton, a decision was made by his father who succumbed to a fever sweeping the Tidewater. Only his death could bring Randolph back to Tarleton. This time when he left, he knew in his heart Duncan would follow, and so he had, leading to this moment of warm reminiscence so far from Virginia.

"Are you sure mother will be all right with father gone?" he asked.

"Of course," Duncan replied. "To be utterly frank I'm not certain she knows he's dead. She was so vague at the funeral. Of course, what everyone mistook for a numbing grief was nothing more than laudanum. My God, what a loveless marriage that was."

"I often wondered about the bastards who invented arranged marriages. Since when is it a crime for two people to marry simply out of love?" Randolph grunted and took a hearty swig of his whiskey. "Damned stiff-necked Virginians!"

"It's hardly just the Virginians," Duncan offered. "The Creoles are even worse. At least at home the girls have some kind of life before they're betrothed. Here they're imprisoned in convents and paroled just in time for their wedding night."

"That's the poet talking," smiled Randolph.

Duncan raised his glass. "*Merci, mon frere.*"

Randolph frowned, no longer able to hide his annoyance. "You're certainly sprinkling your English liberally with French these days. I'm not certain I like it."

"What's not to like? It's simply time for me to become a man of the world. Thanks to Christophe. He's the one who's really helping me explore this city of dreams."

"That wild Creole will turn your dream into a nightmare if you're not careful, Duncan. I know. I've seen it happen."

"What do you mean?"

"As I've told you over and over, the city's extremely dangerous. I'm still angry with you for letting him drag you to that barbaric bull and bear match. You saw the sort of people who attend such horrible events."

"Just part of my education," Duncan dismissed. "There's a whole other world just downriver of the Rue Canal."

"It's called Canal Street on this side," Randolph insisted, exasperated. "I was aware of the other world the moment I came here. The Creoles are all too eager to make certain of that." He took another swig of whiskey and swirled the amber liquid in his glass. "I'll admit there's a certain raffish amusement to be found in occasionally prowling the taverns along the river, but not much else."

"It was on just such a night that we met Christophe, remember? I'm telling you, Randolph, there is much to see in the *carré de la ville*. The women for instance! My God, man! They're all beautiful. Well, maybe not all of them, but they certainly give that illusion. It's one thing to glimpse them on the streets, but when you see them at the opera! That jet black hair, those dark eyes and porcelain skin. And speaking of skin! *Mon dieu!* The *décolletage* is astonishing. Mother would have a fainting spell if she saw it. And without the help of her brandy!"

"Saw what?" Randolph asked, annoyance deepening when he had to ask his own brother for a translation of *décolletage*.

"Bosoms, man! Why it's all I can do to keep my eyes in their proper place when I meet one of those beauties. I mean, I bend down to kiss their hand and next thing I know I'm looking at two half-exposed breasts. There's one young lady who really takes my breath away." He smiled and closed his eyes as he repeated her name in his best French. "Eugénie Duval." He sighed. "I was introduced to her at a Christmas *réveillon* and have been thinking of pressing Christophe to ask her father if I might call on her. That's how it's done, you see. Her father is—"

"I know very well who he is!" Randolph said coolly. "Every banker and broker in the city knows Honoré Duval. He's one of the most . . . may I ask you if you've completely lost your mind? Why on earth you would want to call on any Creole is beyond me. But this one, *this one*, is madness! Don't look at me like that! Do you know anything about this girl's father?"

"No."

"He's infamous, my boy! Infamous! When he's not counting his wealth, he hangs out at some dilapidated tavern in the French Quarter where he and his cronies plot to overthrow us Americans and reunite Louisiana with France!"

"You're exaggerating."

Randolph chuckled bitterly. "Ask your friend Mr. Arnaud. Now I'll admit I'm not overly fond of those people across Canal Street, but this man! He is a mad dog! He would rather shoot you through the heart than let you mention his daughter's name in public."

"You needn't get so excited," Duncan said, alarmed by the rancor in his brother's voice. "But while we're on the subject, why do you despise the Creoles so much?"

"I don't despise them," Randolph amended. "I truly don't. I just find some of them difficult to deal with. From the very beginning they've called us boors and pigs and refused to do business with us. For as long as they could they kept basic city services from the upriver side of Canal. No gaslights or garbage clean-up for the newcomers. Let the upstarts live in darkness and filth."

"Have you ever considered their feelings?" Duncan asked gently, hoping for a rational discussion. Unlike Randolph, he had not inherited their father's temper and whenever he saw the color rising on Randolph's face it triggered long-interred memories too painful to recall. "How would you feel if, say, the Germans suddenly bought the United States and moved in?"

"The French were sold out by their own people," Randolph said defensively. "This colony never made a *livre* for the French kings. Napoleon was only too happy to unload it so he could fight his nasty wars. It is the Americans who have built this city into what it is, the fourth largest in the nation and one of the great ports of the world!"

"You have a point, Randolph, but—"

"Not until 1836 when we got control of the government were we able to get decent services and make any progress," Randolph continued.

"And I'm told the city is more corrupt, more dangerous than ever since that control," Duncan ventured. Before his brother could shout a retort, he hastily softened his tone, adding, "But times are changing, are they not? Christophe says there is more intercourse between Americans and Creole than ever, that they're doing business together, sitting down together at the dinner table, and even intermarrying. That's certainly indication that the two groups are coming to understand and respect one another."

"For money!" Randolph snapped.

"You're impossible!" Duncan said, exasperated. "Christophe is right. We Yankees *are* obsessed with money."

"Listen to me," Randolph said, grabbing the decanter and sloshing a healthy shot of whiskey into his glass. "The Creoles refused to do business with us from the beginning, claiming it was beneath them, that our tactics were crude and mercenary. That was strictly a diversionary ploy. The truth is that they feared we were far better businessmen and would always cut the better deal. Their fears were well-founded, little brother. In the half century since the Louisiana Purchase, American fortunes have soared while Creole enterprises have steadily declined. So these marriages you've just described are based solely on greed."

"Randolph, really—"

"The old Creoles are only too happy to replenish the family coffers with fresh American dollars, while some misguided Americans have mistakenly believed having Creole names and bloodlines will give them a social boost. Are you going to tell me the recent match between Claudelle Moreau and John Townsend is one born of love? My God! The man is over fifty years old and she's barely seventeen. Need I mention that he is an exceedingly rich wholesaler with one of the biggest homes in the Garden District and that her family is virtually destitute?"

"You're being morbid," Duncan said.

"You don't believe me, little brother? Fine. Ask Mr. Arnaud there!"

Duncan had been so engrossed in Randolph's tirade that he hadn't seen Christophe looming in the doorway, top hat in one elegant hand, gold-tipped cane in the other. As he bowed, the cape parted, and light sparkled from a diamond cravat pin. Why, Duncan wondered, had the man suddenly appeared in formal dress?

"Hello, Christophe," he managed finally. Randolph merely nodded.

"Gentlemen," Christophe said. "And what was it you wished to ask me, Duncan?"

"Uh, nothing," Duncan replied, embarrassment flaring. He looked away, momentarily focusing on the vase of gardenias. He didn't realize until now how angry he was or exactly why. He didn't know why he had developed such a deep loyalty to the Creoles, but it was a fact that in two short months he had become enamored of the people and their exotic culture. More than once he had reminded himself he didn't know how much of life he had been missing until he came to New Orleans. He had known only Tidewater Virginia and, true, he cherished the beauty of Tarleton, the serenity of the James River and the rich hush that fell over the tobacco fields at dusk. He especially loved the riverine fog, like silver clouds, making the plantation at once supernal and intensely real.

He had even come to care for his father and mother a little, but, despite warnings from his brother, those people had buried him at Tarleton and it had taken death to rouse him to leave it all behind. His only regret was that he hadn't come sooner.

"We . . . we were just having a discussion."

Christophe's smile bloomed at last. "Judging from the red faces, I'd say I was interrupting some sort of family fun. Might I be included in the merriment?"

For Duncan, the question was an attempt at much-needed levity. Randolph dismissed it as pure arrogance.

"I . . . I don't remember," Duncan lied.

"*Eh, bien,*" Christophe said, unconvinced. Still he was too polite to pursue the matter further. "Do you also not remember that we are due at the Fleury house within the hour?"

"The Twelfth Night ball!" He cried. "How could I have forgotten?!"

"I don't know," Christophe shrugged, hands out, palms up.

"I thought we were having dinner," Randolph protested. "Cook is preparing something special tonight. Your favorite—"

"I'm sorry, Randolph!" Duncan leapt up, grabbing Christophe's arm and all but dragging the elegant figure behind him. "Come along! You can talk to me while I get dressed."

"Go on up," Christophe said, giving him a playful shove. "I'll have a quick word with your brother."

Up until now, Randolph had been civil enough. Nothing had been said about his attitude toward Creoles, but Christophe had heard enough of tonight's conversation to know the truth. It was certainly not the first time he had encountered disdain on this side of the Rue Canal but this one hurt. His new friendship with Duncan was a deep, mutual thing and he had wanted the man's brother to like him too. He knew the pitfalls of trying to undo prejudice but he made the effort nonetheless.

"I heard enough of your conversation to understand your feelings, sir, and I confess they distress me. Your brother seems to have found our Creole customs most amusing. Perhaps you might do the same."

"Perhaps," Randolph conceded.

"Then allow me to invite you to one of our carnival balls sometime. They're really quite gay."

"We have carnival balls this side of Canal Street too," Randolph said coolly.

"Indeed." How Christophe longed to remind this bourgeois American that carnival was a Latin custom and that *Yanqui* celebrations were merely a pallid imitation of the real thing! Instead he responded with an intentionally grandiose bow. "In that case, monsieur, you have my apologies."

He could feel the loathing burn into his back as he followed Duncan up the stairs. Boor, he thought.

"Wonder what the hell he meant by that," muttered Randolph.

He refilled his glass and gulped another slug of whiskey before deciding to go to his club. To hell with Duncan's special dinner. He had no intention of dining alone.

Justine paused before the armoire mirror and studied her reflection critically. A smile slowly bloomed. Madame Clovis' needles had worked their usual wonders and the results glowed like rare rubies. The red gown was a symphony in watered silk, ten yards of a skirt so full it almost made her waist disappear. The hem was elegantly scalloped, scarlet bows blazing from a dozen flounces like velvet flames. Large puffed sleeves decked Justine's creamy shoulders, anchoring a neckline cut in extreme décolleté. She tugged those sleeves lower, baring even more breast before she searched in her jewel box for the final touch. It was her favorite piece, and she prayed it hadn't disappeared like those earrings, necklaces, bracelets, and brooches that had mysteriously vanished over the past few weeks. She knew where they had gone, of course, knew that those garish diamond earrings were now dangling from the ears of some colored girl in the Rue Rampart, just as she knew her grandmother's garnet necklace was probably in the same dark hands. She couldn't help wondering just how dark those hands were and if her husband's mistress was pretty. She was certain if Marie Tonton had her way she would learn everything that would flatter the other woman and throw Justine in a bad light.

She forgot about such unpleasantries when her fingers wrapped around the item in question. Thank goodness Marie Tonton hadn't stolen that too! She took it out and hefted its weight in her palm. It was heavy, this exotic bauble Blancard had bought her in Constantinople during those disastrous years in Europe. Originally part of an extravagant necklace belonging to the Byzantine empress Zöe, it had been broken up by some greedy eighteenth-century jeweler and sold as several smaller pieces. What gleamed in Justine's hand was a brooch, a colorful cloissoné angel surrounded by pearls.

She sat at the rosewood *duchesse* and affixed the brooch to her dress, nestling it comfortably into the cleft of her full bosom. Along with the tiny pearl earrings Blancard so hated, it provided the perfect compliment to the dress.

She released a little laugh, yielding to the urge to rise suddenly and pirouette around the room, whirling in a cloud of silk. The lush rustling sound made her happy, because it meant she was doing something she loved. It was the same when she settled into a box at the opera, slid from the leather interior of a hansom, or whirled around the dance floor with her husband's hand at the small of her back. Well, she thought grimly, perhaps not all the memories were so pleasant.

Justine's mood plummeted at the sound of boots forcing a creak from the eleventh step outside. She hadn't heard it in weeks but it was all too familiar. Skinny Marie Tonton was too light to make that noise. Blancard was coming up the stairs.

Drawing from a newfound reserve of strength, Justine froze in the middle of the room and turned to face the door. She folded her hands over a fan of elegant egret plumes and waited, ticking off the footsteps as he approached her room. She hadn't seen Blancard since responding to the Fleury invitation, and this act—her first without consulting him—might well trigger that mercurial temper.

Her first clue to Blancard's temperament was how he opened the door. It swung open gently. The second clue was his coloring. Blancard was slightly flushed, which meant he had been drinking but not a great deal. It was unsettling because when his mood was this mellow he could be charming, almost irresistibly so. He was dashing in formal dress, top hat in hand, cape slung rakishly over one shoulder. She was further disconcerted when a broad smile bloomed on his face, teeth gleaming white against the darkness of a new black beard. On Christophe, Justine thought idly, it might have been dashing. It gave Blancard the aura of a pirate.

"Well, well! What have we here?" He hadn't been prepared for this dazzling vision of his wife.

"*Bon soir, monsieur,*" she said, gaze dropping to the floor as it often did in his presence. It was nothing he had ever requested, rather something she knew instinctually. It was a statement of obeisance, not unlike that of an obedient servant.

"New dress?" he asked, moving slowly to Justine's left, beginning the first of several long circles around her. She nodded. "Ah, yes. I remember now. Something about the Fleury ball. It's Twelfth Night, isn't it?"

"*Oui,*" she answered softly, trying to control the tremble threatening her hands and voice.

Of course he knew. He knew everything! From that vile-tempered

Marie Tonton of course, and every other spying servant in the household. All but dear Hippolyte. Blancard was toying with her, setting the evil stage before he delivered an all-too familiar performance. He was drawing nearer, closing the circle. She could smell his cologne now, a new scent unfamiliar to her, something heavy, almost vulgar, something, no doubt, that his mistress had given him.

"You are going with Arnaud?"

"*Oui, monsieur.*"

She almost added "with your permission" but held her tongue. Sometimes she could manage him when he was in such a mood, but she had to be careful not to provoke him. The quieter, the more retiring she was, the more she might be permitted. He was behind her now, his breath warm against the nape of her neck.

"Oh!"

"You're as jumpy as a cat," he said, voice low, tinged with amusement. "I was merely righting a strand of hair gone askew. You'll want to look perfect as always. Madame Hilaire Blancard must always look perfect, *n'est-ce pas?*"

Softer than ever, "*Oui, monsieur.*"

Blancard took a breath and spoke expansively as he moved in front of her and paused for a final look. The smile returned, blooming even larger than before. "The dress becomes you, Justine."

"*Merci,*" she whispered, swallowing a sigh of relief. But she wasn't safe yet.

"You'll make my excuses of course?"

"Of course, monsieur."

He nodded curtly, smile vanishing. One more look, this one cold, studied. It sent a shiver to Justine's spine. "*Bon soir, madame.*" He closed the door and was gone.

Justine froze in the center of the room, mentally counting the steps, listening as Blancard's boots creaked on the eleventh stair. She rushed to the door and pressed her ear against it, welcoming relief only when she heard the front door close behind him. When the clip-clop of hooves assured her Hippolyte was pulling the carriage away from the house, she fairly waltzed to the *duchesse*. As she retrieved the forbidden item hidden deep in a drawer, she reveled in her cleverness. The normally reserved Toinette Clovis had been turned into a giggling conspirator, sworn to secrecy when she agreed to purchase the rouge pot and stash it in the folds of the gown before delivering it.

For once, Justine had sneaked something past Marie Tonton!

She giggled too as she opened it and studied the deep red inside. It was darker than she had expected and made her reconsider, made her wonder if she dared. Creole ladies disdained cosmetics as vulgar, claiming their natural beauty was enough. They wore their pale skins like badges of superior ethnic pride, perhaps occasionally rubbing crushed rose petals against their cheeks for a mere *soupçon* of color. Or so they claimed. The Americans suspected that the Creole women used cosmetics in abundance, that those heavily lashed eyes and red lips could not be nature's gift. Yet, they conceded, these women achieved this look with such superb skill that one could never be sure. Justine had never resorted to such artifice, but tonight, with her new gown and her struggling new spirit, she had decided to experiment.

As she touched the rouge gingerly and rubbed it against her cheek, she marveled at the way it blended easily into her skin. Turning up the gas lamp so her reflection was harshly lit, she experimented until she created a radiance that would bedazzle beneath the glow of chandeliers. Yielding to her unexpected skill, she touched a little to her lips as well. She smiled.

"Perfect!"

The shuffle of footsteps alerted her to another unwelcome visitor and she hastily capped the rouge pot and tossed it inside the drawer. When Marie Tonton entered the room, her mistress was sitting before the mirror smoothing her hair. She grunted and jerked her head toward the door.

"Michie Christophe's downstairs."

"*Bon.*" Justine gave her faintly rouged reflection a final fleeting critique and satisfied herself that no one would be the wiser. She rose and faced Marie Tonton, a surge of power prompting a final order. "Clean all the lamps and trim the wicks while I'm at the ball." To assure the job got done, she added, "Monsieur Blancard just complained that this one smokes." The servant grunted again, no doubt disgruntled because she had other plans for the evening. She was unnerved as well when her mistress, whom she believed to be hopelessly naive, issued another unexpected edict. "And stay home. I've heard the drums, girl, and I know you slip out some nights. Monsieur Blancard doesn't approve of *voudou*. I don't think he'd like it if I told him about the *gris-gris* you left in here."

"Wasn't me that put that thing under your bed!" Marie Tonton snapped defiantly.

Justine smiled as the woman fell into her own trap. "I never mentioned *where* I found it, but you seem to know all about it."

She swept by in a grand rustle of silk, leaving the seething mulatress to stew in her own poison. So far the night was a total triumph and Justine fairly ran down the stairs to find Christophe waiting in the parlor. Ordinarily she would have offered her hand for his kiss, or if she was feeling especially gay, her cheek. Tonight she threw herself in his arms and hugged him tight, surprising him as much as herself. And the man watching from the garden as well.

When Christophe told him the Blancard courtyard was one of the grandest in the *carré de la ville*, Duncan couldn't resist exploring. What he saw now, through the glossy dark of magnolia leaves, was far more captivating than the courtyard. This glamourous woman in a red gown, embracing his friend like a long-lost lover, was scarcely what he had expected of the mysterious Justine Blancard. Christophe's carefully delineated portrait of the woman did not imply someone capable of this sort of display, and Duncan watched the scenario with interest. He took a step forward, reconsidered, paused and waited. There was an intimacy inside suggesting it remain uninterrupted, yet there was something else. Duncan was loathe to recognize that what held him back was a most unwelcome twinge of jealousy. But how could this be? He didn't even know the woman.

Finally he responded to Christophe's energetic beckoning and left behind the cold garden. He had never seen Christophe quite so animated and found his smile contagious as he approached these two old friends. He bowed at the mention of Justine's name and when he looked up was entranced as she slowly entered a deep curtsy. Down and down she went, skirts rippling outward as she settled into a crimson cumulus. Dark hair and pale skin startled against so much red, but they were not what caught and held his eye. As Justine listed gracefully forward, creamy breasts swelled against the confines of the neckline, cleavage deepening as she completed the curtsy and began to rise.

She lifted her gaze as she regained her stature, and when she saw where the American's gaze had lit, she blushed furiously. Never had anyone stared so blatantly, so crudely at her bosom. Certainly there were always those gentlemen whose appreciative glances lingered longer than necessary, but this! This was the rude gawking of a schoolboy. Or, she thought, eyes stinging with insult, a crude *Yanqui!* Feeling like a slave on the auction block, Justine snapped open the fan and pointedly draped the showy white plumes over her breasts. Only a vestige remained of her earlier smile, and it vanished when she broke the peculiar silence.

"Parlons-nous anglais ce soir?"

"Of course we'll be speaking English tonight," Christophe said, a bit sternly.

"I'm afraid I don't speak French," Duncan apologized.

"It is of no consequence," Justine said, annoyance unmasked. She hissed something in French to Christophe before adding, in highly accented English, "Shall we go?"

For Justine, it was the evening's first discordant note. For Christophe, it was a sudden embarrassment that she should take such an instant dislike to his American friend. As for Duncan, he was both bewildered and rebuffed by the woman's behavior. Perhaps he had finally encountered one of those aloof, arrogant Creoles he had been warned against. Anxiety replaced his eager anticipation of the evening when L'Eveillé snapped the reins and the coach swayed toward the Rue Condé. Despite all Christophe's talk about the merriment of Twelfth Night, Duncan found himself wishing he had taken his brother's advice and stayed home.

Antoine Fleury's raised cottage, while not the largest in the *carré de la ville*, was certainly one of the most talked about for its gracious but daring marriage of Creole and American styles. It was, carped the diehard Creoles, an ideal reflection of its owners rush to embrace the *Yanquis*. The pedimented portico supported by four Tuscan columns and double stairways curving gracefully from gallery to banquette were unmistakably American while the pastel plaster walls and tall windows flanking the front door were pure French. Just now those windows glowed with much-reflected candlelight, chandeliers strategically stationed before enormous mirrors to glean as much light as possible and throw it back on the giddy, glittering crowd. A crush of carriages flowed around the block as guests streamed steadily from both sides of Canal Street. At this rate, thought Christophe, the house will be bursting at the seams by midnight when the king and queen were chosen. Eager to escape the oppressive silence inside the carriage, he suggested they walk the remaining half block. Equally relieved, Duncan purposely hung back when Justine took Christophe's arm and let the couple move ahead.

As soon as they were out of earshot, Christophe leaned discreetly to Justine's level. "What do you mean he's a barbarian? You've only just met the man!"

"You didn't see how he was looking at me," she hissed. "It was positively vulgar. Outrageous! I've seen boys show less curiosity about *décolletage* than that man!"

"You're too sensitive, *cher*," Christophe said. "I've told you this man is a gentleman and one of my best friends."

"Then you should pick your friends with more care," she snapped. When she saw his pained expression, she hastily apologized. "I'm sorry, Chris. I was so nervous about the evening and wanted so desperately for it to be a success that . . . well, you're right. Perhaps I've behaved badly. Forgive me?"

Ruffled feathers smoothed, Christophe nonetheless wanted her apology directed elsewhere. "It's Duncan who should hear that."

She winced at the notion of the American's eyes boring into her flesh again. "I'll try," she promised. "Just give me a few minutes to collect myself once we get inside."

"That's a good girl," he smiled.

But Justine forgot all about the unpleasant experience when she plunged into the swirl of gaiety inside the Fleury house. As usual there was much fuss over one of her rare public appearances. Héléne Fleury positively beamed when she saw her, thrilled that her ball had been the one to lure Justine from seclusion. No one, including her hostess, dared ask about Blancard!

The women greeted each other with extravagant kisses matched only by extravagant praise for each other's ball gowns. Marie, the Fleury's young daughter, was agog at Justine's dress, but Justine hastily praised the girl's peach taffeta with its showers of chantilly lace and assured her she was the loveliest girl there. Both were dazzled by the beauteous Eugénie Duval, a vision in butter-yellow satin with a dozen flounces trimmed with pink rosebuds and *without* her watchdog father for a change. Her mother Thérése was much more interested in resting her swollen feet than keeping an eye on her ravishing daughter. Claudelle Moreau was only slightly less stunning in pale blue silk, puffed sleeves and skirts foaming with white lace. Her new and rather elderly husband beamed all too happily with this delicate Creole belle on his arm.

"But you should see some of the American girls, Madame Blancard!" Marie gushed. "They're almost as pretty as you and Camille La Sére."

"You shouldn't mention Camille while she's in mourning," reminded her mother. "Now leave Justine alone and help me greet the rest of our guests."

Justine felt her arm taken, grateful when Adéle Boisquet steered her away from the front door. Lucie Dupre had just arrived and was (understandably!) regarding Justine's dress suspiciously. Adéle always overflowed with the most boring gossip, but Justine feigned undying interest as the chubby woman stridently negotiated the crowd. Justine managed a parting wave at Christophe before being swallowed by the revelers.

"She's absolutely nothing like what I excepted," Duncan said when he had a moment alone with Christophe. "Beautiful, yes, but cold as ice."

"I'm afraid you committed a bit of a *faux pas, mon ami,*" Christophe said, snaring two glasses of wine from a passing butler.

Duncan was flabbergasted. "What kind of *faux pas?* I barely said a word."

When he found a spot where he didn't have to shout, Christophe said, "It was what you *did* not what you *said.* You know by now that our Creole women don't mind putting their breasts on display, but their charms are to be discreetly admired. Not stared at. Frankly, Duncan, I'm surprised and not a little disappointed. After all, you told me about how prim and proper the Virginia ladies . . . what on earth are you laughing at?"

"Is that what she told you, that I was ogling her cleavage?"

"*Exactement!*"

"It's too funny!" Duncan said, guffawing anew, so loud that he drew stares from a nearby cluster of young blades. He laughed until tears formed in his eyes, dabbed away by Christophe's hastily proferred handkerchief.

"Will you please lower your voice and explain yourself," Christophe demanded. "If those dandies there discover your disparaging laughter has anything to do with a Creole lady, tomorrow morning it will be pistols for two, café au lait for one."

The very real possibility of a duel sobered Duncan enough to regain his self-control. He pulled Christophe close and whispered in his ear. "I confess her breasts are a wondrous work of nature, my friend, but they were not what so captured my attention."

"Then what, for the love of God, was it?"

"That Byzantine brooch!" Duncan laughed. "I was merely trying to determine if it was eleventh or twelfth century!"

Christophe's whoop brought more curious looks from the crowd. When he and Duncan stopped laughing, he tossed down his wine and said they had to find Justine at once. "I know you'll find this difficult to believe, but Justine loves a good joke. Even when it's on her."

"You find her," Duncan said, smile fading only to be reborn. "I have something more important to do."

Because they had become intimate friends, Christophe knew it could only be a woman putting such a smile on Duncan's face. His eyes followed the trail blazed by Duncan's gaze, lighting on none other than Eugénie Duval. She was sweeping through the crowd like a sleek clipper ship in full sail. The clutch of dandies parted like Moses' sea, but as Eugénie glided through she seemed oblivious to them. While all watched in disbelief, she made directly for Christophe, but in an instant she made it clear it was Duncan who drew her attentions. She offered a hand first to Christophe, then to Duncan who remembered his friend's advice that a hand must be brushed lightly with the lips, never actually kissed. A moustache, he insisted, made it much easier.

"So good to see you, Monsieur Saunders," she said, favoring him with an irresistible smile. "I don't believe I've seen you since the Pradel's *réveillon.*"

"I'm quite certain that was it," Duncan said. "I would never have forgotten another meeting."

While the two exchanged pleasantries, Christophe cautiously eyed the group of wary young blades. Vigilant to a man, their disapproval was blatant as they watched Eugénie deep in conversation with *le Améri- cain.* Unlike their host, they were not so broad-minded and deeply resented this upstart in their midst. Christophe recognized all the ingredients for an ugly encounter, just waiting to be stirred. He had no doubt that a duel was on the mind of at least one of the men. Dominique Duplessy was famed for hot tempers and cold steel, and Christophe determined that his friend avoid both at all costs. He knew the only way to diffuse the smoldering scenario was to separate the parties in question.

"With apologies, Madame Duval, Monsieur Saunders and I must excuse ourselves." His sudden grip on Duncan's bicep tightened, signaling him to follow the plan. "We have some unexpected business to tend to."

Eugénie did her best to conceal her disappointment behind a fluttering fan. *"Bien sûr."*

Annoyed and confused, Duncan carried that parting image of her perfect face behind the dancing ostrich plumes as Christophe fairly dragged him away. At first opportunity he demanded to know what was going on.

"I just saved your life, *mon ami!"*

"You mean you just ruined it," Duncan amended, jerking his arm away. "Was that another of your old Creole customs, separating a lady and gentlemen when they're—?"

"The only thing about to be separated was your head and your shoulders," Christophe hissed. "That group of young dandies was anything but pleased to see Mademoiselle Duval choose the company of an American over them. It was only a matter of moments before you were called out."

Duncan frowned. "Called out?"

"Challenged to a duel!" Christophe grimaced, obviously exasperated. "Don't you remember anything? I explained the Code of Honor to you one night at *Valencia*. Maybe you were so drunk you don't remember."

"If I remember correctly," Duncan said, anger flaring, "it was you who were drunk that night. In any case, I have no intention of having a perfectly innocent conversation spoiled by a bunch of hoodlums who—"

Christophe grabbed him again. This time Duncan couldn't shake off the grip. "They're not hoodlums and, to them anyway, what you were doing was scarcely innocent. Don't look at me like that! It doesn't matter that Eugénie instigated it. It was a serious affront to them, a slight to their pride, a slap at their masculinity. All they saw was the most sought-after Creole belle exhibiting preference for someone other than another Creole. Duels have been fought over far, far less crucial matters. The degree of humidity. The exact width of a river. The merits, or rather *lack* of merits, of a particular soprano at the opera. Anything and everything can be the catalyst for shedding blood on the green."

"You can't be serious."

"*C'est vrai!* But come along. Those boys are still watching us and you have the disconcerting habit of staring at people when I am talking about them. Out of sight, out of mind. They'll soon find another target for their restlessness. Ah, to be twenty with heat in one's blood again!"

At that precise moment, Duncan realized there was a dimension to the Creoles in general and this one in particular that he would never understand. And he would forever be the cool-headed Virginian poet. What an improbable pair they were! Duncan found their friendship at once so absurd and so valuable that he couldn't resist hugging Christophe so hard the Creole almost dropped his wine.

"Eh? And what is this?" he demanded, eyes wide with feigned shock.

"Just testing your sword-happy friends," he teased, adjusting Christophe's crooked cravat. "Do you suppose they'll challenge me to a duel because I prefer you to them?"

"You're impossible!" said Christophe but he loved the joke. "Now may we please look for Justine?"

"*Bien sûr, monsieur!*" Duncan grinned.

They found her huddled with Adéle. Her expression pleaded, *please rescue me from this ignominious fate!* With Christophe in charge, they extricated her from Madame Boisquet and, in the house's only uncrowded corner, Duncan explained his earlier actions.

"With deep apologies, Madame Blancard, while I found your . . . uh, your charms most beguiling it was in fact the brooch that so attracted me."

"Sir?" Justine asked, genuinely bewildered.

"I have a fascination for the Byzantine, you see."

To make his point, Duncan nodded discreetly at the costly bauble buoyed by Justine's bosom. When he did so, Justine caught the twinkle in his eye and found it irresistible. She realized it was possible for a man to admire her flesh without cruelty in his heart. At first she was embarrassed, then relieved. As she studied Duncan's gentle hazel eyes, relief yielded to a welcome calm that in turn flowed into amusement. As Christophe had hoped, she burst into laughter and apologized profusely and genuinely to Duncan. It was as if some sort of dam had broken.

"What a vainglorious fool I have been!" she smiled.

Duncan smiled too. "Hardly. At the risk of being forward, madam," Duncan said, "when one is as beauteous as yourself, the compliments must come like your sudden Louisiana rains."

"I assure you they are not that frequent," Justine said. "I am after all a married woman."

"With apologies again, where I come from it is not improper to praise a woman's beauty, regardless of her matrimonial status."

Justine indulged herself in a daring moment of flirtation. "Perhaps we Creoles have something to learn, eh, Christophe?"

From that moment on, Justine chattered like a bird, and within moments Duncan was completely captivated by her charm. He began to grasp Christophe's fascination for this woman, although he suspected he would likely never be permitted to penetrate beyond her beguiling facade. As they talked, he found her alternately fragile and willful, haughty and humble, a living breathing contradiction. More than anything, and he had no idea why such a recollection surfaced, Justine reminded him of something seen long ago in Richmond.

Scratching for a few pennies, slave children scrambled dangerously high into towering magnolia trees, tossing huge blossoms to friends waiting below. The treacherous descent almost always damaged the creamy petals, bruising them an ugly brown. Those that escaped pure white cost a penny more. And that, thought Duncan, is the image this strange woman conjures. Beneath the radiant flesh, the quick, nervous smile, the mesmerizing cat's eyes, he saw a bruised magnolia.

For Justine's part, she was equally charmed, surprising herself that she felt so comfortable with this tall stranger. Indeed, she was so relaxed that she didn't notice her neck had grown stiff from tilting her head back to look at him. His passion for the Byzantine was, she hungrily discovered, as deep as her own, as was his love for literature and history. For widely disparate reasons, both had retreated into those intellectual realms, fashioning opulent escapes from a world they found unrewarding and unbearably lonely. While Duncan had discovered the intrigue of that long-dead empire on his own, Justine had inherited the interest from her mother, who had told her fabulous stories as a child. She had even been named after Justinian, Byzantium's most celebrated emperor.

It wasn't until midnight drew near, finding them deep in a discussion of the great Justinian's peasant origins, that both realized Christophe had disappeared. They had been alone for hours, conversation overlapping, one completing the sentence of another and beginning a new one to be completed in turn. Anyone overhearing the constant interruptions would have dismissed it as brashly rude, but neither Justine nor Duncan could remember such an exciting interchange.

"Sometimes when I stroll the harbor and see the amazing variety of ships, I'm reminded of what Constantinople must've been like," Justine said. "The towering Venetian galleys, Croatian barques, those graceful feluccas from Egypt . . ."

". . . the caiques from the Greek islands . . ."

". . . and those enormous dromonds of the royal fleet . . ."

". . . the ones that carried the Greek fire . . ."

"*Mais oui!* Byzantium's secret weapon. You know, Mr. Saunders, I've never understood how that mysterious matter worked. I inquired about it while in Constantinople, but the guide gave me a most garbled report."

"It is believed naphtha was the secret ingredient," Duncan answered. "When mixed with sulphur and saltpeter, it—" This time it was not Justine who interrupted. "Where's everyone going?" he asked.

"Everyone's crowding into the dining room," Justine said, rising to smooth her skirts and take his arm. "You're about to celebrate King's Day, Monsieur Saunders. *Le Jour des Rois* we call it, or *Le Petit Noel.*"

"Little Christmas?"

"You know more French than you think, monsieur." She smiled. "Tonight's festivities are a legacy of Spanish rule here and perhaps my favorite of the Mardi Gras traditions."

"I thought Mardi Gras was the day before Ash Wednesday."

She smiled sweetly at his ignorance. "Carnival season commences Twelfth Night, tonight, January 6, the Feast of the Epiphany, and concludes on Mardi Gras which is, as you say, the day before Ash Wednesday. Between now and then is an endless round of balls, parties, dinners, and masquerades. But, hurry and find us a place! They're about to choose the king or queen."

"King *or* queen?" He was confused.

"There's a spot! Hurry!"

Duncan and Justine squeezed in between windows leading to the rear gallery and a dining table which was the focus of much excitement. In the center was the immense king's cake, an elaborate confection adorned with bon-bons, shiny *dragées*, caramels, and more. Duncan's height made it easy for him to see over the heads of the much-shorter Creoles and he watched with fascination as the cake was cut with much anticipation and ceremony. Justine playfully refused to explain why a large linen napkin continually concealed the spot where each slice was removed, telling Duncan only that no one must eat until champagne was passed and all were served.

A hush fell over the packed dining room as everyone ate. Duncan started when the silence was interrupted by an unmistakably feminine squeal. "Some lucky girl found the bean," said Justine. "We have a new queen." Deciding the mystery had lasted long enough, she explained that the chef had hidden a bean in the batter of the *gateau de roi*. The lucky soul finding it in their slice was named king or queen, and they chose a co-regent.

"Can you see her, Monsieur Saunders?" Justine asked, obviously stirred by the thrill of the moment. "Can you see her majesty?"

"It's Eugénie Duval," he replied. "Someone is presenting her with a bouquet of violets and she seems to be coming this way."

"Indeed she does," said Justine when the crowd parted enough to see Eugénie's beaming figure. Speculation in French and English sputtered throughout the crowd as everyone tried to anticipate who Eugénie would choose as her king. When she caught sight of the determination in the girl's eyes, Justine had the answer before anyone else. "Congratulations, Monsieur Saunders," she whispered. "Long live the king!"

"But what do I . . . ?"

Justine hissed instructions so fast she lapsed in and out of English. "When she offers the violets, make *le tour de salon* . . . that is, promenade around the dining room and proclaim, '*Mes sujets, voici votre reine! Recevez ses commandements!*'" She giggled at her own helplessness. "Oh, dear! Well, Eugénie will know what to do."

Along with everyone else, Justine applauded Eugénie's selection as Duncan accepted the nosegay and escorted his queen around the room. Fiddlers provided music for the new monarchs who were toasted and congratulated until Duncan thought he could not say thanks or mutter *merci* one more time without sounding utterly insincere. What had begun as a chaotic evening had metamorphosed into a fairy tale, and Duncan wished Randolph could see him with this dazzling queen.

He also wished, with a disconcerting desperation, that it was Justine beaming up at him, that it was Justine proudly clutching his arm. That and that alone could have made it the perfect moment.

But huddled on the gallery, outraged by the joyous proceedings inside the dining room, was a man plotting to abort Duncan Saunders' reign. For him it was unthinkable that he or any American could share the Twelfth Night crown with Eugénie Duval. There was only one acceptable course and he would pursue it as soon as he found Saunders alone. He rubbed the *colchemarde* at his side, feeling, as did many swordsmen, that the cold steel blade was a necessary extension of his manhood. Indeed he was mightily aroused by the prospect of challenging this impossibly presumptuous *Yanqui* to a duel, but not one of those polite, cosmetic interchanges currently in vogue.

This duel would be to the death.

CHAPTER 8

"**C**ongratulations again, your majesty!" Christophe clambered back into the carriage after seeing Justine to the door and heartily slapped Duncan's knee.

"*Merci*," beamed Duncan, still heady with the unexpected honor. To be chosen king by no less than Eugénie Duval! He still could not believe his extraordinary good fortune.

"But be warned," Christophe continued. "I'm afraid you'll find such royal honors do not come without a price. Literally."

"Oh?"

Christophe explained that, as first King of Twelfth Night, Duncan was obligated to host a lavish ball the following week at Eugénie's house. Duncan was also expected to send his queen a piece of jewelry, the only gift a proper Creole mother permitted her unwed daughter from a gentleman.

Duncan grimaced. "Bad news indeed and not a little embarrassing. When I tell Randolph about this . . . well, you know about his unfortunate attitude toward Creoles. I hardly suspect he will want to contribute to such an event, and God knows the funds are not in my shallow pockets."

"Don't worry, *mon ami*," Christophe said. "Since I got you involved in this predicament, it's only fair that I take care of the matter."

"You're far too generous," Duncan said, genuinely moved by the unexpected offer. How on earth his brother could continue holding such archaic grudges was beyond him.

Christophe waved a hand languidly. "In any case, a new king and queen will be chosen with another king's cake next week, and all this attention will evaporate." He chuckled again. "Along with the expense."

Duncan seemed immersed in thought. "I'm still amazed that she chose me, Chris." The wine and the evening's excitement had made him drowsy, and he sank back in the carriage seat, stretching his long legs as best he could. "Of all the men present."

"You're not the only one. I'm just grateful we got through the evening without incident. I thought for sure Duplessy would cause trouble, but he and his cronies seemed to have disappeared right after Mademoiselle Eugénie made her choice." He rearranged his satin cape more comfortably. "Of course, they're not the only obstacles."

Duncan read him immediately. Randolph's warning about Honoré Duval had haunted him all evening. "Her father, eh?" Christophe nodded wearily. He also was tired, too tired even to toy with his moustache as he always did when confronted with a dilemma. "Has anyone ever been forced to give up the honor of being king?"

"Not that I can remember. Oh, I suspect Duval will do his usual blustering and posturing but, confidentially, the only thing stronger than his hatred of Americans is his love for his only daughter. In fact, this may be just what it takes to drag that old buzzard into modern times. Whoa! What was that?"

L'Eveillé had scarcely drawn the carriage away from the Blancard house when two figures sprang from the shadows and blocked his path. Since slaves were prohibited by law from carrying weapons, he had only his whip to raise in self-defense. Hearing his name assured him this was no robbery, but it did not vanquish a sudden bad case of the trembles.

"Better put that down, L'Eveillé."

While one man grabbed the reins, a second pressed his face against the window of the coach. Although the flickering streetlamps did not yield enough light to identify the intruder, Christophe recognized the raspy voice of Dominique Duplessy. The other man was most likely Étienne Lafon.

"A word with Monsieur Saunders, sir!"

"He does not speak French!" Christophe snapped. "Nor do we converse with unidentified rabble."

"We have no quarrel with you, Arnaud," snarled Duplessy, switching to English. "Although if you continue keeping such questionable company that may change."

"Must I repeat myself?!" Christophe bellowed, shoving Duncan back against the seat when he tried to get out and face his accusers. "Identify yourself or face my *colchemarde.*"

"You would be ill-advised to face my sword, sir," shouted the reply. "You are addressing Dominique Duplessy!"

"And the other?" pressed Christophe in his most imperious tone.

"Étienne Lafon, sir!"

Christophe leaned politely through the window, as though buying a nosegay from a flower *vendeuse.* "Now then. What business have you and my good friend here?"

"It regards his association with Mademoiselle Eugénie Duval. I object to it most strongly. Her choice for King of Twelfth Night is an outrage not to be tolera—!"

"But you said it yourself, monsieur," Christophe interrupted smoothly. "The choice was indeed hers."

Duplessy's anger rendered him unhearing. "This is a matter of honor, not logic, Arnaud. I assure you I speak for her father when I say this outrage will not be tolerated. We will not permit the girl to further disgrace herself with this . . . this bourgeoise *Yanqui!*" He fairly spat the word.

"By God!" roared Duncan. "Let me out of here, Chris! I'll tear that miserable rat limb from limb."

It took all Christophe's strength to block the carriage door as he fumbled wildly for a bloodless solution. "Not that I'm questioning your word, Duplessy, but I'm sure you won't mind a ride to the Duval home to discuss this with Monsieur Duval himself."

"That will only delay the inevitable," Duplessy grunted. "We both know I'm doing what the gentleman is, with all due respect, too old to accomplish himself. The fact is that I am most deeply offended by Monsieur Saunders crude presumption that an American could be king to a Creole queen. It is totally unacceptable." Here it comes, Christophe though grimly. "Therefore, sir, I demand satisfaction."

"*Merde!*" he muttered to Duncan. "Now I'll have to get out of the carriage and make the arrangements."

"What arrangements?" Duncan growled. "I'll beat that bastard within an inch of his life, the little runt!"

"You'll do no such thing! Such behavior, and you should well know this, Duncan, would merely support his accusation that you are bourgeoise *Yanqui* and not a gentleman. Besides," he added as he reached for the door handle, "you've just given me an idea!" He smacked himself on the forehead and chuckled. "It's brilliant! *Mais non! I* am brilliant!"

"Christophe, what on earth . . ."

A finger against Duncan's lips silenced him as he followed his friend from the coach. He was still smarting from the insults, and when he got a better look at Duplessy he could barely restrain himself. Lafon did not seem so repulsive, but despite his fine clothes Duplessy reminded him of a weasel. An elongated Gallic nose overhung an unkempt moustache resembling whiskers, and his habitual slouch reinforced the image of something eager to scurry back to its burrow.

How easy it would be to thrash him here in the street! thought Duncan. I could take him with ease. Both of them even! It had been too long since he had sparred with anyone, and he felt suddenly like a caged animal, ravenous for its prey. Christophe readily sensed this and once more reminded him to remain still.

"Of course I will act as Monsieur Saunders' second," he announced.

"And I will speak for Duplessy," said Lafon. A handsome blade moving with startling grace beneath the moonlight, he struck Duncan as a man who would far rather be home with his family than here, in the middle of a dark street, threatening murder to a man he didn't even know. Duncan couldn't help wondering how many Creoles secretly loathed this antiquated Code of Honor that had long stained the fabric of their glamorous society. "Your choice of weapons, sir?" he asked in flawless English. When Duncan hesitated, he said, "Might I suggest swords?"

"Clubs!" announced Christophe before Duncan could respond. All eyes whirled toward him.

"Why not blades, you coward!" snarled Duplessy, furious because he was a duly celebrated swordsman. He was, Christophe and Lafon knew, only eager to fight when the odds were in his favor and he sputtered his disapproval. "Does the *Américain* lack the courage to face his adversary with a gentleman's weapon?"

Christophe felt Duncan bristle when Duplessy waved a fist in his face. He moved protectively before his big friend when Duncan took a step forward, blocking him from a sword that could flash moonlit steel in a heartbeat.

"My man is no fool, Duplessy!" he snarled back. "But surely he would be if he embarked upon such an unfair match. He is neither marksman nor swordsman. He is instead a boxer of some renown in his home state of Virginia. As well as Maryland and North Carolina." He turned toward Duncan, eyebrows raised as he struggled to remember his geography. "And South Carolina, too, I believe." Duncan was too busy keeping a straight face during this bold lie to respond. He only nodded and held still as the encounter assumed aspects of a comic opera. When

Duplessy rattled his *colchemarde,* however, Duncan was snapped back to harsh reality.

"Be grateful that he had not challenged you to fight him with bare fists!" Christophe cried.

"Unspeakably bourgeois!" snapped Duplessy. "Any Creole gentleman should know that."

"Very well," Christophe said, skirting the slur. "In truth, a man of real courage would forego his known advantage and fight his opponent on equal grounds." He paused before adding with flamboyant flourish. "As would a gentleman."

"Careful," Duplessy warned again. "Or you may have a duel to fight yourself."

Christophe tossed back his head, sneered, and ignored the threat with such drama that Lafon nearly laughed. "Accept our terms, Duplessy, or let word spread throughout the city that it is *you* who are the coward!"

"Clubs it is," said Lafon, obviously wearied of the interchange. Duplessy gave him a withering look lost in the dark.

"At dawn then," said Christophe, opening the door and motioning Duncan back into the carriage. "On Lake Ponchartrain, at the end of the Bayou Road."

Duplessy was instantly suspicious. "What are you up to, Arnaud? Why not the Allard plantation as usual?"

"Because this is a most unusual duel. To begin with, it will be executed in the water."

Duplessy was seething. "Are you insane? What kind of duel is this? Clubs! Water! It's preposterous!"

"It was good enough for Bernard de Marigny," said Christophe with a weighty air of dismissal. He climbed into the coach and called for L'Eveillé to drive on. "Be at the lake or face the consequences." He tipped his top hat politely as the carriage lurched away. *"Bon soir, monsieurs!"*

"What have you gotten me into?" Duncan demanded. "And who the devil is Bernard . . . ?"

"Bernard de Marigny," said Christophe, settling back against the plush coach cushions. "Fascinating man. It's said that he threw a thousand gold Mexican dollars into the cauldron making the bell for his plantation. It supposedly gave it the sweetest, purest tone imaginable."

The man's insouciant digression was maddening. "Christophe, please!"

"Very well, *mon ami.* Calm down and I'll tell you a relevant story. Fortunately it came to mind when you called Duplessy a runt."

Almost in spite of himself, Duncan became spellbound by the strange tale of Bernard de Marigny, one of Louisiana's most influential Creoles, a man whose name was borne by the *faubourg* carved from his plantation adjacent to the *carré de ville*. A fiery orator, Marigny had been elected to the Louisiana House of Representatives in 1817 where he frequently presided over disputes between Creoles and Americans. When Georgia-born James Humble, representative from Catahoula Parish, criticized his overblown speeches, Marigny promptly and ceremoniously challenged the former blacksmith to a duel. No coward, Humble nevertheless sought to avoid the challenge but conceded when peers warned refusing the duel would destroy him both professionally and personally. Marigny was flabbergasted when he received Humble's acceptance which specified that the duel must take place in Lake Ponchartrain in six feet of water.

"With sledgehammers!" cackled Christophe.

"Sounds barbaric," Duncan said.

"But wait! I didn't tell you Marigny was quite short, about Duplessy's height I should think. Humble on the other hand was almost seven feet tall in his stockings!"

Duncan joined the laughter. "I'm beginning to understand your logic. What was the outcome?"

"Marigny was not only amused, he publicly announced he could not fight a gentleman with such an extraordinary sense of humor. As fate had it, the two became lifelong friends!"

Duncan studied Christophe's silhouette, sporadically lit by the flutter of passing streetlights. "Do you think Humble was bluffing?"

Christophe shrugged, palms up. "No." Then, "But we are."

"Nonsense. I'll make mincemeat out of that swamp rat."

"I have to admit that's something I'd personally like to witness. I've disliked the man for years. He's the sort who gives dueling a bad name." Duncan chuckled at the convoluted logic he'd come to associate with his good friend. "*Eh, bien,*" Christophe sighed. "In any case, you will doubtless be elevated in the eyes of the beauteous Mademoiselle Duval."

Duncan sighed too. "She is a jewel, isn't she?"

"The rarest of them all. And if you will pardon an utterly tasteless joke, she is the most heavenly body in the Creole firmament. Perhaps I should have sought her for myself."

"Why haven't you?"

"I've told you before, *mon ami*, I am not a marrying man. Now then. Speaking of the fairer sex, what say we repair to my favorite sporting house and find ourselves some amusement before our early morning rendezvous at the lake?"

Another quintessential Creole suggestion, Duncan thought. *Divertissement* at all costs. He laughed nonetheless. "I am facing a life-and-death situation in a few hours and you want a woman?"

"So do you," Christophe insisted. "What's the alternative? Stewing in your own juices and ruining a perfectly lovely night while you conjecture about this silly duel? Bah! A woman is exactly what you need. You'll see." He rapped the roof of the carriage and called for L'Eveillé to proceed to a shipyard in the *Champs d'Elysees* at the river, "It's high time I showed you the extraordinary and rather bizarre delights in the Rue Gallatin."

Duncan was shocked. "Randolph says that's the most dangerous part of the city."

"Many claim the Swamp in the Rue Girod still claims that dubious honor," Christophe replied lightly. "Perhaps we're only going to the second most dangerous section. But not without protection of course."

"From what I hear, that sword won't be much defense. Randolph says not a night goes by without a murder or two. He also says men conceal blades in their beards and that women hide them in their . . . well, wherever they want."

"All the stories you've heard about the Rue Gallatin are true, *mon ami*. Except none do the place justice. It's a hundred times wilder, more perverse, and more dangerous than anything your poet's mind could conjure."

"Then why in God's name are we going there?"

"I told you my favorite bordello is there. Now no more questions. You must learn to trust your new friend."

Duncan didn't think anything could siphon his thoughts from the peril looming at dawn, but what lurked outside as the carriage swayed through the Faubourg Marigny and beyond proved a powerful distraction. The mansions and prim cottages of the *carré de la ville* fell behind, vanquished by a jumble of dilapidated buildings so wildly atilt a good gust of wind threatened to bring them down. Brown palmettos clattered in a cold wind, and great rotting tree roots loomed like the bones of some ancient beast. The banquettes sagged, decayed, and disappeared altogether alongside ditches heaped high with rotting garbage and raw refuse, both human and animal. The stench was overpowering.

"City services seldom reach this far," Christophe said, raising a scented lace handkerchief to his aristocratic nostrils. "It will be better by the river."

The deterioration continued apace, intensifying as the carriage wheels jounced through bubbling, rancid muck as an arm of the swamp reached for them. Duncan remembered something Christophe had said about having to work the Negro slaves and Irish gangs constantly just to hold the elements at bay, to maintain a stalemate in the eternal battle between land and water. An unattended trickle in the levee might explode into a crevasse flooding the land for miles around. A building succumbing to rot caused by torrid tropical summers lasting most of the year might collapse, bringing down its unsuspecting neighbors. And there was always the threat of invasive weeds and vines sprouting through sidewalks and creeping through shutters. It was only folklore that a resurrection fern had grown on a lady's bonnet while she strolled the levee, but the tale was rooted in an unspoken fear that permeated the life of every New Orleanian.

Order here was an all too fragile thing. The swamp and river engulfed the *Ile d'Orléans,* always lurking through a cloud of mosquitoes or waiting in the fog, hungry for what was once theirs.

Eventually the shadowy shipyard loomed with forest of black masts needling a wintry silver sky. The horse's hoof-clops echoed in the deserted streets, and an atmosphere of isolation and fear settled in with the night air. The first time Michie Christophe had ordered L'Eveillé here, the coachman's hands had shaken so badly he could barely control an equally skittish horse. Even the animal knew better, thought the driver. Now he knew his course and fearlessly sought the lights of a fire glowing alongside a stack of oak knees. This was the nocturnal haunt of the notorious Live Oak Boys, and no sooner had L'Eveillé drawn up the carriage than someone came to investigate the intrusion. The strapping rowdy with the bushy beard was none other than Red Bill Wilson himself, one of the gang's oldest members and, some said, its leader. Swinging from his left hand was the trademark cudgel giving the gang its name. He chuckled when he identified the driver.

"Hey there, Levelay!" He waved his oaken club at the carriage. "That you, Mr. Arno?"

"It is indeed," Christophe answered in English, fearlessly throwing the door wide and holding out a wad of dollars. "My friend and I are after an evening at Pearl's Place. We thought you and some of your boys would like to keep us company." The money was snatched and tucked into Red Bill's filthy pockets with lightning speed as a crooked smile curved his lips.

"Reckon we would at that," he said, swinging into the coach and sitting opposite Duncan. With his pockmarked skin and a nasty scar carved into his jowl, the man could've been anywhere from twenty to forty, and Duncan certainly didn't want to get close enough to learn the truth. "The boys is in the District right now. I was thinking about taking a night off, but I'm always up to do a little business with fine gentlemen such as yourselves."

"Thank you, sir," Christophe said, the picture of *politesse* as he closed the door and called for L'Eveillé to continue. Duncan could comprehend the bizarre tableau that unfolded little more than he could tolerate the miscreant's odor. The stink of rotgut whiskey warred with the stench of unwashed flesh, instantly fouling the air inside the cab. If Red Bill was insulted when Christophe again raised the handkerchief to his nose, he said nothing. Instead he launched into a diatribe about the goings-on in the District, local slang for those two blocks in the Rue Gallatin between Ursuline Avenue and the Rue Hôpital. Duncan was alternately disgusted and spellbound, his poet's mind reeling from the man's tales of macabre things beyond an imagination vivid but limited by lack of worldly exposure.

"You missed a sight last night, gentlemen," he said with raucous enthusiasm. "Yes, siree! You ever been to the Rotterdam? No. Well, it's got a new owner today. The old one, Bridget Brady, they called her One-Legged Brady because she lost her leg in a cat fight with Mary Burke, well, she got into it with her husband Harry. They was tearin' up the place when Harry grabbed her by the hair and dragged her into the backyard. We all followed 'em outside just in time to see him slam her against the privy, take out his knife and stab her about half a dozen times until she stopped screaming." He chuckled, then pulled a small bottle from his filthy pockets and took a healthy swig. Mercifully he did not offer any to the others.

"Just to make sure she was dead, old Harry tore off her wooden leg and beat her brains out." He cackled wildly. "Then he waved it in the air like a pole without a flag! Lemme tell you, gents, that was some sight to see!"

With that final pronouncement, Red Bill slapped Christophe fiercely on the knee and unleashed a blood-curdling howl that pierced the cold night. His tone was so unsensational, so utterly matter-of-fact in discussing murder, that Duncan's stomach turned over.

By contrast, Christophe seemed completely unmoved. "I guess some of those boys can get pretty rowdy sometimes," he observed.

"Reckon they can at that!" Red Bill laughed.

He continued his stories but Duncan's attention was drawn elsewhere. The carriage was still a block away, but the District's magnificently lewd siren was already singing. Balconies and galleries sagged at impossibly precarious angles, raw, rotting, a wooden paean to dissolution. There was not a single structure that did not cry out for paint and repair, reminding Duncan of a hideously aged courtesan who no longer bothered to conceal the ravages of time.

This was an area, boasted the locals, that "snoozed by day and boozed by night." Peeling signs screamed an old story: JOHN RYAN CONCERT-SALOON, TEXAS BOYD'S DANCE HALL, STRADER'S DOG PIT, SOLLMEIER BOARDING HOUSE, JEAN JACQUE'S COCKPIT, EULA ROGERS' HOME FOR SAILORS, PEARL'S PLACE. Through the window, Duncan saw a staggering amalgam of depravity in two blocks solid with bordellos, dance halls, gin mills, and gambling houses, pits for the stomach-turning sports of dogfighting and rat killing. The denizens of the District were an all too idealized reflection of their decrepit environs. Sailors from the ports of the world, country bumpkins, steamboat men, habitues of lazar houses and escaped prisoners, whores and petty thieves, cardsharps and cutthroats, murderers, all undulated together as one massive organism, desperately, hopelessly hurtling backward in evolution. Man was reduced to the basest common denominator of humanity. Duncan was appalled.

Despite the cold, a painfully thin whore in nothing but boots and a tattered robe displayed her disease-ridden wares for anyone to see. The stench of desperation was even greater than that of the garbage heaped in rows on both sides of the streets. The place fairly roared, an unearthly drone punctuated by women's high-pitched squeals, the tinker of piano music and fiddles, and the occasional thud of fist on flesh.

Duncan flinched as a man exploded from a nearby building, careening crazily across the street until he fell, head smashing against the broken cobblestones with a sickening thud. He moaned in agony, unable to resist as a harlot rifled his pockets. She screeched with triumph and held aloft a wallet, a human vulture rejoicing in her carrion booty. For no apparent reason, she gave the body a vicious kick in the ribs before disappearing to count her ill-gotten loot.

As Duncan leaned away from the window, silently wishing he had Christophe's handkerchief, he realized Red Bill was watching him.

"First time in the District, eh?" Duncan nodded. "Well, they have a saying about the place that pretty much sums it up."

"What's that may I ask?"

" 'The only thing cheaper than a woman's body is a man's life.' " Red Bill again roared with laughter as he grabbed the door handle. "Now I gotta get out of here before that perfume you fancy gents is wearin' makes me puke!"

Red Bill swung deftly from the carriage and clung to the door until L'Eveillé stopped before a three-story building with a bright red sign proclaiming PEARL'S PLACE. Christophe exited first and as Duncan followed his eye was caught by a sudden glint of steel. His protector had extracted a blade from his bushy beard and was brandishing it for all to see as he escorted the well-dressed gentlemen inside. Duncan was so mesmerized by the display he tripped over a boot. His gorge rose as he looked down at a badly decomposed corpse poking from an alleyway, limbs locked in grotesque rigor mortis, throat slit in an eternal hideous grin. The stench was nauseating.

"Dear God!"

"Probably got thrown out of that gambling house there," Red Bill grunted. "They leave the bodies of cardsharps on the bars until the stink gets too bad. You know. As a warning to cheaters."

"Dear God," Duncan expelled again.

"Better get used to it, sir," advised Red Bill. He didn't bother concealing his amusement at the American gentleman's distress. "This ain't the Garden District."

"He's right," Christophe said. "It probably won't be the last body you'll see tonight. Come along."

The inside of Pearl's was scarcely more inviting than the streets. The first of two huge rooms was dominated by a long bar. Behind the bar, perched on stools high enough for all to see, were Pearl's bouncers, five monsters gleefully brandishing knives, brass knuckles, and slingshots. Christophe explained that they didn't interfere with fights or even murders as long as Madam Pearl's property wasn't damaged. When Red Bill hastily conferred with two men holding oaken clubs and nodded in their direction, Christophe assured Duncan they had the best possible protection.

"Come along," he said, taking Duncan's arm and ushering him through the mayhem of drinkers. "We're almost there."

The second room was a dance hall where a piano, fiddle, and pitiful cornet made a poor excuse for music that nonetheless drew several couples onto the dance floor. The men were a motley assortment of scraggly bearded recidivists, some with bare chests displaying tattoos and terrible scars, almost all drunk. Their women were an equally rough lot, shuffling through the crowd in scuffed slippers, long hair tumbling around dirty faces, bodies obviously naked beneath thin, knee-length calico frocks. A few women, caught in the drunken madness of the moment, had dispensed with clothing altogether and some of their admirers had followed suit.

"Damn, Chris! Look there!"

A drunken sailor, naked except for his cap and clearly aroused, bore down on a woman who screamed with laughter as he mounted her atop a table. The crowd roared its approval until a burly bouncer pulled the couple apart and cleared the dance floor of another pair attempting the same sport.

Christophe joined the laughter as the sailor tore the clothes off a second whore and tried to mount her instead. "Poor fool obviously doesn't know that sort of thing is off-limits here. Believe it or not, there are *some* rules in the District."

Duncan mopped sweat from his brow. The heat was unbearable. "This is sheer insanity, Chris. Beyond civilized imagination really. I feel as though I've descended yet another rung in Dante's Inferno."

"I promise it gets better, *mon ami*," Christophe smiled. "You must learn to trust me."

Duncan followed him to a doorway guarded by two more bouncers. One recognized Christophe, gave him a vague approximation of a smile and opened the door. Duncan's jaw sagged.

"What on earth . . . ?"

"Welcome to the real Pearl's Place," Christophe smiled. "I told you this was my favorite sporting house in the city. Now you can see why."

"My God, Christophe!"

As the heavy door swung shut behind them, Duncan was transported into another time and place. How was this possible? The appalling stink, noise, and filth of the Rue Gallatin was miraculously left behind, replaced by a quiet room as opulent and elegant as any Duncan had seen. Deeply tufted *bergères*, settees, and *méridiennes* of rich burgundy velvet shown beneath brilliant chandeliers, fragrant candles multiplied in gilded pier mirrors straining toward twelve-foot ceilings. Deepening the startling tableau were a dozen ladies in jewel tones of sapphire silk, ruby satin, and gold velvet, a phantasmagorical departure from the mind-numbing drabness of what lay behind the magical door.

It was, Duncan mused, like stepping off a barren beach into a lush rainforest!

Indeed the women were reminiscent of so many tropical birds, exotic, brilliant, and not a little unreal. In the company of elegant gentlemen they sipped vintage champagnes and listened or danced to the strains of a small orchestra. A narrow but fine staircase barely the width of a hoopskirt led those seeking privacy upstairs where, Christophe whispered, "all the erotic pleasures of the Arabian nights and much more" were readily available.

Duncan shook his head. "I would never have guessed in a million years."

"It's perhaps the best kept secret in the city."

"But how did it come to be here?"

"It's a fascinating story, *mon ami*. And there's the lady who can tell it far better than I—Pearl herself. Come. I'll introduce you."

Ostrich plume fan in one hand, trademark tiparillo in another, Blanche "Pearl" Genois held court in a far corner of the glittering room with a most unlikely coterie comprised of New Orleans' oldest and most recent arrivals. The men were from the most prominent addresses on both sides of the Rue Canal, while the women had been brought, especially by Pearl, from places as distant as New York, Savannah, and Martinique. Her girls were unquestionably the most beautiful, cultured, and costliest in the city, and her clientele the most discriminating. Some of the gentlemen had been calling on her for years. The women, by Pearl's irrevocable dictate, remained no longer than a single season. They were, also by her dictate, all white.

Madam Genois' beauty was under siege but by no means conquered. She was carefully schooled in cosmetic skills unknown to women of the upper classes and always bathed in candlelight giving the illusion of someone much younger than her seventy-seven years. Her face was slender and oval, dominated by a sharp nose and bright, close-set eyes giving her the look of a fox on the prowl. Her thin hoary tresses were concealed by a dark, elaborately coiffed wig made from Italian hair, ringlets and curls throwing calculated shadows on the facets of her face, as did the fan and matching canary yellow ostrich plumes dancing in her hair. No matronly browns and grays and discolored cameos for this woman. Nothing less than a gold velvet ball gown with ermine trim and extravagant jewelry would do. Duncan couldn't help thinking the glistening diamond tiara would cause a full-fledged riot if its existence were known to the rabble just outside the door. Again he was struck by the monstrous incongruity of it all.

"Christophe, *ma cheri!*" she cried. She threw her arms wide and rested gloved hands on his shoulders as he bent to kiss her rouged and powdered cheeks. "You have been away too long, you naughty boy. Clarice has been asking for you."

"I have been busy with a new friend," Christophe began explaining.

Pearl quickly assumed mock indignation. "Ah! So my girls are not good enough for you, eh?"

"*Mais non!*" he said hastily. "You misunderstand, madam. My friend is a gentleman."

The painted face registered shock with practiced measure. "A man? *Mon dieu!* I misunderstood indeed! But for those special pleasures you must call on Madam LaRue in the Rue Girod."

The gathering burst into laughter while Christophe blushed furiously at the racy joke and hastened to introduce Duncan. "Please, madam. Allow me to present Duncan Saunders, a visitor from Virginia."

"*Enchante, monsieur,*" she said, extending a bejewelled hand and switching effortlessly to English. "I have a lovely girl named Virginia here. Although, confidentially . . ." Here she drew him close as though imparting the most intimate of confidences. Instead she whispered loud enough for all to hear. "I fear she is ill-named." A dramatic pause as she glanced from face to face, eyes prancing impishly. "If you know what I mean."

More laughter erupted from the group as Pearl tapped her fan against the couch as an invitation for Duncan to join her. "Any friend of Monsieur Arnaud is most welcome here, sir."

"Like all first-timers, he's curious about the place," said Christophe, wrapping his arm around a petite redhead who knew him from previous visits. "But beware what you tell him, Madam Pearl. The man is a poet and may put your story to verse."

When Pearl smiled, Duncan realized it was the first time she had done so. She revealed a row of perfect but badly stained teeth, doubtless the result of years of cigar smoking. "It's not an uncommon tale, Mr. Saunders. The usual fall from grace although perhaps with a rather unusual ending."

Her flair for the dramatic had already impressed Duncan, convincing him the woman was a born actress. Her delivery of the story was, therefore, artfully done and held him enrapt. Having already heard the tale, everyone else drifted away, to join the dance, share conversation or perhaps disappear upstairs for pleasures of a more intimate nature. Christophe, with the flame-haired Clarice, was among the latter. Once a pretty black girl in a crisp uniform brought Duncan a glass of champagne, Madam Pearl continued with a languid wave of the fan.

"I was born in the Rue St. Louis, across the street from Christophe's home. Both houses were built after the second of the great fires in 1794. Our families shared the same elite society as well as an address, but when I was sixteen my recklessness led me to pursuits unacceptable to those rarefied circles." She drew on the cigar and exhaled a series of perfect smoke rings. "I became *enceinte.*"

All matters concerning pregnancy were taboo in polite circles, and Duncan tried without success to hide his shock. This was, surmised only by the madam, his first visit to a bordello and he was doing his best to appear worldly. Madam Pearl was charmed by his boyish embarrassment and told him so with a squeeze of the hand. Duncan blushed and found, as he stared at his hands, that they seemed uncomfortably large when held in hers.

"My family was understandably outraged and my father would have called the gentleman out had he not, rather conveniently I thought, been summoned home from the colony. We belonged to Spain then, you see, and he was a most charming don from Granada. Javier Sandoval was his name. It's foolish of course but just saying it still excites me to this very day." She shrugged and drew again on the cigar. "When I tried to follow Señor Sandoval to Spain, my father found me out and stormed aboard the ship. I was made a prisoner in my room while he decided what to do. I solved his dilemma by escaping again, but this time I hid were he would never have thought to look." She chuckled at her cleverness. "In the bordellos."

"Oh."

"Don't be shocked, young man. I really had little choice. New Orleans is a big city now, but it was only a struggling Spanish outpost then and everyone knew everyone's business. With the little bit of money I managed to steal from Papa, I bought silence from a madam who hid me until the child came. It was, I'm sad to say, stillborn. In any case, I decided since the elite of the city regarded me as a fallen woman, I might as well play the part. I'm not ashamed to say I did it so well that I eventually became the most successful madam in the city." She smiled with a certain, if sullied, pride. "My attitude was, and remains, 'Evil to him who evil thinks.' Ah, *cher* Philippe!" She extended her hand for a kiss from a departing Creole who masked surprise with a discreet nod when he recognized Duncan from the Twelfth Night Ball. "*Bon soir, monsieur.*"

"*Bon soir,* Madam Pearl." He bowed and was gone.

"Some of these gentlemen are local, the sons and grandsons of my father's friends. They seem to love sharing my secret, dutifully keeping it from their wives and daughters and passing it down from one generation to another. Which brings me to all this." She stirred the smoky air with her plumed fans and gestured at the surrounding grandeur. "Papa eventually fell upon hard times and was forced to auction everything. I bought the furnishings, anonymously of course. I could have purchased the house as well, but this place is as close as I want to be to those people who shunned me. The furniture is, I freely admit, a concession to something still missed, something forever lost." Duncan was touched by the woman's story and believed, correctly, that the gleam of tears in her eyes was genuine. "It has cost me a good deal to remain safe and secure in a place as terrible as this, but it's what I chose. That choice continues to make me a wealthy woman. And famous as well. Gentlemen come here from all over the world because what I offer is the *crème de la crème* of courtesans. All of my girls are educated, speak several languages and . . . well, never mind. I see that one has caught your fancy already."

"I'm sorry, Madam Pearl." Duncan's eye had indeed wandered to a voluptuous blonde singing an impromptu tune with the orchestra. Her plum velvet dress, cinching her waist to impossible smallness, was cut in extreme dé colleté, baring abundant breasts that swelled invitingly before each high note. With the impending duel still nattering the back of his brain, Duncan hadn't imagined he would actually want a woman, but this songbird was quickly changing his mind.

Pearl missed nothing. "Shall I arrange an introduction, Mr. Saunders?"

"Why, yes. Perhaps some conversation would take my mind off an unpleasant bit of business facing me at dawn."

"Conversation?" Pearl smiled. "Why, yes. Yes, of course." There could be, she knew, only one thing a gentleman would be doing at that hour; and she was discreet enough not to name it. "I think you will find the young lady distracting in the most pleasant of ways." She smiled and leaned close enough for him to inhale the peculiar mixture of tobacco and rosewater. "That's Virginia."

Christophe was impatient. Undressing Clarice was usually a pleasure he lingered over, slowly removing every item of clothing himself until the woman was naked. Then he studied her as she lay in bed, posing for him like a model for an artist. When the moment moved him, when he was stirred by the shape of an ankle or the swell of her breasts or perhaps a glimpse of something even more intimate when she assumed an especially provocative pose, Christophe would tell her to undress him with equal slowness. By the time he was naked too, he would be anxious for her. He would explore the curve of her neck and shoulder, linger over her breasts and belly until his light touch triggered a gentle laughter. Then finally, his hand would find the damp quickness between her thighs, the sign for her to touch him likewise.

But tonight he was in a hurry, taking her fast, as though he had to prove something. He didn't understand it himself and, after withdrawing and lying on his back, labored breath finally subsiding, he apologized. Clarice was deeply touched.

"Apologize to a whore? But why, Christophe?"

"I don't know, *ma chére*. I truly don't. For some reason, tonight I am seeing women differently."

Clarice snuggled into the crook of his arm and rested her head on his chest. "How so?"

He reflected over the posturing and portrayal of roles he had witnessed that night, beginning with Justine's indignation that a man should look too long at flesh a male-dominated society dictated be exposed. He considered Eugénie, escaping the dictates of a tyrannical father only to have her happiness challenged by other men. And Pearl, forced into harlotry by a man capable only of damning his daughter rather than helping her. It seemed—was it possible?—unfair. He was truly mystified by this unexpected and most uncomfortable introspection, knowing only for certain that it made him quick with the woman and angry at his own sex.

"I can't explain something I don't understand myself."

"Perhaps it's something to be discussed with another man," Clarice suggested.

He touched her chin with the tip of his finger and turned her face to him. "Do you believe there are things that men and women are incapable of discussing?"

"The truth?" He nodded. "No." She studied his moustache and knew in a moment he would begin twirling it as he always did when he was nervous. "But I am probably not the woman you should be asking that question."

"Ah, but you're wrong, Clarice. I know of no woman, with the exception of Pearl, who would be as honest as yourself."

"An honest whore," she laughed. "Imagine that!"

But he did not laugh. "Other women, *ladies,* are not allowed to be honest."

"Often times they cannot afford to be," she offered.

He frowned and reached for his moustache. "This is all very disturbing, Clarice. And I don't know why it's plaguing me now. Tonight was really no different from any other, and yet . . ." She moved his hand to her breasts where it pressed invitingly against the warm flesh. "Yet it is." As a face, not hers, shimmered deep in his thoughts, he knew why, but he couldn't acknowledge it. He was grateful for Clarice's sudden, skilled diversion. Pearl had never erred in choosing the right girls for her house.

"This is a place of pleasure, Christophe," she whispered, sliding his hand lower still. "We can discuss anything you like, but wouldn't you prefer . . . ?"

When his hand moved farther of its own accord, she knew there was nothing more to be said. This time, partly because his mind was eased and partly because he had just been satisfied, it took Christophe a long time to reach his crisis. Finally, it rushed over him like a caress and he languished afterward on sheets damp with sweat, his and the woman's.

This time she had been with him and he was glad. Perhaps even grateful.

"A little sleep," he murmured. " 'Til dawn."

"Yes," she echoed. "Sleep."

Christophe was dreaming, or was he? A loud scream pierced the room, followed by an anguished gurgle that was surely the woman's last. His eyes flew open and he would have rushed to the window to investigate had Clarice not been snoring softly in his arms. She had not even stirred. He stroked her pale tresses where they fell across his bare chest, listening to another bone-chilling scream. A second woman was following the first to hell, and when Christophe heard a third cry, he could endure it no longer.

He eased himself from beneath Clarice's arm and went to the window. The wintry streets were thick with fog, but he discerned a few shadowy bodies in a loose circle, and he could not make out what or who was in the center. Instead, he looked up, toward the east where the pale reef of dawn challenged the stars.

"Dawn soon," he murmured, reaching for his clothes. "Duncan!"

For a man facing a duel, he thought, hurrying downstairs, Duncan doesn't seem too concerned about the time. As he knew he would, he found Pearl deep in conversation with a customer. She was still on the settee, a distinguished older gentleman hanging on her every word, one of her girls asleep with her head in Pearl's lap. She was always the last to retire in her establishment, and managed a weary smile.

"You are looking for your friend, eh, *mon cheri?*" Christophe nodded and ran a hair through his wild black hair. He was terribly thirsty. "Are you too late for the duel?"

"He told you about that?" Christophe was surprised.

"He didn't have to."

"Why didn't you wake us?"

Pearl laughed. "My dear, I have a cardinal rule about not disturbing a gentleman while he's taking pleasure with a lady." Christophe's eyebrows rose and he smiled. "He is with Virginia. Ah, yes. It made me smile too. He was a man who desperately needed a woman whether he knew it or not."

"I'll have to break your rule, Pearl. I must wake him while he still thinks there's time."

"What a strange thing to say," she remarked, pointing her tiparillo toward the stairs. "You remember the blue room, *cheri*. End of the hall."

"I don't know why we're going to my home first," Duncan protested. Christophe pushed Duncan into the carriage, glad the man was so groggy he didn't notice the night's crop of corpses littering the Rue Gallatin. Curiosity about the screams prompted him to take a closer look he immediately regretted. Three women lay in a pile, as though strewn there like cast-off flowers. Indeed, one in a filthy beige shift, a young girl no more than twelve, reminded Christophe of a bouquet of red roses wrapped in brown paper. Her throat had been slashed, blackening blood covering prepubescent breasts. Pale blue eyes still gaped in horror at her killer.

"Jesus Christ!"

He paid off a half-drunken but still alert Red Bill Wilson and woke L'Eveillé. "Hurry!" he barked at the sleepy coachman. "Get us out of this cursed place!"

"As it is we'll barely have time to make it to the lake," Duncan grumbled. "You said yourself it was imperative that we be there on time or—"

"Forget what I said," Christophe interrupted, deciding the charade had lasted long enough. He ordered L'Eveillé to drive them to the Saunders' house. "There isn't going to be any duel."

Duncan was still groggy and none too happy about being dragged from Virginia's warm arms, but he was coherent enough to question his friend's blunt pronouncement.

"What in hell are you talking about? And why are you taking me home?"

"Duplessy's a hot-headed fool, Duncan, but he's not crazy enough to fight you under those terms. He knows your advantage of size is something he can't possibly overcome." Duncan continued to stare. "He also knows society will excuse him, his honor remaining intact if he politely apologizes and withdraws. Under the circumstances, and especially considering the honorable precedent set by Marigny . . . well, the duel will simply not happen."

Duncan was confused and not a little annoyed. "Don't we have to go to the lake to accept his apology?"

"When we arrive at your brother's house, he will be waiting with a letter delivered by Lafon. It will renounce the duel."

"How can you be so sure?"

Christophe's insouciance was infuriating, as was his characteristic shrug. "As I've said so many times, *mon ami*, you must learn to trust me."

Duncan seethed. "But what if there *is* no letter? What if I am proclaimed a coward because I didn't appear at the appointed site at the appointed hour to fight a duel? That much I do know! Damn you, Chris! Stop playing with your moustache and answer me!"

"None of that will happen," Christophe replied lightly. His coolness was fuel for the fire.

"Did it ever occur to you that it's my reputation at stake? Not yours. Mine!"

"*Bien sûr.*" Christophe managed a wan smile. He was tired again. "That's why I was so careful when I named the terms of the duel."

Duncan was undeterred. "You're being evasive."

For the first time, Christophe looked at him. "We both know the Americans couldn't care less about duels. Indeed, they would respect you more if you refused Duplessy's challenge. The fact is, my dear boy, there's only one person to whom your reputation matters. I speak of a particular Creole and certainly not I."

"What are you talking about?"

"I mean isn't all this talk of honor really about Mademoiselle Duval?"

Duncan started to retort but demurred as the truth smote him hard. Christophe was reading him like a book. While he was with Virginia, Duncan had discussed the impending duel and surprised himself, not altogether pleasantly, when he began taking a certain perverse pride in the matter. When the whore guessed correctly that a woman was the cause, Duncan grew excited to the point of defensiveness. Despite condemning duels as barbaric, he found himself surging with the thrill of the moment. His masculinity was operating full throttle, blinding him to the reality that his life was threatened, so puissant in fact that he took the whore with a ferociousness he didn't know he possessed.

Yes, he admitted to himself. He had felt a deep rush of pride when Eugénie had chosen him from all the others. He had certainly not expected the honor and was equally surprised at the self-satisfaction he received when he and Eugénie promenaded around the dining room to such enthusiastic applause. And, yes, he reveled in the moment when the crown was put upon his head and he was toasted as king. Silly, perhaps, but his exultation was not just of the moment and in truth had nothing to do with Eugénie. What really spawned his exhilaration was Justine Blancard and he could not help wishing it was she at his side. That of course would have been impossible and would only have hastened this dilemma. In any case, he was now forced to participate in an act he eventually saw as honorable, one he could no longer refuse. Christophe recognized this and tweaked him gently.

"It's all right, Duncan. It almost always happens the first time."

"What?" Duncan had his suspicions and although he knew they would humiliate him he wanted them confirmed.

"The metamorphosis is as old as dueling itself, *mon ami.* One feels anger, arrogance, fear, defiance and, all too often unfortunately, rash carelessness. That is the path of the emotions when one is first called out."

"I feel like such a fool."

"Don't." Christophe took his arm as the carriage turned from the Rue Canal into the Avenue St. Charles. "I would have been shocked and even disappointed otherwise." He squeezed the arm. "Believe me, Mademoiselle Duval will be even more impressed by Duplessy's refusal than any victory you may have secured over the bastard. You must realize that you have scored a triumph over one of the most skilled swordsmen in Louisiana. Precious few can make that claim."

Duncan chuckled at the absurdity, even at the horror and unreality of the evening that had just transpired. Kings, queens, whores, corpses, duels, murders. It was like something out of some fairy tale. And the reason why he had experienced it was sitting right beside him.

"You infuriate me sometimes, Christophe. You know that, don't you?"

"Bien sûr, mon ami." Again, the insouciant smile. "But that is much of my charm, non?" Before Duncan could respond, Christophe waved a gloved hand and said, "But enough about such things. Tell me about Virginia. Was I right again? Did you not need a woman, eh?"

The rest of the ride was a trading of male confidences, a comparison of the relative charms of Clarice and Virginia and a confession from Duncan that he had never been to a bordello. But he confined his personal revelations to that and refused, despite all manner of outrageous pleas from Christophe, to reveal how he lost his virginity.

All such talk ceased immediately when the carriage pulled up before the Saunders' house on Prytania Street. Duncan had barely opened the carriage door when a red-faced Randolph burst from the house, waving an envelope wildly in the air.

"I think I'll wait here," Christophe said. "Your dear brother does not seem in the mood for receiving company, especially mine. Shall we have breakfast once you've read the letter? I know a little place that makes the most divine fried croakers. The secret is in their *sauce a la Tartare.*"

"Why not?" Duncan swung from the carriage and strode up the stairs two at a time to confront his angry brother. "Good morning, Randolph."

"Good morning my ass!" Randolph snapped. "Some Frenchman named Lafon brought this for you an hour ago. Woke the entire damned household." He thrust it into Duncan's hand and demanded an explanation. "Well?"

When Duncan finished reading it, he smiled over his shoulder at the waiting carriage. "It is a deeply personal matter, big brother. I'm sorry Monsieur Lafon woke you."

"How personal?" Randolph asked, not so easily brushed off. He eyed the carriage suspiciously. Christophe had lit a cigar and was casually blowing smoke rings through the open door.

"Nothing you should concern yourself over," Duncan said, trying with limited success to sound as confident as possible. Randolph would not be put off. "If you'd like to have breakfast with Christophe and myself, I will be glad to discuss the matter with you."

"I will have breakfast at home," he announced with a withering glare. "And your explanation along with it!"

When Randolph disappeared into the house behind a slammed door, Duncan knew there was no changing his mind. He walked to the carriage, palms up. "You'll have to enjoy those frogs without me, my friend."

"*Eh, bien.* But I must see you later. There is much to be discussed about your upcoming reign with the beautiful Mademoiselle Eugénie." He rolled his eyes. "The Duval castle is going to require a very skillful siege if you are to see your lady fair."

"In all the madness I had forgotten about her father. Does he really hate Americans as much as they say?"

"Let me put it this way, *mon ami.* If you had a choice of befriending Honoré Duval or a bull alligator . . ."

Duncan grimaced. "I'll call for you at noon."

CHAPTER 9

The vision had come to Blancard again, and it taunted him as Hippolyte drove him home before dawn.

He was facing critical business meetings that morning, but it was not their importance that had stolen his sleep. For long hours he had lain awake while Chaillot slept as easily and untroubled as a trusting child in his arms. She had lain naked across him, breasts crushed against his chest, raven hair tumbled wild and careless over her shoulders until he gently pushed it aside so he could gaze at the fine, unflawed flesh of her back.

Her back. It caught and held him, mesmerized him, a perfect invitation to destruction.

He saw the paleness shimmer and the familiar stria reappear, not ribs beneath the porcelain flesh but pink alabaster veins that deepened to a raw ugly red. Close to the surface of the skin, dark streaks metamorphosed into welts and then assumed the color of blood. Beautiful. Perfect! As Blancard touched her back with trembling fingers, he groaned with the stirring in his loins. The ensanguined image had hardened him so thoroughly it was painful. He was consumed with marking Chaillot, as he had marked Medioza and Cossa and the murderous Bricktop and countless whores whose names were long forgotten but for an occasional bloody dream.

And why not? he thought. Chaillot is mine to do with as I choose. Like Justine. Yes, they are both mine, not my slaves perhaps . . . well, not legally. But in any case, who do I have to answer to?

No one but himself, of course, and his conscience was and always had been unblemished. Blancard's power was absolute and utterly thrilling. How lucky he was to be so chosen. How few understood the gratification that came from exploring the darker carnal corners, those obscure regions so few were courageous enough to investigate. He thought, as he often did, of Delphine Lalaurie and how she had pushed limits he had not yet approached. What monstrous power she must have wielded, what brilliance she approached! Yet, what a fool she had been to get caught, to have the world learn her secret. *Their* secret!

What a tragedy that she had been before his time. How he would have adored meeting her! With him she would never have been stopped. And what unimaginable black magic they might have conjured together, what heinous heights they might have scaled. The control, the terrible satisfaction, the unthinkable release it afforded when it was all done. *All* done!

Such images aroused Blancard again. The jouncing motion of the carriage grew increasingly erotic, and he yielded to the urge to drop a gloved hand between his thighs where he massaged the swollen flesh. There was surprising satisfaction in this impromptu flirtation with *frottage*, and the man breathlessly surrendered to it as he watched unfold the dawn tableau that was *La Nouvelle-Orléans*.

When the carriage turned from the Rue Rampart into the Rue d'le Hôpital, he saw a statuesque mulatress balancing a jug of water on her head. She walked the banquettes with a fierce feline grace. Not walked, strutted. Ample hips undulated beneath calico skirts with an ancient invitation bringing a smile to Blancard's lips. His hand pressed a little harder between his thighs as the woman turned toward the carriage. He was so smitten by the dignity in her eyes that he nodded and touched his hat as though she were a white woman! He shocked himself, deeply embarrassed, but it was an easy mistake for a man stricken by raw beauty. Indeed she was a pecan-brown Hebe that would have humbled the men at the *Salle d'Orléans*. She was undoubtedly a slave, yet she wore the invisible shackles of bondage with an exquisite grace that Blancard found deeply disturbing. He chided himself for the inappropriate *politesse* and moved his hand away. The woman was a slave after all, nothing more.

Slaves were all he saw that morning as he watched the city awaken to business as usual. Commerce in this great metropolis could not have moved without them. The success of every contract he negotiated between the Louisiana planters and spinners in Liverpool and Hamburg depended on black flesh that produced, processed and delivered the cotton. Indeed, the sweat of Negroes oiled the machine turning the wheels of the South. Without it, the region would have ground helplessly to a halt and the evidence was everywhere. The woman bearing water for her mistress was only one of thousands. Her brothers in bondage had also risen before dawn, stoking the farrier's fires, mucking stable stalls, delivering firewood. They labored in ironworks, brickyards, cooperages, ropewalks, cotton mills, sugar refineries and distilleries producing the cheap rum called *aguardiente*. They were honeydippers hauling away the waste of privies. They toiled to keep the levees in repair, dug drainage ditches and drove pilings halfway to China for wharves where they would load and unload cargo bound for ships also of their building. Of every color and nameless tribes, they carried out endless tasks, all masterminded by whites. Black hands sewed, cooked and dusted, bathed and pampered white bodies, poured the master's wines and tucked his children into bed at night.

Such white superiority arose from the putrid bloom of human slavery, the egregious enthrallment of one race for the gratification of another, and in New Orleans, that malignant blossom had reached full flower. The largest slave market in the world flourished in the domed lobby of the St. Louis Hotel in the very heart of the *carré de la ville*. Had the abolitionists known, they would have been unspeakably horrified to learned that on Mardi Gras, slaves were put on the auction block in carnival costume.

Blancard saw none of this. As the carriage passed a team of slaves rolling wine casks down the Rue Dauphine, he saw only that: Slaves working as they were meant to. It was the way things were and the way things would remain, despite all that nonsensical abolitionist babbling from the North.

Such thoughts put Blancard in a foul humor. Of course that could always work to his advantage. He always did better business if there was an uneasy edge to his mood. He felt sharper, keener, so he welcomed the anger, decided to mold it to his needs. When he saw the pinched expression on Marie Tonton's face, he knew instinctively that he would find something at home that might well hone it to a fine rage.

"Been waiting for you to get home, Michie Hilaire."

"What is it, Marie Tonton? You look as if you've danced with the devil himself."

"I ain't been the one doing the dancing," she said, opening the door for her master and stepping aside as he clomped inside. She jerked her head toward the upstairs and gave him one of her sourest looks. She looked, he thought, not so much like the cat who had swallowed a canary as one who had pulled its feathers out one by one before the greedy feast. "But someone else has."

"I've no time for games this morning, Marie Tonton. If you know something about your mistress, tell me and be quick about it. And what on earth are you hiding?"

The woman whipped a hand from behind her back and brandished Justine's pot of rouge. "It's hers, Michie Hilaire!" she announced triumphantly. "She wore it last night at the Twelfth Night Ball!"

Blancard's lips curled into a slight smile. "As usual you've done a good job, girl. I'm not forgetting my promise about freedom, but for now this will have to suffice." Marie Tonton shared his smile when he pulled a few coins from his pockets. "Is the madame still sleeping? *Bon.*" He checked his watch. "Have Figaro draw my bath and tell Agathe I want breakfast in half an hour."

"*Oui, monsieur.*"

Marie Tonton dropped a quick curtsy and watched him climb the stairs. She knew her bit of information would precipitate some terrible confrontation and relished it. This would not have been so when Blancard first brought her here. She had been purchased by his father twenty-two years ago when she was fifteen and, although well treated, nurtured a deep hatred for all whites. Blancard firmly believed the Coromantee woman would have radiated hatred and arrogance had she remained in Africa, that her enslavement only exacerbated a natural tendency toward both traits. Still, she did as she was told, for him anyway, and if one ignored her surliness and sharp tongue she was tolerable enough. At least for Blancard who eventually saw an altogether different face from what Marie Tonton showed Justine.

Despite Justine's initial kindness and efforts at friendship, Marie Tonton had remained cool and indifferent. When she saw the relationship between the master and her young mistress changing, she seized an opportunity for finding favor with Blancard. Having no one to turn to after the debacle of the European wedding trip, Justine was desperate enough to hint at the horrors to Marie Tonton. The slave hastened to report these circuitous cries for help to Blancard who promptly punished Justine and warned her against further indiscretions. He also slipped Marie Tonton a few coins for her efforts. These rewards, he assured her, would continue if she brought him news of even the slightest bit of misbehavior from Justine. And, beyond that, the most glorious present of all—freedom.

Thus began the slave's vigilant campaign to discredit and malign Justine. Her natural hatred for any mistress, even one as caring and compassionate as this, was bad enough, but motivated by money and the dream of emancipation she pursued her loathing with relish. She saw a way to use as she was being used, to enslave as she was enslaved. As loyalties to Blancard deepened, she soon held Justine a prisoner in her own home. Nothing Justine did escaped Marie Tonton's hawkeyes, and no complaints to Blancard could prompt him to get rid of the woman. It was only one more tool to hold his wife in thrall. Marie Tonton understood this only too well. So did Justine.

This time Justine hadn't heard the familiar creak on the stairs or the footsteps in the hall outside. She was deep in a dream about the glories of Byzantium and was telling someone, Christophe perhaps, or Duncan Saunders, about the beauty secrets of the Empress Zöe. Then he was saying something about rouge and holding a rouge pot for her to see.

"Justine!"

The man's voice deepened, grew louder and she realized it was not who she thought. It was Blancard holding the rouge pot, thrusting it so close she started from the fragrant, waxy smell. This was no dream! As her husband's face sharpened in her eyes, she pushed herself up in bed, retreating against the pillows and pulling the sheets protectively across her breasts.

"Well?" he asked. "I'm waiting."

Blancard's voice was low, measured. His face expressionless, except to his wife. She had seen this blank, enigmatic look all too often, and she knew it boded only one thing. She drew the sheets higher.

"It was only an ex . . . experiment, Hilaire," she stammered. "I have not been . . . been my . . . myself lately, and I didn't want to go to the Fleury's ball looking like a ghost."

"Creole ladies are supposed to look like ghosts!" he snapped.

"But this was an unnatural pallor," she insisted, grasping at straws. "I didn't want people thinking I was ill."

"So you'd rather have them think you wore rouge, eh? Like some common little whore in the Rue Gallatin?" He leaned closer and the smell of the rouge was dispelled by a woman's fragrance, heavy, exotic. No doubt, Justine thought without caring, it was the scent of his mistress. "Answer me!"

"I didn't think you would mind, Hilaire. I truly didn't. I . . . I had been reading about the Byzantine women and how they fixed their faces and . . . well, it was such a tiny bit on my cheeks no one could have noticed." Her mind raced desperately. "Why, you didn't notice when you came in to say good-night." It was an ambitious lie. She hadn't dared use the rouge until he was gone, but he had been just mellow enough from the whiskey to forget. Justine took a quick breath and continued the lie. "You even told me I looked perfect, Hilaire. Remember? 'Madame Hilaire Blancard must always look perfect.' That's what you said, remember?" His expressionless face was unchanged, a clear sign that he was unhearing. Then he retreated, but only a step, hand dropping to the bedclothes. "Oh, Hilaire, don't! Please don't!"

He seized the counterpane and tore it back. The sheets followed, one torn fiercely from Justine's grip as she sought to keep herself covered. She got to her knees, clutching the towering bedpost with both hands, whimpering with raw fear. Was this it? she wondered. Would this be the time when he did more than ravish her? Was this going to be the moment when he finally marked her outside as well as in? She opened her mouth to scream, but a glare silenced her immediately. Besides, even if someone heard, there was no one to rescue her. No one at all.

When he spoke, Blancard's voice was light, casual, the tone she feared the most, and she whimpered. "You're not the only one who knows something about Constantinople, madam." Still holding the rouge pot, he paced the room, occasionally glancing toward the bed where his victim cowered helplessly. "When we were there, I took a little night tour for gentlemen only. I learned some most interesting things about the women of the sultan's harem." He took a step forward. She retreated until she was crushed against the massive mahogany headboard, watching with mounting terror as he dipped a finger into the rouge pot and approached the bed.

"Hilaire, please . . ."

"The women were prisoners in the harem and went for months without ever seeing the sultan. Prisoners get bored, you know, and they look for ways to pass the time. Do you know what they did to each other, Justine?"

"No!"

His hand shot to her throat where she clutched her nightgown in a pathetic attempt to defend herself. The delicate lace sliced painfully into her neck as it was ripped away and she was hurled naked onto the mattress. Blancard clapped a hand over her mouth as he fumbled in his pocket with the other. He quickly gagged her with a handkerchief before producing the fearsome silk cords. Justine's eyes widened with terror when she saw the restraints, and she wished she could will herself to faint. Instead she felt every bit of pain as her wrists and ankles were secured to the bed posters.

"Perhaps," he said with a malevolent grin, "I'll simply show you what those bored harem women did."

Justine looked away as he dipped a finger in the rouge pot, but it was not intended for her cheeks or lips. He laughed coarsely as, instead, he rouged her nipples, changing their color from pale pink to brilliant red. Justine's nipples responded against her will and to her disgust and shame they were soon firm. Blancard was thrilled.

"So you like this, eh? Then you're going to love what I do next."

Oh, God . . . ! she thought. Oh, dear God!

Blancard gave each of her nipples a painful squeeze before directing his perverse attentions elsewhere. With one finger, he drew a crimson line across her pale belly, circled her navel and moved lower still while she moaned in helpless protest. She trembled uncontrollably as his fingers brushed her pubic down, staining it with the sticky rouge.

"That's right, madam. They shaved their private parts and painted them all sorts of colors, each hoping to attract the attention of their lord and master during one of his rare visits." His fingers splayed across the fleshy mound, gripping hard. The pain was growing. "Well, you needn't worry about such things, Justine. You have my full attention."

The hand moved lower and Justine's silent scream exploded in her head. Oh, sweet Mother of God, no! Please help me. Please!

Her entire body convulsed when Blancard's fingers thrust suddenly between her thighs. The pain was excruciating as he probed, deeper and deeper, shaming her beyond her greatest fears. His hands seemed everywhere at once, stroking, urging, driving her until her pale flesh was streaked with sweat-melted rouge. Justine abandoned all hope and instead prayed that she would faint. Instead she remained fully awake for her final humiliation.

As always, Blancard was greatly roused by the look of utter horror in those innocent eyes. He drew from it ever greater perverse inspiration, his excitement all too evident through his trousers. Justine closed those eyes as he brought his rouged fingertips to her lips and rubbed until they were thickly coated with slippery redness. As he studied her grotesque visage, Blancard was reminded of a whore he had once in the Swamp. She had not liked this treatment either, but what choice did she have? He laughed at the memory.

The faint sound of rustled clothing warned Justine he was unbuttoning his trousers, as portentous a sound as the cathedral bells announcing the Angelus. A hand gripped her throat and held her so tight she could barely breathe. Even with her faint, desperate breaths, she inhaled the unmistakably male odor as he knelt at her head, terrifyingly close.

Oh, God, no! Not this! Please, God! No!

"Whether you watch or not is immaterial to me, madam, but I want the redness of your lips here." He yanked her face hard against his flesh. "Here! Now!"

Justine was dreaming again, or so she thought. There were alarming sounds on the shuttered gallery, peculiar muffled screams or what might have been something dragged from one end to the other and back again. Although the odd noises eventually stopped, the ensuing silence was more frightening.

Stirred by a hot, cloying wetness, Justine opened her eyes. Her face was burning up. Sweat soaked the mattress and there was a pervasive odor of bitterness so potent that she almost vomited. She hovered for a while in that gray zone between waking and sleeping, finally convincing herself she was awake when her elbow brushed against something hard. The empty rouge pot.

"Sweet Jesus!" she moaned. Then, "No!"

Mustering what strength she could, Justine hurled the rouge pot at the door. It cracked and clattered across the room, interrupting the heated conversation at the foot of the steps.

"I've already told you Madame Blancard is expecting me," insisted Toinette Clovis, brandishing her packages. "They're so important that I'm delivering them personally."

"And I've told you she's not receiving." Marie Tonton stood fast, positioning her body between Madame Clovis and the hallway. At the end of that hall were steps leading upstairs, and Blancard had left strict instructions that no one was to enter Justine's room until he returned. Not even Marie Tonton.

"I'm going to say this once more, girl," Madame Clovis said, voice rising sharply. "And you'd better listen well." She was always the picture of control and decorum, but this impudent slave was fast trying her patience. It was not the first time she had locked horns with Marie Tonton. Along with half the city, she knew the Blancard household was run by this emissary from hell. Why Justine tolerated her was a mystery. Another mystery hung in the air like a foul, invisible fog. Something was terribly wrong in this house, and Toinette sensed it in her bones. Marie Tonton's stubborn refusal to let her pass only convinced her she was right and she made a final polite request.

"Madame Blancard asked me to come over here this morning, and you're not going to stop me."

Marie Tonton was furious at having her authority challenged in this house, but she was also fearful of what lay upstairs in the *maitresse*'s bedroom. Stationing herself outside the door as usual, she had heard the familiar scuffling and the muffled screams and could only speculate how Michie Hilaire had extracted his vengeance this time. If *she* had been forbidden to investigate, then the sight was surely not one fit for a stranger's eyes. Especially not this woman.

"You free niggers are all alike!" she snarled. "You think you can walk in anywhere and act like you own the place!"

Madame Clovis seethed at the ultimate insult, and from a Negro

slave no less. She had never struck anyone in her life, slave or otherwise, but she was sorely tempted to do so when she heard the crashing
rouge pot upstairs. That was all she needed to gather her formidable
strength and order the woman out of her path.

"I'm warning you one last time, Marie Tonton," Toinette snapped,
waving her parasol menacingly in the slave's face. "If you don't get your
skinny black hide out of my way, this 'free nigger' is going to hit you
so hard it will probably kill you!"

It was not the umbrella or the threat that made Marie Tonton retreat.
She had seen this kind of determination before, in the face of Michie Hilaire, and had no doubt Madame Clovis was serious. She stepped aside,
vowing to tell her master that her life had been threatened when he
questioned her, as he surely would. She stood by helplessly as Madame
Clovis rushed down the hall and up the stairs, then followed her as far
as the door to Justine's bedroom. When she saw what lay inside, Marie
Tonton shrank in horror. In all her years of cleaning up Blancard's evil
messes, she had never seen anything like this. She muttered something
in Coromantee dialect and turned away.

"Dear God in heaven!" Toinette gasped, parasol and packages slipping from her hands with a thud. Justine lay naked atop the mattress,
a pile of torn sheets piled around her like a cotton fortress. There seemed
to be blood everywhere. Everywhere! "What has he done to you,
child?!"

Justine merely stared, unsure whether she was hallucinating or not.
Toinette Clovis had never been in her bedroom before, and she wasn't
certain she was there now. And if she was, why was she staring with
such an awful look on her pretty brown face?

"Toinette . . . ?" she managed finally.

Toinette moved closer, trying to determine how badly hurt Justine
was. The white woman's body was smeared with blood, caked in spots,
and her hair was wild and wet. Yet, despite the apparent carnage, Justine seemed somehow intact. She retreated behind her pile of stained
sheets as Toinette approached, still unsure of who the visitor was. Perhaps it was death come back again.

"*Cher* Justine," Toinette murmured in her most soothing tone. "Please
let me help you."

Justine frowned. She had never heard a kind voice in this room, her
own room, and it stirred something deep in her soul. As Toinette over-
came her initial shock at seeing this human wreckage, her sweet face
radiated nothing but loving compassion, especially her dark, doe eyes.
Justine burst into tears upon genuine recognition, but when Toinette

rushed to take her in her arms, Justine whimpered and retreated. She stared at Toinette for a long time before gathering the strength to speak.

"Oh, Toinette!" she sobbed. "What will I do?"

"I'll send for a doctor," Toinette said firmly.

"No!" The ferocity in Justine's voice was frightening. "He'll . . ." She stopped herself just short of saying Blancard would kill her. Instead, "I'm . . . I'm all right. Really."

"But the bleeding!" Toinette insisted. Justine looked so pitiful her heart ached. The women were not close friends, but it wasn't difficult to feel compassion for a wounded animal.

"Bleeding?" Justine's eyebrows furrowed, then a look of vagueness settled on her face. "Bleeding?" Toinette gestured toward the red smears on her face, breasts and loins. Justine grimaced. "It's only rouge, Toinette."

Toinette's jaw sagged. "Rouge?! What in God's name . . . ?"

"Hilaire," she muttered weakly, as if his name explained it all. She wrapped a sheet around her nakedness and swung her legs over the side of the bed. She padded barefoot to the wash basin. Catching a glimpse of herself in the armoire mirror, she stopped short. She studied the puffy-eyed, wild-haired creature looking back and, upon seeing the bizarre rouge smears and clotted red cakes, she understood why Toinette was so horrified. Good heavens! she thought. I look like some poor street masker at carnival. My hair looks worse than the cheapest wig!

Justine leaned closer and studied her image, touching a finger to the glass as if to determine which was real. She smiled. To Toinette's horror, the smile widened and then erupted with a maniacal cackle. It grew and grew until the room reverberated from it, indeed the entire upstairs. As Justine began pounding on the mirror with both fists, her desperation metamorphosed into an inhuman wail that echoed off the walls and sent an icy fear to Toinette's soul. The high piercing cry carried a primal plea for help that could only come from someone utterly debased, one stripped of all hope and dignity and reduced to scant more than an animal. Toinette was altogether horrified and not a little frightened. Outside the door at her usual spying station, Marie Tonton heard the unearthly keening and cowered.

Toinette watched the heart-rending tableau until she could bear it no longer. Although it was against the law for a person of color, free or not, to lay hands on a white, she rushed to the hysterical woman, grabbed her by the shoulders and shook Justine until her head wobbled ferociously, like that of a rag doll. The scream slowly faded, choking in a gurgle somewhere deep in Justine's throat. She sagged against Toinette who barely managed to get her back to bed before Justine's legs gave out completely.

"Lie still, dear. I'll be back."

Finding Marie Tonton in the hall, Toinette ordered her to fill a bathtub with hot water. For reasons known only to the angry slave, she did not hesitate. Something about the beleaguered creature in the bedroom had frightened her and she actually hurried to do Madame Clovis' bidding. Toinette returned to the bed and cradled Justine in her arms. Justine seemed very comfortable resting her head against Toinette's breast, and after a long silence passed between them, she gathered the strength to speak.

"It was all because I wore a little rouge at the ball last night."

"A little rouge prompted him to do something like this?" Toinette was scandalized.

Justine shrugged. "He's done worse for less. Once it was because he didn't like my earrings. Another time it was my coiffure. My perfume another."

"But why?" Justine's answer simultaneously broke Toinette's heart and infuriated her.

"Obviously I displease him."

Toinette took a deep breath, trying to control her growing anger. The instinctual dislike she harbored for the man had bloomed into full-fledged hatred last autumn when he had evicted her old friend Lucinde Rousteau from her little house back of town. The elderly Lucinde was displaced, Toinette learned, in order for Blancard to install his new mistress, an octoroon following in her famous mother's footsteps. Everyone in the tight-knit community of *gens de coleur libre* knew of Colette Baptiste, and because Toinette so strongly disapproved of the quadroons' notorious balls she was further outraged by these circumstances. It was hardly news for a white man to flex his legal muscles and quash the rights of a free person of color, but this latest hurt her personally and she had urged her husband to find poor Lucinde quarters elsewhere. Yes, Toinette knew Hilaire Blancard was a heartless man, but she had never suspected him capable of this. She could only wonder at this bundle of cringing flesh clinging to her like an abandoned child.

Toinette could simply not believe this pathetic creature was the celebrated white beauty Justine Blancard!

"How long has this been going on?" she asked, probing gently, fearing she would choose the wrong words and send Justine retreating defensively into silence. Again the woman's words hurt her heart.

"Since . . . since the beginning."

Toinette was incredulous. "He's been beating you from the beginning?!"

Justine shook her head against Toinette's breast, inhaling the comforting aroma of lavender. "He doesn't beat me."

"But what I've seen . . ."

"He never . . . marks me, Toinette. He marks me in ways that others can't see. Inside."

Toinette's breath was dispatched in one long gasp. "Sweet Mother of God!"

"Oh, Toinette!" Justine whimpered, clinging tighter. "I'm so ashamed!"

"You've nothing to be ashamed about, Justine. It is this animal of a husband who should be ashamed. It is he who should have to submit to such unspeakable acts." She shook her head. "Certainly I've heard of cruel husbands before, but nothing, *nothing* ever like this."

Justine sat up and tried without success to smooth her unruly hair. She sniffled and wiped her nose on the back of her hand. Toinette quickly retrieved a lacy handkerchief and pressed it into the woman's hand.

"A few days ago . . . I was alone as usual and felt compelled to go outside onto the gallery. I stood there watching fog roll over the city and something came to me that had happened when I was a child." She told the story of her humiliation at Lake Ponchartrain and the terrible realization that her mother was being beaten. "With a father like that, I had thought all along that this was . . . how things were, *how they were supposed to be!* All I knew of being a wife was something Tante Nanine whispered to me when I was being dressed for the wedding. 'Submit,' she said. 'It is the woman's duty to submit.' It was the same message I had been given by the nuns in school, so when Hilaire smashed up the room that first night and tore my negligee . . ."

She stopped when Toinette touched her lips with a finger. "Hush, child. I've heard enough. I don't think my heart could take more just now."

"But there's one more thing I must tell you, Toinette. I must." She spoke with such conviction that Toinette almost pulled away. The fire in Justine's eyes was a terrible sight, as was the conviction in her voice. "It became more and more difficult for me to believe that God—*my* God!—intended me to live this way. When I confessed my doubts to the priest and told him what Hilaire had been doing all these years, what my father had done to my mother, he said . . . he said . . ."

"What?" Toinette urged.

"He said it was my duty to remain with my husband!"

Toinette's seething condemnation was swift and without hesitation. She too was a devout Catholic, but if she was to be damned for what she believed to be righteous rage, then so be it.

"Priests are not always right, Justine. They're not the ones who have to deal with such villains."

"But we are always taught . . ."

"It doesn't matter what we're taught. Things we're told as children don't always turn out that way in the adult world."

"Is he a villain, Toinette?" Justine asked in a small voice.

The incredibly naive question stunned Toinette into silence. It was just as well because Justine's concentration was abruptly aborted as Duncan Saunders appeared, shimmering in her mind with near palpable vividness. She felt the soothing gaze of his hazel eyes and inhaled the trace of whiskey on his breath, both washing over her like warm spindrift flung from the Gulf. Justine had never sensed such force and wished she could cleave against him and be forever absorbed beneath his potent aegis.

"Ah . . ."

The oddest aspect was that Duncan was not some dreamy image conjured behind closed eyes. She saw him with her eyes wide open, standing right behind Toinette, lips gentle with a smile. She blinked and realized her mistake too late. Duncan's visage had been usurped by that of Hilaire, mouth cruel, eyes bloodshot and raw with evil. She gasped and swallowed hard, somehow summoning the strength to continue with Toinette.

"You must understand things have been this way for so long, sometimes I don't know what's real and what's not, what's right and what's wrong. You see, I thought what happened between Hilaire and myself was . . . well, perhaps not what everyone did, but how was I to know any different?"

"Oh, Justine! Poor, poor Justine! How could anyone venture into the world as unprepared as yourself and fall into the clutches of such a madman? If that is not one of God's injustices, I don't know what is." Toinette frowned at a most unpleasant but natural suspicion. "Of course he's threatened you, told you not to tell anyone, didn't he?"

Justine nodded, trembling as the old fears resurfaced, the terror of discovery, the threat of retribution, the unthinkable that had spawned her horrifying dream of death. Toinette recognized those fears and swiftly addressed them.

"You're not alone now, *mon cher.*"

"But what can I do?"

"I don't know yet," Toinette admitted. Both turned toward a knock at the door and heard Marie Tonton's announcement that Madame Blancard's bath was ready. Toinette retrieved a robe from the armoire and eased Justine into it. Justine grimaced when pain shot through her shoulders, a reminder of her struggles with the hated restraints. "We'll talk about it more while you clean up. Come along. You'll feel much better once you've bathed."

"I don't know, Toinette," Justine lamented. She stood shakily and leaned against the woman as they crossed the room. "I just don't know."

Later, as she lingered in the tub, the room a dense cloud of steam, Justine's thoughts cleared enough for her to confront her greatest fear: Blancard's reaction when he learned she had told someone of his evil deeds. It was inevitable, of course. He would know as soon as Marie Tonton got to him. She voiced this fearsome reality to Toinette, who had dismissed the slave and was tending to Justine's bath herself.

"I cannot make a move without it being reported to my husband," she explained. "Right now that evil woman is probably listening at the door."

"She is Coromantee, *n'est-ce pas?*" asked Toinette, lowering her voice. "Eh? I thought so. That explains her arrogance and ill temper." Her quick mind probed for a solution. "They're almost all *voudous,* you know. Does she go to the ceremonies?"

"I don't know, Toinette," Justine answered tiredly. "Can't remember." The hot water and steam were steadily draining her.

"It's important," Toinette hissed. "Think!"

Justine closed her eyes and inhaled the rich wet plumes of steam. Toinette was right. She felt better already, her mind clearer. "Yes. I remember Hilaire chiding her on several occasions, warning her away from those strange meetings. She denied attending them, but it was clear even to me that she was lying. I doubt if she's given them up."

"One rarely does," Toinette said solemnly.

"Hilaire doesn't approve of *voudou.*" She thought for a moment, as though seized by a revelation. "I actually think he fears it. Strange. I never thought anything could frighten him."

Toinette's thoughts raced elsewhere. "So Marie Tonton is *voudou,* eh? Then I know just what to do. Where is that girl?"

Justine nodded toward the door. "Just outside there, unless I miss my guess."

Sure enough, when Toinette flung the door wide she found Marie Tonton not lurking so she could run away before being caught, but sitting where she might hear everything. She stared defiantly at Toinette, amber eyes brimming with hatred. Such boldness riled Toinette because it revealed how much Justine was a prisoner in her own home.

"I want a word with you," Toinette said. "Alone."

She closed the door behind them, and Justine soon heard raised voices. She did not try to understand them, did not even care what was discussed. What did it matter? There was no force on earth that could keep Marie Tonton from exposing Justine's betrayal to Blancard. Finally she rose from the tub and toweled herself dry, grateful for the heat of the nearby brazier. She knelt before it and toweled her wet hair before drawing on her robe and returning to her room. All she wanted now was to get back into bed and await Blancard. The sooner he meted out the inevitable punishment the better.

Justine was surprised to find her bed freshly made and a peignoir laid neatly on the counterpane alongside her favorite dimity dressing gown. She donned them both and stretched out on the bed, suddenly exhausted again. She was just drifting toward sleep when Toinette returned. The woman had a look of grim determination on her pale brown face and those warm gray eyes, so common among quadroons, flashed fire.

"Your secret is safe, *mon ami*," she said, firm-set lips melting into a smile as she sat on the edge of the bed. "I thought of the one thing that could buy Marie Tonton's silence."

"But what on earth could that be?"

Toinette took her hand and squeezed gently. She was pleased that much of Justine's color had returned. "Not what. Who."

"Who then?"

"Marie Laveau."

"*Mais non!*"

"She is just what I need, Justine. The greatest, most feared *voudouienne* in the city. Her powers are legendary among the *voudous*. She is their undisputed queen."

Of course Justine had heard of Marie Laveau. Who in all New Orleans had not?

"And you know this woman?"

Toinette smiled. "Your Marie Tonton was most distressed to learn that Marie Laveau is my cousin. Distant to be sure, but I know her well enough." She snapped her fingers. "She would help me like this!"

Justine winced. The very notion of the forbidden African religion terrified her almost as much as Blancard. She knew it existed of course, feared it like most Creoles, and she certainly didn't want it touching her life, no matter how tangentially.

"Oh, Toinette! Let's hope we don't have to resort to *voudou*."

Her hand was squeezed again. "It's too late, *mon cher*. The wheels have already begun to turn. Even now word will be spreading through the Negro grapevine that someone is looking to put a curse on Hilaire Blancard. Within the hour, Marie Laveau herself will know about it."

Justine was stunned. The idea that this petite woman in prim gray, black hair in a tight chignon, eyes behind gold-rimmed glasses, could have any connections with the notorious *voudous* was beyond her ken. "You . . . ?!"

Toinette laughed gently. Although the white woman's naivete could obviously prove dangerous, here it was amusing. "Let's just say that I am not a regular at the ceremonies, my dear, but that should not suggest I do not have my connections. Connections that, as you will see, come in quite handy. You are hardly the only one who bears a grudge against Hilaire Blancard."

Frightened, Justine demurred. "I don't know if I bear a grudge against him or not, Toinette. He is my husband after all."

Toinette was repulsed by such denial, but unsurprised by it. "That does not give him the right to abuse you!" she snapped. "Few slaves are mistreated this badly. And don't remind me what the priest said or what the nuns taught you. I'm wearied of all of them today. Nor will I listen to anything approaching an apology from you, Justine. It's time someone told you that you're married to an evil bastard who deserves to be taken to the calaboose and beaten like a runaway slave!"

"Toinette!"

Justine didn't know what shocked her more—Toinette's rage, her slurring of the church, or her damnation of a white man. Under the *Code Noir*, such verbal attacks were considered crimes. But they were all things Justine needed to hear things she had studiously avoided for years.

"There!" Toinette announced triumphantly. "I've spoken my mind and I don't regret a single word!"

Justine hung her head, suddenly tired again. "Toinette, I don't know where you get your strength. How I envy you!"

"Nonsense," Toinette soothed. "I'm the one who should envy you. To think that this madness has been going on for all these years, yet you could appear at the opera or in my shop and dazzle everyone with your smile and your sweetness. Why, the beauty and poise of Madame Blancard is legendary. I could never have achieved such a grand charade."

Justine frowned. Such a thing had never occurred to her. "What . . . what would you have done in my place?"

"Seen Marie Laveau first and then . . . well, whatever it took to stop him. The most drastic steps necessary, if things were that desperate."

"Toinette! I could never imagine you doing such a thing."

"But we both know appearances are deceiving, eh, Justine?" A disturbing, near malevolent sparkle waltzed in the gray eyes.

"It would seem so." She pondered Toinette's unthinkable allusion. "Do you mean . . . murder?"

"I might."

"But could you really bring yourself to do such a thing?"

Toinette smiled, encouraged by Justine's slip. "I made no mention of murder, *cher*. That was your word. No human truly knows his capabilities until he is cornered. I know only this, Justine. The life you have is no life at all. What's the point of living if every day is in fear, every night is filled with humiliation and debasement? You are as much a slave as Marie Tonton!"

"It wasn't all bad . . ." Justine began.

"*Stop it!*" Toinette interrupted fiercely. "I will not hear this, Justine! I will not listen to you utter another word in that terrible man's defense. Don't you understand there is no defending the indefensible?" Justine moaned weakly. "For God's sake, woman! Why gainsay the the truth? You're with me now. A friend. Someone who cares for you, who will be with you always to help any way that I can."

Toinette's pledge of loyalty moved Justine to tears. Certainly Christophe had been a splendid ally, but in her adult life she had never had a real woman friend, never one with whom to share confidences, to compare experiences, nothing. And to think her first such confidante was a free woman of color.

"But why would you do all this for me?"

"Let's just say that your road is not altogether unfamiliar to me. I can tell you no more. Not now."

Justine was suddenly overwhelmed and slipped off the bed onto her knees. Eyes brimming with tears, she smiled at Toinette before burying her head in the woman's taffeta lap. Toinette stroked the long black hair, still damp from the bath, and thought she had never seen anyone so desperately, hopelessly sad in her life.

"Mark my word, Justine. We'll find a way out of this." Justine murmured something that Toinette didn't understand. "This very day I will call at that little cottage in the Rue Ste. Anne. I will personally speak to Marie Laveau herself!"

Justine continued her silent prayer, only half hearing as she thanked God for this colored angel of mercy. For the first time since her wedding night, she believed her prayers might be heard. She picked up the thread of Toinette's conversation only when she felt her hand gently taken.

"And now, *mon ami,* I must have something from you. Something that can begin your journey from this hell." Justine frowned. "And *under no circumstances must it be missed!* If we're discovered by that wretched Marie Tonton, everything will unravel. Promise me!" When Justine hesitated, Toinette squeezed hard. "Justine, listen to me! If you never promise another thing in your life, promise me this. You must!"

Weakly, "Yes. I promise."

"*Bon!* Now this is what I need from you . . ."

PART THREE

Shrovetide

Si on me presse de dire pourquoi je l'aimais,
je sens que cela ne se peut s'exprimer,
qu'en répondant:
"Parce que c'était lui; parce que cétait moi."

If I am pressed to say why I loved him,
I feel it can be explained only by replying:
"Because it was he; because it was me."
—Montaigne

CHAPTER 10

Duncan waved a final time and watched the Arnaud carriage disappear down Prytania Street. As he reluctantly trailed Randolph inside in the house, he wished he had left with Christophe. He rarely quarreled with his brother, but the distress on Randolph's face assured him there were going to be cross words.

There was nothing Duncan wanted less. He had traversed so many emotional peaks and valleys over the last twenty-four hours that there had been no chance to digest them all. He wanted nothing more than to sleep for a few hours and then seek a way to put his bizarre experiences into words. At long last, there was a poem seeking escape from his brain, and he sought to divert his angry brother by mentioning as much.

"I'm going to start writing again!" he called, trying his best to sound cheery as he steered the subject away from Lafon's letter. His hopes for reprieve evaporated with his brother's terse reply.

"It's high time you did something productive since coming here, and I have plans for just such activities. We can discuss them while we eat." He glared. "Among other things."

Duncan's appetite was fading fast, and he watched with disinterest while Junon served breakfast. Fried oysters on toast came first and Randolph plunged into them with relish. Duncan's nostrils flared with repulsion and he again sought escape. "Randolph, could we please postpone this until you return from work tonight?"

"There are no pleasant times for confronting unpleasant matters," Randolph replied coldly.

"But I'm thoroughly exhausted and desperate for sleep. There was all that excitement at the ball and the business with Duplessy and then Gallatin . . ."

Duncan caught himself but not fast enough. Fatigue had caused him to drop his guard, and at the mention of that notorious thoroughfare, his brother exploded.

"Is *that* where that wild Creole took you last night? Good God, Duncan! Have you lost your senses? Is that how you got involved in a duel? What happened to the Twelfth Night Ball? Was that just a ruse so the two of you could go whoring?"

The throb in Duncan's head grew as he reeled from so many questions, especially the ugliness of the last. But he knew there was no escaping Randolph's interrogation and proceeded to explain the night's activities as quickly and simply as possible. He hoped to end on a civilized note by announcing that he and Eugénie Duval would be hosting a ball the next week, but Randolph was unmoved. He angrily forked a broiled oyster and popped it into his mouth, staring at his brother as he vigorously chewed. Duncan thought he would never swallow the thing.

"I'm going to say some things that you're not going to like, little brother. Because it's my duty. I know you're twenty-seven years old and don't need a mentor but I'm most concerned that you've fallen in with the wrong crowd. Please don't look at me like that. Just listen. And believe I'm telling you this only because I love you." Duncan nodded because he knew it was so. "It seemed to take me forever to have you with me again, and now that you're here I'm frightened for you. Terrified, if you want to know the truth. You're all I have, Duncan, and I don't want to lose you."

Duncan loved him too and was moved to silence while his brother attacked Christophe, the Creoles, the dangers of New Orleans, and Duncan's apparent obsession with hedonism, not to mention constant flirtation with danger. While he talked, Randolph managed to devour a fried perch with hominy and lyonnaise potatoes, cornbread drenched in Louisiana syrup, and several cups of coffee. His conversation was liberally sprinkled with unpleasant references to the perils of attending bull and bear matches and cockfights, of the justifiably notorious reputation of Gallatin Street bordellos, and the obvious consequences of duels.

"I didn't bring you all the way from Virginia to have you die at the hands of some damned hotheaded Creoles, Duncan. You can talk all you want about their opera and theater and grand balls and beautiful women, but that scarcely compensates for the barbarity of dueling. I've never heard of anything more uncivilized in my life! Surely you've heard some of their absurd excuses. Because the humidity is distressing or because the river is too high or too low. Bah! Absolutely barbaric!" He glanced over his shoulder. "More coffee, Junon."

The quiet, slender Negro filled Randolph's cup and retreated, watching silently. Randolph had acquired him during his years in Charleston, rescuing him from a discordant French Huguenot household and bringing him here where loyalty to his master grew. Junon was deeply disturbed by the unpleasantness between the brothers. Like his faithful manservant, Randolph was on the retiring side, choosing tranquility over turmoil at all costs, unless he was angered or faced a crisis in his brokerage offices. Or, like now, fought for something dearly loved.

"You're a grown man, Duncan. I can't order you about, nor do I want to. I'm merely asking you to spend more time with me and your own kind. Why, you've not even begun to scratch the surface of what we have to offer on this side of Canal Street. There *is* an American New Orleans, you know, and we have a carnival season as well. Matter of fact, I've just involved myself with a group of gentlemen who want to save Mardi Gras from itself."

"How so?" Duncan was grateful the subject had shifted away from himself and allowed Junon to serve him a plate of the steaming oysters. Their Gulf redolence had rejuvenated his appetite as had the rich aromatic coffee.

"As I'm sworn to secrecy about our plans, I'll explain later. I'll say only that if things go as planned, Mardi Gras this year will be unlike anything the city has ever seen. The world even! The Creoles have let it degenerate into such a dangerous catastrophe it's fallen to us to resurrect it."

Duncan nodded patiently, knowing the Americans were also blamed for carnival's decline. The Creoles cited a crime wave that began with American domination. The street parades had been taken over by drunken whores and vicious petty thieves, and the denizens of Gallatin Street wore only guns and knives. This outrageous public nudity continued because no policemen would venture into the District to make arrests! The European custom of tossing flour at the revelers was banned after hooligans tossed lye instead, burning some celebrants, nearly blinding others. Horrified Creole ladies viewed the parades from the safety of lacy balconies, if at all, and only those taking great care not to be unmasked dared brave the dangerous streets.

Only last year the Creole newspaper, *L'Abeille,* expressed no sorrow that "this miserable annual exhibition is rapidly becoming extinct. It originated in a barbarous age and is worthy of only such." The American's *Daily Orleanian* attacked a masker dressing as a priest in order to take "unspeakable liberties with unsuspecting ladies" and called for an end to masking. The *Daily Delta* detailed the excessive public drunkenness and fighting, citing the overflowing jails and costumed corpses as the legacy of "this reign of licentiousness." Regardless of who was to blame, Mardi Gras was clearly in trouble with many city fathers, both French and American, hoping it would embrace a quiet death.

Duncan resisted the temptation to remind his brother as much, just as he reined the urge to tell Randolph that the potent brew and most of the breakfast menu were pure Creole. Now was hardly the appropriate time.

"By all means continue to see Arnaud if it suits you," Randolph concluded, "but exercise caution where you take your pleasure. The very notion of you going to Gallatin Street sends chills down my spine. And as for that business with the duel . . . well, I hope you've learned a lesson."

"I have," Duncan conceded. His head was pounding worse than ever. The strong coffee had only worsened the discomfort, and he waved Junon away when he endeavored to refill his cup. "And I apologize for any pain I've caused you. I'm trying to see it from your viewpoint and I agree that I've been like a child in a candy store. There has been glittering temptation everywhere I looked."

Randolph nodded. "You've never traveled outside Virginia and I'll be the first to concede that this city can be a tempting bauble. You just need to proceed with caution. I'll help with a little gathering next week. Saturday night perhaps. Some of my friends have some enchanting daughters, and . . ."

"Some other evening perhaps," Duncan interposed gently. "That's the night of the next ball. The one I am to host with Eugénie Duval."

Randolph dabbed his mouth with a napkin and drew an envelope from a pocket in his waistcoat. "I think this is as appropriate time as any to give you this, little brother. It came shortly after the letter from Mr. Duplessy. These letters have kept us busy this morning, haven't they, Junon?"

"Yes, sir," Junon replied softly.

Duncan suspected the contents before he opened it. The message was in French, and he frowned as he struggled to identify a word here, a phrase there that he might comprehend. He was helpless and not a little embarrassed when he looked up at his brother.

"Junon understands French, but of course he can't read. If you read it to him, perhaps he can translate." Even with Duncan's awkward mispronunciations, the terse message was easy enough for Junon to grasp.

Monsieur Honoré Duval regretted that his daughter would not be able to attend the upcoming ball!

Duncan crumpled the letter and tossed it into the fire. "The old bastard!"

Randolph was surprised by the venom in his brother's voice. "Does the girl really mean so much to you?"

Duncan was bone weary, fatigue forcing a confession he'd not even made to Christophe. "No." He raised a napkin to conceal a yawn, eyes burning as a woman's face danced inside his head. "We've only seen each other once, but she captivated me. I've never met anyone like her. She's so knowledgeable about the Byzantine and when we talked it was as if no one else was in the room. In the world! She . . . no! That's not right." He stopped when he realized he was describing Justine. "Forgive me, Randolph. If I don't go to bed my face is going to fall right into these oysters. Please excuse me."

Duncan's feet grew heavier with each step as the fatigue finally swept over him full force. He stripped off his dress clothes and tumbled into bed in his drawers, not bothering with a nightshirt. Junon hadn't stoked the brazier since last night and the room was cold. The heavy counterpane felt good as Duncan snuggled underneath.

As Duncan drifted quickly toward sleep, a face hovered hazily in his fading thoughts. He didn't recognize it although he was certain it was female. She seemed to be a strange synthesis of Virginia and Eugénie and even Molly Lewis. And someone he didn't know at all.

The sleep that overtook him was swift and deep, soothing him into a world of blissful oblivion. He dreamed not at all until the end, when he was teased by images of the Bayou Road. He and Christophe had driven to Lake Ponchartrain on one occasion, pausing along the way to admire the primordial beauty of the swamp. Duncan found it at once frightening and compelling. Ancient cypress brooded in obsidian waters, rising from great, swollen stumps, woody offspring in phallic clusters at their feet. Their moss-graced branches soared toward an ashen sky, knitting a canopy so dense the sun seldom reached a ground more water than earth, a dark reflection of what hovered above. A water snake disturbed that ebony mirror, dispatching ripples as it fled the intrusion of man. A snowy egret, mysteriously left behind from the migration, aimed an inquisitive beak at the men, lacy white plumes startling against the daytime blackness. It was as if the earth's palette had been leached of all color.

As Duncan surrendered to the dream, there was other movement in the swamp, and it was no longer winter. He had only heard of the canicular torpor of the deep delta summers but now they steamed to life, overwhelming and smothering like deep sleep itself. There were colors too, vivid, shimmering greens and the jewel-tones of butterflies and exotic lilies. Such colors hurt his eyes as he slogged knee-deep into the dark waters, oblivious to danger as he was lured by a recurring flash of whiteness always just beyond the next tree.

Nothing was quite in focus. The heat shimmered in lazy waves, emanating from the core of the earth to simmer on the muddy floor of the swamp. It smote Duncan's nostrils along with the sweet, fecund odor of birth and decay that forever embraced this place. It was shocking and new, this heat that could be tasted and smelled as well as felt. It set his bare flesh on fire, especially his sex.

A high laugh pierced the ponderous stillness and he caught sight of the fleeing creature again. Like him, this elusive nymph was naked, pale flesh so glaring in the emerald swamp that he shielded his eyes. He pursued her without choice, slogging through the black waters, his noisy invasion stirring birds into flight and lesser creatures into retreat. A sleeping log yielded a pair of ancient yellow eyes, watching, waiting before the great reptilian tail swished, silently propelling the alligator below the water and out of sight. Duncan saw none of this, blinded by his pursuit of the woman. He caught her on a low reedy hummock swelling from the floor of the swamp, seized her by the wrist and spun her around.

"Justine . . . !" he murmured sleepily.

The taunting laughter faded as he drew her down beside him, into the soft, damp earth. She succumbed easily, writhing beneath him like a serpent, baring her teeth as he entered her hard and sharp. Her nails raked his flesh, stinging and drawing blood like a fine crimson spiderweb across his back. He felt no pain except hers as she opened her mouth and released a scream so primeval that it triggered his explosion. Mouths and loins were crushed together, melded by sweat and the fervent, relentless heat. They, he and the woman, were drowning in the primordial ooze. White limbs were entangled in the reed-riven mud, drenched in a rich, all-consuming darkness that sucked her away from him. He lunged toward her as she began fading, whimpering painfully as she vanished into the poisonous, obsidian waters.

"Ahhh!"

Duncan moaned awake, loins still tingling as the dream evaporated. But the image lingered, imparting with it a satisfying warmth, and he called her name again.

"Justine!"

He started at a knock at the door and Junon's voice drifted in from the hall outside. "You all right, Mr. Duncan?"

"Just . . . just had a bad dream!" Duncan lied. He struggled to stir the mental cobwebs. "What time is it?"

"Half past nine, sir."

Duncan had been sleeping almost three hours! Oh, well. Still plenty of time for him to bathe and dress and catch the St. Charles mule-car. He considered his lingering tumescence, puzzled by the need for release when he had so recently had satisfaction with the whore. No woman, even in adolescence, had ever spawned such a sensual dream and he marveled at the power Justine wielded over him, even in absence.

He slipped from the bed and tossed off his damp drawers. "I'll need a bath, Junon! At once!"

"Yes, sir."

Within the hour, Duncan was contemplating the fabled houses of the Garden District as the mule-car clipped along St. Charles Avenue. Such cars were a recent arrival in New Orleans, replacing the sluggish omnibuses when city fathers learned iron wheels upon iron rails both eased and speeded a horse's workload. Duncan enjoyed the leisurely ride until he reached Canal Street where the noise was overwhelming. This intersection of the city's two major thoroughfares choked in a sea of buggies, cabs, drays, carts, and delivery wagons, a crashing cacophony of horseshoes against cobblestones, of chanking harnesses, of frustrated drivers shouting. When an enormous flat-bedded wagon precipitous with cotton bales threw a wheel, Duncan and several other passengers swung down from the car, deciding they'd make more progress on foot.

Once he was free from the noise, Duncan was invigorated by the cloudless day and a chilled wind gusting off the river. He glanced at his watch and, realizing he had a half hour to kill, opted for a stroll up bustling Canal Street and then right along the Rue Rampart. He'd heard so much about the neat little cottages lining this street. They were mostly the legacy of *plaçage,* built by Creole gentlemen for their mistresses of color. Many were still used for that purpose, others were boarding houses operated by women whose unions had ended. Others were home to those who quietly lived alone with their memories, generously provided for by long-departed lovers who financed a household complete with slaves.

On this cold January morning, glowing beneath a brilliant winter sun, Rampart Street struck Duncan as unbearably bittersweet, and he drew a piece of paper from his coat to scribble a few notes. It was the beginning of his first New Orleans poem.

He wandered as far as Congo Square where the slaves congregated on Sundays to dance their frenzied *calenda, bamboula,* and *chica,* all under the vigilant eye of white policemen. Today the square was deserted, all four gates closed. Duncan felt something odd emanating from there too, a primitive force unnerving and forbidden, but it did not register. He made a few more notes and tucked the paper away.

He crossed the Rue Rampart into the Rue Ste. Anne, drawn to a squat, unimposing house with a sloping red-tile roof and a small yard dense with banana, bamboo, and bracken. A high fence almost hid it from the street, and except for a crowd milling about on the banquette outside he would have passed without a second thought. He approached another tall gentleman who was peering atop the sea of heads, face flushed wildly with excitement. Duncan touched the brim of his hat and nodded politely.

"Please excuse me, sir, but might I ask why this crowd has gathered?"

The stranger looked at him in wonder. "We're all waiting to see her, of course."

Duncan frowned. " 'Her'?"

Another disdainful look. "The queen of course. Marie Laveau!" He seemed utterly flabbergasted when Duncan asked who she was. "She's the most potent *voudou* in the city," the man replied. "Why, visiting New Orleans without seeing her is like missing a famous sight. I'm from St. Louis myself." Facing another blank stare, he was about to ask if Duncan knew what *voudou* was when the door of the little cottage opened and a well-dressed, heavily veiled white woman emerged, an American as best Duncan could tell. "One of the rich ones who comes for Marie Laveau's darker work. Doesn't want to be recognized. That would be my guess."

As the woman threaded her way through the restless crowd, there was a collective heave forward. An ancient Negress chose the next lucky acolyte, a small, smartly dressed quadroon who glanced warily over her shoulder before hurrying inside.

Duncan shuddered, noting that the bright noon light was disappearing behind a fast-rolling cloudbank. He was suddenly in need of company and hurried toward Christophe's home in the Rue St. Louis. He turned up his coat collar and moved on.

Before she was ushered into Marie Laveau's house, Toinette had seen the tall American and wondered who he was. His considerable height had easily set him apart from the crowd, but there was something else drawing her to him. He had a look of barely controlled desperation about him, a neediness she didn't suspect he sought to erase through *voudou.* Her suspicions were confirmed when he wandered away. She wondered if she had seen him before, perhaps in her husband's shop, perhaps with a lady in *La Mode.* For the Creoles, *La Nouvelle-Orléans* remained a very small town.

Toinette forgot about him as the Negress closed the door behind them, obliterating all sunlight and sucking her into a dark, oppressive atmosphere at once unnerving and supernal. If Marie Laveau had not been a relative, albeit a distant one, she might have been frightened, but she was not. Besides she had been there on other occasions . . .

"Wait here, madam," the Negress said in French. "I will tell her you're here."

"Merci."

When Toinette's eyes adjusted to the gloom, she shuddered in spite of herself. The small, wildly cluttered room was smothered with so much filthy drapery it was like being inside a tent. She put a gloved hand to her mouth and coughed, victim to an overwhelming scent of must and decay and something she couldn't identify.

Her eye was drawn to an altar against the far wall. Three tiny votive candles flickered beneath statues of the Virgin, St. Peter, and St. Marron, a colored saint who, Toinette was certain, was unknown to the Vatican. She was sure Rome would have been horrified to know of his existence and supposed powers.

After a few moments, the claustrophobic, malodorous room and the dancing candlelight grew mesmerizing. Toinette felt a little dizzy. The brightness and reality of the outside world began to recede, vanquished by an eerie ambience carefully orchestrated by the tall woman lurking behind drawn portieres, who adjusted an earring and indulged herself in a rare smile. It would be business as usual of course, but it would be good to see her pretty little cousin. Madame Laveau had always thought Toinette could have been one of her highest-paid girls if she'd only gotten to her before Bernard Clovis. *Eh, bien* . . .

Toinette's hand flew to her throat when the portieres parted with a loud clank and the room flooded with the unsettling presence of Marie Laveau, New Orleans' undisputed *voudou* queen, the most powerful and feared woman in the city. She had been ruling so long no living soul was certain exactly when she ascended her mysterious throne. Legend, myth, reality, and not a little fear, had long ago churned together in a confusion leading some to claim this was only a daughter of the first Marie Laveau, a woman born when the flag of Spain still flew over the city. Others weren't so sure, but no matter. All were lured, black and white, the rich and influential, the poor and desperate, all seeking the same thing: the *voudouienne*'s help in solving the problems of life and love. Or, in the case of the Missouri tourist, something to talk about when he got home.

The tales were endless, thrilling, terrifying, stomach-churning, and Toinette had heard many of them. There was nothing Marie Laveau would not do to to achieve her ends, and there was proof positive of her omnipotence in the number of rival queens left toppled in her determined, destructive wake. This was no trifling *voudou* who contented herself with erasing impediments to marriage or securing the return of a wayward lover. This was a woman whose dark escapades were retold with fevered relish among the Negro populace and discreetly whispered about among her white believers.

It was nothing for her to leave *gris-gris* on a doorstep or dance with snakes in *le Plaçe Congo*. It was expected that she would skulk about in the cloak of night to deposit coffins or blood-drenched conjure balls in side yards. And everyone knew of the lascivious services the *voudou* queen conducted on the shores of Lake Ponchartrain, those drawing aristocratic masked white participants as well as slaves. What transpired at those shameless orgies included the most scandalous of all subjects, miscegenation between white women and Negro men. That was one unspeakable topic that did not insinuate its way into the parlors on either side of Canal Street.

And there was the talk of her participation in human sacrifice, the terrible tales of her drinking human blood? And the poor infant's skeleton she supposedly kept in an armoire . . . " 'Tite Toinette!" Marie Laveau said. The smile flickered again and died. "So you've come to me again."

There was no familial kiss exchanged. It was, for both, unthinkable. For Marie Laveau, it was a matter of distancing herself from ordinary mortals, of maintaining the carefully spun web of superiority and puissance. For Toinette, the idea was merely repulsive.

It was certainly not because the woman was ugly. Indeed, Marie Laveau was a tall, strikingly handsome *sang-melée* with carved cheekbones the reputed legacy of Colapissa blood. Her face was framed by jet-black hair with only a hint of curl, lips rouged to fullness. Although it was impossible to tell in this light, Toinette knew her cousin's skin was a light, burnished bronze and that her black eyes bore pupils like misshapen stars.

She wore her trademark dress of deep blue cotton, cinched tight at the waist and hugging an ample bosom. It was buttoned from neck to waist. A blue *tignon* and great gold hoop earrings completed the picture. Her carriage, thought Toinette, always bordered on regal.

But there was something about her that was as dreadful as the stench of evil. It enveloped her in a noxious cloud, preceding her and lingering long after she was gone. Toinette recoiled, as she had on other visits, and fought to keep from defying the smell with a handkerchief to her nose. Unlike other foul odors, this one did not vanish gradually with acceptance and defied identification. Rather, it hovered as some sort of reminder of Marie Laveau's macabre omnipotence.

The *voudouienne* spoke in a low voice, edged with power. "It is not Bernard who gives you trouble. But the husband of another woman, eh?" Toinette nodded. "A white woman."

It was not a question, but Toinette nodded and coughed. She wished she could open a window or crack the door. When the woman moved closer, the stench burned her eyes. It emanated from her entire body. Stale sweat, the passage of time and that mysterious something else.

"A friend," Toinette managed finally.

"Tell me more."

The *voudouienne* listened enrapt as Toinette recounted tales of Justine's abuse at the hands of Hilaire Blancard. She nodded occasionally, bright red lips pursing and then straining into a taut, narrow line. She shook her head and raised a silencing hand.

"I need hear no more," she pronounced. "He is pure evil, this man. For what we need we must go to another room. Come!"

As Toinette followed, she was overwhelmed with foreboding. She had not been there, but she had certainly heard about the infamous "back room" where all manner of maleficence transpired. Where the worst curses were cast. Where Marie Laveau kept the giant snake that devoured small children. Where dark gods were invoked with rituals too horrifying to think about. For the first time, Toinette wished she had not come. Marie Laveau sensed her fear, smelled it like a predator and she whirled on her cousin.

"Do not be afraid. What I do for you I do for myself as well."

Toinette didn't understand but obeyed. The second room was smaller and darker and, if possible, more cluttered than the other. Toinette found it increasingly difficult to breathe, heart pounding as her eyes sought to hone fuzzy images in the blackness.

Another altar loomed, dominated by what seemed to be animal statues. Toinette eventually discerned a lion, a tiger, wolf, and a bear, flanking an enormous open book. All rested on a heavily carved box that bore the unmistakable scent of a living creature. As Toinette moved cautiously into the macabre inner sanctum of the *voudouienne,* she heard movement in the box and was horrified when she remembered stories about it. Some said it was the giant snake from Africa. Others said it was the devil himself. Without thinking, she hastily crossed herself. Marie Laveau laughed, a low throaty sound as much animal as human. The huge hoop earrings flashed gold in the candlelight as she reared back and pointed.

"Sit! There!"

Marie Laveau indicated a seat to the right of the altar and Toinette slid into place. She watched as the *voudouienne* closed her eyes, muttered unintelligibly and reached into one of two huge pockets in her voluminous skirts. She opened her eyes again, flipped a few pages in the book and placed something dark and shriveled in the crease between them. She looked at Toinette and extended a hand.

"His picture. Did you bring me a picture?"

"Yes."

From her other visits Toinette had remembered what the woman would need to work her spell. She withdrew the daguerreotype of Hilaire Blancard from her muff and passed it to the waiting hand. She recoiled from the malevolence that instantly materialized on Marie Laveau's face. The fine chiseled features contorted, scarlet mouth vanishing as she squeezed her lips in rage. The eyes were furious slits and when she spoke the voice was raw vitriol.

"Ah, yes! I know this man. That monster cost me my poor Josette. She came to me for help but it was too late. Hilaire Blancard discovered what she had done and . . ." She shrugged, palms up. "The next day she was dead."

"Josette?" Toinette ventured.

"The child of an old friend who also died young. I didn't raise Josette but I saw that she wanted for little. Like so many desperate young women, she saw the balls as an avenue of escape and went when she was only fifteen, a beautiful thing. On her debut night she met this man—*this monster Blancard!*—and within the year she was dead."

Toinette's heart turned to ice. "Did he . . . ?"

"Kill her? I would say yes. Others no. He reported that she died with a miscarriage but I saw the body and I assure you it was not any unborn fetus that took her life." Toinette didn't dare ask how the woman had access to the corpse of Blancard's young mistress. "There is only one thing that could have so hideously contorted that child's body. It was fear, pure and simple. That girl was scared to death. I swear to you there is no limit to the evil in that man. He can kill without touching!" Marie Laveau hissed suddenly and snarled like a tigress. "Such powerful art lies in the hands of the very few!"

Toinette crossed herself again as images of Justine's bruised nakedness materialized. *"Mon dieu!"*

"I told Josette what I always tell women with bad men. Take a towel that's been used in lovemaking and wave it in his face. That always stops the beating. Guaranteed. But as I said, with Josette it was too late. When he learned she had come to me, spoken to an outsider of their peculiar little arrangement, he flew into a deadly rage. I know."

"*Mon dieu!*" Toinette sighed, echoing herself. Blancard was worse than she had imagined. Much worse. She was frightened but somehow drew strength from the bizarre woman determinedly pacing the room and muttering incantations as much to herself as her dark spirits.

"I knew our paths would cross, his and mine. I tell you what, Toinette. For this picture I will waive my usual fee. This undoing I want to work myself. I must be clever though. Very clever. This man has superb powers, although I suspect he doesn't know it."

She studied the daguerreotype, one taken of Blancard shortly before his marriage to Justine. What looked back at the *voudouienne* was a smartly dressed gentleman still dashing in his thirties. A casual observer might remark on the man's handsomeness, but Marie Laveau's view was scarcely that of lesser souls. The clue was, she knew, in the eyes. Lurking in their darkness was a potent rage, a smoldering anger just waiting to be stoked. Poor Josette had roused it, as had Justine. Marie Laveau could only wonder how many others had fallen victim to the man's sickness. Then she smiled, but it was not the sort to warm any hearts.

"Often, my dear Toinette, the darkest powers are the simplest to invoke. For example, all I need to do is bury this picture. When it fades, and it will, he will die a terrible death. And not without knowing the evil he has done."

Marie Laveau touched the smooth surface of the daguerreotype, held her fingers there only a moment before jerking them away, as though the picture seethed with heat. Earrings jangled as she shook her head. "Potent, this man. Very potent!"

"How . . . will . . . he . . . ?"

"I cannot tell you how he will die," dismissed the *voudouienne*, "only that it will happen before the eve of Ash Wednesday." A wave silenced the question Marie Laveau knew Toinette would pose. "I cannot act faster because his powers are too strong. As it is, we must catch him napping."

"Marie, I—"

"Say nothing!" the *voudouienne* commanded harshly. "It is finished between us. But I tell you this: you leave my house knowing that the days of Monsieur Hilaire Blancard are numbered. I, Marie Laveau, *La Reine des Voudous*, swear it!"

Before Toinette realized it, she was back out on the banquette, jostled by the milling crowds and inhaling the sweet, cold riverine air. It took a few seconds before her feet moved her away from that strange little cottage in the Rue Ste. Anne. Not until she rounded the corner of the Rue Royale and saw Soona through the windows of *La Mode* did she at last identify the terrible smell wrapping Marie Laveau in a malignant cloud.

It was the scent of scalded blood.

CHAPTER 11

"I've been absolutely desperate to spend time with you, Michie Marius." Chaillot beamed as she took his arm and Gautier was stirred. "You know I love *maman* dearly, but she always seems to be around whenever I steal a moment away from Blancard. Of course it's you I want to see when I go home."

"Isn't home the house in the Rue Rampart now?" Gautier asked cautiously. He well remembered her recent outburst, but he didn't want anything to spoil their outing at Lake Ponchartrain. As things were, they would barely have time to catch the last train. He adored Chaillot but punctuality was something she found maddeningly elusive.

"Never!" she hissed.

"Do you still hate him so much?"

"Oh, I don't know, michie." She shrugged and twirled her parasol. "Perhaps not so much. Or perhaps I am just getting used to the wretched routine. I must admit he gives me nice things."

"So I see."

Chaillot stroked the mink trimming of her new muff and giggled girlishly. Sometimes, Gautier thought, she seemed the most weary courtesan in the world; at others she was still the little girl play-acting with Combas. She would, he decided, make a great actress.

"You know what helps me get through it, Michie Marius? I tell myself that I am playing a part in a grand play. And you know what else? I think of his gifts as applause." She looked up at him, sapphire eyes flashing as she read doubt where none existed. "And I *will* be an actress!"

Gautier's laughter was so loud that people boarding the train turned to see the source of his amusement. "But you should consider a career as a mind reader first, *ma petit chou*. That is precisely what I was thinking!"

"Oh, no!" But her reaction was to something else, and Gautier frowned as she fumbled frantically inside the muff.

"What is it, *cher?*"

"My pass!" she hissed. "I left it behind!" She glanced frantically at the cars marked with stars, those reserved for slaves and *gens de coleur*. "I'd better hurry home and . . ."

"There isn't time," Gautier said.

He did not hide his annoyance as this was a dangerous bit of carelessness Chaillot could ill afford to indulge. The law of the State of Louisiana was strict and clear. Persons of color must carry identification at all times, proof of their status as free man or slave. It was something Chaillot should consider as much a part of her person as the flesh itself, for the consequences could be dire.

Gautier made an instant, daring decision. "We'll go anyway."

Chaillot was horrified. "But what if I'm questioned?"

"No one will stop you as long as you're with me. Now come along. We'll take that car."

The lanceolate eyes widened when he indicated the unstarred car at the front of the platform. It was reserved for whites only. Chaillot held back, visibly cowering. "I don't dare!"

Gautier leaned so close his lips brushed her ear. "Consider it practice for when you go to New York. We both know you're going North to seek more than an acting career."

"Michie Marius!"

Dear friend though Gautier was, Chaillot had not dared reveal that deepest of secrets, her hope of passing for white. Indeed, because it was a deception tinged with arrogance, shame, and not a little danger, she dared not confess it to anyone.

"You needn't bother play-acting around me," he chided sweetly. "Now come along. You have to begin the madness some time, and you may as well start passing now." He smiled and nodded at her chic traveling costume. "Besides, my dear, you're already gowned for a dazzling dress rehearsal!"

Fortunately in the gush of the steaming train, bawling conductors, and chattering crowd, no one heard their conversation. But a pair of close-set eyes followed when they walked to the other end of the platform and boarded the Whites Only car. As they sought seats on the crowded car, Chaillot's gloved hand gripping Gautier's arm so tight it hurt, no one noticed anything unusual about the handsome couple except their exceedingly fashionable clothes and the exceptional beauty of the blue-eyed young woman.

Gautier held his breath when a gentleman quickly rose to offer his seat. In a velvety voice, Chaillot thanked him and slid into place, smoothing the folds of her long coat and dimpling prettily.

The trip was scarcely more than five miles but Chaillot feared it would take a lifetime. The sun streaming through the windows was warm, but not enough to cause the beads of perspiration threatening her forehead and upper lip. Despite the elegantly insouciant way she played with her parasol handle and fussed with the contents of the muff, she was inwardly terrified. Pretending to be white with Combas was one thing, but this was exceedingly dangerous.

Occasional glances at Gautier helped, but Chaillot's best solution was spinning herself into a sort of trance as she imagined actresses did when they assayed an especially treacherous role. With her mind so fixed, time at last unfroze. She all but shivered with relief when the conductor bawled the last stop.

"Milneburg! Ponchartrain Hotel and the lake! Last stop! All passengers off! Last stop!"

Chaillot's face remained a beguiling, enigmatic mask as she took Gautier's arm. Quietly, they strolled the pleasure gardens of a hotel built within the walls of the old Spanish fort. Gautier was pleased but not surprised at the grace Chaillot displayed in acknowledging the tipped hats of passing white gentlemen and the polite nods of their ladies. But his pride in Chaillot was short-lived. As they neared the doors of the hotel, she shied like a skittish horse.

"*Non!*" she hissed. "I cannot!"

"It's all right, *cher*," he said. "You're with me."

"But I . . . oh, not yet, Michie Marius! Not yet!"

"Very well. Come along then. We'll stroll the lake."

Chaillot took no notice of the bath houses, shooting galleries, or the lighthouse towering over the relentlessly flat terrain. She wanted only to escape all other human beings, to find sanctuary where she could shed this skin she found not nearly so comfortable as she'd imagined. Not until they were well out of earshot of everyone, close only to a handful of screaming boys flying kites, did she dare speak.

"I've never been so frightened in my life. I tell you I can't do it again today, michie. When we go home, I'm going to ride in the colored coach."

He acknowledged her genuine fear but had to laugh. "Don't you think that's rather like announcing who you are?"

"But it *is* who I am!"

"Use your brain, Chaillot. There are people who saw you in the white car. What will they think if . . . ?"

"Oh! I didn't think of that!"

"There are endless things to think of when you pretend to be someone you're not," he warned. "You must be on your guard all the time. Not just when you remember to be. Always. *Always!*"

The blue eyes narrowed at the ferocity buoying his words. She seemed to notice something in him that had never been there before. "I've never heard you sound so serious. You . . . frighten me a little."

Gautier scanned the heavens as though looking for something. When he didn't seem to find it, he looked back at her. "*Ma petit* Chaillot. You're barely sixteen and although there's so much you know, there's also a great deal you've yet to learn."

"You mean about being white of course."

"No. Well, yes, that too. But . . . no, *cher.* I mean other things." He shaded his hand and watched five pelicans glide by, all in a row until the first spotted something in the lake and plunged after it. The others continued on, oblivious to their missing leader, continuing to scan the glassy lake surface for fish.

Chaillot was also lost in her own thoughts. She too studied the pelicans and for some reason, these great grotesque clowns stirred her emotions. She had loved them as a child and would miss them when she was gone North. Indeed there was much she would miss, but there were other, far more important things she would not.

"You've been gone so long you don't know what it's like here, michie. Things are changing in *La Louisiane,* and the changes are scarcely good for people of color."

"What do you mean?"

"There's more and more pressure being put on us to leave the state. Other things too. Just last week Bernard Clovis, Monsieur Blancard's tailor, was denied a loan to expand his shop in the Rue Royale. Monsieur Blancard told me that a white man was given a loan to buy that same property, at much more favorable rates. He should know. It was his bank!"

"A terrible thing," Gautier conceded.

"But it's not just that," Chaillot continued. "It's the fear that more and more things will be taken from us. According to *maman,* it's merely a continuation of what's been happening for years."

"*C'est vrai.*"

Like other compassionate Creoles and white Southerners, Gautier was sympathetic to the plight of the *gens de coleur libre*. For well over a century they had lived in a shadowy world, neither black nor white, not slaves but neither completely free. Certainly not like whites were free. They posed problems unique to Louisiana, and local legislation, along with the conscience of white Southerners, still wrestled with how to handle them.

The first real problems began with the arrival of the Americans in 1803. The newcomers didn't know what to make of this largely literate, well-educated community of French- and Spanish-blooded blacks who carried firearms and actually owned slaves of their own! They absolutely could not conceive of Negroes owning prosperous shops and fine houses, wearing fashionable clothes and occupying boxes at the opera. Indeed over a quarter of the city's finer houses were owned by free people of color, mostly single women! The first American governor, Virginia-born William C. C. Claiborne, was aghast at the aggressiveness of the free blacks and the freedom with which they associated with whites and comported themselves in the streets. It was, he surmised, further proof of the colony's utter decadence.

And as for the quadroon balls . . . !

The Americans were further alarmed when revolution in *Saint Domingue* flooded New Orleans with thousands of refugees, doubling the black population by 1810. Under considerable pressure, Claiborne reacted by ousting every free man of color from *Saint Domingue* over the age of fifteen and requiring all blacks to carry iden'.ification passes stating their status as freeman or slave, a deep insult to those born into freedom, especially those owning slaves of their own!

Matters worsened in 1830 when newly emancipated slaves were ordered to leave the state. More degrading laws prohibited press favorable to Negroes and forbade rights to assemble or testify against whites in court. Slaves could no longer be educated. The last straw came in 1842 when contact with the West Indies was severed and all recently arrived blacks were ordered to leave Louisiana. The result was a mass exodus as over nine thousand free people of color sold their property and fled to France and Mexico. Their population in New Orleans had been more than halved!

These harsh realities danced bitterly in Chaillot's mind. "Bit by bit, our rights are being stripped away," she concluded, "and I don't want to be here when we are left with nothing."

"I'm afraid it will be outside forces accomplishing that," suggested Gautier. "Before our Louisiana politicians get the chance."

"You mean the war of course." He nodded grimly. "Well, either way, my people will lose. If the South triumphs, we'll continue down the path to destruction. If the North wins, slavery will end and my people will be reduced to the status of freed slaves."

"You're a smart girl, Chaillot." Politics was scarcely an appropriate topic for young ladies, and today's discussion had been a rarity. Finding Chaillot open to it, however, Gautier pursued the issue. He suddenly saw it as a segue to the real reason for their afternoon sojourn to the lake. "Are you also smart enough to know the South doesn't stand a chance against the superior manpower and industrial strength of the North?"

"I . . . I never gave it much thought," she conceded.

He smiled grimly. "I'm afraid you're typical of too many white Southern gentlemen. They think they can fight a war with courtly manners and a slave-based economy, when what they need are foundries and a population triple in size."

"It all seems so hopeless," Chaillot lamented. "Unless . . ."

"Unless you can move North and begin living the lie," Gautier finished.

"*Oui,*" she conceded.

This time there was neither hesitation nor denial. In truth, it felt good to unburden herself from the secret she had nurtured since childhood. It was a relief to share this deepest, most forbidden dream with someone as understanding as Michie Marius.

"It's a treacherous thing, this business of living a lie," he warned gravely. "I know what it's like, *mon cher.* So does your *maman.* And Simon Guedry and Narcisse Villeneuve."

"What do you mean?"

That strange edge to his voice had returned, tinged with rage and sorrow. It unnerved Chaillot and she took his arm to reassure herself. They had turned around where the boardwalk ended and were heading back toward the lighthouse. Gautier's thoughts splintered and he struggled to keep them from foundering. He *must* talk to her. Colette was adamant, and she was right. Their great lie was often so onerous as to be unbearable. It was time they eased their burden by sharing the truth with Chaillot.

"Michie Marius? Have I lost you?"

"No, *cher.* Come. Sit here for a moment. There's something we must discuss."

"You sound so serious," Chaillot said as she lifted the folds of her heavy coat and perched on the bench. "And that terrible look on your face, michie. It frightens me!"

"I didn't mean to scare you, *ma petit.* I only want to erase something between us once and for all. You see, I asked you here for a reason. To explain something your dear mother wanted to tell you the night I returned from Paris, when you announced your intentions to leave Monsieur Blancard."

"A night I shall not soon forget," Chaillot sighed.

"It involves . . ." He swallowed hard, and for a moment neither he nor Chaillot thought the words would come. The story remained agonizing to consider, much less to relate. "It involves Monsieur Guedry and what happened after he killed Bernard Lestain in the duel."

"He became *maman's* protector, *non?*"

Gautier pursed his lips as he considered his response. This, he knew, was where things would grow complicated. "Yes, he did. But their liaison was to be, surely, the most unusual in the city's history."

"*Pourquoi?*"

"Because it was never what it seemed. You will remember he had amassed a great fortune in shipping, but what you couldn't know was that he could have had any woman he wanted."

"He was so charming," Chaillot sighed. "And so dear to me."

She shuddered from the twin pangs in her heart, one for Simon Guedry, the other for Narcisse Villeneuve, both lost to fever in the Great Plague of '53. They had been so precious, so endlessly generous with their love and caring in a child's world populated exclusively by white men and women of color. They alone were the stars in that penumbral world, one so fragile she was often forced into retreat with Combas. They, alongside Gautier and *maman*, had fought to protect her from the harsh realities of her peculiar life, and when the ugly arrows of racism inevitably pierced her little heart, they consoled her with a compassion she could still feel. She drew strength from it now as she waited for Gautier to continue.

"Indeed he was," Gautier said at last. "But his appeal was on many levels. Such fantastic wealth as Monsieur Guedry amassed spoke volumes, my darling, even in the innermost Creole circles. In any case, you must understand that he was not interested in a wife. Rather he was only interested in having the Creoles, and the Americans as well, *believe* he had a mistress. It was either that or a wife, and the latter was impossible. There was talk enough because he wasn't married. You know the Creoles. *La famille* is *everything.*"

"True," Chaillot said. Curiosity swelled with each new revelation. "But why didn't he simply . . . ?"

"There was nothing simple where this fine man was concerned," Gautier said. He smiled sweetly but it seemed to Chaillot that his heart was breaking. "Your mother made a grand show of returning to the *Salle d'Orléans*. She even pretended to be serious about a few offers. Her performance was so successful that it led to the suicide you mentioned. And other duels as well. So you see she wasn't being evasive when she asked which duel you meant. In any case, she accepted Simon Guedry as a protector, your *grandmere* approved the arrangement, and the contracts were signed.

"You can't imagine the shock and outrage that roared through the city," Gautier continued. "Absolutely every gentlemen so inclined wanted your mother desperately. Except, as the fates would have it, Guedry himself."

"My head's swimming," Chaillot cried.

"Patience," Gautier repeated. "This is so difficult I mustn't get ahead of myself." He took yet another deep breath of the cool lake air. "Guedry already had a lover, Chaillot. All he wanted from your mother was the illusion of a mistress. When he confessed the truth, she made a confession as well. While she was still under Lestain's protection, she nonetheless managed to acquire a lover of her own. Guedry not only didn't object; he was all too eager for her to continue the affair. That way, they could both have what they wanted and no one would be the wiser."

"I'm so confused," Chaillot lamented. "Why would it matter who knew what? And why was my father so anxious for everyone to think he had a mistress?"

Gautier slipped from the bench and knelt at Chaillot's feet. He took her hands in his. "Guedry loved you with all his heart, my darling Chaillot, but he was *not* your father."

Chaillot's head reeled. "What can you mean?"

Gautier repeated the words slowly, with meaning. "Listen to me. Simon Guedry was not your father."

She was incredulous. "But he was! I called him papa always. I was told from the time that I was . . ."

"Indeed you were. But what you were *not* told was the truth. The truth, you see, would have brought down those two carefully arranged, fiercely guarded liaisons like a house of cards. It was essential that you believed, like everyone else, that your father was Simon Guedry. Nothing could be left to chance."

In a very small voice, "Then . . . who?"

"Your father was Narcisse Villeneuve."

"*Mais non!*"

"Yes," Gautier assured her.

"*Mais non!*" she said again, utterly bewildered.

The truth roared at her, deafening. Narcisse was her mother's lover? Narcisse was the man who bounced her on his knee and looked into sapphirine eyes so like his own and told her he wished she were his daughter. *Mon dieu!* How perverse the gods could be! It seemed to take an eternity before she could clear her mind and seek the final piece of the puzzle.

"Then who was Michie Simon's lover? Do I know her?"

The pain on Gautier's face was almost palpable. "Oh, this is so difficult, Chaillot. If only you were older. If only . . ."

"If only *what?*" Chaillot asked, thinking she would go mad from it all.

Gautier took her hands and brushed them with his lips. A low moan escaped with a breath so hot it pierced her gloves, at once shocking and heart-wrenching as he prepared to provide the final truth. He could almost hear Colette's voice, shrieking frantic encouragement.

"Do it, man! Tell her! Tell her NOW!!"

"Mademoiselle Baptiste, I believe!"

Chaillot and Gautier had been so absorbed in their conversation that they hadn't noticed a shadow falling across them. Both turned toward a pudgy white man struggling to catch his breath. He had obviously hurried down the beach. She didn't know him, but law dictated that she stand to address him.

"Do I know you, sir?" she asked, hastily rising.

"No," he said. A nasty smile flickered on his face and grew as he raked her with his eyes. The glaze in his tiny porcine eyes was due more to whiskey than overexertion, and she and Gautier both sensed trouble. "And I only know you by reputation. From the *Salle d'Orléans* of course."

"I was there only once, monsieur," she said icily. "Perhaps you confuse me with someone else."

"Indeed I do not!" he insisted, stung by her cool tone of dismissal.

Alarmed, Gautier stepped in. Suppose this was someone who recognized a woman of color on the white train car!

"Perhaps I might be of assistance, sir." He touched the brim of his hat and bowed. "Marius Gautier at your service."

"My business is not with you, Monsieur Gautier," the man snapped. "Unless you'd care to explain what you are doing here with Hilaire Blancard's girl."

"I explain nothing to a gentleman who does not identify himself," Gautier replied haughtily.

The plump man gave him a perfunctory nod. "Meilleure, sir. Henri Meilleure. I am an old friend of Blancard."

"A gentleman of estimable renown," Gautier said hastily, mind racing. Clearly the man was drunk and could make considerable trouble if he chose. Gautier and Chaillot tried desperately to remember if they'd seen him on the train, but neither could recall anything. Suddenly Gautier had it.

"And one who would surely not object to her mother's protector taking her daughter to the lake."

Meilleure frowned. Porcine nose primed for scandal, he hadn't planned on uprooting something so innocent. "You're Colette Baptiste's protector?"

"Indeed," replied Gautier, pleased with his lie. The bewilderment on Meilleure's face told him it was working. "Since the death of Simon Guedry, in fact."

Meilleure's frown deepened. He was thrown off the scent but did not give up quite so easily. "How come I never saw you at the balls?"

"Not all connections are arranged at the *Salle d'Orléans,* Monsieur Meilleure," Gautier said evenly. "And now we must be going. I believe the last train is about to leave."

"Uh, yes. Of course." Meilleure nodded in confusion, the redness in his face deepening. "My . . . my apologies, monsieur. I had no idea . . ."

"Then you will excuse us, sir?"

"Of course," he said again. He turned away, weaving unsteadily toward the hotel.

Chaillot was ashen. "He'll tell, Michie Marius! I'm sure he'll tell. And what will Michie Hilaire do? Oh, I'm frightened."

"Don't be," Gautier said, putting an arm around her waist as they followed Meilleure's portly figure at a discreet distance. "There's a good chance the man won't remember this at all. He's certainly had enough to drink."

"But if he does?" Chaillot pressed.

"Then repeat the lie I just told that fat old fool."

"Tell him you and *maman* are lovers?"

"It's just one more lie to live," he said with a smile. "Frankly, I would be greatly honored for the city to believe me the man lucky enough to keep your mother. She is still a great beauty, you know. And much sought after. There are many who would like to see her return to the balls."

"She's too old!" Chaillot snapped, shamed by the jealousy flooding her voice.

"At the risk of speaking in clichés, *ma petit,* your mother is like a fine wine. Aged to perfection. There is much to be said for youth, but there is also a voice for those no longer young."

He chose his words carefully. After all, Chaillot had been bred every bit as carefully as the white Creoles girls, and her fragile sensibilities were not to be offended. He was still reeling from Colette's raw frankness the night she had called herself and her daughter whores! He had chided her after Chaillot had left, but Colette was adamant. "The balls are in decline, my dear Marius," she had insisted. "I can no longer protect my daughter from change. The more Chaillot understands about her untenable position as a free woman of color, the better prepared she will be for dealing for life's little inconsistencies."

"And those women," Gautier finished delicately, "who have a wealth of experience in their repertoire."

Chaillot nodded but her focus remained on the web of deception so carefully spun around her these many years. Actors everywhere!

"Lies," she mused. "I feel shrouded by them today. And now we're about to embark on another."

"Then I'll even the score by answering the question you posed before Mosieur Meilleure so rudely imposed his presence on us." He took her hand as though savoring the pale softness. "You asked if you knew Guedry's lover, and the answer is yes. Rest assured I do not speak in jest when I answer you at last."

For the second time that afternoon Chaillot thought she was going deaf. She felt her lips move and heard her voice, very small, very distant as she uttered the one word.

"*You?*"

"Yes, *ma cher.*"

"*Mais non!*"

"*C'est vrai.* We met a year before Guedry and Lestain dueled. With a single look we knew we were the answer to the other's prayers, the sanctuary at the end of a torturous journey. We were together for fifteen years." He blinked hard but Chaillot saw no tears. "And that, my dear Chaillot, is the last of the lies. I have done your mother's bidding. The story is complete."

"*Maman* and Michie Narcisse," she breathed. "And you and . . . Michie Guedry." He nodded. "All that time together and I never suspected!"

"You were a child most of that time," Gautier reminded her. "And just when you were old enough to start suspecting things, your mother packed you off to the Cane River. To Palmetto. Oh, my darling! Did I shock you?"

"No!" Chaillot insisted. "It's not shock you see, but confusion. It . . . it will take a while for me to digest it all, but I understand. I truly do."

"Your mother had her doubts. I didn't."

"I'm not the naif *maman* thinks I am," Chaillot insisted. "Or rather the one she wishes I were."

"You do your mother an injustice," Gautier insisted. He sighed with relief, grateful that the subject was shifting away from him and his dead lover. "She considers you her greatest accomplishment."

"Then why did she send me to the balls?" Chaillot asked. Like him, she was eager to speak of other things. Regardless of her claims to the contrary, she had only a vague notion of men being together, and just now it was too much to think about. She knew if she tried to picture Guedry and Gautier, her cheeks would flame!

"It was all she knew. And all her mother knew before her," Gautier said. "She naturally assumed that with your grace and beauty you would form an even better connection than she. Indeed you could have done far worse than Hilaire Blancard."

Chaillot's blue eyes blazed and calmed. She spoke slowly. "She never gave me a choice."

"Did you ask for one?"

After a guilty pause, "No."

"Then you cannot fix blame on her," he said sternly.

"What you say is true," she conceded, "but I'm still unhappy with the arrangement. It's not as if this has always been a tradition in my family. *Grandmere* was not a *placée.*"

"She was a slave, was she not?"

Chaillot nodded, heart warming as she remembered her beloved *Grandmere* Chocola, dead almost nine years. "And black as the night. Pure Ibibio. And, oh, what a glorious voice! When she sang in church, *maman* said she could make the angels weep!" She fell silent for a moment, and Gautier knew she was reminiscing. "Did you know she earned her freedom, michie? It was easier, she said, during the Spanish regime. Her master allowed her to hire herself out and in time she made enough money to buy her liberty." Such pride glowed in her voice that Gautier understood, for the first time, how difficult it would be for this girl to shun her true heritage. She talked a good game, but time would tell.

"Her former owner became her lover after that, and they were together until he died. My great-grandfather Sosthéne Barriére. It was *grandmere's* decision, as a free woman, to be with him, and I've always envied and admired her the most because of that. Because she chose him of her own free will!"

"As you chose Hilaire Blancard," reminded Gautier.

Chaillot bristled. "That's not fair, michie. It is not the same, and you know it."

"Agreed. Forgive me?"

Chaillot suddenly brightened, mood mercurial as always. "There is nothing I would not forgive you, Michie Marius. Nothing! And I mean that with all my heart." Her profession was clear. "I love you. I always will."

"If I thought Meilleure weren't watching I'd kiss you, Chaillot. As it is, I'll make you promise me a kiss when we get home."

"Home!" Chaillot shouted. She pointed frantically as the little train belched a cloud of smoke and rattled noisily from the station. "Look! There goes the last one!"

"*Bon.* I had no intention of risking more trouble with that meddlesome Meilleure. I'll go to the hotel and hire a hackney to get us back to the city."

"But what will we do when we get to town?" she asked, alarmed anew. "Oh, Michie Marius! Why must everything be so difficult, even an innocent trip to the lake?" If she was discovered riding in a carriage within the city limits, the consequences could be severe.

"We'll do just what we did on the ride out here," he shrugged. "We'll simply take our chances!"

"You risk too much for me, michie."

He took her hands. "If it's in my power, there is nothing I would not do to protect you, Chaillot. Nothing. Remember that, *ma cher.*"

"I *am* remembering," she smiled. "You promised me that when I was little. Both you and Michie Simon."

"We meant it then. I still do."

"I do love you!" Chaillot smiled. Then, mercurial as ever, she shrugged. "*Eh, bien.* At least the driver won't care where I sit. Oh, look, Michie Marius! Those clouds there across the lake. They look like the lighthouse." She shaded her eyes from the sudden glare, transfixed by a glow that turned her skin golden. "And see how the sun peeks through, just like a beacon. No. Like the flame of a lighthouse. It's perfect! God drawing in the clouds. But how fragile and how sad when He erases it."

When she turned to Gautier, he was astonished to see the lanceolate eyes brimming with tears. Yes, Gautier thought as they watched in silence. She will make an extraordinary actress indeed!

The sudden shadow drew Duncan's concentration from his poetry to the reef of high flying clouds dimming the sun. He watched them for a moment, remembering the lazy Virginia summers when he and Randolph lay on the hillside searching, like all children, for castles in the clouds. None here, he thought a little sadly. Just the remains of a strange tower steadily shredded by lofty winds.

Duncan dipped his quill again and drew the nib across the page. The muse had returned that sunny winter day, steering his hand as the words flowed easily for the first time since he came to New Orleans. He smiled. He was pleased with what he had written. He feared it was little more than a pallid imitation of his idol, Samuel Coleridge, but he persisted nonetheless in his dreamy evocations of Byzantium and her ladies fair. He didn't realize it until the work was complete that he had been delivered of a love poem, his first. It puzzled and pleased at the same time. It's this place, he thought. The spell of New Orleans had permeated every aspect of his life, and now that he had begun writing again, he saw the city's exotic embrace in his poetry.

He shivered. Despite Junon's gentle scolding, he had been writing in the garden in just his waistcoat, taking advantage, he insisted, of a sunny day with little wind. New Orleans winters were deceptive, the butler warned. Mr. Saunders would catch cold in the tropical dankness, and now, with the wind decimating the clouds, Duncan knew what he meant. The garden turned suddenly cold and the damp penetrated his shirt sleeves. He shivered again. When he turned to go inside, he saw a stern-faced Junon through the windows. The black face was a study in disapproval. Duncan was chilled to the bone and admitted as much when he hurried inside.

"Weather here's lots different from Virginia I 'spect," offered Junon as he slipped a jacket on Duncan. "I used to tell Mister Randolph the same thing in Charleston. You think maybe because they's palm trees out there it don't get cold."

"I've learned my lesson, Junon. Next time I'll wear a coat."

"Next time, sir, maybe you'll do your writing indoors."

Although Junon was Randolph's age, Duncan felt like a reprimanded child, but he was scarcely offended. He smiled gratefully as a brandy was slipped between his fingers and his boots were tugged off so he could turn his stockinged feet to a fire built just for his comfort.

Duncan sipped the brandy as he picked up his poetry and scanned it, relieved that he was still pleased. He was his own worst critic and had destroyed works that suffered after a second reading. Yet he smiled as he indulged himself with his own images of Byzantine domes and oriental maidens, his deliciously fanciful if slightly overblown imagery. Yet it was nothing as chimerical as Coleridge's *Kublai Khan,* and Duncan couldn't help wondering what he might produce if he too wrote under the influence of opium.

He was pondering that alternative when the jingle of harness bells told him Randolph was finally home. No doubt he'd been to one of his mysterious meetings, which were coming with increasing frequency these days. Duncan raised his glass in greeting and insisted Randolph join him by the fire.

"You're absolutely flushed with excitement," said Randolph. He took the brandy from Junon and shrugged his cloak into the waiting black hands. "Is it the brandy or . . . no! Don't tell me! You've started writing again!"

"All afternoon."

"Splendid!" Randolph clapped him on the shoulder and sat opposite, enjoying the heat of the hearth. The air was pungent with the crisp smell of the cedar chips Junon had scattered into the crackling flames. "Are you pleased?"

"Very! I tell you, Randolph, it's unlike anything I've ever done. Oh, I know I've said it before, but this city casts a strange spell on me. It's even changed the way I write."

"How so?"

"Don't tease me, big brother, but I've written a love poem of sorts. You know I've never done such a thing."

"A love poem?" Randolph asked suspiciously. "For whom? Surely not Miss Duval."

Duncan shook his head. "She, I have sadly learned, was merely using me to rile her papa."

"Ah, women!" Randolph sighed. He drank deep of the brandy and sighed again. "What are we to do with them?"

Duncan laughed heartily. "Why, woo them, marry them, and make them the mothers of our children, of course. Not to mention reap the considerable pleasures of the marriage bed!" Duncan laughed again until Randolph's smile faded. His enigmatic look prompted Duncan to venture into waters rarely plumbed. Since Randolph's heartbreak over Molly Lewis, he rarely sought female company and, to Duncan's knowledge, had no intentions of changing. "Do you not concur?"

"Women are no longer for me, little brother. I'm a born bachelor."

"But . . ."

"Junon takes care of me well enough." Randolph's firm interruption warned further queries were useless. "Now then, about your poem. For whom is it written?"

"For all women and no woman in particular," Duncan confessed, not altogether truthfully.

"Spoken like a true lover!" Randolph smiled, ebullience returning. "As well as diplomat. Will you share it with me after dinner?"

"Not until it's finished. But then. I promise." He smiled. "But I am not the only one flushed with excitement. Tell me why you're in such good spirits. Did you make a small fortune today from some witless planter with more cotton than brains?"

"Hardly," Randolph answered. He didn't approve of the joke but laughed nonetheless. "I've been to another meeting of that new gentlemen's club. Things are going even better than we hoped."

"Such as?"

"I've told you more than I should already."

"You've told me nothing," Duncan insisted. "Except that it has something to do with saving Mardi Gras from itself."

Randolph frowned. "Then it must've been Junon I told. Hmmm. I am getting truly forgetful."

Duncan tried to hide his hurt at being less of a confidante than the manservant. "Then at least share what you've told him."

"I'll tell you only this," Randolph said, studying his brother over the rim of the snifter. "On the night of Fat Tuesday, something is going to happen in the streets of New Orleans that has never happened before, something that will have people talking for years afterward."

"Something this new club is planning, I assume."

"Exactly."

Duncan was frustrated. "We've never had secrets before, Randolph. Why do you insist on starting now?"

Randolph chuckled. "Never had secrets, eh? How about the secret life you were leading in the French quarter? Whores! Bulls and bears! Cockfights! Being chosen King of Twelfth Night and a duel, no less! I am hardly the secretive one!"

Duncan conceded, basking in his brother's good-natured jibe. "Touché. But at least tell me the name of this club. Don't tell me that's a secret, too."

"It won't be after Mardi Gras," Randolph said with some satisfaction. "And I don't suppose it will do any harm to share it now." He leaned close, as though relating an intimate confidence, and only then did Duncan realize he took the matter of the secret club very seriously. "We are named for a masque written in 1634 by one of your favorite poets. It praised chastity and portrays the eponymous god as a sorcerer."

Duncan knew the poet immediately. "John Milton." He paused to think further. Of course!

"Comus!"

CHAPTER 12

Iris and Catin huddled in the kitchen. Wintry gusts tore around the tiny building, but it was not the bitter wind that kept the women cowering before the fire.

Through the lace-draped windows, they watched the silhouette of Hilaire Blancard pace back and forth. It periodically blocked and revealed the glow of two argand lamps. Aside from the fire Catin had built for him, they were the only lights in the house. That Blancard's anger grew as he waited for the absent Chaillot was obvious. What he would do when she returned was anyone's guess, but the terrified servants had done their share of speculating. Their short time in the peculiar household had already taught them to expect the unexpected from Hilaire Blancard. His moods were as fast-rising as the winter storm that had descended on the delta, and sometimes just as dark.

"I told her to be back before he got home," Iris wailed.

"You know Missie Chaillot listens to no one but herself," Catin ventured. "Now she will pay."

Inside the main house. Blancard lit a cigar and sat at last, settling into a chair facing the front door. As he waited, fury seething, he took deep breaths and reconsidered Meilleure's poisonous words.

The man had gone straight to the bank, all but flaunting his drunkenness as he burst into Blancard's offices with the nasty news. At first, Blancard hadn't believed him. It was inconceivable that his adoring Chaillot would publicly keep company with another white man without first asking permission, even if the gentleman in question was her own mother's keeper. She didn't ask, Blancard decided, because she knew he would refuse. The only white man she could be seen with was himself. It was an unspoken, understood rule and she had broken it. But what to do with her? He took a long sip from his whiskey and drew deeply from his cigar, plotting, planning.

It was in a wreath of pungent smoke that Chaillot found him. Her heart skipped a beat and she gasped, her hand flying nervously to her throat.

"Michie Hilaire!" she gasped. "Why, you look like Lucifer himself, lurking in that glowing cloud. Such fire and brimstone!" She rushed to kiss him but his words froze her in her tracks.

"My dear Chaillot," he said in a leaden voice, "have you ever wondered if I might, in fact, be the devil himself?"

"What a thing to say!" she said, giggling uncertainly.

Chaillot tried without success to will her feet to move. She struggled desperately to read his mood, to gauge how drunk he might be. She wondered if that awful man on the lakeshore had somehow managed to get to Blancard with news of her whereabouts. Her speculation ended when Blancard rose suddenly and took her in his arms. He kissed her with deceptive tenderness and brushed her cheek with a fingertip.

"I've missed you terribly, *ma cher*. You cannot imagine how utterly bereft I was to come here and find you out."

"I'm . . . I'm sorry I wasn't home," she said. "I was—"

"To pass the time," he interrupted, "I went out again and bought something for you." He nodded toward a beautifully wrapped package atop a marble-topped table.

"You are too generous," Chaillot said, feeling a little relief. He wasn't mad after all; he had even brought her a present. She would explain her absence in due time. "May I open it now?"

"Not now."

"Very well, michie. Then shall I ring for supper? You must be famished. I know I am."

"I'm famished," he said, bending down to taste her throat. "But not for food."

Chaillot smiled. Things were going better than she had expected. His enunciation and the intensity of whiskey breath revealed his exact level of inebriation, and she knew he was just mellow enough to desire her.

"Then I'll ring for Iris," she said.

"Not this time," Blancard insisted gently. "Might I not have the pleasure of undressing you?"

Her blush, all too real, inflamed him further. As did her courageous, calculated reply. "Of course, michie. If that is your desire."

"It is," he said. Then, "I want us to be completely alone tonight. I've told the girls as much. They won't disturb us."

"How romantic!"

Flooded with new confidence, Chaillot offered her lips for a kiss, and for once the man's touch did not repulse her. Certainly she did not welcome it, but neither did she find it disgusting as usual. Could it be that she actually liked Blancard a little? But she was too tired, her mind brimming with Gautier's shocking news, to entertain such a bizarre possibility.

"Shall we?" he smiled.

As they left, Blancard swept the present up with one hand while resting the other on Chaillot's neck. In the bedroom, he set the package on the dressing table, amidst the usual chaos of perfume bottles, and lit the fire. Glancing over his shoulder as he knelt at the hearth, he noted with satisfaction that the girl's eye went repeatedly to the mysterious box.

Greedy wench, he thought.

He took his time undressing her, deceiving her with his seeming serenity. He kissed wherever he removed an article of clothing, replacing her stockings with his mouth, her chemise with his lips. When she was naked at last, Chaillot reached for the sheets to cover herself. Although Blancard was always excited by her modesty, he also dismissed it as intrusive, even laughable. This woman, no matter how beauteous or impeccably mannered, would never be anything more than his colored whore.

"No," he insisted, reaching for the light and turning up the flame. "I want to look at you. And I want to see your pretty face when you open your present."

"As you wish." Chaillot smiled as the box was slipped into her small hands and, like a child, could not resist shaking it when she heard a strange clink inside. "Why, whatever could it be?"

"I suppose there's only one way to find out," he smiled. He watched closely as she tugged at the elaborate bow. "Oh, I almost forgot to ask. Where were you this afternoon?"

"Nowhere special," she replied lightly. And without thinking.

"Did you miss me?" he asked, fury stoked. Now he could add deception to the sin of disobedience. How dare this girl think she could misbehave so insolently and then hoodwink him into believing nothing untoward had occurred?

"Of course." Chaillot giggled girlishly as the ribbons fell away at last and she opened the box. Inside was a dark green velvet bag tied with gold tassels. She shook it again, mystified by the strange rattle. "Is it something to wear?"

"What a clever puss you are!"

Chaillot drew the cord, opening the bag so that its contents spilled onto the bed. The lanceolate eyes widened in shock and then a numbing fear. She started to speak but Blancard's hand closed swiftly over her mouth.

"They're the latest rage in Paris, my dear," he said, dangling iron slave shackles in her face. "I just hope they're not too large for these petite wrists!"

Chaillot was so stunned she was helpless to react. Blancard flipped her onto her bare belly, wrenched her hands behind her back and shackled her wrists together.

"Michie, don't . . . !"

She regretted the words instantly. Blancard twisted her head, cruelly wrenching her neck so that she faced him. "Don't what?"

In a very small voice, "Don't hurt me."

Blancard's smile turned her bowels to ice. "You know I would never mark anything so beautiful, so perfect." Chaillot had no time to consider the peculiar promise before he seethed once more. "So you're not asking why I'm doing this, only asking that I not hurt you. Well! Why is that, Chaillot? Is it because you know the answer already? Have you surmised that I had a most interesting visit this afternoon from a certain Monsieur Meilleure?"

Dear God! she thought. He knows about Marius! He knows and he's leapt to all sorts of terrible conclusions!

"Michie, please. Let me explain. It was a perfectly innocent train ride to Lake Ponchartrain. Many people saw us. Nothing was hidden."

"Except your devotion to me!" Blancard snarled. He stepped back and studied his tethered trophy, a perverse smile curling his lips when Chaillot struggled vainly to escape. The mere sight of her helpless writhing sent tingles of excitement to his loins, and he reached for the buttons of his waistcoat. Time for him to undress too.

"Why didn't you ask for permission?"

"I . . . I didn't think it was necessary," Chaillot insisted. Remembering Gautier's bold lie, she hastily added, "I visit *maman* all the time without asking permission. Monsieur Gautier is only her keeper. Michie Hilaire, please listen to me! He is a fine gentleman, nothing more."

"Perhaps this fine gentleman has an eye for something younger than your mother," Blancard snapped, stripping to his underclothes. The evidence of his arousal made Chaillot turn away. She shuddered when she felt his hand stroking her flanks, eventually insinuating itself between her thighs and brushing her pubic down. "The fabulous Colette is a prize indeed, but nothing can compare with meat this fresh."

"Please don't talk like that, monsieur," Chaillot pleaded. "It frightens me!"

Her timidity made Blancard roar with laughter. She shrank from him. "How dare you make demands of me, mademoiselle? You must never forget who and what you are. Or, more importantly, who *I* am!" His open palm caught her squarely across the buttocks. "Never!" Chaillot moaned as the man continued to rain blows, staining her derriere with angry pink handprints. "When I heard what you had done, I remembered how my *Nonc* Michel used to discipline his slaves. That's what my girl needs, I thought. Ah, yes! Some discipline!"

Chaillot's fear was turning to anger, a rage she was helpless to rein. She knew it was useless to resist, but she could not help herself. All the loathing she so carefully controlled bubbled forth in one long defiant hiss.

"I'm not your slave!"

She regretted the words as soon as they were uttered. She screamed when Blancard's fingers shot between her thighs, driving suddenly and sharply into her tender flesh. A second scream was stillborn when a pillow slip was shoved hard into her mouth.

"You are whatever I say you are!" Blancard railed. "You have no voice in this arrangement, no say-so in the matter of *plaçage*. If you act like a disobedient slave, you must be treated like one."

Chaillot shook her head like a dog with a bone, struggling to dislodge the gag and scream until her lungs ached. She was helpless. She rocked her body with every bit of strength she could summon, fury mounting as though fueled by Blancard's roars of coarse, humiliating laughter. She writhed and whimpered like the most pitiful of trapped animals, fighting to keep her flesh from further violation.

But in the midst of the madness, she realized the man had retreated and was laying beside her, lightly stroking her shoulder. A comforting croon had replaced the hideous laughter.

"Shhh," he whispered. "It's all right now. You've had a little scare, but I'm here to protect you."

Chaillot could only guess at the depths of the man's insanity as he turned her gently toward him and removed the gag. He crushed his mouth to hers, so tight she could barely breathe, and gripped her shackled wrists. He held the chain tight against her flesh as he nudged her knee high with his, parting her thighs.

"Now," he sighed.

Chaillot moaned with surrender as he entered her. Having no more spirit to fight and bewildered by his madness, she closed her eyes tight and willed herself into a dark, impersonal void where she felt nothing, least of all his crude, insistent thrusts. Mercifully it ended quickly. She scarcely heard the guttural groans when the man's crisis passed, but she was all too aware of what was said afterward.

"You know I would never really hurt you, don't you, *ma petit?*" She moaned, rubbing sore wrists as the shackles were removed at last. "Don't you?" he pressed. She nodded against his chest, believing herself only slightly less than she believed him, especially when she heard his poisonous addendum. "Just as you know if you ever tried to get away from me, I would hire men to track you down to the ends of the earth." She nodded again. "*C'est bon.* Now open your eyes, Chaillot. I've something to match them."

Catching the firelight, the stones so dazzled Chaillot that she actually covered her eyes. When she looked again, she thought herself dreaming. Blancard was dangling a spectacular necklace of diamonds and sapphires.

"If you had behaved yourself, *ma petit,*" Blancard said, "you could have had this without the *bracelet.*" He retrieved the shackles from the tangle of damp sheets and dangled them from his other hand. He watched with no small satisfaction as Chaillot's eyes went from one to the other and back again. How he loved toying with inferiors! "The choice will always be yours, Chaillot. Pleasure or pain. Your behavior makes the decision. Remember that." He coughed hard, voice catching deep in his voice as he grunted the last words. "Or better yet, remember Josette."

Chaillot was far too terrified to ask what he meant. The hideous hunger in his eyes warned her to promise in a very small voice, "I'll remember."

"Good girl." Blancard kissed her on the forehead like an obedient child and draped the heavy necklace around her neck. "I was right. It does wonderful things to your eyes."

"It's heavy," she whispered, not knowing what else to say.

"Somehow women always manage to bear such burdens," Blancard grunted tiredly.

As always, sex wearied Blancard. In a matter of moments, he was snoring against Chaillot's bosom. She studied his once-handsome face, coarse and puffy with drink as it rose and fell with her own breathing. The hard mouth had softened and the eyelids concealed a malevolence that had all but exploded from his gaze, yet an undeniable cruelty emanated from this man to whom she now belonged.

I was wrong, she thought bitterly. When I told him I was not his slave I was wrong. I am his property as surely as if he had bought me under the dome at the St. Louis Hotel. And unless I break free of him I am just as doomed. But how? Is escape from this man really possible? Surely he *would* track me to the ends of the earth.

Chaillot fingered the necklace. It was by far the most extravagant gift Blancard had ever given her and, therefore, the most valuable. She and her mother had discussed Blancard's wealth and generosity at length and, with Colette's expert coaching, she had grown skilled in estimating the value of fine jewelry. Unless she missed her guess, this item alone was enough to ensure financial security for the rest of her life.

But what would that life be worth if Blancard came looking for her?

The din of the *Café de Aguila* faded into oblivion as Christophe read the poem, toying with his moustache as usual. While Duncan watched nervously, the fingers tugged, twirled, and stroked, reacting to Christophe's mood. His dark eyes danced at first, then hardened as the poem provoked serious thoughts. The full lips were set in a grim line until something saddened him with amazing swiftness. A tear slipped from one eye and trailed into his moustache where the busy fingers massaged it away.

"It's beautiful, *mon ami!* Absolutely beautiful. All that glorious Byzantine imagery breaks my heart. I would never have thought a *Yanqui* could have such exquisite feelings of love."

"Oh, the devil with you!" Duncan said, snatching the poem from his friend and tucking it carefully inside his waistcoat. But his annoyance was scarcely heartfelt. Try as he might, he could never be truly angry with Christophe. "You French didn't invent passion, you know."

Christophe's response was utterly guileless. "We didn't?"

His performance triggered a burst of laughter from Duncan. "Oh, dear Christophe! What am I to do with you?"

"*Mais non!*" Christophe insisted, gesturing wildly. "The question is what am I to do with you? Here you are, a man overflowing with passion and feeling and desire, a marvelous zest for living, and I didn't even know it! If you can write such things without a woman, imagine what you could do *with* one! But perhaps I am wrong! Tell me, where did you find such inspiration? Eugénie, no doubt? What's this? You are shaking your head. Then I shall guess again. Ah! I have it! The whore at Madame Pearl's! What was her name?"

"Virginia."

"Virginia!"

"It was not Virginia," Duncan said. And if I told you the truth, he thought, you would not believe it. "And there will be no more guessing games. A poet's inspiration is sacred."

"As you say," Christophe conceded, retreating gracefully but with discontent. He understood his friend well enough to know there were deep pockets in Duncan's soul that he could never reach, and he masked his disappointment with humor. "I feel exactly the same way about making love."

"That's quite a segue," Duncan laughed.

"I suppose. Nevertheless, it's true. I'm deeply inspired at such moments and my inspiration is sacred, too."

"Oh, I'm quite certain of that," Duncan said, ill-concealing his amusement.

"Which reminds me! Suppose we make a return visit to Madam Pearl's tonight? I know of no man who leaves that place unmoved. Including yourself."

"Oh, I don't know, Christophe." Randolph's warnings still rang in his ears.

It was more a desire for privacy than the din in the coffee house that made Christophe leaned close to Duncan's ear. "The body is like a hotel, my boy. Instead of many rooms, it has many appetites, and if they aren't all filled, the entire building suffers."

"If that's an example of your imagery," Duncan said, roaring with laughter, "I should advise you to steer clear of poetry!"

Now it was Christophe pretending to be hurt. "In any case, we could both use some sport this evening. What do you say we begin with a little supper at my house, some billiards and perhaps even a turn at the *Salle d'Orleans* before calling on the ladies at Madame Pearl's?"

"It sounds very exciting," Duncan conceded, "Especially the quadroon ball. I have to admit I enjoyed it the first time."

"Then you'll go?"

Duncan shook his head. "I'm deeply tempted, but I must decline. I want to write tonight. A poet is seduced when the muse is courting."

"*Eh bien!*" Christophe stood and whipped on his cloak with great flair, very nearly dislodging his cup of café au lait from the table. "So I must leave you to be seduced by some ancient Greek entity when you could instead partake of the voluptuous fruits of some flesh and blood . . ."

"Off with you!" Duncan laughed. He stood as Christophe kissed him on both cheeks before cutting a swath through the cloud of cigar smoke and disappearing into the Rue Royale. Duncan chuckled to himself and ruminated over the last of his coffee before deciding a morning stroll would clear his head.

Outside, a few weak shards of sun pierced the otherwise leaden skies. For no particular reason, Duncan turned toward the French Market. It was one of his favorite places to explore, as it was for many tourists, especially those from the North. If the casual visitor had not been immediately smitten by the city's exotic flavor, a trip to the market with its Babel-esque ambience convinced them. Like Duncan, they were baffled by the amalgam of languages; they easily identified Spanish and German, and of course the mellifluous Creole French, but were mystified by the Turkish, Greek, and Choctaw which fell on the ear with as much cacophony as Maltese.

The market stretched along the bustling levee across from Jackson Square. A squat structure with a low-pitched tile roof and thick-columned, arcaded sides, it housed over a hundred stalls offering freshly slaughtered lamb, pork, beef, and mutton, and fowl that included turkey, guinea fowl, duck, and pigeon. Enormous woven osiers overflowed with red fish, lake and river shrimp, croakers, crab, frogs, and terrapin and many fish Duncan couldn't identify. Baskets and crates were heaped with cabbage, lettuce, chicory, beets, and carrots, and fruit stands flashed the bright hues of bananas, apples, cherries, oranges, lemons, and all variety of grapes. Duncan was astonished at the bounty Louisiana yielded in the dead of winter.

Like Gallatin Street just two blocks away, the French Market was nearly impassable at three in the morning but now, as the clock approached nine, the crowds had considerably thinned. Still, it required patience and a certain amount of navigational skill to thread one's way through the throngs of shoppers bearing every imaginable type of basket.

Nuns in stiff white headdresses rubbed elbows with prostitutes from the District, both perusing oranges and comparing discordant notes. Negro mammies sold pralines with pecans or pink and white cocoanut. Indian squaws squatted atop filthy blankets, delicately woven baskets filled with filé powder to thicken madame's gumbo, while their braves half-heartedly hawked blowguns as souvenirs indispensable for the visitors from Philadelphia and Boston. Duncan was startled by a brilliant flash of scarlet and emerald green as a Colapissa Indian thrust a blur of feathers in his face. The jungle macaw obligingly spread his wings and accompanied the gaudy display with an ear-piercing screech. Shaking his head vigorously, Duncan retreated and caught his breath.

Most out of place and yet a presence almost from the beginning were those who sought the chaos of the French Market for other purposes. Clandestine meetings of all sorts, most hasty, some lingering, transpired hourly. Many involved the exchange of *billet-doux*, sometimes between agents, other times between the lovers themselves. Duncan smiled watching a desperate Creole youth stalk his beloved, carefully slipping an envelope in her hand while her chaperone haggled over the price of bananas. If the distracted *tante* did not witness the bold deed, she was the only one in the market who did not. Duncan guessed that such women had been seeing and not seeing such things for generations, and, in their youth, had likely been in the girl's place.

The smells were as captivating as the sights and sounds, everything from crab and crawfish to roses and freshly fried *calas*, coarse rice fritters so dear to the hearts and bellies of the Creole. Duncan now knew enough French to translate the cries of the vendors calling *"Bels calas, bels calas, tout chauds!"* Beautiful and hot! he thought. A statuesque Negress, elegant in her multicolored *tignon*, sold steaming coffee to chilled *domestiques* shopping for their mistress's dinner while their masters bought nosegays to wear to work that day.

Duncan surrendered willingly, eager to be swept up by this exotic tableau that could be played out nowhere in the world but New Orleans. It was a colorful collision of Europe, the Mediterranean, Africa, and the Caribbean that had improbably impacted on the Mississippi River delta. The unreality of it all was hypnotic.

The sun felt good on his face as he lingered on the periphery of the chaos and watched the unfolding of endlessly intriguing vignettes. It was, as Christophe once said, the greatest free show in town, one which never wearied Duncan. He perched atop a stack of empty crates in an effort to get more comfortable when something caught his eye that was all the more arresting because it was so unexpected.

Seemingly oblivious to the ebb and flow of the crowds, her arm linked through that of a chicly dressed quadroon, the woman moved through the madness like the most graceful sailboat imaginable. She was completely covered in a hooded, street-length cape of navy merino that revealed nothing but her face. It was a face that brought Duncan swiftly to his feet and set his heart pounding. The name burst from his mouth.

"Justine!"

He started toward her and froze. At first he wished Christophe were present to guide him through the etiquette requisite for approaching the woman. Then he was grateful to be alone, for what he intended to do was nothing his friend need know about. Not yet, anyway.

Strange, Duncan thought, as Justine grew nearer and he felt his body flush with the heat of an unnatural sun. What the mind battles and the body resists, the heart can command. As though hypnotized, he moved into Justine's path and stood until she approached. He was helpless to resist her charm, just as he could not keep from stripping away the cloak and envisioning her as he had in his dream.

It seemed everything about this woman was unexpected.

Justine moved on, unaware. When at last her gaze sought his from the dark depths of the hood, her heart clutched so hard as to be painful. Her response was frightening because it was spawned by a man she had met only once, someone who had entered and exited her life like an operatic tenor with but a single aria. Now he emerged, in the wan, wintry sunlight, as something far more than that, a man who, she learned only now, loomed deep in her soul. For a moment, she thought she would go mad.

Oddly, neither could find their tongue and it was left to a perplexed Toinette Clovis to interpret. "Do you know him, madame?" she hissed. Justine nodded, pale face flooding with color. Like Duncan, she wished and did not wish that they were alone. When Justine remained mute, Toinette curtsied and introduced herself, hoping to prod a name from the tall *Américain* blocking their way.

"Duncan Saunders," he managed at last. Then, after another awkward, lost pause, "I am an acquaintance of Madame Blancard."

"And you must forgive me," Justine said, recovering along with him. "I was surprised to see you." Toinette eyed them both suspiciously as Justine's hand slipped from her cloak and into his. "How delightful, Monsieur Saunders."

"The pleasure is mine, Madame Blancard."

As he bent over her hand, Duncan cursed the gloves blocking her flesh from his lips. He lingered longer than necessary, something that did not go unnoticed by either woman. When he released Justine's hand, she blushed anew and tucked it back in her cloak. Then, abruptly, she steeled herself and addressed him frankly.

"I have not seen you since your Twelfth Night coronation, monsieur. You have been well?"

"As well as a dethroned monarch can be," he smiled. When he received a blank look, he asked Justine if she had not heard about his forced abdication.

"I have not ventured out since that night," she explained, "but since I pay no attention to gossip I wouldn't have known anyway." She grimaced. "These feuds between Creole and American can be so tiresome."

"I agree."

She tilted her head back and sought his eyes with hers. "Personally I thought Eugénie made an excellent choice."

"In all modesty," Duncan laughed, "so did I!"

When the laughter died, Toinette extricated herself from the heavy silence that ensued. While she pretended to browse a stack of osiers teeming with iridescent crab, Justine surprised herself as much as Duncan by taking his arm. They strolled toward the levee, not venturing far from Toinette. Justine had reasons for remaining close to her new friend.

"And you, Madame Blancard. Have you been well?"

"Why, yes," she replied, lying with a skill mastered long ago. Her radiance gave no clue that she had endured so many terrible, intimate in-clemencies.

"Might I ask why you have stayed at home all this time?"

"You may not, sir," she replied, battling the memory of Blancard at-tacking her with the rouge. Coming from anyone else, Duncan would have been offended by the dismissal, but in fact he not only respected her response but found it intriguing.

"I didn't mean to pry," he said.

"I'm sure you didn't," Justine agreed. "And I certainly take no offense from the query."

"There's so much I don't know about protocol with French ladies," he lamented. "Christophe has tried to coach me, but . . . well, obviously I'm still quite awkward."

"To the contrary. I find you most charming. And at the risk of ap-pearing too bold myself, I must add that I cannot remember when I've had a more invigorating conversation than the one we shared Twelfth Night. You see, Mr. Saunders, you are perhaps the only gentleman, American, Creole, or otherwise, who has ever spoken to me as if I pos-sessed a brain."

"Indeed!"

She nodded. "I've no doubt you understand my inference. I've heard enough about Tidewater Virginia to know it's an aristocracy consider-ably older than ours, one that also finds it necessary to ensconce women on pedestals and leave them there when conversation, or anything else for that matter, turns serious."

"Your comments are bold indeed, madame," Duncan said, smile blooming. "I find them most refreshing. I too felt something special about our conversation on the Byzantine. I found myself discussing things I'd never discussed with ladies."

"Then we're off to a fine start, eh?" she asked, returning his smile. She tossed her head and the hood fell away, revealing a tightly bound chignon. The sunlight remained pale, but the ebony hair caught it and he was stunned yet again by her beauty. "C'est bon," she said, almost as an afterthought.

They paused, watching the slow upriver passage of a heavily laden Indiaman, riding dangerously low in the water. Although there was probably a safe distance between them, the vessel seemed hellbent on a collision course with a blunt-nosed trading brig heading toward the Gulf. Justine gripped Duncan's arm until the moment of danger, imag-inary or otherwise, passed.

But her thoughts were not on the ships, rather the hideous chimera of her past, which Duncan had stirred with his gentle touch. As it soared through her mind, tormenting her as it sought safe harbor, she rebuked it. Instead she considered Toinette's ardent assurance that men like Hilaire Blancard were monstrous rarities and that gentler male souls overwhelmingly prevailed. Justine knew Duncan Saunders was such a soul. He had communicated as much with no more than a smile, a fragile touch, as though he feared she might break, a glance that stirred her in ways she had always associated with terror. Was it possible that what happened between her and Blancard would be different with other men? Could it be, again as Toinette insisted, that kindness and consideration could replace the ugliness that Blancard always brought to the bedroom?

This sort of musing deeply shocked Justine, not only because it was something ladies never thought about, much less verbalized, but also because the man who had inspired such yearnings was standing beside her. She was at a loss to understand her thoughts, bewildered by her reaction to this near-stranger. When his hand discreetly closed over hers, pressing ever so slightly where it nestled in the crook of his arm, Justine understood. And her heart was wild with the realization.

Duncan Saunders thrilled her in ways that Blancard terrified her! For the first time in her life, she enjoyed the touch of a man, even one as chaste and innocent as this.

"Tell me!" she gasped, so loud Duncan was startled.

"Madame?"

"Tell me if you have written anything since we last spoke. You mentioned that you felt great inspiration from New Orleans but had yet to put quill to paper."

Now it was Duncan's turn to blush. The poem tucked in his waistcoat was fragile indeed, but suddenly it had the weight of a tome and seemed to crush his chest. "I wrote my first poem. It's about . . . the Byzantine. A love paean of sorts."

The enormous eyes widened. "To be bold again, monsieur, might I read it some time?"

"I would be honored, although I must warn you it might be considered indelicate in part."

"I assure you I am capable of approaching it from a purely intellectual standpoint," she said, immediately wondering if she spoke the truth or not.

"In that case," he said, releasing her hand long enough to retrieve the poem, "here."

"Oh!" Justine smiled as she took the poem. "I didn't expect you to have it with you. Shall I read it now?"

Duncan coughed into a glove, freeing the words stuck in his throat.

"No, Madame Blancard. Please take it with you and peruse it in private. It would embarrass us both if you read it now."

"But why?"

This time the words came easier, as though rehearsed. "I know it is caddish and coarse because you are a married lady, but I could not help myself. The poem was written for you and about you." Justine's lips formed a little "o" of benign shock. "You are the maiden in the orchid pavilion, floating in the restless, sun-silvered seas. It is you who sorely tempts the . . ."

Justine's gloved finger stilled his lips. "Tell me no more, monsieur, lest I have no need to read it myself!"

"You are not disgusted by such impetuosity?"

"To the contrary, monsieur, I am deeply flattered. As you say, I am a married lady." She dared squeeze the inside of his elbow. "But I am also a woman." She gave the man a moment to consider the provocative pronouncement before withdrawing her hand and offering it in farewell. "And now Madame Clovis and I must be on our way. We were merely taking a detour through the market before going to her shop in the Rue Royale. *La Mode.*"

"She is your *modiste* then?" Duncan asked as he escorted her back to Toinette.

"Oh, much more than that. Toinette is a dear friend and a great lady. I'm not ashamed to say it."

"I see."

Duncan did his best to hide his shock. It was common enough for whites to form a close bond with Negroes, slave as well as free, but it was quite another for Justine to distinguish the woman as "a lady." Yes, he thought. Madame Blancard is a personality of many, most unexpected facets.

"Then I look forward to hearing your critique of my poem upon our next meeting."

"And when might that be?" Justine blurted. Then she giggled at her brashness as well as his bemusement. "This seems to be our day for shattering conventions, eh, monsieur?"

But Duncan heard only her first words. "You need only name the place and time, madame. I am your servant."

How I wish that were true, she thought. "Here. At this hour. Tomorrow."

"I will be here without fail."

He kissed her hand, pained with longing as she withdrew and took Toinette's arm. He felt as though a part of him had been ripped away and mourned its passing as Justine drew the hood over her head and disappeared into the throng.

"*Adieu,*" he whispered. "Until tomorrow."

Justine was aware that Toinette had seen her tuck the poem inside her cloak. She knew her good friend was discreet enough not to question her, but in truth she could not wait to tell her what had happened. More than that, of course, she was desperate to be alone to read the poem.

"I know this sounds impossibly vulgar," she hissed to Toinette, "but I must tell someone or I will surely explode. Thank goodness you are with me."

"What on earth did that man say to you?" Toinette asked. "I've never seen you more radiant, not even at the opera."

"Nothing," Justine said. "That's the miracle I believe."

"I don't understand."

"Neither do I, Toinette. All I can tell you is that the man has stirred something in me that I didn't know existed. And it has been there ever since we met a week ago."

"I'm more confused than ever."

But Justine was unhearing. "I know this is sinful to say, but I'm so glad that Eugénie Duval didn't sink her claws into him."

Recognition dawned on Toinette. "I thought his name sounded familiar. Monsieur Saunders is the one she chose as her king on Twelfth Night."

"You know about that?"

"Of course," Toinette laughed. "Good heavens, Justine! You are perhaps the only one in New Orleans who doesn't know. What a scandal that was! And the *almost* duel that followed!"

Justine gripped her arm tight. "I want to know every detail, Toinette. Every single detail. Leave out nothing!"

"Since when have you cared anything for gossip?"

"Since it involves Duncan Saunders!" Justine announced with unfeigned ferocity.

Inside her cloak she moved the poem closer to her heart. She could not know it, but that small piece of paper would catapult her life to an unimaginable apogee.

CHAPTER 13

It was not merely the imagery that swept Justine high over the walls of *La Mode*'s quiet little garden. It was confirmation that she was indeed the inspiration for this rich tapestry of a poem.

As she read of the moon-drenched seas and gilded deserts, the impudently phallic fountains, and fertile plains, she knew she was the maiden of whom Duncan Saunders so ardently wrote. It was she, not Roxelana, who was the *raison d'etre* for this mystical, mythical love paean, the whore/goddess who seduced the sultan's son and toppled a dynasty as old as time itself.

It was she whom Duncan loved!

Her hands trembled as she folded the poem and tucked it inside her cloak. She closed her eyes and drifted, face warmed by sunlight unleashed by the January wind. It seemed, at that moment, that she had always been cold, that not until now had she felt any real warmth in her soul. It did not, she knew, come from the sun. Something was happening to her, something she was helpless to rein, just as she was powerless against the recurring ravishments of her husband.

Justine drifted, mind, body, and soul wrapped in a cocoon of obsession, her thoughts dominated by one thing, one man. Even though her eyes were closed, she saw Duncan. His strong face, kind, gentle, compassionate, perhaps even a little ingenuous, locked away everything else, and for a rare moment Justine forgot all else. There was, for now, no terrible past, no tenuous present, and no conception of a future.

Justine knew what it was because it was innate to every human being. For some it blossomed immediately; for others it required careful nurturing. For others still, such as her husband, it was tragically stillborn. It had lain dormant in her, pummeled into submissive silence and never allowed to grow, first by her father, then by Blancard. Was it possible to be stirred this late, and by a man she had met only once, a man she scarcely knew and yet felt she had always known? Was it possible at all, with him, with anyone?

Did she love Duncan Saunders?

Justine's thoughts tumbled and collided, rippled and melted one into the other. They were at once cogent and indecipherable and as exotic as the Byzantine love poem. She burned, although not from the sun, but from a burgeoning heat of the heart that had smoldered undetected, like fire in the hold of a ship. It was threatening to ignite now and consume the entire vessel, and she had never, not even with Blancard at his worst, been so terrified in her life.

"Some coffee, Madame Blancard?"

Justine's eyes fluttered open and she awoke as though from a deep sleep. She saw Nicole's smiling face and nodded. "Why, yes. *Merci.*"

"Madame Clovis will be out directly. She's with a customer just now."

"Fine."

"Are you feeling better? You don't seem so pale as before."

"Yes. Sitting here in the sun seems to have helped."

Nicole nodded and left her alone again. After leaving the French Market, Justine's heart had raced so wildly that she had all but collapsed in the Rue Royale. Something lingering from the encounter with Duncan had trailed and clutched at her soul, so undermining her strength that she had sagged against Toinette and nearly fainted. Now, after reading the poem and being soothed by the quiet of the jewel-like garden, she felt much better. Indeed she had an aura of robustness when Toinette came to study her patient over the familiar gold-rimmed glasses.

"Ah! You look much improved."

"Much," answered Justine. She sipped the steaming café au lait. "And this is perfect. What's this? The coffee seems to have a bite."

"A bit of brandy never hurt anyone," Toinette smiled. "Some might even say it does the coffee good. I'm having a little myself." Justine nodded and sipped again.

"Can you tell me now what happened? You seemed fine one moment, so animated and alive, and the next . . . well, my dear! You gave me quite a fright."

"I gave myself one too," Justine conceded. "And, yes, I will explain as best I can. Perhaps I should begin by letting you read this."

Like Christophe, Toinette's emotions registered easily on her face as she read the poem. She smiled, frowned, and wiped away a tear before returning the paper.

"It's exquisite. But what has it to do with you?"

"I am Roxelana," she sighed blissfully. "And the poem was written by Monsieur Saunders."

"Is that what he passed to you in the marketplace? *Oui?* How bold! I never dreamed it might be a *billet-doux.*"

"Nor I."

Justine rose and paced the tiny garden, the hem of her cloak raking bushes laden with camellia blossoms. She took no note of the shattered petals left in her wake. Soon the narrow path was strewn with pink and white blooms gleaming in the deepening sunlight. The garden was warm now, one of many tropical oases in the chilled *carré de la ville.* Justine was reminded of that chill when the wind-tattered banana leaves clattered in the stillness.

"And yet it's so very peculiar," she continued. "I was shocked when the man gave me the poem, even more so to learn that he had written it about me. Yet once I read it I felt it the most natural thing in the world."

"You know what it is, of course. This feeling."

"I think so," Justine nodded. "But I'm afraid to say the word."

"It's no wonder, considering the wretched journey Blancard has taken you on!"

Toinette all but snarled. She could hardly speak the man's name without dripping vitriol. She wondered, not idly, about the daguerreotype moldering in the backyard of Marie Laveau's house. She conjured images of the man's portrait as it melted and faded, deteriorating into dust. And she prayed to someone other than God that the evil man himself would suffer the same fate.

"Do you want me to say it for you?" she asked at last.

Justine nodded.

"He's in love with you, *ma chére.*"

Justine spun around, hood falling from her hair. "And I with him!"

Toinette rose slowly. "But how is this possible?"

"If I had the answer, I would be the sphinx herself," Justine replied. "I cannot explain it. In truth, I did not even like the man on our first meeting. I developed a certain fondness later that same night but it meant nothing to me. Only now have I come to realize the truth. Today. When I saw him in the marketplace."

"But you're married!"

Justine's face darkened but briefly before responding to the hasty pronouncement. "You of all people should realize the meaninglessness of that statement, Toinette."

"You're right, of course. I spoke without thought." She thought, mind racing, of the inescapable barriers that would strangle such a hopeless liaison. "But your love for this *Yanqui* who writes romantic poetry does not alter the fact."

Justine was unhearing. "Yes, he is romantic, isn't he? I never knew the meaning of the word until today." Her tone changed abruptly when she added, "I've told you what happened on my wedding night." Toinette repeated her dire warning. "It alters nothing except that I now feel like a changed . . . no, a different woman. Somehow not as helpless as before."

You didn't even know you were helpless, Toinette thought grimly. You thought all husbands were like Blancard, that what went on in your bed was echoed in the boudoirs of the world. But it was hardly the time to bring this up. It was something she had all but hammered into Justine since that sickening moment when she found her naked body covered with rouge.

"I'm loathe to spoil a beautiful moment," Toinette said slowly, "but again we must speak of the truth. The consequences for adulterous love are enormous. You well know that with Blancard they could be fatal."

"Blancard!" Justine fairly spat the word. She returned to the small iron bench and perched among its graceful black swirls. She thought for a moment, eye drifting to a purple banana pod sticky with nectar. "How could I be such a fool? There is no way I will ever escape his madness."

"How has he been of late?"

"When I've seen him, which has been most infrequently, he has been a perfect lamb," Justine said. She lamented the fact because this was inevitably the calm preceding the storm. She nodded politely as Nicole returned with more steaming coffee. "I've told you how wildly his moods fluctuate. He can be gentle as a kitten one moment and bare lion's claws the next. When I hear his feet on the stairs outside my room, I never know which man will darken my door." She sipped the coffee, pleased that it too was laced with brandy. "There is, however, one thing that helps me predict his mood."

"What's that?"

"His mistress."

At the mention of Chaillot, Nicole froze, then pretended to notice the garden path littered with camellia petals. She fetched the broom propped in a corner and proceeded to sweep quietly.

"I can only assume that he's as brutal toward the poor girl as he is to me."

"You astonish me, Justine. Not only do you acknowledge your husband's mistress, which is highly unconventional, especially when the confidence is made to another woman of color, you actually pity her."

"I understand far more about slavery than most white women," Justine said with meaning. Toinette thought her heart would break. "In any case, I also assume when this girl sates his evil appetites that he chooses to let me be. Now, because he shows me virtually no interest, I imagine he is most content in his perverse liaison."

"Dear God," Nicole sighed.

Toinette spun around, suddenly aware of the woman's presence. "Leave the sweeping until later, Nicole. There's more important work inside." When they were alone again, Toinette took Justine's hands in hers and asked what she was going to do now.

"Make a novena and pray for guidance," Justine said. "And meet Monsieur Saunders tomorrow at the marketplace."

"*Mais non!* You don't dare!"

A shadow passed over Justine's pale face, mirroring clouds as they dispatched the winter sun into seclusion. "Perhaps. Perhaps not." A long, heavy pause told Toinette this woman had a newfound determination not easily dissuaded.

"I see."

"What you said earlier," Justine edged, "about the consequences of discovery. What is the worst that could happen?"

"You know yourself," Toinette replied darkly.

"He would kill me."

Toinette grimaced. Was it truly possible they were discussing something as unimaginable as murder while they, two well-born ladies, sipped their coffee in this lovely garden?

"Possibly."

"Probably."

"You know him better than I."

"All too well I'm afraid. But my point is this, Toinette. My life now is scarcely more than a living death. At least it was until I met Duncan Saunders. If I am to die pursuing the one thing that makes me want to live, then so be it. I would rather be dead than continue as I am now."

"Oh, my darling Justine!" Toinette wailed. "That a person such as yourself should have to make such a terrible choice!"

Chaillot stood in the doorway of the cottage, waving tiredly as Blancard climbed into the carriage. Blancard was especially pleased with himself. He had been with the girl four straight days, and in that time she had drunk deep from his well of degradation and depravity.

What changes he had wrought since introducing her to the handcuffs! And how delicious it had been to see her wearing them as though they were the most precious of diamond bracelets. Indeed, the image he carried with him as Hippolyte drove him home was one of Chaillot as she had been last night, kneeling in the middle of the bed, hands draped between her thighs. She had been naked except for the handcuffs and the sapphire necklace, and the spectacle had roused Blancard to an almost painful stiffness.

"*Magnifique!*" he muttered, the exquisitely erotic memory very nearly rousing him again.

It had been difficult for Blancard to gauge just how much Chaillot enjoyed his handiwork. She could be quite the little actress. How diligently he had sought to attain that golden moment when her moans were a perfect amalgam of ecstasy and pain. How carefully he massaged her nipples and stung her buttocks with his fingertips, eliciting thrilling little whimpers as he watched the pale flesh turn rubicund. Even now the memory imparted the familiar rush of power he so craved.

Such omnipotence must sometimes be reined, however. Once when Blancard had Chaillot cuffed and turned onto her belly, he had been sorely tempted to enter by the other gate, but he decided she was not yet ready for such an invasion. It was a naughty alternative introduced to him by the lusty, amoral Bricktop, but he had not worked its perverse pleasures on a woman. In time, he told himself. In time he would try all of it and more, much more. Perhaps even the ultimate, as he had done with Josette. The pursuit of that satanic *ne plus ultra* had gripped Blancard's soul of late and begun to eclipse everything else in his world. For the first time in his life he had ignored business, for the last few days choosing the bedroom over his office as he languished with Chaillot and pushed his demonic desires to new depths. He felt his life changing because of this woman and surrendered to her as she surrendered to him.

Neither had any true choice.

In Chaillot, he thought triumphantly, he had found the perfect pilgrim for his exotic, misunderstood mission. She was nowhere near completely malleable, and, oh yes, she would be capable of serious resistance for some time, but isn't that what made it exciting? For now, any disharmony or misunderstanding on her part was a minor thing soothed with something as ridiculous as a necklace or, if necessary, a few well-aimed disciplinary blows. She would yield soon enough. All did. Besides, he thought with no small degree of satisfaction, what choice did she have in the matter? It had cost him dearly, but with that cottage and its furnishings, the gowns and the jewels, he had bought Chaillot as surely as he if had purchased a new slave.

Like Josette, she would never escape him.

But he forgot about Chaillot and abandoned the memory of her as the carriage turned onto the Rue Dauphine. Replacing it was Justine. Her image arose as soon as Blancard saw the house. It was ablaze with light, making him wonder if there might possibly be company. But Justine never entertained. Marie Tonton assured him of that. She had not even entertained Christophe Arnaud since that fateful Twelfth Night, when he had had to punish her for her vanity. He hadn't really wanted to, but he had had no choice. Indeed, what husband could let his wife comport herself like a whore without treating her accordingly? Certainly no responsible gentleman he knew!

Justine, he thought. Poor Justine. He considered his handiwork with her virtually complete. He supposed it was inevitable, but the girl no longer excited him. She was utterly submissive now, a sad, whining thing that aroused him only by accident. The rouge incident was a perfect example, and a sad one for Blancard. He rued the day when the woman herself did not naturally incite his furious arousal. Only through accidental misbehavior did she have any appeal, and now even that had all but ceased. He couldn't imagine that spineless soul doing anything to stir him, so she was best forgotten. No, he decided. Chaillot is more than enough for now. The woman rouses my greatest artistry, while Justine . . . well, she is only a wife.

As usual, Marie Tonton rushed to open the door while Figaro lurked obediently behind. "Do we have company?" Blancard asked.

"No, michie," she replied, eyes downcast as she dropped a curtsy. "Madame Blancard asked that we wait dinner in case the master returned. It's been that way for the past four days."

"Really?" Blancard asked, pleased in spite of himself. "The past four days, eh?"

"*Oui, monsieur.*"

He gave Marie Tonton his hat, cape, and gloves and surprised her by not asking for a report on her mistress' activities. It was just as well. Ever since Toinette had threatened her, Marie Tonton had been afraid to follow Justine anywhere, especially with Toinette in attendance. She was relieved when Blancard asked only where Justine was.

He found her in the parlor, immersed in a new book on the Byzantine. She wore an unusual but elegant gown of bronze watered silk, trimmed with gold lace and cut in modest décolleté. Pearl earrings and a small cameo at her throat were her only jewelry. Regardless of his numbed passion, Blancard conceded she was still a stunning woman.

"*Bon soir, madame.*"

"Good evening, Hilaire." She closed the book and rose, hastily smoothing her long skirts and risking something she had not done in years. She approached and looked directly in his eyes. "May I get you a whiskey?"

"*Bien sûr,*" he said. He glanced past her to a dining table covered with a snowy cloth and gleaming with china and silver. "Marie Tonton says you've waited dinner."

"As I now do every night, monsieur." Before Blancard could comment, she hurriedly added, "I know it's an indulgence on my part, and I most definitely should have asked your permission, but it was something I thought would please you. Although you take most of your meals elsewhere, I know you still have a fondness for Agathe's cooking." She smiled. "She reminds you of your childhood, does she not?"

"Why, yes, she does," Blancard agreed, puzzled by the uncharacteristic concern. He watched Justine hurriedly pour the whiskey, pleased when she remembered to be especially generous. When she slipped the glass into his hand, he muttered a low, "*Merci.*"

Justine's smile faded as she spoke in a far more serious vein. "Of course, if you are displeased we can repair to the bedroom whenever you like."

"Since when do matters of the boudoir interest you?"

He frowned, instantly on the alert. She had not welcomed him into the bedroom since their wedding night, and such comments made him suspect the notion was not her own. His scowl made Justine worry that she had overplayed her hand. For a moment she was reminded of the absurd charade that used to be played out in the opera, when Blancard excused himself from the box upon Christophe's arrival. Such scenes must be executed delicately and she quickly reined herself.

"They interest me only because they interest you," she said smoothly.

"Unhh." Blancard seemed placated when Justine deftly focused attention back on him.

"In truth, I have thought of nothing but pleasing you after my grievous error with the rouge, Hilaire. I am determined to do nothing so ill-conceived, so improper again. I have sought to make it up to you and want only to please you."

"You said that twice," Blancard grunted.

"So I did, but that is only because I am a bit nervous in my new role. I hope you can forgive me."

"As you well know, madame, I forgive nothing. Nevertheless I confess I find your attitude satisfactory and the idea of dinner appropriate, at least for tonight. There is something important I would discuss with you."

"I'm most anxious to hear it, monsieur."

Over Agathe's lamb cutlets with a delectable sauce *soubise*, Blancard made a stunning pronouncement. "We have been together almost thirteen years now, madame, and I find the need for certain connubial pleasures has waned. At least in this house."

Justine's stomach churned like a Mississippi paddlewheeler. Where on earth was this conversation going?

"It may or may not be news to you that I take such pleasures elsewhere, just as your approval or disapproval of the matter is of no consequence to me. To be frank I should be content to live permanently apart, but for obvious reasons that is impossible. We must maintain some semblance of respectability and I am convinced the old solution remains the best." He forked a mouthful of baked yams and watched her until he swallowed. "You will inform Monsieur Arnaud that he is to resume his role as escort." Justine's eyebrows rose, heart racing when she heard the addendum. "On an indefinite basis."

"As you wish," Justine said, hanging her head so that he would not see the smile fighting for freedom. It was too good to be true!

"I see no reason why he shouldn't take you to all the requisite carnival balls or why he shouldn't keep you company when you leave the city for the summer."

"As you wish," Justine said again.

Their dining continued in silence; there was nothing else to be said about the old arrangement, or anything else for that matter. Justine looked up only when Figaro appeared with a steaming *pouding a la Reine*. Ordinarily she found the bread pudding soaked in whiskey too sweet, but that night she relished the taste of currants and raisins and even indulged in a second helping.

Before Blancard retired to the parlor with his brandy, he made a final pronouncement. "From now on, you will instruct the servants to prepare dinner only for you. My appearances here will be most infrequent and there is no need to give them extra work." Justine could not remember when the man had ever given a kind consideration to anyone, much less a slave. She was further flabbergasted when he came to kiss her forehead with astonishing and thoroughly unexpected tenderness. "What you sought to do was most considerate. And now, *bon soir.*"

Justine was so shocked by her husband's bizarre behavior that she could not find the strength to leave the table. She watched him disappear and sat mesmerized by the dancing candle flames until Figaro inquired if she wanted anything more.

"*Non,*" she murmured. "Nothing."

Blancard's declaration was too dreamlike to be substantial, yet Justine forced herself to recognize it as fact. When she had decided to plan these late suppers for Blancard, she had no clear idea what lurked behind her motivation. Nor did she know how long his latest proclamation would last. The unexpected was the rule rather than the exception with this man, but Justine was optimistic because he had never before indicated he wanted the arrangement to go on indefinitely. It was simply a Godsend!

As she rose at last and floated upstairs to her room, Justine's mind spun uncontrollably with ways to include Duncan Saunders in this new arrangement. With Toinette again safely at her side, she had seen the man once more since their chance encounter in the marketplace, and in that even briefer interlude she had confessed how overwhelmed and honored she had been by his poem. Duncan had devoured her every word and pleaded with her to make their meetings a regular thing. Justine had been sorely tempted, but had refused. She was afraid. She desperately wanted to see him but knew she had to be wildly discreet. Two meetings in the marketplace were acceptable, for everyone in the city strolled those bustling arcades, but three would be tempting fate. Marie Tonton had kept her distance ever since Toinette threatened her, but caution was still imperative. For all Justine knew, Marie Tonton had engaged someone else to do her spying. No, she decided. Difficult though it would be, she must not see Duncan for a few days and when they met again it would be far from the French Market. She would send word when the time was right.

But, oh, how she wanted to send word now! How she wanted to dispatch Hippolyte with a message for Christophe telling him to come at once. She would have to wait of course, endure a night of restless dreams, none of which she would remember the next day. For the first time in years, she awoke with a smile on her face, and if Marie Tonton thought it suspicious when she brought breakfast, she nonetheless remained tight-lipped.

"I could eat a horse this morning," Justine announced, lavishly ladling her batter cakes with Louisiana syrup and plunging into them with relish. She even tasted a bit of Agathe's delectable creamed chicken and the steaming *omelette aux Confitures.* "Delicious!"

Marie Tonton drew the curtains wide and paled the room with wintry sunlight. "Humph," she snorted. "You keep eating like that and you won't be getting in any of your clothes."

Justine's fork paused in mid air, dripping syrup onto the plate. Was it possible this evil, enigmatic soul had a shade of good after all? "Why Marie Tonton!" she teased. "I didn't know you cared!"

"I don't," came the quick reply.

"But you must," she said. "Otherwise why would you say such a thing?"

"I don't know," Marie Tonton grumbled. She adjusted her *tignon* and stared out the window, momentarily distracted by a seagull soaring high over the convent a few blocks away. "Seems like there's a whole lot of things I don't understand lately."

"Like what?" Justine asked, scarcely believing they were having the semblance of a conversation.

"Like you," she replied, still addressing the morning light. "And your involvement with this Clovis woman."

"She is to be addressed as Madame Clovis," Justine said coolly. "I'd advise you to remember that."

"Well, whoever she is, she scares the devil out of me," Marie Tonton said. "You don't know what you're doing, taking up with an old hoodoo woman like her."

"I will remind you once again to be more respectful when you speak of my good friend," Justine insisted. "And what makes you think she has any involvement with *voudou*?"

"She went to see Marie Laveau, didn't she?"

"I'm sure I don't know any Marie Laveau," Justine lied, immediately regretting the turn of the conversation. "Besides, I'm sure whom she visits is her own business. Not mine. And certainly not yours."

Marie Tonton turned at last, rheumy eyes narrowing. "You know plenty about Marie Laveau," she accused. "You be using her to get back at Michie Hilaire."

"What you're saying is nonsense," Justine said, appetite rapidly diminishing. "And what goes on between myself and my husband is also of no concern to you." She added with meaning, "Not now!"

"Maybe," Marie Tonton said curtly. "And maybe not. You want me to take the tray now?"

"Yes," Justine said, suddenly wanting to be rid of the woman. "But leave the coffee. And tell Agathe to make more. I'll ring later."

Marie Tonton paused in the door with the tray of food. When she spoke, her tone reflected the sort of caring that Justine found anything but comforting. "Madame Blancard, we both know that anything that goes on in this house is my business and I'm telling you something for your own good. That Madame Clovis is an old hoodoo woman and you'd better be careful of her. She may look like a schoolteacher, behind those glasses and all, but she's got herself a dark side that don't bode good for no one."

"How dare you talk such rubbish!" Justine snapped.

"I'm just warning you," Marie Tonton said. "It's those who appear to be so innocent. They're the most dangerous of all. I know, Madame Blancard. I've seen it with my own eyes too many times."

"Get out!"

"I been asking questions, Madame Blancard. You better start asking some yourself."

Justine was livid. "Out! Do you hear me, woman? Out!"

Justine still seethed after the door closed behind the slave. She sipped the coffee, angrily pursing her lips when she realized it had turned cold. In fact the whole room suddenly seemed chilled, as though an icy specter had settled nearby.

"This business about Toinette is nonsense," she muttered to herself. She reached for the robe at the foot of the bed, drew it on and paced the room. "Utter nonsense."

But was it? It would not leave her, Marie Tonton's accusation that Toinette was a *voudouienne* and the warning that Justine shouldn't be fooled by the quadroon's prim appearance. As muddled as her thoughts had been that day, the same thought had occurred to Justine when Toinette revealed her relationship to Marie Laveau. But there had been more. Justine tried to remember Toinette's words, and with effort they finally formed in her brain.

"Let's just say that I am not a regular at the ceremonies," Toinette had said, "but that should not suggest I do not have my connections. Connections that, as you will see, come in quite handy."

And there was more, a later, enigmatic comment that rushed back at Justine with all of its original impact.

"Let's just say that your road is not altogether unfamiliar to me. I can tell you no more. Not now."

Still more, the most frightening remark of all, one causing Justine to shudder with the remembrance.

"You should have seen Marie Laveau first and then done . . . well, whatever it took to stop him. The most drastic steps necessary, if things were that desperate."

Perhaps even murder!

"*Mon dieu!*"

Justine dropped to the *prie-dieu* and hastily crossed herself. Toinette a *voudouienne*? It was possible of course. When *voudou* was involved, anything was possible. Like miscegenation, it was hardly discussed in polite parlors, but its presence was as undeniable as the countless *sang-melées* strolling the city streets.

Voudou? To feel its presence pound in the brain, one had only to listen to the drumbeats subtly punctuating the city's stillness, especially on velvety summer nights, or keep alert for what might go unnoticed by the uninitiated. Justine was typical of most Creoles. She denied being superstitious, yet she was quick to recognize a conjure ball or the infamous *gris-gris*.

Other whites similarly dismissed *voudou* as so much hogwash, but secretly feared it, terrified when it crossed their paths. Most often it was the work of slaves who disliked their masters for injustices either real or imagined. Justine had heard women complain of feeling strange lumps in their pillows. Invariably it was the work of a servant who rolled feathers into tight balls or tied them into rooster-shapes. That the pillows were never opened was proof of the white's deep-seated respect for *voudou!*

The same masters and mistresses might find other, far more unpleasant signs of a servant's discontent. A particularly nasty *gris-gris* was a black paper sack containing a mixture of saffron, salt, gunpowder, and pulverized dog feces. The vile concoction usually lurked in dresser drawers, behind draperies, even inside pianos. A Creole belle making her debut at the opera might have the magical moment ruined by opening her bag and finding a similarly repulsive article in her purse. Accusations, if made at all, were naturally met with claims of innocence by the slaves, and they were rarely punished. Indeed, the master or mistress often sought to treat their servants with a lighter hand lest more drastic *voudou* measures be taken.

"But she can't be!" Justine hissed. "Please, dear God, no! She can't be!"

The marble was cold against her hands and there was little warmth shed by the flickering votive candles. Justine swore the room was growing colder by the second, and she suddenly wanted out. She crossed herself again, deciding against further prayer in her urgency to flee the room.

She dressed hurriedly, not bothering with all the buttons. No one would see them under her cape, and she could ask Toinette to finish the buttoning. That was who she had to see immediately, the only one who knew the truth. Toinette! She would confess; she would not keep dark secrets from such a good friend. But were they really friends? Did the woman have an ulterior motive, was she seeking something else from Justine? Was it possible that she and Marie Tonton were in league with one another, somehow helping Blancard to plot her undoing? Why just last

night he had virtually said he would seek to end the marriage if he could!
Mais non! she thought again. It can't be!

Justine was down the stairs and halfway down the street when she stopped her mad flight. She leaned against a lamppost in the midst of the Rue des Ursulines, oblivious to passers-by, some familiar, some not, as they nodded, tipped hats, murmured *"Bonjour."* Her heart pounded frightfully and as she paused to catch her breath she experienced something tantamount to an emotional epiphany.

It was not fear of Toinette's *voudou* making her crazy, driving her to think such terrible things. Rather it was Blancard who had so intimidated her with his perverse attrition that her mind had ceased to function logically. She was so fragile that she had allowed an infinitesimal seed carefully planted by Marie Tonton to blossom into a garden of purest evil. Even away from Blancard, she still suffered under his malignant spell. She had to stop believing he was her only world and that his evil dictates were infallible, just as she had to start trusting Toinette, Christophe, and, yes, Duncan Saunders. The very thought of the man invigorated her, infused her body and soul with a new strength buoying her on to Toinette's shop. Far from fearing and condemning Toinette for her *voudou* connections, she now saw them as a means of escape. She could not deny her doubts of the church, and while the idea of embracing *voudou* was anathema, who was to say it could not help her where she believed her own faith had failed?

It was an unsettling notion, yet one Toinette happily confirmed as soon as Justine arrived at *La Mode* and blurted all that had happened since the night before. Toinette was thrilled.

"Something wonderful has just happened," she chirped. Justine thought she looked especially pretty in a creamy tarlatan that set her skin aglow. "You have made that crucial first step and started thinking for yourself."

"I have?"

After herding Justine into the dressing room where she finished buttoning her dress, Toinette continued her praise. "Indeed you have! You should take enormous pride in the deed. Women such as yourselves, men too, can take the rest of their lives to heal themselves after such an ordeal. Thirteen years of hell on earth! *Mon dieu!* It's a miracle you have a mind left at all, much less one strong enough to sift so astutely and separate the lies from the truth. I know slaves so badly mistreated by their masters that they're reduced to little more than human jelly. They speak gibberish and have minds like sieves."

"I wasn't so sure of myself at first," Justine said, ashamed of the doubts she had entertained about Toinette.

"It doesn't matter, as long as you understand the facts now. Let's begin with Marie Tonton. Naturally she would seek to put doubts in your mind. After all those years of spying on you, she must be frustrated beyond belief now that her *raison d'etre* has been erased. What easier way than to attack your new friend and try to frighten you with her own brand of *voudou?*"

"She very nearly succeeded," Justine sighed, embarrassed again.

"As I said, that's not important here. What matters is that you were able to overcome those years and form thoughts and opinions of your own. You've even been asserting yourself in ways you don't yet understand."

"What do you mean?"

Toinette finished the buttons and ushered Justine into the garden where she had been having the usual morning coffee with Nicole and Soona. A wave of their employer's hand sent them back inside, but Nicole purposely left the French doors ajar so she could eavesdrop.

"There are reasons, my dear," Toinette continued, "why you decided all on your own to start waiting dinners for Blancard."

"I'm not sure I know why myself," Justine confessed.

"Not surprising," Toinette said evenly. "There are other forces at work here. Now then. Let's talk about Blancard. Why do you suppose he handed you that first, tiny bit of praise? Why this sudden reinstatement of Christophe in your life? And why did Blancard speak of ending . . . relations, of ending the marriage itself? None of these things are typical behavior, are they?"

"Definitely not. Oh, he's certainly let me keep company with Christophe before, but he's never been adamant about it. He as much as said that he wants me out of his life."

Toinette smiled and smoothed her hair with an open palm. Justine considered it a nervous habit because the woman's hair was, as always, brushed until it shone and coiffed to perfection. Then she leveled the disconcerting gray eyes.

"Don't you see, my dear? It's all of a piece."

Justine frowned. "I don't understand."

Toinette leaned close and took Justine's hands. "Remember the daguerreotype of Blancard I took to Marie Laveau?"

"What did she do with it?"

"That's not important," Toinette said hastily, knowing Justine would not understand and probably would ridicule the simple act of burying the picture. "All that matters is that the woman's powers are potent and whatever she has done is working. Slowly, to be sure, but working nonetheless. Think about it. In less than a fortnight, you have a husband who has shown affection and given you permission to lead a separate life. Not only that, a gentleman has appeared who offers the opportunity for much more than romance."

"It is most strange," Justine conceded. "It reminds me of something Christophe used to say. 'Sometimes things can be too much of a coincidence to actually *be* a coincidence.' "

"Christophe sounds like a wise man."

Justine giggled in spite of herself. Christophe was many things—dashing, witty, madcap, and hopelessly charming—but she had never considered him wise. "If only you could meet him, Toinette."

Toinette smiled too, but she was not yet ready to relinquish the subject. "I'll never deny my connections with the *voudous*, Justine. It was scarcely my first visit to Madame Laveau when I took her the picture. I will say only that I find her talents extremely advantageous. What you choose to believe is up to you."

"I appreciate your honesty."

"And I expect the same from you, my dear." She squeezed Justine's hands. "Can you not see that we have a most extraordinary relationship, Madame Blancard? For a free quadroon and a white woman to enjoy this sort of deep confidence is rare indeed. It is so precious that we must be careful not to let anyone interfere with it." When Justine started to insist that no one could do such a thing, she remembered what had happened only that morning. Toinette easily read the recognition on her face. "Do you see what I mean?"

"Only too well."

"*C'est tres bon!*" Toinette stood and patted her hair again. "And now, *mon ami*, I must get busy. I have none other than Madame Dupre coming by this morning. You well know how difficult she can be." She slipped an arm around Justine's tiny waist as they reentered the shop. "You know, only once did she pick up a gown on time."

"Don't tell me!" Justine laughed. "It was the red gown you let me have for the Twelfth Night ball."

"*Exactemente!*"

"Well," Justine said, feigning seriousness, "she can't have it back. That is my lucky dress. I was wearing it the night I met Monsieur Saunders!" Justine kissed Toinette's cheeks and wiped away a tear. "I cannot thank you enough, dear Toinette. If you had not happened by that morning and forced your way past Marie Tonton, I shudder to think where I might be today. What a stroke of fate!"

Toinette felt briefly sickened when she remembered poor Josette. Indeed, without her interference, Justine might well have suffered the same destiny. She opened the door and smiled as Justine stepped onto the banquette.

"It was not fate, my dear. Always remember that."

CHAPTER 14

hristophe yawned luxuriously and nestled his head deeper against
Clarice's voluptuous breasts. He had never realized they made such
superb pillows, especially when one's head throbbed so horribly.

"How long have I been here, *mon cher?*"

"Four days," Clarice smiled, tugging the sheet higher when the
wind's icy fingers stole between rotting shutters.

"*Mais non!* Is it possible?"

"Oh, it's possible all right. Madam Pearl decided to send your coachman home the first morning. She said she knew a man about to go on
a debauch when she saw one." Clarice pushed a greasy curl off
Christophe's forehead. His hair, like the rest of him, was in dire need of
washing.

"My mother will be sick with worry!"

"Madam Pearl took care of that too," Clarice said. "Sent a note with
the carriage driver, explaining you'd be with a sick friend for a few
days."

"God bless her, she thinks of everything," Christophe sighed. He
sighed again. "Four days, eh?"

"You were determined to forget something about a poem," Clarice
said.

"Damn you!" he groaned. But the words were without malice. He was
his own worst enemy in this, the real target of his misery. "You made
me remember the one thing I wanted to forget."

"All the drinking and wenching in the world ain't gonna make you
forget her," Clarice said.

"Who?"

Clarice shrugged. "You didn't mention her by name, but there's nothing but a woman can make a man act like this."

"Mmmm."

Christophe turned his face again to her breasts and hoped a soft nipple would distract him from his throbbing temples. Clarice shifted her weight to make them both more comfortable. The whore indulged him, reminding herself she was there to give him pleasure. It was something she shouldn't have to remember, but the simple truth was the man had wasted her with his lusty attrition, worn her until her loins ached. Clarice couldn't recall a man with such inexhaustible passion, much less one stemming from pure melancholy. Oh, how he wanted to lose himself! Something had injured this fine gentleman deeply, enough to send him on a four-day spree in the District. Clarice had come to care for Christophe and loathed seeing him in such pain.

He had simply lost all concept of time since reading Duncan's revealing poem in the *Café de Aguila* and ultimately recognized his personal tragedy. Duncan was clearly in love with Justine Blancard, and Christophe could not have been more shocked or disappointed. He only dimly remembered his reaction in the coffee house, asking Duncan who inspired the poem while secretly guessing the source. He had babbled something about a night on the town and fled, very nearly knocking over the coffee cups. And he had fled here, to Madam Pearl's place, where he whored with a vengeance and repeatedly drank himself into oblivion.

A soft rap at the door stirred another moan from the man. "Tell them to go away!" he muttered into Clarice's breast. But she ignored him, knowing Madam Pearl would interrupt only if it was important. A young quadroon maid entered quietly and gave Clarice an envelope. Clarice playfully pricked Christophe's bare bottom with a corner of the envelope.

"For you, monsieur."

"Ouch!" he said. "Read it to me."

"You know I can't read."

"*Merde!*" he muttered, struggling into a sitting position. His head rebelled but after a moment the painful pounding ceased and he took the letter with a shaking hand. "So it's come to this, eh? Christophe Arnaud is getting his mail in a whorehouse!" Clarice snickered, grateful that his sense of humor was returning. She had always loved him for that. She studied him as he read, his face a panoply of emotions.

"It's from her, ain't it?"

"The sender is of no concern to you," he said, not unkindly. "But what on earth is behind this? What can Blancard be up to now?" Christophe absently scratched his left nipple and grimaced at his reflection in the armoire mirror. With his unruly hair, sunken eyes, and four days' growth of black beard, he looked a good decade older than his twenty-eight years. "Good God! Draw me a bath, woman! I need to erase my tracks through hell before I call on this angel."

Clarice slipped dutifully from the bed, muttering to herself. "It's her all right."

An hour later, freshly bathed, shaved and cologned, wearing clothes Pearl had thoughtfully cleaned for him, Christophe emerged into the dubious daylight of the Rue Gallatin. He took a deep breath, surprised that Clarice's scent still lingered in his nose. As usual, Red Bill was still in tow, although now so drunk as to be little use to anyone. Fortunately, two of his fellow gang members were playing a lively game of cards and keeping a close watch on the Arnaud coach. L'Eveillé, wisely, refused to get out. Christophe passed a wad of bills to the men and climbed into the carriage.

"The Blancard home," he called to L'Eveillé.

He reread the letter and hoped he wasn't still drunk, that hallucinations had not conjured this moment. It had been years since he'd received such an invitation, since he'd been asked to stay at the Blancard home longer than it took to fetch Justine for an evening out. Blancard may have entrusted his wife to the man in public places, but it was rare indeed when that faith extended to his home. Not, thought Christophe wryly, that the man was ever there.

Christophe reread the letter a third time. It puzzled him anew, but one line in particular he found almost exhilarating. "Hilaire insists that you be my permanent escort. Not just during the carnival season but into the summer. And who knows? Perhaps the fall as well. Oh, Christophe! We'll have such fun!"

"Indeed we will!" Christophe breathed.

There was now no impediment to being together like the old days, he thought happily, just the two of them. He might occasionally invite Duncan along, as well, if he could stand it. Justine knew nothing about the man's love and would surely never find out. She was, after all, a married lady, relegated to a lofty plane excluding her from anything more than matronly respect and chaste admiration.

Then again, Christophe thought, maybe not. The fact that Duncan had dared pen such a frank romantic pledge to a married woman gave him serious pause. If Duncan was this bold, it might not be beyond him to tell Justine of the poem, perhaps even allow her to read it! But no! Duncan would never do such a thing. Someone of his fine breeding and background surely understood the consequences. If the poem were ever discovered, Blancard would challenge him to a duel. At the very least, Duncan would be permanently ostracized from Creole society. At most, he would be killed by Blancard's bullet. Or would he? Blancard had once been lauded as one of Louisiana's crack shots, but he had not called anyone out in years. And if his drinking was as voracious as Christophe had recently heard, it was unlikely the man was the marksman he had once been.

"Stop this!" Christophe muttered. "You'll drive yourself crazy!"

Deep down, of course, he knew this was not what was driving him mad. It was his own unrequited love for Justine, one he had secretly nurtured since they were children together, one forever murdered when her father sold her to the rich, older Hilaire Blancard. It was that selfsame love that steeled him against gossip, vicious talk about why he never called on other women, why he consented to escort Madame Blancard for her whoring, phantom husband, why he threw himself so wholeheartedly into a romantically doomed relationship. Christophe cared nothing for what anyone said or how anyone interpreted his association with Justine. He loved her with all his heart and would have done anything for another moment stolen with her. Anything, that is, except confess his love.

It was simply not something a gentleman would do.

"*Cher* Christophe!"

Justine greeted him as though nothing had happened since he brought her home from the Twelfth Night Ball. She offered both cheeks for his lips and took his hand, leading him into the parlor where Figaro was setting up for tea. Odd, he thought. Marie Tonton was nowhere to be seen. He knew something else was afoot the moment he saw Justine, but could never have imagined what had happened during those days of oblivion lost at Pearl's.

"You're my oldest friend," Justine began, bracing him for an obviously weighty confession. She had never used those preparatory words before, and Christophe's heart raced when he considered the possibilities. There was only one that truly meant anything of course, but he dismissed it as hopeless as ever.

Yet now, with that look in the iridescent eyes, the radiance in her cheeks . . . did he dare the unthinkable?

"I have something to tell you that must go no farther than this room, Christophe. Oh, don't worry. I've sent Marie Tonton to the market. We're alone except for Agathe and Figaro."

"You're so flushed," Christophe said, not a little concerned. "Are you well?"

"Never better in my life, *ma cher!* And may I tell you why?"

"Please. Before I die of suspense."

"So much has happened since we last spoke. I didn't dare put it all in the letter. Blancard no longer wants anything to do with me. I'm free to spend as much time as I like with you and, well, the news could not have come at a more propitious time." Justine took his hand and pressed it to her cheek. "I know you will find this difficult to believe, my dear Christophe. I know that because I can scarcely believe it myself." She kissed his fingertips, making the hair on his neck stand on end.

"I'm in love!"

Christophe's vanity and his desperate, long-suppressed hopes were ugly conspirators. He seized her hands and waited anxiously, heart in his throat as he let his guard slip ever so slightly. "Tell me, Justine. Let me hear the words at last."

"Why, Chris," she said, frowning. "What a strange way to put it."

"Is it?" he asked, instantly retreating, a terrified sea creature withdrawing into its nautilus.

If Justine read the truth in his request, she revealed nothing as she continued her confession. The frown lifted like a winter fog burned from the river, and she fairly blurted her confession.

"I'm in love with Duncan Saunders."

Christophe's unsettled stomach churned dangerously. He swallowed hard, willing away the wave of nausea coursing through him. He wanted to scream, to smash something, to curse the name of his best friend. But he swallowed again and composed his face into the very mask of *politesse.*

"Indeed," he said slowly. He could manage no more.

Justine was disappointed. "Is that all you have to say? 'Indeed'! I thought you would rail at my gross and improper behavior, accuse me of being mad, tell me there's no hope for such a thing."

"It seems to me," Christophe said evenly, "that these are things you have already addressed yourself." He reached for the tea cup, decided his hand was shaking too violently, and retreated.

"Of course I have," she confessed. "A thousand times. When I told Toinette about it . . ."

"And who is Toinette?"

"My seamstress."

"The quadroon with the little shop in the Rue Royale? Why, her husband is my tailor." The black eyebrows rose suspiciously.

"Oh, it's too long to explain, Christophe," Justine insisted. "Let me just say that Toinette has been a Godsend. In only a week, she has taught me more about myself and my marriage than I had learned in thirteen years."

"What was there to learn?"

"Far more than I knew. And far more than my priest knew. Or would tell me."

Christophe was utterly lost and not a little hurt. "And so you confessed this . . . love for Duncan to this . . . colored woman?!" He made a face. "How can you expect me to take you seriously when say you shared something so intimate with a perfect stranger?"

Justine demurred. Then, with an aching sadness in her voice, "I didn't ask you here to cross-examine me, Christophe. And I was hoping that you, of all people, would understand."

"But what is there to understand? You yourself said there is nowhere for this thing to go. Why torture yourself over something that can never be anything more than a glance here, a smile there? Why let yourself be consumed with a hopeless passion . . . ?"

Justine interrupted with a smoothness that cut Christophe to the quick. "Are you speaking of me, dear Christophe, or of yourself?"

Stung, he rose and strode to the marble-topped table glittering with decanters. He grabbed the closest one and sloshed several fingers of whiskey into his glass. Justine grimaced as he downed it in a single swallow. It was followed by a second and then a third, and then she heard a faint voice drifting through a near palpable silence.

"*Goddamn!*" Then, with painful slowness, "To hell with being a gentleman!"

"What?"

He could not look at Justine, facing instead a portrait of her mother. He had loved her almost as much as Justine, yet now, with her long hair piled high and her bosom half-bared, Adéle Fonteneau cast a warning, seemed to discourage his efforts on behalf of her daughter. It both infuriated and disappointed him, but he forced the confession nonetheless.

"I . . . have . . . always . . . loved you."

Justine closed her eyes and took a deep breath. *Please, God! Help me!*

"Turn around, Christophe, and look at me when you say it."

It was the most difficult thing he had ever done, facing the woman he had loved all his life and uttering a truth that seared his heart with every accursed word. She looked more beautiful than ever, even with a face scalded by tears.

"I have always loved you."

She spoke without hesitation and straight from the heart. "And I, my darling Christophe, have always known it."

He was incredulous. "Was I so obvious?"

"Only to me, *ma cheri.*"

She was in his arms then, holding his head to her breast as he unleashed tears that had been building for years. He didn't care that she saw him weep. He had no shame before her now, no secrets. He was far more naked than he had been with Clarice, yet somehow, after a while, he began to feel cleansed. He experienced a peculiar relief.

"I'm so foolish," he said at length. "I should have known better than to hope for the hopeless."

"We don't choose who we fall in love with," Justine soothed. "It just happens. I didn't think it possible because what I had known with Blancard was anything but love. But when Duncan gave me the poem . . ."

Christophe withdrew so fiercely that it threw Justine off balance. She hastily grabbed the arm of a *bergére* to keep from tumbling to the floor. "For heaven's sake, Christophe! What is it?"

"I never imagined he would show you the poem, that's all."

"Why not?"

Christophe tried to keep from bristling. "You know very well, Justine. There were parts of it that were . . . indelicate, to say the least. It's hardly the sort of thing a gentleman would show a lady."

"Maybe I'm not the lady everyone believes me to be."

"Justine!"

"*Je regret.*"

"No, no. I'm the one who should apologize. No doubt jealousy played a part in my reaction. In any case I'm not above admitting I've learned something today. I've learned how truly strange love can make one act."

Justine took his hand and led them back to the couch, grateful that Christophe set the whiskey aside. His hands no longer shook when she poured the tea. When he had calmed, she said, "He didn't tell me he showed you the poem. But then, we had such a brief time to talk." While Christophe listened intently, she recounted their encounters in the French Market. "While I read it I was transported somewhere I'd never been before. To this day I don't know where I went, but it was as if I was whisked right out of Toinette's little garden and hurtled through the cosmos like a cannonball."

Christophe nodded, for her sake forcing himself to be generous. "Until I read the piece I wondered if the man was really a poet or someone merely claiming as much, but now I see he has considerable talents. I found the poem reminiscent of Samuel Coleridge."

"I thought so too," Justine said. "One of his idols, I believe."

"Mmmm."

Both sipped their tea, allowing the warmth of the moment to wash over them, purifying what had careened perilously close to disaster. They knew what had nearly happened and were deeply grateful that their friendship had survived. Love between friends is rarely equal, but when the scales are tipped so wildly, all can be lost. Indeed, an over-abundance of love can be more destructive than none at all. Justine considered that painful reflection and prayed she wasn't rushing things when she asked Christophe for help.

"I must ask a great deal of you now, Christophe. A great deal of your generosity and selflessness because I cannot pursue this business without your help. Certainly I cannot confess my love."

"What exactly is it you want?" He swallowed again. The words were as bitter as gall.

"Merely to include Monsieur Saunders in our plans from time to time. Nothing more. Believe me, I know this is asking a great deal but I do so because you are a great friend."

"You know I could never deny you anything," he said after a long, difficult pause. "To be frank, I feel no small amount of disappointment and perhaps a bit of anger as well. No, Justine! Don't interrupt. This is something I have to say. And there's more. At this very moment, looking at you, eyes aglow, a genuine radiance you've never had before, I believe this love of yours is real. Therefore I must tell you that if I can contribute to your happiness, then I must do so. There now. I've done it."

"You've no idea how happy that makes me," she beamed. She wanted to embrace him again but did not, knowing it would be awkward for both of them.

Christophe could not resist a touch of humor to smooth a rough moment in his heart. "Well, you know I'll do anything to get at a woman, even if her heart belongs to someone else."

"Thank you," she smiled.

"It is nothing. Now then. What are we to do first?"

Justine retrieved an elaborate invitation she had been using as a bookmark. Christophe recognized the novel as one he had given her at Christmas. "Have you received yours yet? To the Duvals' *bal masque?*"

"I've been away for a few days," he said. Knowing Justine would ask, as always, about his whereabouts, he had prepared an elaborate lie, but when she didn't, Christophe told himself he'd have to get used to the fact that her interest was in Duncan Saunders.

"No doubt your invitation is waiting for you at home. And I see no reason why all three of us cannot go together. The invitations allow guests."

"Are you crazy?" he laughed. But the twinkle in his eyes told Justine he was more than a little intrigued. "Have you forgotten what happened when Eugénie chose Duncan as her king? Not only did her father publicly insult Duncan over the incident, but you can be sure there will be no *Yanquis* at Honoré Duval's ball."

"Then perhaps it's time that changed." Justine smiled when Christophe began twirling his moustache, a sure sign that he was plotting something naughty. "Oh, don't pretend you don't like the idea, Chris. I know you too well. You think it would be a delicious lark. Admit it!"

"I suppose," he conceded. "We'll be masked, of course. Still, there are certain risks . . ."

"What's the worst that could happen? If Duncan is discovered, it certainly won't be the first time he's been shunned by Honoré Duval!" Christophe burst into laughter when she added, "The old goat!"

"Justine!"

"Oh, I'm so bored with the Duvals and the Favrots and the Cassards and the Materres and all the others who cling to their cherished dreams of Creole glory! It's time they acknowledged what happened back in '03. We're part of the United States now, and everyone would be better off if we acted like it. Especially that ridiculous Lucie Dupre, who crosses the street rather than pass an American on the banquette. The fatted calf!"

Christophe was deliciously shocked by Justine's uncharacteristic, refreshing irreverence. He laughed so hard he had to set his tea aside lest he scald his lap. Through intermittent chuckles, he asked who had put such ideas in Justine's head. Duncan, no doubt. Or, more accurately, her love for him.

"No one," she said defiantly. "Perhaps I'm just voicing what I've thought all along. And is it so inconceivable that I might occasionally have an original thought of my own?"

"Of course not," Christophe said. He dabbed his cheeks with a fine lace handkerchief, erasing tears of mirth where tears of sorrow had been just minutes earlier. He was feeling much better about himself, Justine, and even Duncan.

"Then you agree?"

Christophe shrugged agreeably. "Why not? The more you talk about it the more exciting it sounds."

A trace of uneasiness still plagued Justine, one having nothing to do with the Duval ball. "You're certain it will not be too difficult for you, having Duncan with us?"

Christophe spoke from the heart, the caring in his words unmistakable. "I love you and Duncan both, Justine. That is all I need to say."

"He need not know about your love for me," she ventured carefully. "Nor mine for him."

"In time perhaps he will," Christophe said. "In time perhaps we will want to tell him ourselves."

Justine thought that a preposterous remark but said nothing. In his own fashion, Christophe could be as mercurial as her husband, albeit never in harmful ways. She had certainly witnessed a vast range of his emotions today, enough for the personalities of several men. But that was part of why she cared so deeply for him. In his own way he was larger than life, and in his magnitude he found a place to hide her. For that she would be eternally grateful.

He studied the ball invitation for a moment before replacing it in the book. "And what about costumes?"

"I've not had time to think about it, but I'm sure Toinette's girls can make something appropriate. Any suggestions?"

Christophe picked up the book and flipped through the pages. The novel was filled with fine illustrations which immediately inspired him. "I do indeed," he said. "Perhaps the irony is too great, but no one enjoys a joke on me more than myself."

"What are you suggesting?"

He gave her the book. "It's too perfect, my dear. Why, Monsieur Dumas' *Three Musketeers* of course!"

Colette looked especially engaging as she brought Gautier's whiskey, preferring to serve him herself that night. She dazzled in red lace that hugged the swell of her bosom and shrank her waist to nothing. Marius lavished praise as he often did. To him, great beauty was without gender, a thing to be admired and cultivated. If only Colette were a man, he thought, a gentleman radiating such natural raw concupiscence, a man with those piercing eyes and that insouciant self-assurance. *Eh, bien . . . !*

"It's a pity to waste such glamour on me," he said as she studied him over the rim of her glass. Unlike most well-bred ladies, colored and white, she was not above taking a little whiskey now and then. Especially with an old friend.

"It's not wasted," she said sweetly. "You and dear Simon were never ones to ignore beauty of any kind."

"I was just thinking that," he smiled.

She smiled too, then the black eyes danced wickedly. "Tell me, *cher.* Did you ever wish I were a man?"

"*Sacre bleu!* Sometimes I think you are a sorceress, woman!" Gautier's cheeks coloring suddenly. "But let's not speak of such things. They are far too intimate for us."

"Your true feelings betray you, Marius. As well as that charming blush. But don't concern yourself. The subject is closed. Besides, I'd far rather hear what you think about the slaughter in the Rue Gallatin."

"Colette!" he laughed. "Must you always choose topics unsuitable for ladies?"

"I've never concealed my fascination for the macabre," Colette replied evenly. "It was something Narcisse and I shared. We used to read about crimes and discuss them at length. Besides, this latest business is certainly no secret. The newspapers have been full of it. *L'Abeille* says there's a murder in the city every week now."

Gautier nodded grimly. "It seems the blood has barely dried when the paper reports it. In turn, the *ink* has barely dried when another similar incident displaces it. The sheriff of Orleans Parish is calling the city a hell on earth. He claims nothing can stop the madness except making it penal to carry firearms. It seems that everyone is carrying guns these days."

As though checking the time, Gautier calmly reached into his waistcoat and withdrew a fob chain with a tiny derringer pocket pistol where the watch should have been.

"Marius!"

"This is the latest thing," he explained, holding it up for her inspection. "Two barrels holding a shot apiece and not even four inches long! *Très chic, non?*"

"It's tiny!" Colette gasped. "Does it work well?"

"What a leading question!" he laughed.

"But we have so few secrets, eh, *mon ami?*"

"I'll say only that there are at least two hooligans who would give my little gun a vote of confidence. They made the mistake of thinking me drunk when I left a waterfront bar at a disgraceful hour."

Colette's eyes widened. "Did you kill them?"

"I didn't linger to check their pulse, but the amount of blood was terrible." Gautier smiled grimly. "Frankly so was the amount of satisfaction."

"Good," Colette said. "I hate such incidents, but, well, what is a decent populace to do? Especially when the criminals are so audacious!"

"*C'est vrai.*"

They were not the only concerned citizens. Even though the incident transpired in the District where hourly crime was a fact of life, the brutality and daring involved shocked even the most jaded denizens of Gallatin Street. Three of the Live Oak Boys, Red Bill Wilson not among them, had stormed a dance house called Babylon and torn the place to pieces. The whores had wisely escaped upstairs, but less fortunate patrons were caught to face the whiskey-fueled fury of this deadly trio. Bouncers and bartenders, patrons and even musicians, all were caught in the murderous crossfire as the Boys boldly helped themselves to the till. Tables, chairs, gaslights, windows, all were smashed to bits before the rampage concluded, and when the Boys left, fleeing on a cloud of maniacal laughter, five men lay dead on the filthy floor. Four were stabbed, two shot, and one had even been strangled. Eyewitnesses likened it to the Biblical plague of locusts, an unexpected madness descending from nowhere and leaving utter devastation in its wake.

"Who knows when those men will decide to invade some respectable establishment?" Colette worried. "It's not inconceivable that they might invade a ladies' coffee shop or a gentleman's billiard hall in the Rue Royale and wreak equal carnage."

"I should hope the occasional police presence on that street acts as some deterrent," Marius ventured. "I understand that the police no longer venture into the Rue Gallatin unless they're in force. Everyone knows they haven't gone into the Swamp on Girod Street for decades."

Colette sipped the whiskey. She admired its amber glow as Senegal tossed a log onto the fire, unleashing an explosion of sparks. "It's all so very disturbing, Marius. What do you suppose makes a man do such a thing?"

"They can't help themselves of course. Murderers are born, you know."

"So they say."

"I don't understand it of course." He waited discreetly until the servant had left them alone again. "Any more than I understand why one human being sees fit to own another."

Colette nodded. It was hardly the first time they had discussed what Yankees called the South's peculiar institution. "As you know, that's why I insist on hiring free Negroes. It was not a difficult decision since *Grandmere* Chocola was a slave. Chaillot knows I don't approve of her owning slaves, but that's Monsieur Blancard's decision. She says every time she broaches the subject, he's adamant."

"So are many *gens de coleur libres* who own slaves."

"True. Some were once slaves themselves," Colette offered a bit wearily. "I puzzle over that too, dear Marius. Especially when I hear tales of cruelty, of master beating slave without cause." The fine, limoges-hued face darkened with her mood. "Which brings me to a bit of unpleasant business."

"Oh?"

"Just last week Nicole came by here with a most unsettling tale. It seems that her employer was deep in conversation with Monsieur Blancard's wife, Josephine . . ."

"Justine," Gautier corrected.

"You know her then?"

"Simon and I met her on several occasions and often saw her at the opera. She is a great beauty, but has a distressing sadness about the eyes. Simon once ascribed it to melancholy."

Colette pursed her lips and continued. "Nicole was unsure of the exact words because they were only overheard in the garden, but she seems to think Blancard may be a bit of a brute."

Gautier's forehead furrowed. "How so?"

"As I said, Nicole didn't hear clearly and she didn't dare ask Madame Clovis about it afterward, but Madame Blancard made some remark about his evil appetites."

"Whatever can that mean?"

Colette shrugged. "Who knows? I intend to ask Chaillot about it next time we speak, but who can say what she will reveal? She was always a secretive child, hiding away with that strange little doll Combas. I've often believed she only says what she wants me to hear. That's why her talk of leaving Blancard and fleeing North to pass for white came as a complete shock. She revealed more of herself that night than in all the years I've known her."

"When did you see her last?"

"It's been five days. I know that Monsieur Blancard has been with her all that time, and of course I don't dare call on her when his carriage is parked before the house. That in itself is most unusual, his long-term presence I mean. I know him to be a consummate businessman and for him to miss days at his office . . . well, it just seems strange to me."

"Perhaps Chaillot has beguiled him more than we think," Gautier suggested, hoping to ease Colette's concern. "As you say, we have no idea what sort of tricks she has up her sleeve."

"I think it's more important that we know about what tricks Monsieur Blancard has up his sleeve," Colette ventured grimly. She shook her head and watched the fire a while. It smoldered quietly, digesting the damp cypress with difficulty. "There's something about the man that disturbs me, Marius. Something about him that touched a raw nerve the night he approached me at the *Salle d'Orléans* and asked to be Chaillot's protector. I've never mentioned this to anyone, least of all Chaillot, but I now question my wisdom in allowing her to speak with Monsieur Blancard."

"You're being too hard on yourself, Colette. Every mother who takes her daughter to those balls has the same worries. Did she make the best possible connection for her girl? Should she have refused offers from certain gentlemen? Will her daughter resent her for recommending the wrong man? Besides, the ultimate choice was hers. No one forced Chaillot to choose Blancard."

"*C'est vrai,*" said Colette. "But my role in the arrangement is unquestionably a large one."

"You worry too much."

"At the risk of annoying you, my dear Marius, I must remind you that you would think differently if you had a child of your own."

"The truth scarcely offends me," Gautier smiled. "Besides, Simon and I often thought of Chaillot as the daughter we could never have. It wasn't difficult since he pretended daily to be her *papa*. In truth, she could not be more dear to me if she were my own flesh and blood." He smiled, suddenly flooded with fond memories. "What a beautiful child she was, so full of life and love for everyone. Even when she was naughty, playing with that awful Combas, I found her irresistible. I do love her, Colette. As dearly as I love you."

"Then you think I should drop the matter of Blancard?"

"Not at all, *mon cher.* In fact, I will question Chaillot myself when we next meet."

"We both should," Colette offered. She sighed and sipped deeply from the whiskey, relishing the warmth as it crept into her bones. The chill of the night was a most unwelcome reminder that she was no longer a young woman. "Sometimes I think you know her better than myself, Marius. I was most surprised when you told me about her reaction to the news of her father, and to the truth about you and Simon. Oh, I prayed she would be accepting, but to embrace such shocking news so easily . . . well, I never thought her capable of such compassion."

"Did she discuss it with you?"

Colette shook her head. "I mentioned it once, to open the door, so to speak. She was rather cool, saying only that the past is past and something rather frivolous about a leopard being unable to change its spots. Whatever *that* meant."

"She's right of course. After all, what is there to discuss?"

"Women aren't like that, Marius. We need to know things, to say things to one another."

"Not Chaillot."

"*Vraiment*. Sometimes I can hardly believe she's my child."

"But I am, *maman*. Another fact that cannot be changed."

Both spun toward the doorway. They had been so engrossed in their conversation that neither heard Chaillot enter. Her sudden appearance was not the only thing unsettling them. She was wrapped in a gold evening cloak, a silk confection that should have enhanced her porcelain beauty. Oddly, this latest gift from Blancard emphasized an unnatural pallor.

"But sometimes you sell me short."

"It is a two-way street," Gautier added, reminding Chaillot of their conversation at the lake, of her unwarranted criticism of Colette.

But Colette, fighting tears, was aware only of her daughter's presence and rushed to embrace her. "This past week without you has seemed like an eternity, my darling." She kissed both cheeks them stroked them gently with her fingertips. "You could use a touch of rouge, my dear."

"That's so like you to think of such a thing," Chaillot said icily. "How different our priorities are."

Colette was so delighted to see her daughter that she skirted all attempts at sparring. "I hope you've not come here seeking a quarrel, Chaillot."

"No," Chaillot conceded. "I have not. I came only because I've not seen either of you in too long. I apologize, *maman*."

Colette nodded and smiled. "It is forgotten." Contrition was true in Chaillot's voice and for that Colette was grateful. It seemed that Chaillot's affections were maddeningly erratic of late. Or more accurately since she debuted at the *Salle d'Orléans*.

Chaillot paced. "I've . . . I've not been myself lately."

"You look lovely," said Gautier, taking his turn to kiss and embrace her.

"Lovely," echoed Colette.

"God love you for being such sweet liars," Chaillot said, moving before the fireplace where she sought warmth from the frail blaze. "I have mirrors. I know how terrible I look."

"Perhaps a trifle fatigued," Gautier suggested gently.

Chaillot's response was a wan smile. "No matter. Now tell me what you wanted to speak to me about, *maman*."

Colette sat close and took her daughter's hand. "I will waste no words, Chaillot. Is Monsieur Blancard treating you well?"

A tension gripped Chaillot's hand delicately, yet it did not go unnoticed by her mother. "Why, yes, *maman*. Why do you ask?"

"There has been some talk, that's all. Nicole heard something at the shop."

"Oh?"

"An exchange between Toinette Clovis and his wife, suggestions that he mistreated Madame Blancard." When Chaillot did not respond, Colette added, "Rather badly it seems."

"Madame Blancard said this?"

"She did indeed," Gautier answered, knowing this was difficult for Colette. He repeated the story, adding the few ugly details Nicole heard, and left it to Chaillot to break the silence.

"Nothing more than gossip from a bitter wife," she dismissed. "Surely you encountered the same thing in your connections, *maman*."

"From what I understand, Madame Blancard is not the sort of woman to criticize anything. Except perhaps her husband."

"What a strange thing to say," Chaillot said, turning toward the crackling fire. She was acting her heart out.

"You're certain there are no problems then?" Colette pressed, not altogether satisfied. She knew something was amiss when her daughter avoided looking at her.

"*Absolument,*" Chaillot insisted. She pulled away and opened her cloak so she might display the dazzling gown underneath. It was an aquamarine satin affair with an avalanche of creamy Chantilly lace, accentuating hemline, puffed sleeves, and a daring neckline. Even Colette was shocked by the amount of bosom displayed, yet she said nothing. Like Gautier, she was distracted by the sapphire necklace nestled against Chaillot's abundant cleavage. As if that weren't enough, Chaillot tossed off the hood of the golden cloak to reveal matching sapphire earrings. "I only came by to show you my new dress, and of course the jewelry." She smiled, but, as Gautier later confided to Colette, it was a desperately vacant gesture. "Your little girl is doing all right for herself, *n'est ce-pas?*"

"Indeed." Colette had to turn away lest Chaillot see her eyes once again threatened by tears. "I'm very proud of you."

Chaillot swept by her mother, leaving a cloud of perfume in her wake. She faced Gautier, so close that their lips might have touched had she been as tall. "And you, Marius? Are you proud of me as well?"

"I am happy if you're happy," he said, ever the diplomat.

"Oh, I'm happy," Chaillot said, purposely fingering the necklace. She smiled again, another failure. "Do you know what Michie Hilaire said?

He said that women always adjusted to the weight of jewelry, no matter how heavy."

"How I wish that could be the only burden my child will ever have to bear," Colette sighed.

Chaillot turned slowly until her eyes locked with her mother's. Colette endured a look that iced her soul and silently prayed to God that she would never have to endure another one. For some reason she thought of those luckless people in the Rue Gallatin who had been so cold-bloodedly murdered.

"So do I, mother. Although I constantly surprise myself with what I'm capable of . . . well, I just surprise myself." She looked away, pinching her cheeks until she was satisfied with their pink glow. "I must be off now. Monsieur Blancard will be calling for me soon. I just wanted to show you my new things."

"You're not walking!" Colette said, horrified.

"Why not?"

"Have you lost your senses, girl? Do you not read the papers or listen to talk? Heaven knows this is neither the time or place for a lone woman to be about, especially one dressed such like a Mardi Gras queen!"

"I'll take you home," Gautier insisted, his firm tone warning Chaillot there would be no further discussion. He discreetly touched his chest, reminding Colette of the pocket pistol. "We'll be fine in my carriage."

"Then we must hurry," Chaillot said, reluctantly conceding. She knew when she left home that she was taking a grave risk, but then that seemed to be what her life was all about of late. "I dare not let Michie Hilaire catch me in your company again, Marius." She dimpled and tried to coquette, another dismal failure. "He's so jealous!" She kissed her mother good-bye and took Gautier's arm, pausing in the door as though remembering the true reason for this visit. "Oh!"

"What is it, *cher?*" Colette asked.

"Do you know anything about Josette Beaulieu?"

The question so startled Colette that for a moment she couldn't remember the girl's identity. Again Gautier came to her rescue. "Blancard's last mistress."

Colette said slowly, "Only that she died in childbirth."

"Oh."

"But why do you ask?" Colette pursued.

"If it involves Michie Hilaire, I must be interested." With a flourish, Chaillot was gone.

It was with a wildly sinking heart that Colette watched her daughter depart. She finished her whiskey and rang for another one, downing it, too, by the time Gautier returned. He could tell by the unnatural sparkle in her eyes that she was not a little inebriated.

"She's lying, you know."

"About what?"

"Everything to do with Blancard." Gautier knew only too much whiskey or wine would permit Colette to drop the proper term of respect for a white person. Addressing another gentleman by only his surname was common between Creole gentleman, but for a woman of color it was unthinkable. He ignored the breach of etiquette. His relationship with Colette was, after all, scarcely governed by convention. "There is something terrible between them."

"But how do you know?"

"I know my daughter better than she thinks, Marius. I know when she is playing a part, and believe me the performance we witnessed tonight was a *tour de force*. Except in her mother's eyes." She leveled her gaze. "To me she was absolutely transparent!"

Gautier fell silent, knowing Colette was about to launch into one of her frequent monologues requiring only his attention, not his participation.

"You saw her, Marius. She looks ghastly. Of course, ghastly for Chaillot is something most women would aspire to, but I digress. She is pale and her hand trembled terribly when I asked how Blancard was treating her. An even greater sign than the pallor in her cheeks is the light in her eyes. It looks as though some ill wind had blown out the beacon in a lighthouse. I know you noticed it." It was in fact the first thing that Gautier had noticed, but he said nothing. "My *grandmere* Chocola always said a person's eyes were a window into his soul. From what I can tell, my friend, the light in my child's eyes is dying, and if that's true . . ."

"You're letting the whiskey run your imagination wild," Gautier interposed gently. "I'll admit Chaillot looks a bit fatigued, but it's not as desperate as all that."

"You're not her mother," Colette said, a trifle sharply.

Gautier knew it was the whiskey talking and was not offended. Still, he made a hasty suggestion. "Shall we have some supper now? Senegal said the cook has things prepared and waiting."

"We shall indeed," Colette said, rising unsteadily. She smiled when Gautier deftly caught her arm. "I know I've had too much to drink, *mon ami*, but I do not apologize. I only ask for your tolerance while I remind you of another experience, aside from being a parent, that you couldn't possibly fathom. And that is the predicament of a free woman of color. Don't look away, *cheri!* I have no intention of belaboring my lot. I will only say that at times, such as now, a little too much whiskey helps ease the pain. It is only a temporary solution, I know, but it helps nonetheless. You see, with a bit more bourbon I can forget the woes of my daughter and myself and the loss of my precious Narcisse."

"Come along," Gautier said, easing her into a seat at the dining table. He smiled as Senegal brought the first of several trays in from the kitchen. Though tightly covered, they still steamed tantalizing aromas of green turtle soup, bouillabaisse of redfish, and snapper and Creole sweetbreads. "Ah, dinner at last."

"I don't know how you do it," Colette said. "You seem so good at handling dear Simon's loss, although I'm at a loss to explain how you do it. Doesn't . . . sometimes doesn't the—pardon me, doesn't the goddamned pain eat you alive?"

A profanity too, Gautier thought sadly. He nodded. "Every day, my dear Colette. Every night and every day. It's why I know I can never love again."

"What do you mean?"

"I mean that I could not bear to lose someone I loved to such excess again. Such endurance is simply not in my power."

"But what would you do if it happened?" Colette pursued. "Suppose tomorrow you met a gentleman who . . ."

"I would refuse it," he said firmly, "because I must. Because I would rather die than suffer such loss again. It's really quite simple."

His heartfelt confession disarmed Colette, and she exchanged the bourbon for a bowl of fragrant soup. As they ate, Gautier decided he didn't know this beautiful woman as well as he thought. Behind the glittering facade, the elegant poise, and measured smile lurked a soul of devastating sadness. Only at rare moments such as this, when the onus became too much, the charade too tiresome and demanding, did the celebrated Colette Baptiste lower her guard for a sympathetic friend.

It was obvious, Gautier reflected sadly, where Chaillot inherited her talents as an actress!

PART FOUR

⊠

Mardi Gras

High on a throne of royal state, which far
Outshone the wealth of Omus and Ind,
Or where the gorgeous East with richest hand
Showers on her king, barbaric pearl and gold,
Satan exalted sat, by merit raised
To that bad eminence; and from despair
Thus high uplifted beyond hope.
                    —John Milton, *Paradise Lost*

CHAPTER 15

"It was incredible," Duncan said, studying the bright buckles of his equally golden boots. "What the *Daily Picayune* wrote was a virtual obituary. Have the French newspapers been as critical?"

Christophe dismissed the remark with a languid wave of his glove and peered through the window as they approached the Rue Canal. Already L'Eveillé was slowing the coach. "None of the newspapers have said anything kind about carnival in three years, not since the Company of Bedouins paraded. Ah, what a spectacle that was!" As L'Eveillé navigated the mayhem of traffic where St. Charles approached Canal, Christophe described the extravaganza in a dreamy voice.

"There were thousands of maskers in that parade, people dressed as Arabs and sultans and pashas, riding papier-mâché camels, chanticleers, and horses, real and imaginary. There were dozens of carriages, most of them lavishly ornamented, the horses beautifully caparisoned. And lesser carts and wagons too. I remember them being bombarded with flour and bonbons. All the newspapers gave it a glowing report, especially *L'Abeille*."

"What happened to change their minds?"

"Well, there is definitely truth to some of the criticism. I'm afraid Carnival Day has degenerated into a sad public spectacle, attended only by cutthroats and drunken whores. No real lady would ever venture forth, masked or otherwise. Those nasty murders in the District have nothing directly to do with Mardi Gras, but the papers are trying to make a connection. The headline in yesterday's *L'Abeille* screamed

'Madness Is King of This Year's Carnival!' *Mon dieu!* Mardi Gras is still three weeks away!"

"It's as if they've begun a campaign to stop carnival."

"*C'est vrai.* The Creoles blame the Americans for the sad state of affairs, and naturally the Americans blame them right back. It's the old story."

"Randolph is involved in something he claims is going to give Mardi Gras a fresh start," Duncan ventured.

"I've heard the rumors," Christophe said. "What do you suppose he's talking about?"

"He's very closed-mouth. He would tell me only that he belongs to some sort of men's organization, something to do with Comus."

"The Greek god of revelry, eh?" Christophe gave another insouciant wave and toyed with his exaggerated lace cuffs. He was always a bit restless when his opinions were not the core of conversation. "That's all very interesting, but it seems to me that there are two serious problems both sides would be wise join forces and address."

Duncan removed his hat and toyed with the orange plumes. He'd never costumed before and secretly thought he looked very dashing as one of Dumas' musketeers. He hoped Justine would think the same. "What are they?"

"What I mentioned before, the cutthroats and whores. Unfortunately, the longshoremen from the Irish Channel have made it their carnival sport to attack free Negroes. They hate them because they work the docks for lower wages, and on Carnival Day the Irish take to the streets looking for trouble, hiding behind masks, of course. The city is always left to count the bodies on Ash Wednesday."

"And the whores?" Duncan asked warily.

"New Orleans is overflowing with them, and they take to the streets in amazing numbers, riding in decorated carriages and wearing the most scandalous costumes."

"That sounds more like fun than a problem," Duncan laughed.

"It should be, but it's not. They bare entirely too much flesh and yell all sorts of obscenities, at gentlemen naturally, but especially at any luckless lady who gets caught in their path. They don't confine their nastiness to attacks on the innocent citizenry either. Rivalry among the red light districts is acute. Those from the District will march on the Swamp and vice versa. Shouting matches quickly escalate into full-fledged assaults with fists, knives, rocks, and clubs. When it's all over, it's another occasion for counting bodies. There are always surprises for the coroner because many of them dress as men."

"No!"

"And some of their men dress as women. Pearl has told me some outrageous tales about carnival in the District. If the weather permits on Fat Tuesday, many people take to the streets wearing nothing at all. If it's too cold, they do the same inside the saloons and dance halls." He paused and chuckled. "Well, I shouldn't say they're entirely naked. Pearl says some of the women tuck plumes in their hair and most all of them carry some sort of weapon."

Duncan spoke as though in a trance, obviously transported to some sort of voyeuristic reverie. "How exciting. Perhaps we could get Red Bill to arrange something for us."

Christophe let out a whoop. "Could this possibly be the same conservative Virginian I met just three months ago?"

Duncan felt color rising in his cheeks. "I'm so embarrassed. What could I have been thinking?"

"*Mais non,* my boy!" Christophe insisted, "Apologies are *not* in order! I'm glad to see you surrendering to the spell of the city."

"I'm not exactly a stranger to her sorcery," Duncan confessed, thinking of Justine, the muse inspiring his return to poetry. "But I'm still embarrassed."

"Don't be. In all honesty, *mon ami,* I had entertained the same thought. After all, carnival is meant to be an escape from social restraints, a season for reveling and indulging in mischievous merrymaking of all sorts. It is a time when the Lords of Misrule are in control."

"I suppose," Duncan laughed. "Otherwise I wouldn't be appearing in public dressed as a musketeer."

"With a woman dressed likewise," Christophe added. "But that's the spirit! Regardless of what those doomsayers print, whores and miscreants won't stop the revelry. There will be over a thousand balls before the season is over."

"How is that possible?"

"Oh, they won't all be extravagant. Many will be small affairs in private homes, much smaller than the Fleurys' ball. The one tonight should be especially lavish, though. To be frank, Honoré Duval has more money than he knows what to do with and he loves opening that tight purse this one time a year. It will include a *galopade* and a—"

"A what?"

"A long theatrical performance of some kind, often entertaining, often tedious. It will end at midnight, which is when the dancing begins. That always lasts until dawn."

Duncan grimaced. "I'm afraid I'll never stay awake."

"Didn't I tell you to take a nap this afternoon?"

"No," Duncan lamented. Then, "Christophe, I'm so nervous I feel like I'm about to jump out of my skin!"

"Justine *naturellement.*"

"Of course. And this business of going to a ball where I know I'm not welcome."

"It's merely a little harmless mischief," Christophe insisted. He decided on a ploy of distraction to calm Duncan's frayed nerves. But how he longed to be in the man's shoes! "You will not be the only one there playing a little trick on our host. No doubt a gentleman or two will be present with whores on their arms."

"No!" Duncan was horrified, mind racing with other, equally shocking possibilities. "Do they bring their mistresses as well?"

"Certainly not if she's a woman of color, my boy, *Sacré bleu!* That's one propriety they dare not break!" He sighed with relief when L'Eveillé finally broke through the crush of carriages and trotted the horse smartly across the Rue Canal and into the *carré de la ville.* "Which is more than one can say for the white ladies."

"What do you mean?"

"I mean that certain very prominent Creole ladies are rumored to have invaded the *Salle d'Orleans* during Mardi Gras. Masked and costumed to the teeth of course."

"But why?"

"Act your age, boy. To see what their husbands are up to of course. Or perhaps just to satisfy one of their oldest curiosities, to see for themselves if the balls are as grand, the building as elegant and of course the women as beautiful as rumored."

"The city never ceases to amaze me!"

"But don't you see, Duncan?" Christophe said, waxing expansive as ever. "That's the true beauty of Mardi Gras, something the Latins knew centuries ago. Everyone wants to see something he's not supposed to, to be something or someone he's not. Carnival gives a man that chance."

"Obviously it gives women that same chance!" Duncan joked.

He turned toward high-pitched feminine squeals and roars of masculine laughter as an open landau jounced alongside. It was filled with colorfully costumed merrymakers who raised their wine glasses and toasted the two handsome musketeers waving back. Duncan was beginning to catch a little of the inevitable carnival fever Christophe promised, but it did not entirely undermine the apprehension he felt about seeing Justine.

The woman was, he reminded himself again and again, a married lady with whom there was no chance of anything more than the most casual friendship, one that would doubtless always have Christophe in attendance or at least close at hand. There would never be an opportunity to be alone, truly alone, but even if that were possible, would it not merely exacerbate his agony? He was in love with Justine, pure and simple, and he didn't know if he could keep from telling her as much. The fear of revelation gnawed at his entrails like a ravenous rat because he knew once she learned his true feelings, she would be required by social dictates to terminate further contact.

I must be insane to agree to this, he thought. I must be mad to allow myself to be drawn into this simultaneously chaste and perverse *ménage à trois*, this simulacrum of a liaison destined to end in frustration and misery. Why am I subjecting myself to such humiliation?

He had no answers of course, except for the obvious. Duncan Saunders was a man in love. Had he known Justine was a woman in love, he might have been even more blindly stuporous as L'Eveillé drew the carriage before the Blancard mansion in the Rue Dauphine.

"Oh, God," he murmured, the words fleeing him in a single release of breath.

"What is it?" Christophe watched him closely.

"Nothing, *mon ami*," Duncan replied, pleasing Christophe as always when he attempted a little French. "Nothing."

For his ball, Honoré Duval had chosen the St. Louis Hotel, unquestionably the smartest hostlery in the Creole district. Opened in 1838 and rebuilt after a disastrous fire just two years later, it was a five-story domed structure dominating half a block along the Rue St. Louis and included both an exchange and arcade of smart shops. It was one of Justine's favorite places, although like all ladies she avoided the rotunda by day when the place was given over to the auction of slaves. Their bare black feet stood on the very site where, tonight, white feet shod in fanciful shoes would swirl to the dance. But Justine thought of none of that, excitement focused on Duncan's confession that he had never been inside.

"Shame on you, Christophe," she chided, playfully poking him in the ribs as they alit from the carriage. He had never seen her so giddy, and it disheartened him to know the reason. Yet he struggled to keep his promise, to both her and himself, to be happy for her doomed passion. "How could you be so remiss as a tour guide? Why, after Jackson Square, this is the second heart of the city."

"I've taken him *other* places instead," Christophe retorted with a broad hint of mystery. "Places that others might say are the *real* heart of the *carré de la ville*." His naughty tone warned Justine not to pursue the taunt and she laughed gaily as he swept off his plumed hat to execute an elaborate bow. "But I nonetheless offer my apology, Madame Musketeer. Would you like to challenge your brother to a duel?" He drew his *colchemarde* and sliced the air dramatically.

His gesture drew bemused stares from passers-by who were quick to notice the three glamourous maskers. Toinette's seamstresses had done a marvelous job outfitting them in lush satins and embroidered brocades, hats trimmed in outrageously tall ostrich plumes. She had put Christophe in scarlet, Duncan in gold, and Justine in a blue that turned her eyes into bottomless pools. They also drew attention with their stair-step heights. Duncan was a good head taller than Christophe who in turn towered over the diminutive Justine. Some wondered if they might not be brothers, until they heard the woman's laughter. It was deep, throaty and, to Duncan, oddly arousing.

Justine's ebullience was contagious, and he couldn't help thinking that even dressed as a man she remained beautiful and utterly feminine, her attempts at masculine swaggering comic at best. Even in tunic, tights and high boots, her curves were undeniable and Duncan discerned the shape of her derriere and legs with considerable excitement. It was a rare and improper treat indeed, as ladies inevitably covered themselves in layers of clothing designed to display shoulders, bosoms, and tiny waists, never any part of the anatomy farther south. He could scarcely take his eyes from her.

Nor she him. It wasn't his looks that so compelled her, however, for in truth, Duncan was not handsome. But his quick smile suggested genuine warmth and the strong features were those of a man who could offer unassailable refuge. Having known neither, Justine wanted to fling herself into his arms, but at the same time was puzzled by her impulsiveness. The man unknowingly tempted her to cast aside everything she had been taught by *Tante* Nanine and the nuns, to forget she was a married matron and behave like she'd never behaved before.

The insistent urges were not altogether comfortable. She had told herself that she could manage a platonic relationship with the American, but since she had admitted to herself and to Christophe that she was in love with the man, she was making a liar of herself. She had not anticipated the glow Duncan's frequent gazes stirred on the nape of her neck or the light-headedness that, for once, did not come from whalebone stays laced too tight. She was experiencing something so altogether new that it was frightening, but with the same grit she summoned to face Blancard's most ferocious moods, she plunged into it headlong. For Justine, the most exhilarating aspect was that, deep in her soul, she had no idea where it would take her. For once in her life, she was embarking upon a reckless journey willingly and with all her heart.

Stepping between the men, she took their arms and sought to turn Christophe's omission into an advantage. "Then I will pretend to see the hotel through your eyes," she told Duncan, "so that I might also see it again for the first time." Duncan was utterly beguiled.

The St. Louis Hotel was deceptive, far more from within than without. Approaching from Exchange Alley, the trio of musketeers entered beneath a shallow portico and crossed a vestibule stretching 127 feet. Duncan felt Justine squeeze his arm when the ceiling suddenly retreated, opening into a dazzling rotunda soaring nine stories. It was crowned by a magnificent dome supported by sixteen marbleized Corinthian columns, each forty feet high, with bases of iron and capitals of striking black cypress. The walls were ornamented with arabesques and fresco paintings representing great cities of the world, and sixteen medallion portraits of great American heroes. Justine insisted her favorite was Lafayette while Christophe preferred, of all people, Amerigo Vespucci. Duncan was impressed by everything.

"It never fails to take my breath away," Justine confided, struggling to make herself heard over the din of masked revelers. The dome was magnificent but scarcely an acoustical triumph. "It's hard to believe the place burned just two years after it was completed. In a manner of speaking, this is a reproduction."

"It's absolutely remarkable," Duncan said. He tilted his head back to see the fourteen-foot wide oculus, which flooded the rotunda floor with sunlight in the daytime. Justine sputtered and laughed when he brushed her face with the plumes of his hat. "I'm afraid this thing takes some getting used to," he smiled.

"As does wearing tights," Justine confessed a bit sheepishly.

If Duncan thought anything of her bold remark he gave no notice. He barely had time to admire the grandiose dome before he was swept up in the madness of the moment. It was his first *bal masque,* and it was not an altogether pleasant experience. He was momentarily disconcerted by the inability to see faces. It didn't matter that he would have recognized no one: until the privilege was withdrawn, he didn't realize how much human reaction and interraction was based upon another's expression.

"It's strange at first, isn't it?" Justine said. "I remember my first masked ball as a child. I was actually frightened in the beginning."

"Understandable," Duncan said. He looked down at her, seeking a glimpse of her eyes through the slits of the silk mask. He found them, sparkling in the glow of a thousand gaslights. "You're not afraid now, are you?"

Justine's heart clutched. You couldn't possibly know, she thought. You couldn't possibly fathom the serenity I feel right now, the comfort I feel from nothing more than your presence. It was as if a blinding light had been turned on, obliterating the darkness that has been her half-existence with Blancard.

"For the first time in my life, Monsieur Saunders, I can honestly say no. This time I am not afraid."

As Christophe had said, there was the requisite *galopade,* which, to everyone's relief, was an obscure but highly amusing piece by an Italian playwright no one knew. It was filled with harlequins, punchinellos, and a fabulous scaramouche that kept the audience constantly shaking with laughter. Duncan was grateful for the end, however, because it signaled the beginning of the dance and the opportunity to hold Justine in his arms for the first time. Both were careful to see that Christophe had his fair share of dances, and although all three were having a wonderful time, Christophe suggested they leave well before dawn.

"But why?" Duncan asked, reluctant to bring an end to his time with Justine.

"Because as the night wears on, so does the drinking and there's always a rowdy or two who insists on looking beneath everyone's mask."

"He's right," Justine said. "We'd be wise to steer clear of such an event, owing to our host's prejudices."

"But isn't it too early to go home?" protested Duncan.

"Of course," Christophe grinned, noting that his friend had successfully banished all threats of fatigue. "Since Justine is in disguise, we can patronize the men's coffeehouses in the Rue Royale."

"And maybe take a short drive first," Justine suggested. "We ladies are always warned against the night air, but I could certainly use some just now. It's stifling in here, especially beneath this mask."

"An excellent idea," Christophe said. "Shall we go?"

Their spirits were still soaring when L'Eveillé turned the coach onto the Rue St. Louis and headed away from the river. Christophe had given him no instructions in particular, requesting only a short drive. When L'Eveillé protested that it might be dangerous, Christophe pointed to the crowds on the street. All of Creole society was at the Duval ball that night, and the banquettes fairly teemed with revelers.

Unlike L'Eveillé however, the trio inside didn't notice the sudden and drastic change when the coach crossed the Rue Rampart. The sidewalks were empty here in back-o-town which skirted *La Cypriére,* that trackless, virtually impenetrable morass stretching between the city and

Lake Ponchartrain. It was pitch black except for a few flames flaring sporadically before huts of palmetto fronds and shacks of the most wretched sort. Only the poorest, most desperate citizens lived in this dense cypress swamp where the mosquito, snake, and alligator still ruled. L'Eveillé realized his mistake and executed a hasty saccade. It was too late.

Their path was blocked by two men with large clubs, dark figures that had sprung from the shadows with lightning speed. One grabbed the horse while the other tore the door open and ordered the passengers out. Justine screamed, pushed back by Duncan who quickly blocked the doorway with his big body. Christophe peered over his shoulder, struggling to identify the source of the trouble.

"You there!" he shouted. "If you want to take me, you'll have to fight like a gentleman! I demand satisfaction!"

"Chris, for God's sake!" Duncan snapped, too late.

He watched in disbelief, Justine in abject terror, as Christophe forced his way out of the coach and confronted the two hooligans. They were big men, and their menacing manner made their bulk seem even more dangerous. Obviously they were prepared to make short work of this slightly drunken fool in his ridiculous silks and plumes.

"And who might you be?" chuckled one.

"The King of the Fops, I'd say!" laughed the other.

Undeterred, Christophe drew his sword and shouted, *"Engarde,* you filthy swine!"

Christophe's pitiful warning slashes were comically executed and drew more uproarious laughter from the thugs. Christophe lunged so carelessly that he tripped and sprawled at their feet. Even in his fear, Duncan couldn't help remembering the bumbling scaramouche they had watched in Duval's *galopade,* but he reminded himself this was quite serious. As the men moved against Christophe, Duncan sprang from the coach, intending to station himself between the thieves and his fallen friend.

"You've more to deal with than him," he warned. He was totally inexperienced in fencing and drew still more gales of laughter when he fumbled with his *colchemarde.* It flew from his hand and splashed helplessly into a dark pool of swamp water.

"My God, man!" muttered Christophe as one of the men helped him to his feet. "You're even clumsier than me. And I was only pretending."

Duncan was baffled, especially when Christophe slapped both ruffians on the back and politely inquired after their health. Knowing Justine would be frightened out of her wits, however, Christophe brought a hasty end to the charade.

"These are a couple of the Live Oak Boys," Christophe announced. The mere mention of the deadly name brought a whimper of fear from the carriage. "It's all right!" he called. "I know these men."

Justine poked her head warily through the coach window, not yet able to comprehend what she had just seen. Fear had made her heart throb high in her throat. "Wha . . . what on earth?" she stammered.

"The hows and whys don't matter just now," Christophe said. He reached in his costume and extracted a wallet, wisely overpaying the men for their trouble. "Just be grateful that it was these boys who attempted to waylay us rather than some who might be not be so understanding."

"You're very generous, Mr. Arno," grunted one.

"Indeed," agreed the other. "Perhaps we might accompany you away from here before something else happens."

"An excellent idea!" said Christophe. His pulse was racing from the excitement of the moment and he suddenly wanted to do something daring. He turned to Duncan. "You mentioned earlier that you wanted to explore the District. I say now is as good a time as any."

"Are you mad?" Duncan spat. He jerked his head toward the coach. "What about . . . ?"

"In the coach with you!" Christophe cried hastily. "You boys can ride on top with L'Eveillé. You remember him."

"Indeed we do," said one, swinging high into the coachman's seat and making L'Eveillé feel none too comfortable. If he lived to be a thousand, he'd never understand his master's obsession to flirt with danger. He snapped the reins when he heard the unpleasant command.

"The Rue Gallatin, L'Eveillé."

Inside the coach, Justine whimpered and clung to Duncan, all pretenses of propriety destroyed by raw fear. Christophe tried to melt the tension with a joke. "Is that any way for Aramis to behave toward Athos? I think not!"

"I . . . I thought we were going to die!" gasped Justine. "Just when I thought I was going to start living!"

That, thought Duncan, is something I must ask her about later.

They rode in silence for a few moments, each lost in a private terror of more disastrous consequences. Neither man mentioned that they had been discussing crime earlier that evening. Nor did Justine want to dwell on her recent discussion with Toinette of the Gallatin Street murders, but they returned to mind when she considered Christophe's order to L'Eveillé.

"Good heavens!" she gasped. "Why are we going there?"

"I thought it would be amusing," Christophe answered lightly. "And there's no need for you to protest that you are a lady. Duncan and I know that only too well. As for the others . . . well, the less they know about you the better."

"Just now my sex is not the issue," Justine protested flatly. "After what nearly happened, I should think the Rue Gallatin is the last place we should want to be."

"She's right," Duncan said. "The coffee houses on Royal Street are a much wiser choice."

"For shame!" Christophe taunted. "Do you think this is the way the musketeers would have behaved? *Sacre bleu,* I think not! Where is your spirit of adventure?"

"I'm afraid it's back there in *La Cypriére,*" Justine moaned. "Lying in the swamp alongside Duncan's sword."

"What a pair of cowards I'm with! Don't you know these men are the best possible insurance, that no one would dare raise a hand against us with them in tow? Why, the very mention of the Live Oak Boys sends a chill through through the District!"

"What on earth makes you think they can be trusted?" Justine asked.

"They probably can't," Christophe conceded. "But Red Bill Wilson can, and they know very well that I will report any misbehavior to him."

"And pray tell who is Red Bill Wilson?"

"The unofficial leader of the gang. Miscreants like these have few loyalties, but old Bill somehow manages to squeeze it out of them. I assure you, Justine, we will not be harmed. We'll be in the safest place in the District."

"I may be a sequestered Creole lady," Justine said, "but I'm not a total fool! Everyone in New Orleans knows about the dangers of the Rue Gallatin. Why, I've known about the place ever since I was old enough to read the newspapers. How could there possibly be a safe place in that hellhole?"

"Justine!" Christophe gasped.

"I'm only quoting *L'Abeille,*" she snapped. "Just this morning it said, and I quote, 'The Swamp is a festering sore in the American sector while the Rue Gallatin remains a living hellhole in the downriver bowels of the *carré de la ville.*' So there."

"I stand corrected," Christophe said, laughing softly. "You know, Justine? Tonight you are so different, so candid, so utterly unlike yourself that I can hardly believe I'm with the person I've known all these years. You continually surprise me."

"Myself as well," she conceded. She looked at Duncan. "You must think me terrible, Monsieur Saunders. Why, I've all but behaved like a fallen woman."

"Nothing could ever dislodge you from the high plateau to which I have elevated you," Duncan said.

"Spoken like a true poet," Christophe said, tempted to add that those were also the words of a man in love. "Very well, Justine. I'll tell L'Eveillé to change course."

"You'll do nothing of the sort!" Justine smiled, good spirits, along with no small dose of confidence, returning. "You're right. This should indeed be a night of adventure. Gallatin Street it is!"

"You're quite sure?" asked Duncan.

Like Christophe, he was astonished by Justine's bold behavior. It was as though she had changed personalities along with her clothes, play-acting the part of a roguish musketeer instead of a highborn Creole. Once he had adjusted to the shocking difference, he eagerly embraced it. After all, Justine the lady would never have permitted more than the slightest physical contact. She most certainly would not have leaned so daringly close as now, when the coach bounced into the rutted streets of the lower *carré de la ville*.

"I'm quite sure," she replied. "Although for my own peace of mind I would like to know about this mysterious haven in the middle of such danger."

"Fair enough," said Christophe. "We are going to visit a lady named Blanche Genois."

"No relation to the family who lived across the street from you, I'm sure."

"The same."

Justine was flabbergasted. "But they were as old as the Arnauds and the Fonteneaus. I remember when they lost their fortune, but surely Madame Genois could not be . . . !"

"She is now called Madame Pearl and she operates the most exclusive . . . well, since we're breaking all sorts of taboos tonight, I'll say the word."

"Bordello," Justine laughed. "There! I've said it for you."

"But how could you know about such things?" Duncan asked.

"You have a great deal to learn about women, Monsieur Saunders. Fallen and otherwise."

Duncan leaned so close Christophe could not hear. "Teach me."

"I believe I shall," she whispered back. "But such education is, I believe, a two-way street."

The first thing Justine noticed about the District was the stench. It preceded Gallatin Street by several blocks, a noxious wave blending fish and waste, rotgut whiskey, burning tar, and decay of all sorts, including human. Like all New Orleanians, she was not unaware that the city stank, that it was like a fragrant swamp lily shimmering uneasily atop a cesspool, but after a while it was absorbed and forgotten. This appalling stink was a fetid reminder, and it took a moment before her nose embraced it. The men noticed it too, but they had expected as much and waited for the unpleasant moment to pass.

Justine also accepted the wildness in the street. With her mask again in place, no one could gauge her reaction, but Christophe was well aware when she gripped his arm too tightly. Or leaned, trembling, against Duncan. The interior of Pearl's shook her every sensibility, and despite her pretenses of worldliness, she was utterly horrified. The sight of the bedraggled women, foul-smelling, drunken, and unkempt, many half-naked as they plied their trade with equally miserable men, was almost too much. So were the ragged bodies shoved in corners, some drunk, some beaten and cut, some dead and lying right in her path. Like everyone else in the city she knew death; she had seen too many corpses during the plague years not to recognize it, but this one . . . *mon Dieu!*

"Chris!"

When he saw that Justine was not going to faint, Christophe helped her over a body grotesquely contorted with rigor mortis. "I'm afraid death is a close companion of life here, *mon cher.*"

"But how can someone be left to . . . ?"

Christophe shrugged with disturbing nonchalance. "Eventually someone will get around to throwing the poor soul into the street. In the meantime, what's one more body found in the Rue Gallatin?"

Everyone seemed scarred, battered, damaged, and it was discomforting when she found she could relate to their despair and humiliation as human beings. How had they come to this? How had any human being sunk to this low water mark of existence? That drunken, wild-eyed whore straddling the sailor's lap, thighs widespread to offer the most shocking of vistas, hadn't she once been some *maman's* precious little girl? And what about that man shivering in the street outside, half his face a bloody pulp, his moans still tugging at Justine's heart. Hadn't he been some father's darling, bounced on papa's knee and given a pony? She knew, of course. And she knew how, beneath her silks and satins, sequestered in the fine townhouse in the Rue Dauphine, she was little better off than they. She was perilously, hideously close to being one of them.

She was forced to keep moving, to plunge deeper and deeper into the hellish realm, yet with each step she wanted to turn back and run screaming from the place. But she was trapped between Christophe and Duncan, hemmed in by the ferocious Live Oak Boys. More and more she was grateful for the mask and told herself she must never take it off.

"Safe harbor lies behind that door there," announced Christophe, shouting to be heard above the din.

Justine nodded, unsure what to say. She was shaking so badly Duncan yelled that they should take her home, but Christophe couldn't hear. In another moment, they were inside the warm richness of Pearl's private apartments, the vile, unwashed horrors of the bar replaced by soft music, the swish of satin gowns, and the fragrance of jasmine and sweet olive. Such lushness could not have been more unexpected, but respite arrived too late. Justine had barely been presented to Pearl when she was gripped by powerful nausea. The madam quickly summoned a Negro servant girl to whisk Justine away. When she returned some time later, mask tucked under her arm, she was ashen but steady.

Christophe was immediately at her side. "My deepest apologies, *cher*. I should never have brought you here. What on earth could I have been thinking? Dare I blame it on the whiskey?"

"Blame it on me for not refusing," Justine dismissed. She scanned the room, drinking in the luxurious appointments, and conceding that the women were both comely and most fashionably dressed. She wondered idly if Toinette was their *modiste*. "This place is truly unexpected. How on earth did it come to be in this . . . this . . ."

"Hellhole?" offered Duncan. They all laughed, and Justine felt much better. "That's a story you should hear from Madam Pearl."

"That's the one once called Blanche Genois?"

"The same, honey." Pearl had come to inquire after the woman's health and insisted that she come to her private quarters. She knew women like Justine were destined to be overwhelmed by a plunge into the *demimondaine* and wanted to give her a chance to recoup. "We'll enjoy a feminine conversation while the boys amuse themselves."

Duncan's look pleaded that he wanted only to be by Justine's side, but Christophe drew him away. When they were alone on a tufted settee as luxurious as anything in the Blancard house, Pearl smiled and patted Justine's hands. Ordinarily Justine recoiled at a stranger's touch, but she found the madam's touch oddly comforting. "I've known that mischievous Christophe for years but I never thought he'd do anything as outrageous as this. You're welcome of course, but what possessed you to let him bring you here, dear?"

"I'm afraid we were all simply caught up in one of carnival's insane moments," Justine replied. "Certainly I should have told him no, but I . . . well, lately I've not been myself."

"What do you mean?"

The old woman's tone was inviting, but as brazen as Justine had been these past few hours, she refused to discuss intimacies with a total stranger. And certainly not the madam of a brothel!

"I'm afraid it's very personal."

"As you say." Pearl withdrew her hand and drew a tiparillo from her jeweled reticule. While Justine watched in shock, Pearl lit the cigar, took a long draw and exhaled a stream of bluish smoke above her head. "I'd offer you one, dear, but . . ."

"Oh, no, thank you!"

Justine smiled politely as she considered such an absurdity. But the incongruity didn't seem so far-fetched when she saw herself in a mirrored screen nearby. Each of three panels reflected different angles of an elegantly gowned, cigar-puffing elderly woman sitting beside a musketeer. Justine burst out laughing.

"You know what, Madam Pearl? I've traveled as far as Constantinople, but never have I felt as far away from home as I do at this very moment. This place is like something out of a dream."

"One reached only after traversing a nightmare, eh, my dear?"

Justine nodded. "I should like very much to hear about the journey that brought you here."

She watched the woman exhale another plume of smoke before she began her story. She was enrapt by the tragic tale of the woman's fall from grace and her bizarre retreat into a place such as this. She tried not to reveal her shock at some of the more prurient details but could not prevent color from rushing to her cheeks when Pearl graphically described her moments of ecstasy with the dashing Javier Sandoval.

"But you are a married woman," Pearl said finally. "Such talk shouldn't embarrass you. Surely you and the other ladies commiserate about matters in the boudoir."

"Certainly not!" Justine said, tone a bit too sharp. "That is to say, I don't." She started to add that, except for Toinette, she had no close women friends, but thought better of it.

"But I forget," Pearl apologized with a wry smile. "Things under the Spanish regime were not quite so prim. The French Creoles had not yet had time to create such a delicate breed of ladies. Oh, we were proper too, mind you, but never to this degree. You started to say something, my dear. What was it?"

"It's so embarrassing, so bold, I don't know if I can," Justine confessed.

"Nonsense!" Pearl took her hand again. "Believe me, Madame Blancard, nothing is too bold for these ancient eyes and ears. I assure you I have heard it all."

Justine swallowed hard, wondering where she found the courage for such an improper question. "Did . . . did you simply manage the . . . place or . . . ?" Her cheeks flushed again as the words refused to come.

"Or did I work here, too? Of course I did! I say it and without shame. For a woman like myself with no family and no aptitude for anything except choosing the proper gown or arranging flowers, there were precious few options. Since I was being ostracized as a scarlet woman, I chose to play the part. And you know what, honey?" She leaned close to make her confidence and revealed a row of even but tobacco-yellowed teeth. "I had a good time with almost every man I was with."

"Oh!"

"Don't look so surprised, Madame Blancard. If I didn't know better I'd think your husband has provided little pleasure in the boudoir."

"None. Ever!"

There, Justine thought. I've said it. And I don't care!

"*Mais non!*" The old madam was incredulous. "A beautiful woman like yourself? What can be wrong with the man?"

"With all due respect, Madam Pearl, my story is ignominious."

"Pardon?"

"I . . . I cannot tell it. It's too ugly, too shameful."

"As you wish, my dear. But tell me this. Has he a mistress?"

"*Oui.*"

"Of color?"

Again, softer, "*Oui.*"

"This damnable *plaçage!*" Pearl snarled. "It brings nothing but evil to countless lives, all except the men who invented it, of course. A wife *and* a mistress, the whole condoned by society. If ever there was a way for a man to have his cake and eat it too, this is it! *Merde!*" She fixed Justine with an angry glare. "Did he, as the saying goes, put you on a pedestal and leave you there while he amused himself elsewhere?"

"In part," was all Justine could reveal.

"Then you don't really know the pleasures a man can bring a woman?"

"I didn't know such a thing existed," Justine conceded.

"I'm hardly surprised," Pearl lamented. "If only men and women talked about such things. If only men knew women could receive as much excitement as themselves. If only . . . ."

"You mean there's more for a woman than submission?"

"Oh, my poor child! *Mais oui!* Much more." Although they were alone, she leaned close and whispered. Justine's ear burned when she heard the perverse pronouncement. She couldn't fathom allowing a man to do that, not even with Pearl's astonishing promise of sheer ecstasy.

"*Non!* It's unthinkable. More than that, it's impossible!"

Pearl shook her head. "*C'est vrai, ma petit.* You can have the very same excitement as the man."

"I don't understand," insisted Justine. "If what you say is true . . ."

"Believe me, *cher*, it is!"

"Then why does everyone conspire to deny it? Mothers, fathers, certainly the church. *Everyone.* Why are women not allowed this knowledge?"

Pearl shrugged. "In fairness, most men probably don't know. It is, after all, up to the woman to explain what pleases her. Men are not mind readers. But even if they knew the facts, I doubt they would take the time to share the pleasure. Men are too often in a hurry to please only themselves. Men are . . . well, men."

Justine rose and paced the room slowly, *colchemarde* banging absurdly against her thigh. Her eye was repeatedly drawn to an alcove behind the settee, a most astonishing piece of furniture glimpsed through crimson portieres. It was a massive bed in the shape of a boat. An elegant swan graced the prow, a lantern gripped in its beak, the mahogany darkness looming darker because of the bright white *mosquitaire* draped above. It was elaborately carved with what seemed to be cherubs, garlands, and things she could not identify from a distance. She had never seen anything like it.

"I see you've noticed the bed." Pearl said. Justine's back was to her but she knew the woman was smiling. And with a strange pride.

"It's remarkable!" Justine went closer to investigate. "Is it one of the pieces you bought from your family?"

"My grandfather found it in Venice. It was carved in the sixteenth century for some doge's favorite. It was always my favorite piece and I longed to sleep in it as a child." Justine passed her hand over the prow, amazed by the sweep of the swan's long neck, which seemed to be cut from a single piece of wood. The feather detailing was astonishing. She didn't realize how long she stood there massaging the wood until it warmed to her touch. "I was never even permitted to get into it, much less sleep there. But I certainly made up for it in later years."

Justine nudged the stepstool leading into the huge affair. "I think if I got in there I'd never want to come out."

"Believe me, my dear, there were times when I felt the same way. I never use it now. These old bones aren't as supple as they used to be and I find those little stairs difficult to climb." She was amused by Justine's fascination. "By all means see what it's like."

"Oh, I couldn't!"

"Like all great ladies, you deny yourself too much," Pearl said, the edge in her voice just the thing to propel Justine into the fantastic bed. It was filled to overflowing with pillows of brocade and satins, trimmed with tassels and fringe and the most elaborate passementerie she'd ever seen. It belonged, she thought with no small amount of wickedness, in the Sultan's harem at Topkapi.

"When I got up this morning," she said from the depths of the bed, "I knew it was going to be a new day, a day filled with surprises. What has happened is all that and more, much more. To be frank, I don't know if I can digest it all."

"May I tell you how much I admire you, Madame Blancard?"

Justine sat up. *"Merci.* But what an odd thing to say."

"Not really. You see, I see much of myself in you at your age. I know what a shock it has been for you to come to a place like this. I was perhaps only slightly less shocked when I found myself here too. What I'm admiring is your spirit. While I don't know what's troubling your marriage, I know that you've taken some daring steps outside it tonight. And it's my guess that Duncan Saunders is the reason why."

"Perhaps," Justine smiled, not bothering to deny it.

"Then let an old lady do the worst thing imaginable, and give you some advice," Pearl said.

"I should be honored," Justine said as she returned to the settee. "Please do."

"I know a great deal about the cruelty and loss of family. Although you've not said so, I suspect you do as well. All I will say is, be as prepared as possible to handle the consequences when they come. And they surely will. If you end up shunned and ostracized like myself, you may end up with this."

"But what you've created here is wonderful," Justine said.

"Beautiful, yes. Wonderful, no. Never forget that all this glamour lies in the heart of a human cesspool." She rose slowly and took Justine's arm for support as they walked to the door. "My life is all illusion, dear Madame Blancard. Don't make the same mistake. Find something substantial." Both blinked as they moved from Pearl's dimly lit quarters to the brilliance of the chandeliers. "Ah, there's your gentleman now, waiting for his mistress like an anxious puppy."

"So he is," Justine said, returning Duncan's smile as he rose and approached them. "Would you say he looks substantial, Madam Pearl?"

"Mais oui, ma chére! Mais oui!"

CHAPTER 16

The house was dark when Justine arrived home at dawn. Blancard's carriage was absent as usual, and with the exception of Agathe, already stirring in the kitchen, the servants were fast asleep. Good, she thought. Perfect for what I want.

She climbed the stairs to the third floor where a small door concealed a narrow staircase leading to an attic filled to overflowing with the debris of past lives. Justine was no stranger here and had long ago carved for herself a tight path to one of the dormer windows. Not without difficulty, for it always stuck, she pushed it up and, boosting herself on an old sea chest, clambored through.

"Ah," she sighed, breathing deeply of the cool delta air. "Just as I hoped."

This point, some forty feet above the streets, was one of the highest vantage points in the *carré de la ville,* and she cherished it as hers alone. She had created this private retreat when she desperately sought solitude and escape from the prying eyes of Marie Tonton. The servant knew about it, but for reasons known only to herself never disturbed her mistress there. Such uncharacteristic consideration made Justine wonder if, deep down, the terrible woman had a heart after all.

She sighed again and leaned full length against the slate roof tiles, quickly feeling the cold dampness penetrate her costume. She shaded her eyes as dawn surged toward the city on a brilliant tide. A dense orange reef was forming over the Gulf, turning the great bend in the river a pure, molten gold. The new day was not coming gently, but announcing itself with a bold sheen that hurt Justine's eyes. She found it deeply satisfying and altogether appropriate.

"Today I no longer know who I am, and from the look of things, the world is also hungry for a new beginning."

From her lofty perch, Justine felt the weak winter sun strengthen, deepening its strokes over the city, crawling into the nooks and crannies of courtyards and iron-fringed galleries, down chimneys and deep into colonnades. And into Justine's very bones. Its warmth fed her, sustained her, gave her the will to weigh the madness of the past twelve hours.

"It's as if I set out to do everything to disgrace myself," she murmured. "Almost nothing I did this evening was appropriate for a lady, but then perhaps Pearl is right." A smile curled her mouth. "Perhaps the cost of being a great lady is too high. Especially when a man like Hilaire Blancard is setting the price."

Justine well knew what had brought her here, knew what she was going to confront as she struggled to sort through all that had happened. She had felt it in her soul before she talked with Madam Pearl, and when she had laid in that fabulous boat bed she knew her course was set.

She would tell Duncan Saunders of her love!

She barely considered the consequences of discovery. She had little doubt that Blancard would kill her if he found out but, as Toinette had said, her life as it was now was no life at all. Of course, Duncan Saunders had given her a precious *raison d'etre* but his mere presence was, strangely, not enough. Something in her had been stirred, a rapacity she did not know existed. Duncan had awakened the appetite, Madam Pearl had whetted it, and now she was setting out to satisfy it.

She would take Duncan Saunders for her lover!

She was terrified, of course. Was it possible that Madam Pearl was exaggerating, that what she claimed existed between men and women was a figment of her prurient imagination? She had been, after all, a whore. But no. Toinette was a fine lady and she had insisted that Blancard was a monster, that what he did in the boudoir was a despicable perversion. She believed—she *had* to believe—that there was more to lovemaking than what she had known.

Justine contemplated the shadows stretching across the banquettes far below. It was not the first time she had studied the distance between herself and the streets. Once she had come here with a ripe tomato and tossed it into the air to see what would happen. Its blood-red explosion had sickened her and momentarily discouraged her thoughts of suicide.

So much had happened so fast that she was dizzy from it. By surrendering to the forces of passion, she had found the strength to go up against Blancard and Creole society itself. Never had she felt so satisfied, but the accompanying terror was exhilarating. Such exuberance coursed through her body that Justine felt she could join the screeching seagull orbiting overhead, its wings tinged with gold as it circled beneath the sun.

She also sensed the maleficent angel of her past hovering as well, but she denied it. More than that, she pronounced it dead. Blancard had said it himself. Their marriage was over. She closed her eyes and delivered a silent, evil eulogy for that which was lost but unmourned.

She would discover, with Duncan, that wildly intimate secret Madam Pearl had just revealed!

Justine closed her eyes and filled her lungs with the sun-warmed air, exulting in her self-proclaimed emancipation. She remained on the rooftop while the sun heated her eyelids, listening to the city as it stirred and rose from sleep. Without looking, she listened to the creak of wagons bearing slaves to work, in the distilleries or the brickyards and munitions factories downriver. There was also the music of carriage bells as the Gallé family returned from the Duval ball. After a while, Justine opened her eyes, dazzled by dawn's deepening gleam on the thicket of ship masts at the foot of the Rue des Ursulines. It promised to be a glorious day, one she would have enjoyed more if she had not been so fatigued. But she did not go downstairs without a heart-felt paean for her home city.

"*Ah, La Nouvelle-Orléans,*" she sighed. "I've never thought you more beautiful than at this very moment. But this is as it should be for I am seeing you through the eyes of a new woman."

Marie Tonton had turned down her bed hours earlier, and Justine shed the musketeer's costume easily. As she tugged on her nightgown and snuggled beneath the sheets, she smiled at the recollection of Madam Pearl's outrageous bed.

"I will have, you, Duncan Saunders," she sighed. "That's a promise to myself I refuse to break."

When Justine turned onto her side, the nightgown slipped above her knees. She closed her eyes, willing away the church's excoriation for what she planned to do. She could almost see the damnation in Sister Anunciata's eyes as her hand snaked sleepily between her thighs, exploring the forbidden region the old madam had so vividly described. She trembled as her fingers brushed the damp down, half expecting a fatal bolt of lightning through the ceiling. When nothing ensued except a delicious desire for more, she ventured further, sliding her fingers toward the cleft beyond.

"*Mais non!*"

She hastily withdrew, paralyzed by a memory of fear strong enough to make her whimper. Only Blancard had touched her there and always left her reeling in raw, rough agony. She had never entertained the possibility that her loins held anything but pain, but now she reconsidered Madam Pearl's assertion that a man's touch could be exciting. Just imagining the man was Duncan rekindled a desire to explore again.

Slowly, the old woman's words returned, goading Justine to seek the promise of exquisite release. Justine dwelled a moment on a description of anatomical matters so graphic as to be unrepeatable, yet it prompted her to probe further and seek the tiny button of flesh in question.

"Oh!"

It was there! What Pearl had promised was there! Its reality shook Justine to the quick. The pleasure was so superb it ignited her very flesh, radiating a tangible heat when she imagined it was Duncan's sweet touch rather than her own. Her forehead blazed, and she jerked her hand away as though it had been thrust into a flame, but it was not for any ingrained fear of Catholic condemnation. The promise of such ecstasy frightened Justine, and she hastily decided it was not something she should explore alone.

"Duncan will be my guide," she murmured with immeasurable anticipation. "Duncan will touch me like no man has." And then, because she could not help herself, she crossed herself and whispered, "God forgive me!"

She had hoped for dreams of Duncan and of their future together, however unsure, but instead there were nightmares of the basest sort. She imagined herself in Pearl's Place, saw herself as one of the girls working there with a long line of men stretching from the boat bed outside to the street. Each was filthier, more vile than the last. The Live Oak Boys were waiting their turn, and Blancard too, in a soiled, blood-stained dinner jacket, along with the corpse Justine had seen sprawled on the floor of Pearl's Place. He had risen from the dead to take his pleasure too, and she could not shake the memory of his putrefied visage.

Justine awoke, damp with sweat and fearful of returning to sleep. She willed herself to stay awake but found herself again drifting toward a cloying fuzziness of sight and sound. Blessedly, there was nothing but a vacuous darkness and when she awoke again it was to the sound of the noon angelus. She rose dutifully to kneel at the *prie-dieu*, but this time it was not only Christ she celebrated. It was her own incarnation, resurrected and made manifest at last.

Justine's exuberance stayed with her as she rose and rang for Marie Tonton. Nor did it retreat with the sound of the woman's footsteps approaching down the hall. She even smiled as the woman eased a tray of coffee onto the bedside table.

"No breakfast," she ordered. "A full lunch. I'm ravenous."

"You want it in bed or downstairs?" Marie Tonton asked, sounding more mechanical than ever. Since she had been ordered from Justine's room after warning her against Toinette, Marie Tonton had assumed a new persona, one that reminded Justine more of a machine than a human being. If there had been no warmth about her before, what emanated now was queerly cold. But Justine would not allow the woman's icy indifference to discolor her mood.

"I'll have it here. And afterward you'll dress me for an afternoon out. The rose taffeta will do. I want to look especially nice." Justine was thrilled when Marie Tonton's facade dropped just long enough for her to take the bait.

"Where are you going?"

"Why, to call on my good friend, Toinette Clovis of course," she replied, relishing every word. "Now hurry up, girl. I told you I was starving!"

She stifled a laugh as Marie Tonton vanished in a cloud of dark Coramantee muttering. She no longer dreaded the woman. Indeed she now almost relished confrontation. Toinette's intimidation had given Justine the strength to discipline the servant as she should have done all along, had it not been for Blancard's interference. It pleased her deeply, this new assertion, because it reflected a further break from the old ways.

Toinette's high spirits faded the moment Justine entered the shop. Only Justine's deserved self-absorption kept her from noticing anything unusual about the modiste's behavior. They had not seen each other in a week, and ordinarily Toinette would have hung on her every word, but she listened only half-heartedly as Justine recounted her escapades. Justine made no secret of her delight at Toinette's shock.

"But how could you?" Toinette gasped. She was so stunned by Justine's most unorthodox behavior that she momentarily forgot more pressing issues. "Taking Monsieur Saunders to the Duval ball! And then venturing into the Rue Gallatin! My heavens, Justine! People are killed there every day!"

Justine shrugged. "I began thinking, dear friend. Since I am punished without provocation whenever Hilaire has a whim, I decided I might as well have an adventure or two. To justify his actions as well as mine."

"You mustn't think such things," Toinette warned. "You're making excuses for him again."

"Not really. In any case, I have to have fun while I can. It's only a matter of time before he's up to his old tricks again." She pursed her lips, nurturing a hope, not for the first time. "Although this time I think it may be quite a while before he pays me much attention. He's got such a lovely new plaything these days." She sighed, adding as a perverse afterthought, "Poor thing."

"But Justine!" Toinette cried, ignoring the impropriety of referring to Hilaire's mistress. "You were such a fragile creature that awful day I came calling. Who is this new person I see? And where on earth do you get such daring?"

"Why, from *you* of course," Justine smiled. "Your strength has been with me from the beginning. I draw from it daily."

Toinette frowned. "You must not make so much of my advice, Justine. I am no miracle worker with all the answers. I was merely trying to help someone in sore need."

"You are too modest, *ma chere*. Much too modest."

Toinette waved away the flattery as she remembered who was due at the shop any minute. She took Justine's arm and steered her toward the door. "It's always wonderful to see you, of course, but I'm afraid you've come at a bad time for a visit. My day is filled with fittings. You've no idea how hectic things get as carnival draws near. All sorts of people are making desperate last-minute requests." When she saw the embarrassment on Justine's face, she hastily added, "Present company excepted. I was only too happy to make the musketeer costumes."

"I won't keep you then," Justine said, disappointed that Toinette didn't have time for her. "But I will inquire as to the progress of my Byzantine costume."

"It is a little behind schedule," Toinette said, heart racing when she spied familiar faces coming down the banquette. "But with some extra effort from Soona it will be ready on time. Now you really must excuse me, *mon ami*. I have much to do." To Toinette's deep distress, Justine balked. Instead of leaving, she insisted on perusing some bolts of pale blue silk Nicole was setting out for display.

Toinette had no choice but to open the door to admit Colette and Chaillot Baptiste.

While a Creole woman might know of her husband's involvement in *plaçage*, it was never acknowledged and under no circumstances discussed. Such was not the case for the mistress who often had to listen to her lover's complaints and sometimes praise regarding his wife and their children. While the mistress might therefore know a great deal about the wife, the reverse was never true. The wife knew nothing of the mistress, not even the woman's name.

That their paths should cross was highly unlikely but not impossible, as neither ventured frequently from the *carré de la ville*. Toinette silently lamented her fate that such an encounter should happen in her shop. Of course Justine would know nothing of the fair-skinned colored beauties entering the shop, but the Baptiste women were all too familiar with the name Hilaire Blancard—and his wife.

Toinette took a deep breath and greeted the new arrivals. "Madame Baptiste. Mademoiselle Baptiste." She nodded, speaking as softly as possible. "Always an honor when you come to my shop. Your note said you were interested in something special. Some brocade, I believe."

"It is Chaillot who needs the new gown," Colette replied rather coldly. Toinette had been quite outspoken in her criticism, indeed condemnation, of the quadroon balls, but only in private. However, Colette had seen too much disapproval not to recognize it in the woman's gray eyes. She remained polite but distant. "Tell her what you want, angel."

"That bolt there," Chaillot announced firmly. "It would be heavenly with my eyes."

Toinette's heart leapt again when she saw where Chaillot was looking. "But that's silk, mademoiselle. I thought your interest was in brocade. We have some exceptional material just off the boat from Paris. I'm sure . . ."

"Later perhaps," Chaillot dismissed.

The helpless *modiste* was horrified and helpless as Chaillot swept by her to inspect the same fabric passing between Justine's fingers. She held her breath as the two women nodded politely and exchanged pleasantries. Colette watched too as the beauties cast critical eyes upon one another, evaluating everything from coiffure to dress. It was Justine who finally broke the ice.

"I've always wished I could wear that color," she said, nodding at Chaillot's smart coat of burgundy merino. "It makes me look haggard."

"I can't imagine anything unsuitable for you, madame," Chaillot said honestly.

She was genuine in her praise, nodding discreetly for Colette to look at Justine. She was rarely moved by the beauty of another female, but this one was different. Perhaps, she thought as Justine returned the compliment, it was because this woman seemed to be without a trace of vanity. That was certainly more than she could say herself, and the selfish notion brought a smile to her face. It did not go unnoticed.

"But you should smile more, my dear," said Justine. "You seem so serious."

"I'm afraid my life has been all too serious of late," Chaillot said guilelessly. After a moment she realized Justine was studying her and not the fabric. "Is something wrong, madame?"

"Forgive me for staring, mademoiselle. It's just that you don't look familiar. Are you visiting someone perhaps?"

Dear God, thought Chaillot. She thinks I'm white!

She cast about helplessly, searching for the words to explain herself. But before she found safe harbor, the situation worsened. A numbing shiver shot down her spine as Justine extended her hand. Toinette, watching every move, was paralyzed with horror.

"But where are my manners?" Justine said, chiding herself. "Allow me to introduce myself. I'm Madame Hilaire Blancard."

The name turned Chaillot's insides to jelly. Dear God! How was it possible?

But she had no time to consider the reality of meeting Michie Hilaire's wife. She must first circumvent the threatening breach of etiquette posed by Justine's hand. Chaillot wisely retreated, gathered the folds of her coat, and dropped a curtsy.

"I am Chaillot Baptiste, Madame Blancard." She choked back the bile buoying the requisite words to her lips, "A free woman of color."

"Oh!"

Justine's hand plummeted to her side, cheeks blazing as the impact of the *faux pas* washed over her in a deeply discomfiting wave. But then, remembering the game she often played with herself, trying to guess the secrets of the most porcelain of the *sang-melées*, she burst out laughing. She had been wildly mistaken about this young woman.

"Madame?" Chaillot bristled. "Is something wrong?"

"Not at all," she said, boldly squeezing Chaillot's arm as though such intimacy would erase all awkwardness. It helped, but the moment still weighed heavily on both. "Forgive me," she said at length.

"But no apology is necessary," Chaillot pleaded, confused and not a little piqued. She nodded politely and sought to withdraw, but Justine's grip was firm. "Is there something else, Madame Blancard?"

"*Oui,*" Justine replied, discreetly lowering her voice. "As a matter of fact, there is."

She looked into the lanceolate eyes with such ferocity Chaillot was unnerved. Was it possible she knew? The truth rushed at her with such bold swiftness she felt her knees sag. She hoped the white woman didn't notice when she gripped the display table for support.

"Madame?"

"And we both know what it is, don't we, Mademoiselle Baptiste?"

Despite her cool, even haughty composure, Chaillot was terrified. She glanced helplessly at her mother, who was deep in conversation with

Toinette. She opened her mouth to answer, but the answer, the truth, was locked away somewhere deep in her soul and she could not summon it. Not even when the white woman deepened her grip. It might have hurt—Chaillot didn't know. At that moment, she knew only that she wished she could will herself a thousand miles away.

"Then I will say it for you," Justine said, leaning closer still. So close that Chaillot found herself inspecting that perfect face for any telltale discoloration that would hint of bruises. She saw only a disconcerting warmth flowing from the other woman's eyes, eyes that bore a trace of melancholy so misbegotten it hurt her heart. She didn't need to be told what this woman had endured at the hands of Hilaire Blancard. The pain was written in the pale palimpsest of her skin for anyone who dared to look close enough.

"I have heard the name Chaillot before, mademoiselle," she said slowly. Then, "From my husband."

"The name is not that unusual," Chaillot insisted, casting about frantically for help.

"Quite the contrary. It's most unusual, and so are you. And with your exceptional looks, there is no doubt." The voice grew forceful, undeniable, cutting off all retreat. "It's all right, Chaillot. I know." Again, softer, "I know."

"But . . ." Chaillot was lost. Then, "He dared tell you . . . ?"

Justine nodded slowly, full lips a thin, unreadable line. "He did indeed."

Chaillot was genuinely frightened. She was also appalled at this latest of Blancard's transgressions. That a white man would speak to his wife of his mistress of color was unconscionable, embarrassing Chaillot as much as Justine. She was again at a loss for words and felt some relief when she saw her mother approaching with Toinette at her heels. There was no doubt left that the unspeakable truth had just revealed itself, and Colette was girded for battle. But she misunderstood the white woman's grip on her daughter's arm, just as she underestimated the formidable Justine.

"Madame Blancard," she began. "I . . ."

A single look hushed her. Toinette felt it too, this silent reminder that they were in a state where people of African descent, no matter how diluted, were by law not citizens, and therefore subject to the whims of the white race. Justine's utterly emotionless stare reminded all three women that she could have them thrown into the calaboose for the slightest insubordination, real or imagined, and, if she desired, have them flogged. When she finally spoke it was in that tone whites reserved for Negroes when their superiority was not to be questioned. Colette had no avenue but retreat while Justine addressed herself to Toinette alone.

"Mademoiselle Baptiste and I require a moment of privacy, Madame Clovis. Would you be so kind as to arrange it?"

Toinette's mind raced desperately. The shop was filling with customers, and every female eye was on the drama threatening to unravel. Some knew the Baptistes were women of color, others did not, but that something was amiss was a given. The tension was near palpable.

"Bernard!" Toinette said suddenly. When she was met by Justine's unreadable gaze, she added, "My husband's shop is not open this morning. His small office is therefore vacant." She pointed toward the rear of *La Mode*. "Our stores are connected through there. Come. I will show you."

"Chaillot!" Colette hissed. She made no move to intervene, was merely crying out for her daughter. This time it was Chaillot, not Madame Blancard, who reacted.

"It's all right, *maman*," she insisted, voice surprisingly steady. "Madame Blancard wants only to talk, *oui*?"

"We shall see," Justine replied coolly. "Come along, girl."

She released Chaillot's forearm and trailed Toinette to the rear of the store. Chaillot followed with a desperate backward glance at her mother. She had never seen Colette frightened before, never even imagined her redoubtable *maman* capable of that emotion. It did nothing to shore up her own desperate apprehension.

When Toinette returned, she made every effort to conduct business as usual while Colette retreated to an uncrowded corner to pace. Nicole, who had watched the peculiar interchange, rushed to quiz her, dark head shaking as Colette explained.

"This is unthinkable!" gasped Nicole. "That the man would mention a mistress to his wife—and by name!"

"I don't know which is worse," Colette lamented. "That indiscretion or the two women meeting in a public place."

Nicole shook her head again. "What do you think is happening?"

"For once I cannot even hazard a guess," Colette replied. She gave Nicole a discreet shove. "Get back to work. People are curious enough without you adding to their suspicions. For heaven's sake, girl. You look like you've seen a ghost."

Easily intimidated, especially by Colette, Nicole hurried back to the bolts of new cloth. She busied herself with their arrangement while Toinette flitted merrily from one customer to another. Colette stewed, again and again checking her gold watch, a gift from dear Narcisse.

Oddly, although there was probably little he might have done, even as the girl's white father, Colette missed him desperately at times such as this. It was strange when he came to mind, not always in memories of shared things such as brandy in bed or the secret trips to Palmetto, her brother's plantation on the Cane River. No, it was peculiar moments, when she least expected it, when she suddenly conjured his beguiling smile or felt his fingers touch, ever so lightly, the nape of her neck. Times such as this. No one, with the possible exception of Marius, understood the depth of her grief.

Colette eventually wandered to the front of the shop where she idly observed the traffic in the Rue Royale. She was watching a slave sweep the banquette before a billiard parlor when she heard a door click open. Justine appeared, oddly radiant, and whispered something in Toinette's ear. She nodded politely as she approached Colette who felt somehow obliged to open the door for the white woman.

"*Merci,*" Justine said. Then she was gone.

Colette turned just as Chaillot entered and was horrified by the girl's puffy eyes. That Chaillot had been crying was obvious, and her mother rushed to her side. "*Ma petit! Ma petit!* What happened? Was it terrible for you?"

"*Mais non, maman.*"

"But you've been crying!"

"Not out of fear," Chaillot said calmly. She turned as Toinette joined them and smiled sweetly. "And now, madame *modiste.* May I see some patterns?"

Colette's hand shot out and gripped her daughter's wrist hard. "What's the matter with you?!" She lowered her voice to a husky whisper. "For God's sake, girl! You're the mistress of that woman's husband! Do you mean to tell me nothing happened?"

"Nothing at all, *maman,*" Chaillot insisted. "At least nothing I can discuss."

"You mean nothing you can discuss *here,*" Colette amended. She refused to relax her grip.

"Nothing I can ever discuss," Chaillot said. "What Madame Blancard and I talked about is between us and us alone."

Colette was seething. "Chaillot, you're not saying you won't tell me . . . ?"

"She made me promise," Chaillot said evenly. "And it is a promise I intend to keep." When she saw the hurt and frustration on her mother's face, she hastily added, "Madame Blancard is a great lady, *maman.* A very great lady indeed."

"Amen," sighed Toinette.

Colette turned to the *modiste*. "And you, Madame Clovis! Can you not tell me what she just said to you?"

"Of course," Toinette smiled. She patted Chaillot's cheeks. "She said your daughter is a most remarkable young woman. I agree."

"*Merci*," Chaillot said in a small, grateful voice.

"And now, ladies," Toinette said firmly. "Shall we look at some patterns?"

Duncan had never seen Randolph behave so mysteriously, or exude such excitement. He was reminded of those golden boyhood moments when his idolized big brother included him in some harmless mischief or insisted they sleep together when the Virginia countryside rumbled under the assault of crashing thunderstorms. Randolph's ebullience practically overflowed as the carriage swayed down a deserted St. Charles Avenue and into the drowsing Faubourg St. Marie. It was not yet dawn and Duncan was still puzzled at being roused at such an ungodly hour. And not a little sleepy.

"Why won't you tell me where we're going?" Duncan asked groggily. "And why now, for God's sake?"

"Because no one must know of our secret mission," Randolph insisted. "That's why I insisted on driving. We must be alone. Not even my fellow conspirators much know. They'd probably throw me out if they knew what I was up to."

A clue at last, thought Duncan. "So this has to do with the men's organization you've joined."

"It's called a krewe," Randolph explained, spelling the strange word. "The Mistick Krewe of Comus. We've been meeting in the old Gem Saloon on Royal Street."

"Are we going there now?"

"Patience, little brother," Randolph said. "I will explain everything. Well, most everything. But you must promise to hold everything I tell you in absolute confidence. You promise? Good!"

Duncan was fascinated as his brother unfolded a tale that began in neighboring Mobile twenty-five years before. In 1831, young men organized the Cowbellion de Rakin Society, which brought the Alabama city some glamour by parading on New Year's Eve. When some of the Mobileans settled in New Orleans and despaired over the disastrous decline of Mardi Gras, they decided to rejuvenate it. Last fall, six of them had met in the rear room of an uptown drugstore and made a list of eighty-three of the city's most prominent businessmen. Randolph Saunders was surprised and deeply honored to learn he had been included on the exclusive roster. A parade was planned, floats designed, and a dress committee formed. The chairman of that committee was, Randolph explained, in Mobile at this very moment, checking on costumes, which were being sewn in the utmost secrecy.

"Come Mardi Gras, New Orleanians will witness something unlike anything they've ever seen!" Randolph insisted. He drove by what looked to be an abandoned warehouse, pointing out some shadowy figures before circling around to the back. "Guards," he explained. "No one must know what's inside that warehouse. Especially anyone who might leak the information to the French newspapers. They'd love to damn our efforts before they're ever implemented, simply because they're American." Thinking immediately of Justine, Duncan bristled at the slur but said nothing. His brother's enthusiasm was too important, and he wanted nothing to spoil the moment.

Randolph drew up the carriage at the rear of the warehouse and hissed for Duncan to get out. There was no door and only a few high-placed windows. Randolph indicated a stack of crates and climbed up, holding out a hand for Duncan to follow. Duncan joined him and the two peered through the windows as the first rays of morning sun pierced the filthy glass. It took Duncan's eyes a moment to adjust to the dim lighting and what was illuminated inside. When he discerned the first float, he gasped.

"It's magnificent!"

"Indeed," said Randolph, with no small amount of pride.

"Is that for some sort of throne?"

"Yes. Now look at the one behind it."

Duncan shaded his eyes. More shards of sunlight invaded the warehouse from the side, and as he watched the whole interior was bathed in dusty gold. He blinked as the sunlight twinkled on pyramids and turrets and what looked like mounds of diamonds.

"And boulders of gold! What on earth is it, Randolph?"

"I can tell you no more!" his brother hissed. He grabbed his coattails as a sign to leave. "Now come along! We've risked enough for one morning."

Duncan shared his brother's excitement as they drove home through the growing dawn. He had seen something wondrous indeed. He grinned, envisioning the dazzling sunlit spectacle.

"All that gold, and those diamonds! They'll be blinding in the sunlight."

"It's to be a night parade," said Randolph.

"But what a shame! Such fine detailing will be lost in the darkness."

"Who said anything about darkness?" Randolph grinned.

"Oh?"

"Another part of Comus' surprise."

"You intend to light things somehow, eh?"

"With *flambeaux*." Randolph chuckled good-naturedly at his brother's silent ignorance. "At long last, little brother! I know a French word you do not!"

"Touché," Duncan laughed. "In any case, I certainly approve anything that will bring the French and Americans closer together. It sounds like a wonderful idea."

"We're not doing it for that reason," Randolph corrected. "We're doing it because the French have allowed carnival to fall into such disrepute. Someone has to do something to resurrect it."

"Please, Randolph," Duncan said with a yawn. Suddenly he was sleepy again. "Let's not have this same argument again."

"I want no argument either, little brother. I only want to state some facts. The French are doing nothing to revitalize Mardi Gras. We are. That should tell you something. A great deal actually."

"How do you know the French are not planning something as big and secretive as your Mistick Krewe of Comus?"

"They're not," Randolph answered flatly. "You'll be pleased to know there are some very prominent Creoles in the krewe, and they assure us nothing similar is happening in the *carré de la ville*. Nothing at all in fact. So you see, they cannot care too much about their tradition. When that happens, it is time for change."

Duncan muttered unhappily, "How many Creoles exactly?"

"Six," Randolph answered reluctantly, hoping Duncan would let the matter alone. He knew better.

"Out of eighty-three?" Duncan was incredulous. "Aren't we supposed to be living in a democracy? Is that any kind of equal representation?"

"A true democracy hardly includes slavery or people with less rights guaranteed under the law," Randolph reminded him.

"Don't change the subject, Randolph. Surely you don't think this Comus business is fair!"

"The Krewe of Comus is an American organization formed by Americans," Randolph announced. "We were not bound to ask any Frenchmen to join at all. In fact, there were a number of men who opposed the idea."

"Were you among them?"

"No," Randolph admitted, expelling his breath in a tired sigh. "I know my views on the Creoles vacillate, perhaps even seem contradictory. It's only natural since I'm trying to change. I've not made any secret of my dislike for the arrogance of the French, but I see no gain in alienating them further. My love for New Orleans is greater. The city can benefit only from unity, not divisiveness."

"Well said!" Duncan studied his brother as they turned onto Prytania Street. "You've never lied to me, Randolph, so what you've said makes me very happy. Especially under the circumstances."

"What circumstances?" Randolph asked, immediately on the alert.

"Since this seems to be the time for sharing secrets, I may as well share one with you too."

"Oh?"

A deep breath and a silent prayer. "I'm in love with a Creole."

"My God, Duncan!"

"I'm afraid there's more to it than that," he said. "She's married."

Randolph's face went white. "My God, boy! I truly regret having to ask this so often, but have you completely lost your mind?"

"Yes," Duncan said in a faraway voice. He looked out the window and saw Justine's image shimmering in the fog-shrouded dawn. "Perhaps I have at that."

They rode the rest of the way in silence. When they entered the house, appetites were roused by the smell of breakfast in the dining room. Randolph had instructed Junon to have it ready at 7:30, and the man had not disappointed him.

"Shall we discuss this lady over breakfast?" Randolph asked.

"I wasn't sure you'd want to hear more."

Randolph turned his back to Junon as the cape was slipped from his shoulders. "You are many things, Duncan. Impulsive, willful, argumentative. Impossible at times. A damned dreamer if I ever saw one. Those things may change, but there's one thing you will always be."

"And what's that?" Duncan smiled, noticing the telltale twinkle in Randolph's eyes.

"My brother. Of course I want to hear about her. Just try not to say anything to upset my stomach. As the Creoles say, 'Nothing is worth a fit of indigestion.' "

"Quoting the Creoles are you?" Duncan laughed, draping an arm around Randolph's shoulders as they walked to the dining room. "That's encouraging."

"It would seem that some things are inevitable," Randolph conceded.

"Indeed they are, big brother," Duncan said, naturally thinking of Justine. "And when you least expect them."

Randolph grasped the implication all too quickly. "Pour the coffee, Junon."

"*Café au lait* for me, please," Duncan added with a smile.

At Randolph's insistence and under Junon's watchful eye, the cook had become an expert at preparing Virginia dishes. As delectable as Creole cuisine was, the Saunders brothers frequently yearned for the comforting food of childhood. That morning they breakfasted on a country ham stuffed with greens, red eye gravy, snowy grits, corn pudding, beaten biscuits, and more.

Fork poised with a slice of smoking ham, Randolph asked, "Well? Tell me about your mystery lady."

"Might we speak in private?" Duncan asked. His nod indicated Junon, poised as always behind his master's chair. Randolph frowned.

"You do my man an injustice. Although I agree with our great fellow Virginian, Thomas Jefferson, that servants should not be privy to intimate family matters, Junon is an exception. As I've said to you before, he and I have no secrets. He is hardly one to gossip and scarcely a part of the slave grapevine." Although it wasn't necessary, Duncan apologized. Randolph beamed, as did Junon.

"The lady in question is Madame Hilaire Blancard."

Randolph was horrified. "And I thought Eugénie Duval was a dangerous choice! Good Lord, Duncan. I know of this woman's husband, have done business with his bank on occasion. He is a powerful man, and I understand he can be quite ruthless in his business dealings. I can't imagine how he might react if he thought someone was after his wife." Duncan was silent. "What do you plan to do about the lady?"

"I've had no time to think about plans. No time to think about anything in fact. Except perhaps how much I love her."

"But how did all of this come to be?"

"It's most peculiar," Duncan said. Steam brushed his face as he sipped the *café au lait* and explained the unconventional social parameters Blancard had delineated for his wife. He told Randolph a little about their time together, wisely deciding to exclude the visit to Gallatin Street.

"Utterly bizarre," Randolph said. "How could Blancard . . . ? Well, perhaps you're right. The man must be completely preoccupied with his new mistress."

"An obsession that satisfies me as well, because it enabled me to meet my muse. You see, it is because of Justine that I began writing again."

"Then that first poem, the one you said was about all women . . . ?"

"Was all about Justine Blancard."

Randolph frowned. He remembered when Duncan had finally shared the poem, reading aloud while a winter rain pounded the garden outside, beating a monotonous symphony on the banana trees while steadily shredding their leaves. Randolph had never paid serious attention to his little brother's work until that moment. The combination of soaring, lyrical passages and the aching sentience in Duncan's voice mesmerized Randolph and moved him, a man rarely given to deep emotion, nearly to tears. The realization that Justine Blancard was the inspiration, the muse who had delivered his brother of such passion, such yearning, was both revealing and disturbing. And not a little enviable.

"My God, Duncan. If you feel half as strongly as that poem suggests, I pity you."

"I take that as a compliment."

"It was intended as such. And yet . . ."

"And yet?" Duncan urged.

"I'm frightened for you, little brother," Randolph conceded. "I well remember what I felt for Molly Lewis. I felt strongly enough to attack her fiancé and risk expulsion from school. It was all I had to gamble at the time, and I did not hesitate. I behaved not as a gentleman, and went against everything I had been taught. And for what? A woman without whom I did not think I could live."

"Do you regret your actions?"

"I don't believe in regrets," Randolph replied without pause. "They gain you nothing and make you miserable. You simply have to glean from what remains after a debacle such as that and continue with your life."

"So why are you frightened?" Duncan asked. For the first time he noticed the beginnings of silver at his brother's temples. "Eh, Randolph?"

"Because I don't want you to suffer as I have suffered."

"But you just said . . ."

"Continuing with one's life does not mean there is no pain. It's inevitable that one remembers, that one wishes, that one . . . sometimes weeps for what is lost."

"So you're suggesting that it's inevitable that Justine will be lost?"

"I'm saying only that you must be realistic, little brother. Madame Blancard is a married women. More than that she is a Catholic. Even if the woman so desired, there is no hope for divorce. Therefore no hope for a future together."

"Oh, we will have a future together," Duncan said firmly. "I have no doubt of it. It is merely the quality, the complexion of that future which remains to be explored and established."

"You're saying you could be content with a platonic affair?"

"Yes!" Too quickly. Then, "I don't know."

"And there's where the trouble lies," Randolph said sadly.

"But would you have me deny my true feelings?"

"Given the chance, I would have you deny only unhappiness," Randolph answered gravely. "And the lady? Does she reciprocate?"

"We have never discussed it."

"And you? Have you told her of your love?"

Duncan shook his head. "But my feelings were made clear in the poem."

Randolph was incredulous. "You let her read it? But it was shocking, Duncan! It is one thing for a lady to read such a work and secretly ponder the object of all that passion. But for her to know that she herself is the woman in question, that she is responsible for unleashing all that—dare I say it?—raw emotion, for stirring those 'phallic minarets' and offering the 'swell of breasts like Byzantine domes' . . . well, it's unthinkable!"

Duncan smiled. "I'm amazed that your quotes are so close to accuracy."

"Never mind about that," Randolph said. "Any true lady would have been appalled."

"You don't know Justine," Duncan said softly.

"True. Therefore you must tell me, explain her to me."

"I cannot," Duncan said. "At times like this, I fail as a poet and the right words elude me. She is the most paradoxical, contradictory soul I have ever encountered." He had a fleeting image of her sitting beside Madam Pearl, heads together as they chatted like long-lost friends. "She would be equally at home in a convent or a bordello."

"Impossible!"

Duncan's smile deepened. "Again, with all due respect, you don't know the lady." His jaw dropped at his brother's response.

"Then I shall have to meet her," Randolph announced. "I shall have to see for myself this creature that has so bewitched and beguiled my little brother." His heart was stirred when he saw love dancing in Duncan's eyes, for himself as well as the enigmatic Justine Blancard.

"You would do this for me?"

"As I said before, I'm trying to change my attitude toward the Creoles. Having one at my dinner table will be a first." Duncan's eyebrows rose. "Yes, that's it. I will invite her to a small supper. Is that the sort of thing her husband would permit?"

"He has no restrictions on his wife, as long as Christophe is present."

"Then I shall invite Christophe and he can bring her along. Will that fit the criteria?" Duncan nodded. "Utterly bizarre," Randolph said again. He motioned for Junon to slice more ham. "Don't you agree, Junon?"

Making a rare show of his insightful sense of humor, Junon smiled, too, and spoke with a frankness his master always welcomed. "I find the more I know about white people, the less I understand them."

The Saunders brothers dissolved in laughter.

CHAPTER 17

"The way I see it," Christophe said with typical expansiveness, "you and I and the lady in question have merely explored the tip of the iceberg. The Duval ball and the sojourn to Pearl's last week were nothing more than tests."

"What sort of tests?"

"Tests of what we could really get away with if we put our collective minds to it."

"You're in a wicked mood today, *mon ami!*"

"Guilty!" Christophe laughed. He had drunk too much wine with lunch, but Duncan didn't mind. He had indulged as well.

He took Christophe's arm as they strolled the fashionable Rue Chartres, breathing deep of the warm afternoon air and enjoying the special sounds and smells of this part of the old city. Owing to the mildness of the day, most of the cabarets had their doors flung wide across the banquettes, spilling forth the tinkle of a piano and an occasional singer. Banjo music pursued them from a billiard parlor, along with the roar of a crowd betting heavily on a fierce game. Duncan glanced inside and saw a cluster of well-dressed men gathered around the pool table, their heads a restless sea of black silk chimneys.

They passed a row of gleaming confectioners, cookies and candies especially tantalizing in the golden glow of sunlight. Duncan's nostrils flared at the sugary scent and he ducked inside to buy pralines for both. The taste had not left his mouth when he smelled strong coffee and suggested they chase the sweetness with some café au lait.

"Whiskey would be a much better idea," Christophe said. Then, exuberantly, "Ah! I have it! What do you say we head for the waterfront? Return to that bar where we met . . . when was it? Three months ago?"

"It's much too nice a day to spend in a dark, smoky bar," Duncan insisted. "Let's find a *divertissement* outdoors."

Christophe grunted. For reasons known only to himself, he was far more interested in whiskey than sunshine, but he conceded. "We can go anywhere you like, as long as we go some place afterward and plot our strategy."

"*C'est bon!*"

Christophe thought for a moment. "What day is it?"

"Sunday."

"Ah! *Le Place Congo!* That's it. That shall be our destination."

"About time," Duncan said. "I've been hearing about it ever since we met. The closest I ever got was hearing the drums one afternoon when you and I were out for a drive."

"One cannot see all of *La Nouvelle-Orléans* in a few weeks, *mon ami.* She is like a beauteous woman, formally gowned for the ball. To understand all her secrets, she must be undressed a little at a time. A hemline lifted here. A neckline lowered there. The petticoats, the corset. The chemise. You understand."

"Sometimes," Duncan said, amused by the sensual imagery, "I think you should be the poet."

"*Mais non!* One poet among our three musketeers is quite enough I think." Something dulled the gleam in his eyes, and Duncan knew Christophe was thinking of Justine. He didn't pursue the notion.

"Congo Square it is!"

The official name for the plot of open land on the Rue Rampart just above the Rue St. Anne was Circus Square, but it was known to blacks and whites of the city as *Le Place Congo* or Congo Square. Under the French and Spanish, *les bruts Africains* were legally forbidden to gather in any significant numbers, an effort to quell the omnipresent fears of a slave uprising. The Americans thought otherwise, deciding in 1805 that such gatherings could be greatly beneficial if properly and closely monitored. It was vastly preferred to allow slaves to positively channel as much discontent as possible through socializing and especially through their native dance. Congo Square was chosen by the mayor as the sole official site for these gatherings and Sunday the only day when they would be permitted. Initially, it was, with the exception of the police, an exclusively black affair, but when the dances grew more elaborate, the crowds of slaves larger and more enthusiastic, it attracted the attentions of a white populace curious to see what all the fuss was about.

In time it was the thing to do, a sight for male tourists second only to the quadroon balls. White ladies attended as well, although often protesting that the dancing was far too savage and indecent for their taste. The men, after all, were almost naked, wearing scant more than tattered breeches. Disapproval notwithstanding, many Sundays would find an almost racially balanced audience, local whites as well as visitors, both awed and appalled but inevitably mesmerized by the spectacle of the *calinda,* the *chica,* and *bamboula* performed with a feverish, purely African frenzy.

Carrying the requisite written consent of their masters, the slaves began arriving at the fenced square well before the dancing was to begin. The spectators were, as Christophe pointed out, a sight to see, proudly sauntering about in the cast-off trumpery of *maitre* and *maitresse.* One extraordinarily tall Ibibio was a sight in a well-worn top hat brushed until it gleamed. His woman was no less a spectacle as she sashayed in a oft-mended but spotless calico frock with a matching dotted *tignon.* Either, observed Duncan, might have been a tribal king or queen back home. Ribbons, scarves, feathers, fans, anything and everything was ingeniously improvised to put on as gay a show as possible. Even the slave children were included. Little girls had kinky African hair tortured into braids and tied with bright ribbons, while the boys preened and romped with colorful scarves around their necks.

"It's quite a spectacle," said Duncan.

"And the dancing hasn't even begun," Christophe grinned. "Come. That praline has whetted my appetite for more sweets."

The men threaded their way through the forest of hawkers, trays around their necks bearing lemonade, steaming coffee and *biére douce,* the ginger beer dear to blacks and whites alike. Since the leafless sycamores gave off no shade in winter, the rows of tables were draped with cotton awnings. They offered roasted peanuts, cakes, candies, pies and a refreshing drink called *la bierre du pays.* Christophe explained it was an amalgam of fermented apples, ginger root, and mellow pines, and a favorite of children.

"We always pretended it was ale," he laughed. "And that's another favorite. *Estomac mulâtre.*"

"What on earth is mulatto's stomach," Duncan asked. "And why is it called that?"

"Ginger cake." Christophe's reply was followed with a hearty laugh. "And for once, I haven't an answer. Isn't that strange? I've been eating it and calling it that as long as I can remember, but I don't know why." He bought pieces for himself and Duncan and they ate as they strolled deeper into the crowd. When they secured a good vantage point by the Rampart Street gate, Christophe checked his watch and nodded at a policeman. "In a few minutes, he will give the signal to that big slave there, in the center of the square. He'll start rattling enormous jawbones on a cask covered with a sheepskin, a sort of a drum. Called a *tam-tam* I think. That will summon the dancers, and . . . *mon Dieu!* She's coming! I always heard she attended these things—commandeered them even!—but I've never seen her before now."

Without exception, every eye locked on the figure moving through the restless crowd with a determined grace. While some people rushed out to touch the hem of her long skirts, others hurriedly retreated from the tall mulatress who swept through like Moses parting the Red Sea. Christophe stood on his toes and craned his neck for a better look. The taller Duncan had no difficulty noting every detail about the woman. She wore a plain blue dress with matching *tignon* and clutched a large wicker basket to her bosom, and as she approached the policemen guarding the gates, a murmur grew that swirled around the square like a tornado.

"If what I hear is true, he won't stop her!" Christophe hissed. When Duncan gave him a blank stare, he added, "Only slaves are supposed to pass, never free coloreds. They are not even welcome here, the slaves hate them so. See! Aha! I was right."

The policeman, expression vacillating between sheepishness and outright fear, stepped aside as the woman approached. No one dared interrupt her progress to the very center of the square where she set down the basket and turned slowly until she had looked a full 360 degrees around, as though plunging every face, black and white, into a bottomless memory. There were some squeals and moans, by no means all from children, when she finally opened her basket and extracted, very slowly, a huge snake. The dramatic gesture was obviously anticipated and much was made of it as she held up the writhing serpent before fearlessly draping it around her shoulders and parading around the center of the square.

"Christophe!" Duncan hissed. "For God's sake. Who is she?"

"Marie Laveau, of course!"

At first the name was unfamiliar, and then Duncan recalled the afternoon he had happened upon the *voudou* queen's little house in the Rue St. Anne.

"What is she doing here?"

"Staking out her territory, I suspect." He lowered his voice and leaned close to Duncan's ear. "Like some kind of jungle animal."

"You sound like you don't like her!" Duncan hissed back.

Christophe pursed his lips and seized one end of his moustache between two fingers, twirling nervously. "The stories about her are the stuff of legend, *mon ami*. There are those who say it is she who really runs the city. It's no secret that many of our most prominent politicians seek her advice. And more."

"What do you mean?"

"Spells, of course. Curses. Whatever you want to call them. You see, years ago she was a hairdresser for the rich white ladies and they foolishly shared enough confidences to give Marie Laveau considerable powers, all based on blackmailing. She's parlayed that privileged knowledge into something dangerous. Whether or not you believe in her powers is up to you, but I . . . well, I am not foolish enough to dispute them."

Duncan frowned. "Are you frightened of her?"

"Quite!" Both jumped as an open palm crashed upon a drum and the sound reverberated through the unnatural hush, again and again. "Now be still and watch!"

The drumbeat was acknowledgment of Marie Laveau's powerful presence as well as her signal to begin dancing, and every eye remained on her as the strange performance commenced. It was brief, commanding, a series of slow turns that escalated until she was spinning like a whirling dervish with the snake held high above her head. Her long skirts billowed like sails, becoming a hypnotic blue blur. How she executed it without growing dizzy was a mystery to Duncan until she slowed enough for him to see her eyes. She seemed lost in a self-induced trance, and there was no lack of others similarly lost. Then she fell perfectly still and the drums faded. Just as Duncan was lulled by a new, even more unnerving silence, more drumming began.

This time it was the Negro with the huge jawbones. He rattled them against the *tam-tam* while two more men approached, intensifying the crude discordance with an African version of the tambourine called a *bamboula*. To this was added the blowing of wooden horns carved to resemble those of cattle, and the African orchestra was complete.

At first, Duncan found it only so much noise, but as he watched the dancers begin, the sound drifted elsewhere, eventually settling inside his head. The men, naked to the waist and barefoot with ribbons, bells, or bits of tin tied to their ankles, were a variety of heights and colors, ranging from obsidian to *ivoire* and representing as many tribes. But their movements were the same. The men circled each other like stalking predators and then, acting upon an unseen signal, they leapt high into the air and landed as one. They also stamped as one, a disembodied caterpillar whose myriad feet alit simultaneously. Their shout was also one and the same, and it grew in volume as the leaps increased in height.

"*Dansez Bamboula! Bou doum! Bou doum!*"

Duncan was so fascinated by the wild, yet graceful leaps that it was a while before he noticed the women. Forming a colorful line around the men, their feet planted firmly on the ground, the Negresses also moved as a single organism, bodies swaying with a primitive concupiscence as ancient and dark as Africa itself. Their words were different, less explosive but no less insistent. Duncan and Christophe both found it reminiscent of a dirge, the insistence plaintive, the words unintelligible. But not those of the men.

"*Dansez Bamboula! Bou doum! Bou doum!*"

The sound had gone full circle and returned again to Duncan's consciousness, intensely hypnotic and tinged with danger. Duncan was unnerved and a little embarrassed to realize he was swaying with the music. To his amazement, so was Christophe!

"*Dansez Bamboula! Bou doum! Bou doum!*"

The hundreds of bodies throbbed and pulsed all of a piece, conspiring to convert the entire square into one great black writhing organism. The mournful female chants, the men's shouts, the boom and thrum of bone against sheepskin, the jangle of bells and chink of metal, all coalesced into a maddening cacophony that reverberated in Duncan's skull.

"*Bou doum! Bou doum! BOU DOUM! BOU DOUM!*"

"It's hurting my head!" he shouted. "Please, Christophe! Can we go?"

But Christophe was lost. He had been swept high by the pulsating, discordant drone, transported somewhere into the dark African jungles where no white man had been or need go. The stony rapture on his face was disconcerting to Duncan and he grabbed his friend hard by the arm. They were away from the square, across the Rue Rampart and well into the *carré de la ville*, before Christophe realized they had gone. His head snapped as he turned toward the sounds of the fading drums. Then he gave Duncan a queer look.

"Why did you want to leave?"

"I told you. It was making my head hurt." He frowned. "Obviously it had an entirely different effect on you."

"Did it?" Christophe said absently. "Perhaps it was the wine."

"It was not the wine." Duncan was adamant. "I watched you, my friend. You looked hypnotized, carried away by it all. You didn't even hear me when I shouted at you."

Christophe was still unhearing. "Did you watch her, Duncan? Did you see how she moved? How she looked at the crowd?"

Duncan was exasperated. Now it was he who wanted a drink! "Who?"

"Marie Laveau, of course. She's . . . she is *magnifique!*"

"She's a witch doctor with a snake and a tired bag of tricks," Duncan retorted. "An actress playing a part to a gullible audience. And an ignorant one as well."

Christophe gave his friend another strange look and then, very slowly, smiled. As the smile grew, Duncan was as disconcerted as he had been when Christophe had been so mesmerized a few minutes ago. The uneasiness grew into confusion when Christophe threw back his head and laughed. He barely remembered to slap his hand on the brim of his tall hat to keep it from toppling into the gutter. He laughed until Duncan wanted to shake him, and just when his hands were itching to the point of no return, Christophe stopped.

"Amazing," he said.

"What's amazing?"

"I thought you were growing to understand New Orleans so well, but now it seems that you don't understand us at all."

Duncan's face flamed. "What's so complicated about a gang of slaves singing and tribal dancing and making terrible music on makeshift instruments?"

"Is that all you saw?" Duncan nodded. "And you consider yourself a poet?"

"You're making me angry, Chris!"

"Then what she did was working."

"What, for God's sake?"

"The evil in that *voudouienne's* body, my friend. I could feel it, radiating from her like fire, burning into me, hurting my heart with its black poison. Don't you see what she's done, what she's capable of doing?"

"I see nothing at all!" Duncan growled. He tried to retreat as Christophe took his arm, but the grip was firm and sure.

"You don't see that she drove a wedge between best friends, even for a few moments? Didn't you feel hatred for me?"

Duncan considered the macabre possibility. "I don't know what I felt," he confessed.

"Good," Christophe said, taking control now as he steered Duncan toward the waterfront where the rich brown river bore the scent of sudden rain. "It's a start. Now let's find that whiskey, eh, *mon ami?*"

More than ever, Duncan felt the disembodied spirit of the city hovering over him as the sun sank toward Lafayette and Carrollton. The sun had taken the heat with it, burying it in the rich dankness of the bayous and releasing instead numbing dampness. He was suddenly chilled to the bone and wanted nothing so much as a fire and a glass of bourbon. And Christophe to explain what had happened. But it was not to be.

"It's . . . it's so strange," he murmured. "What happened back there is so strange."

"Not when you think about it. If nothing had happened, *that* would have been strange."

"I've never known you to be so metaphysical, Christophe."

The conversational door swung shut with the insistence of the deafening *tam-tams.* "It's turning bitter very fast, *mon ami.* Let's hurry!"

In a few moments, all was behind them. Duncan and Christophe were comfortably ensconced at the Mermaid, whiskies in hand, moods rising as surely as the storm clouds swarming across the river. It wasn't long before the crackling fire, the company of good friends and, of course, the whiskey had them busily making mischief. Christophe, Duncan noted with amusement, was plotting like a man possessed.

"A boy's frock coat and trousers for Justine!" he cried, thumping Duncan's knee. "That's what we need. Not too snug, mind you. Nothing must spoil the illusion."

"What illusion?"

"And a mask of course. I have one that should be perfect. Or she could use the one she wore as the musketeer. *Non!* Someone might recognize us. We must leave nothing to chance."

"Tomorrow night's ball is no masquerade, Christophe."

"I'm talking about afterward," Christophe grinned. "Haven't you guessed yet? Think, old friend. What could be even more outrageous—and fun—than sneaking Justine into Madam Pearl's Place?"

"I don't know. Surely you don't mean the Swamp?"

"That crazy I'm not!" Christophe laughed. "Guess again."

With the unspoken communication of true friends, Duncan studied Christophe's face and suddenly understood. As recognition brought the words to his lips, Christophe's glee blossomed.

"The . . . quadroon . . . balls!"

"Mais oui!" Christophe cried. "You are brilliant!"

"And you *are* crazy!" Duncan laughed. "I remember what the *Salle d'Orléans* was like. There was not a white woman to be seen."

"Because they are banned from the balls, of course, as are men of color. But who's to say we cannot costume Justine so that her obvious feminine charms are not so obvious?"

"It would take a magician," Duncan said dubiously.

"You are looking at one, monsieur," Christophe said, leaping to his feet to execute a quick bow. "When it comes to costuming and cosmetics I can work as much magic as Marie Laveau herself."

"You?"

Christophe made a pyramid with his hands and propped his chin atop it, staring with a fixed smile. "When I was much younger, I went to a *bal masque* dressed as the Empress Catherine of Russia. I shaved the moustache, applied the right make-up, wore a wig, a gown without dé-coletté, and *voilà!* I had gentlemen lined up begging to dance."

"No!" Duncan exploded with laughter as he conjured an image of Christophe in a ball gown, skirts flying as he was swept around a dance floor in the arms of another man. It was uproarious. "You are too much, my friend!"

"Illusion was practically invented in this dreamy place," Christophe insisted. "You saw that just this afternoon."

"So I did," Duncan conceded, uncomfortable with the terrible memory of Marie Laveau and the black magic of Congo Square. He hastily changed the subject. "But what if Justine doesn't like the idea?"

"Oh, she will. We are witnessing a metamorphosis, my good friend. We are watching a woman break from her cocoon and spread her wings for flight. You don't know the lady that well."

"True," Duncan conceded.

"I have seen more changes in the past week than I have in all the years I've known her, and I must admit that I am not comfortable with all of them." He took a deep swig of his whiskey. "The truth is they frighten me."

"Because you think her husband will change his mind and end things like before. Justine told me all about that. So strange. Like the man had two personalities."

"It's more than that, Duncan. There's a part of Justine that I've never been able to reach. A dark side. A desperate side. It's something Hilaire Blancard created because it wasn't there before she married him."

"Now you're frightening me, Chris."

"You shouldn't concern yourself," Christophe insisted. His mood was rapidly turning dark, and Duncan felt a chill that did not come from a bitterness settling upon the city like a glacial canopy. "Nor should Justine."

"But why not?"

"Because I'm frightened enough for both of you."

"I'm glad you arrived early," Justine said. "It will give us time to have refreshments before the ball. To be frank, I adore Patrice and Mathilde, but there is always such a crush at their parties that no one can get anything to eat. I know it's unfashionable to admit, but all that dancing makes me ravenous."

"As usual you're full of surprises these days," Christophe observed good-naturedly.

"I suppose I am at that." She smiled and indicated Figaro, who stood waiting to serve drinks. "What's your pleasure, gentlemen?"

"Champagne!" Christophe said without hesitation. "Tonight is a very special occasion."

"Champagne it is," Justine agreed. When the butler was gone, she asked Christophe what made the night so special.

"Oh, you will see soon enough." He glanced around as though there might be spies in the woodwork. "Where is Marie Tonton?"

"With Hilaire," she replied. "For some days now he's taken to having her with him. Heaven knows what they do over there. Surely he's not too cheap to buy that girl a maid. Oh, I'm so sorry! Forgive me, Monsieur Saunders. That was most indelicate."

"He likes it when you're indelicate," Christophe announced, plopping himself in a *fauteuil* and brashly draping his knee over one arm. Justine was amused by his brashness, but there was an undercurrent to his words that cut. She understood it only too well. "Don't you, Duncan?"

Duncan didn't know what he knew at that moment. When Justine had swept into the room, he had seen a confection of white satin showered and flounced with ivory chantilly lace. Tiny pearls peeked from her ears, and an ancient cameo shone dully at her throat. Her luxuriant hair was piled high atop her head in a gleaming ebony chignon, a few wisps escaping at the side. Duncan the poet was grateful for those wayward strands, fearing he would find pure perfection unbearable.

"Duncan!" Christophe laughed. "Have you lost your tongue?"

No, he thought. It is my mind that has gone astray. He looked at Christophe as though asking for permission. "A . . . a word alone with Madame Blancard if I . . . may," he stammered.

"Of course," Christophe said. He started to rise, but Justine was too swift.

"You wait here for the champagne, Christophe. Monsieur Saunders and I will retreat momentarily to the courtyard. Last night's terrible cold has passed and the evening is refreshingly warm."

"On one condition," Christophe announced. Both turned, puzzled by the urgency in his voice. Neither knew what to expect, but smiles blossomed when they heard his amusing edict. "I insist that you begin addressing one another by your Christian names. I find such formality among the three musketeers most inconvenient."

Justine went directly to her old friend, took his chin in her hands and kissed him on both cheeks. *"Merci, Christophe. Merci beaucoup."*

She took Duncan's arm and they wandered into a courtyard smelling of shattered gardenias and Spanish moss. She searched the branches of a tall Japanese magnolia for the bright green of wild parrots, disappointed to find only darkness. "Those terrible winds took some liberties here last night," Justine said, touching the toe of her satin slipper to the white swansdown of a broken camellia. "Oh!" She started when a drop of cold rainwater oozed from a banana leaf onto her bare shoulder. Duncan was quick to whip a handkerchief from his waistcoat and boldly wiped away the water. The heel of his hand burned where it rested on Justine's flesh. It glowed golden beneath the gaslight spilling through the tall French windows.

"I'm grateful for Christophe's benediction," Duncan said slowly. "About our Christian names. It suggests he knows what I'm about to say."

"And I as well," she added softly.

"You will not be offended by my declaration then?" he asked, daring to take her gloved hand and press it to his heart.

She shook her head. "No more than you should be offended by my eager response."

"I didn't dare hope!" he gasped. "Is it truly possible . . . ?"

"Shall we say it together?"

"We shall," he said.

Their damning confessions soared as one. "I love you."

The words thundered in Duncan's ears, a deafening roar that sent everything rushing from him, the house, the city, Christophe, his brother, everything except the angelic vision shimmering white before him, too tenuous to be more than a dream. In Justine the confession spawned a bloom of serenity, one that faded almost abruptly as it had arisen but left her shaking long after its intensity had peaked and passed. Oddly, it was she who recovered first.

"But what are we to do with this precious knowledge, Duncan?" It was the first time she had spoken his baptismal name, and she savored the word like a fine wine. "For surely it is too fragile to endure."

"How I wish I could disagree with you!" he moaned. "But I know this is true. I have lived this moment and felt its consequences more times than I can recount. How I wish . . . ."

The tip of Justine's gloved finger stilled his lips. "It is no use wishing for more, *cher* Duncan. We can change nothing. Therefore we must be grateful for what we have and learn to live with it."

"I cannot help myself," he protested.

"Then I must help us both. I must tell you there is no hope. I learned long ago that one must be cautious about investing too much love, especially when it is given without reservation. Something or someone can always arise to destroy it, and that has been my lot."

"You mean Blancard, of course."

"He is only the most recent. No, Duncan. This began long ago. With my father."

Duncan recalled his own father and a childhood that would have been unbearable except for Randolph. "Was he unkind?"

"Cruel to the point of genius," Justine said flatly. A bitter smile froze her lips, hovered for a moment and was forever lost. "Strange. I would never have been able to say . . . no, *admit* that a few weeks ago. Not to you. Not even to a priest. But there's no advantage in looking back, unless you learn from it."

She looked again for the missing parrots then back at Duncan. For a moment, even in the flattering glow of gold lanternshine, she looked drawn and unbearably sad. She was utterly guileless.

"I am thinking of something most strange, something I want to tell you although I don't know why. Not yet anyway."

"Please do."

She paused long enough for Figaro to bring the champagne. Through the windows, she watched Christophe light a cigar. He was, she decided, all right for the moment.

"It happened my fourteenth summer. Like everyone else, we had fled the heat of the city and were at an uncle's plantation upriver. Sweet *Nonc* Adolphe made me a gift of a colt, but of course papa said I could not have it, that I was too irresponsible. When I begged and pleaded . . . I don't know. Perhaps I embarrassed him into letting me have my way. He gave in, but he made me promise to make that colt my responsibility. I remember hearing that word 'responsible' over and over again. I promised everything, of course. I'd never wanted anything so much in my life! I named him Sultan and spent every moment with him. The Negro grooms taught me everything about grooming, and soon they weren't needed. I curried that colt until his black coat shone like ebony. I was so proud of Sultan. And of myself, as well. I had proven something to papa, pleased him at last. Or so I thought."

She sipped the wine, distracted when the bubbles tickled her nose. She did not smile.

"Somehow he ate some poisonous weed and fell gravely ill. The veterinarian said Sultan could survive if he was tended all night, so naturally I set out to do just that. My *Tante* Elizabeth was giving a ball that night, attended by people from all over the parish. Papa came out to the stables and dragged me into the house, ordering me to dress."

"Knowing how sick your colt was?"

In a small, sad voice. "Yes." Justine blinked, but the time for tears was long past. "It was the one time I defied my father, but it did no good. It was the most miserable night of my life, trying to smile and be polite when all I could think of was my poor baby out there in the stable, needing me. When the ball ended around midnight, I finally managed to slip outside. Belhomme, the groom, was waiting outside the stall, and when I saw his face I knew Sultan was dead." She swallowed. "I went into the stall to say good-bye. I don't remember how long I was in there but I remember waking up with my head against Sultan's mane. My father's voice woke me, loud, filled with revile. *Nonc* Adolphe was there too, and *Tante* Elizabeth, pleading for him to calm down, but papa was unhearing. He was a man with a mission."

"A mission?"

"To tell me, in front of my aunt and uncle, and the overseer and all the grooms and other slaves, that I had killed that colt. That because I was irresponsible and didn't stay with the animal that it had died."

"My God," Duncan breathed.

Justine shook her head, as though clearing it of painful cobwebs. "Poor old Belhomme knew how much I loved that colt. If he hadn't known the consequences of hitting a white man, I swear he would have struck my father senseless."

"That kind of cruelty is unimaginable to me," Duncan said. "Especially directed toward a child. Your mother said nothing?"

"My poor *maman* had been dead for eight years, along with my sister Céleste. Lost to the fever. But she could have made no difference. She and Céleste were as powerless as myself."

"The man was an ogre."

"The incident with Sultan was, I'm sad to say, only one of many, but by far the most painful. Now that I've told you about it, I know why."

"Oh?"

She moved close, so close that his nostrils flared with her scent. Something more than her body heat surged through his flesh, not without arousing Duncan. An undeniable strength burgeoned in his loins.

"I've loved nothing since that long ago moment in that stable!" Justine cried. "Nothing until now. Until you. And I see only devastation and disappointment, just as before. I'm sorry, Duncan. I cannot help myself, I cannot deny this truth that burns my heart."

The great weight of Justine's ebony chignon grew suddenly unbearable, so heavy against the back of her neck that she swooned against Duncan's shoulder. He caught her, held her tight as his mind was torn with what to do. He felt her head tilt back, knew she was looking up at him, knew what should happen next. Then he saw Christophe waiting at the window. As he froze with Justine in his arms, Duncan thought he had never seen such agony. His heart sank when Christophe, his face a mask of desolation, moved slowly away.

"I will find a way," Duncan vowed. "I don't know how or when or where, but I will find a way for us to be together. Beginning tonight, that is my mission."

"And mine," Justine whispered.

CHAPTER 18

Because Mathilde de Longueval had a passion for nostalgic dance, guests at her ball were encouraged to take a turn with the gavotte, the minuet, and more. Justine and Christophe were in the midst of a saraband when he whispered his outrageous plan. She was so shocked she barely clung to her composure through the remainder of the stately dance. When they finally cleared the gleaming floor she sequestered him in a remote corner and questioned his sanity.

"I think you and Duncan must have been well into your cups to propose such a thing! Even if I agreed to such madness, white women are not permitted in the *Salle d'Orléans!*"

"But white men are," Christophe smiled. "And thank heavens you're not pretending you've never heard of the place."

"I would have if we had not agreed to a moratorium on conventional manners until Ash Wednesday. But what do you mean about white men?"

"You know the old saying, *mon cher.* Clothes make the man. Or in this case, clothes make the woman *into a man!*"

"*Mais non!*"

She clapped her hands together, at first frightened and then exhilarated by the sheer outrageousness of it all. It was not completely unheard of, of course. Some of the most enduring New Orleans rumors concerned this jealous wife or that curious fiancée who had somehow secretly insinuated herself into the forbidden world of white men and their ladies of color.

"Do you really think I dare?"

"I think you will if *I* dare!" Christophe roared. "Besides, I can see the challenge is on your brow like a fever. What do you say?"

"I say you've created a monster!" she laughed.

"But surely no monster was ever so beautiful," Duncan said, hearing the last of the conversation as he joined them. He smiled. "I take it then that Chris has told you our idea."

"He has indeed. But how do we go about it?"

Christophe could barely contain his excitement. "It's all arranged, thanks to your good friend Toinette Clovis."

"But what has she to do with this lunacy?"

"At our request Madame Clovis has secured a young man's frock coat and trousers from her husband's shop. She will also help you dress."

"Surely she knows nothing of our intent!"

"Of course not," Christophe assured her, fingers busily working his moustache. "She simply thinks it more of my lunacy." His eyes danced wickedly. "Did you tell her about Madam Pearl? Aha! I thought so."

"But what if we get caught?" Justine asked.

"No one will suspect anything," Duncan smiled. "Not with you stationed between us the entire time."

"Hmmm," Justine grumbled. "What if you forget and ask me to dance?"

All collapsed in laughter at the image of two gentlemen invading the dance floor of the *Salle d'Orléans,* and when the merriment finally eased, they discussed it deliriously. The more they talked, the more enthralled Justine became. The enthusiasm of the men was as contagious as swamp fever, and she found herself urging them to leave the ball at once. As they promised, Toinette was at *La Mode,* working feverishly on last-minute Mardi Gras costumes. Soona and Nicole were at her side, but she sent them from the dressing room while she helped Justine change. Since Monsieur Arnaud had first approached her on this matter, she suspected discretion was paramount.

"What foolishness are you up to tonight, *ma chére?*" Toinette turned Justine away and deftly opened the row of tiny buttons she herself had sewn on the ball gown.

"Since I have no secrets from you I see no harm in telling the truth," Justine hissed. "We're going to the *Salle d'Orléans.*"

"*Non!*"

Justine giggled as Toinette unlaced her corset. "You needn't waste time with any arguments, dear Toinette. I'm sure I've considered them all."

"But what if . . . ?"

"What if my husband found out?" Justine finished. "What do I care? I'm in love!"

Toinette spun Justine around so hard and fast both nearly lost their balance. "So that's what this is all about, eh? *L'Américain* out there? I should have known it wasn't only me putting these wild ideas in your head."

"You know me better than anyone," Justine said.

"But think what you're doing, Justine. Look carefully at the course you've taken, the dangers you're courting, and consider the odds. It's only a matter of time until you get caught!"

"I don't believe that," Justine said defiantly. "Besides, so what if it's true? I've spent an entire life being punished for things I didn't do."

"You've said that before," Toinette reminded her. "I suppose I should start believing you by now."

"*Merci beaucoup,*" Justine said, high spirits quickly flooding back. "Besides, it's carnival! Now let's hurry!"

"I'll help you only on the condition that we don't hurry," Toinette said, with concern. "It will take time to make this work." She gave Justine's voluptuous figure a critical eye, taking in the swell of breast and hip, the graceful throat, the soft, unlined complexion protected for years by parasols, gloves, hats and shawls. "And it won't be easy."

Outside in the coach, the men took turns swigging from Christophe's flask. Duncan repeatedly looked at his watch. "I have always wondered why women take forever to dress."

"Because they have much more to put on," Christophe said.

"Then it shouldn't take Justine so long, eh?" he laughed. They roared with laughter until Christophe had a coughing fit. Duncan was busily slapping him on the back when a small man peered through the carriage window. Duncan started to ask what he wanted when he caught himself.

"Justine? Is it possible? Christophe! Stop coughing and look here. It's our beautiful monster!"

Toinette's handiwork was remarkable and, despite her disapproval of the perilous lark, she beamed from the banquette. Not only had she dressed Justine to perfection and removed all trace of expertly applied cosmetics, she had concealed Justine's long hair by unbinding and carefully tucking it inside a top hat. From Bernard's shop, she had retrieved a cape with a high collar that hid the back of Justine's neck, but Justine refused the suggestion of a malacca cane as a finishing touch. Canes of any sort released the floodwaters of too many terrible memories. The *coup de grâce* was a pencil thin *faux* moustache Toinette had purchased from a novelty shop in the Rue Toulouse. Not even Christophe knew about this flourish, and he pounded his gloved hands together in approval.

"*C'est magnifique!* If I had a little brother, you are what he would look like!" Christophe grinned. "But that's it!"

"What's it?" asked Duncan.

"If anyone asks, I'll introduce her as a distant cousin from Paris. If anyone addresses you," he warned, "remember to keep your voice low and say as little as possible. The place is usually so noisy no one would suspect anything anyway."

"I wasn't having last minute doubts until now," she lamented.

"No more talk!" The three scrambled back into the cab while L'Eveillé gave Toinette a disgruntled look. He secretly shared Junon's thoughts on the insanity of white people.

With Mardi Gras only a week away and carnival exuberance at fever pitch, the *Salle d'Orléans* was thronged. Outside in the Rue d'Orleans, a noisy swarm of carriages and hackneys disgorged white men of all ages, alone, in pairs and in drunken groups. Christophe was glad for the chaos; it meant someone as petite as Justine would easily be lost in the shuffle of white gentlemen massing to peruse the colored beauties. They would be far more fascinated by café au lait complexions, bare shoulders and daring *décolletage* than a small stranger.

As they alit from the carriage, Justine's grip on Duncan's arm was ferocious and she froze on the banquette, momentarily transfixed by the reality of the place. She stared up at the second story windows, slightly ajar to catch the breeze of the unseasonably warm night. Music floated through the windows, from an orchestra of colored men silhouetted against the panes, their violins throbbing the most sensuous of waltzes.

"Hurry!" hissed Christophe. "The carriage behind is full of impatient rowdies. We don't need any untoward attention."

"I want to," Justine whimpered, "but I can't! Help me!"

Each grabbed an elbow and lifted Justine off her feet, bearing her swiftly into the crowded vestibule. The few men glancing in her direction assumed she was drunk and laughed approvingly. Christophe was grateful for Duncan's size when they were caught in the tangle of men checking hats, capes, and canes. He told him to make quickly for the stairs. He knew tonight's crowd would be an unfashionable mix of maskers, and no one would pay undue attention to a drunken tourist in top hat and cape.

Justine froze again when they reached the top of the stairs. It was one thing to know about the forbidden balls but quite another to see them in the flesh. The place was dazzling, albeit lavishly vulgar with its abundance of gilt mirrors, outré paintings and statues of undraped women. The cypress floor was certainly impressive, gleaming like glass as it reflected and buoyed an elegant ocean of dancers. It took Justine a few moments before she could register any faces, and she was sorry for the effort. Certainly she was stricken by the beauty and grace of the women for, of the dozen ballrooms catering to such exotic tastes, this one drew the *crème de la crème* of quadroon and octoroon beauties and their prospective protectors. But there was an unrelenting sadness as she watched the men move among the women, evaluating them as they might a slave, inspecting them with a brashness that would've earned a slap from a proper Creole lady.

"It was a mistake," Justine hissed to Duncan. "I find it unbearable."

"I found it shocking too, the first time," Duncan conceded. "Certainly nothing like this would ever be allowed in Virginia, but if you observe it as a social phenomenon it can be quite fascinating."

"I said unbearable, not shocking," Justine insisted, disappointed by what she misread as a lack of compassion. "Do you not find the whole spectacle unbearably sad?"

"I do indeed," Duncan concurred. "But those of us who approach slavery—and that is what this is on a grand, gracious scale—with anything other than a wholehearted embrace . . . well, it's nothing to discuss with a lady."

Justine warmed to his reply. "I might remind you that I am no lady tonight. But you are right, of course. Frankly I try to never think of slavery, try to put it permanently out of my mind, but it's impossible when it's everywhere you turn."

"Especially in New Orleans," Duncan said. He considered something, withdrew it as inappropriate, and changed his mind again when he remembered tonight's agreement. "Did you know that during carnival, slaves being sold in the St. Louis Hotel are auctioned in costume?"

"I had heard that," Justine offered. "I'm afraid it's only one more aspect of *La Nouvelle-Orléans* that sets her apart from other cities. More of our laissez-faire attitude toward everything, even human bondage. I'm embarrassed by it and . . . well, there! I've said it!"

Duncan's eyebrows shot up. "You're not an abolitionist, are you?"

"Certainly not," Justine replied hastily. "I told you I try not to think about it, that's all. It's too unpleasant."

"You two are getting much too serious," Christophe insisted. He had overheard enough conversational snippets to deem them inappropriate and moved things toward a lighter plane. "What do you think of the gowns, Justine?"

"I think most of these women are better dressed than the Creole ladies," she conceded. "Of course with their dark skin, they can take daring chances with colors that would make me look ill. Take that divine buttercup creation over there. And that maroon satin. Why, on me . . . oh, *mon Dieu!*"

Christophe saw them too, and now it was his turn to be frozen to the floor. Blancard had appeared at the top of the stairs. On his arm was Chaillot, resplendent in a gown of pale blue and a necklace of dazzling sapphires. All eyes were on the new arrivals. As Chaillot had not returned to the *Salle d'Orléans* since her debut, it was indeed a special occasion. And while it was not unheard of for men to bring their mistresses back to the ball, as it was the only place where they might enjoy the dance together, it was unusual.

Of course, Blancard had a special, perverse motive. In a recent drinking bout with Meilleure and some other men, Blancard had wagered none of their mistresses could approach Chaillot's beauty. Since two of the men had not been present when Chaillot made her debut appearance, they had only Blancard's word and, considering him as full of boasts as he was of whiskey, they accepted his challenge. The judges would be five men randomly chosen at the ball. The women, of course, were told nothing of the heartless wager, merely instructed to wear something special for the occasion. They were innocents on display, preening and strutting in their new finery like peacocks, unaware that a small fortune had been wagered solely on their appearance.

"Who are they?" asked Duncan, awed as much by Chaillot's beauty as he was disgusted by the elegant wastrel with her.

"My husband and his mistress," Justine said evenly. She shook her head, a wry smile tugging her lips. "Why, I even told her that material would be wonderful for her eyes."

"We'll leave at once," Christophe said, so disconcerted he didn't question her revealing remark.

"But why?" Justine joked guilelessly. "Don't you want to pay your respects?"

"Don't be absurd!" Christophe snapped. "I'm afraid our brave little charade is over."

"Not just yet! But distance yourself from us. It's quite possible Blancard would recognize me if he saw me in your company." She grimaced. "Although he appears drunk as usual."

"But why stay?" Christophe demanded, nearly frantic. This was more than he had bargained for, much more. If Blancard ever knew . . . but the consequences were too dire to consider.

"Because I want to see them dance together," Justine said, her response as sweet as it was enigmatic. "Now away with you!"

As Christophe separated, Duncan moved closer to Justine. He studied her as she watched her husband, mystified by the aura shrouding her face like a malignant miasma from the swamps. It was unreadable but so unsettling that he, too, looked at Blancard.

Again Duncan was met with questions that had no answers. Doubtless Blancard had been handsome once, but now it was inconceivable that Justine could be wife to such an old, ravaged soul. And the inevitable idea of them in the boudoir . . . well, it was an image much too repulsive to conjure. It merely served to reinforce Duncan's desire to find an escape for Justine.

"Pardon?" Justine's voice had been so low he didn't understand.

"I said he used to be such a wonderful dancer. He still manages to move a woman with a fair amount of grace, *n'est-ce pas?*"

Duncan said nothing. It was incomprehensible that she would have anything remotely complimentary to say about a man Christophe repeatedly maligned, damned as a boor and an uncaring brute. One who had bought Justine from an equally unloving father for something tantamount to thirty pieces of silver. As for Justine, she had been as reticent as Christophe had been vocal, her sole comment being, "Blancard is, I fear, the devil himself." Duncan had wanted to know more, but Justine remained adamantly, maddeningly quiet. There was, she insisted, no more to add.

Knowing so little naturally stoked the fires of Duncan's imagination. He surmised enough to recoil as Blancard circled the dance floor again and again, sweeping so close the hem of Chaillot's gown brushed the toes of Justine's boots. It was more than Duncan could endure. He wanted to kill Blancard! He had never really wanted to kill anyone, not even Dominique Duplessy, but he had a nearly uncontrollable urge to wrap his fingers around Blancard's throat and choke him lifeless. He didn't realize the depth of his rage until Justine whispered he was hurting her. He released her arm, horrified when she rubbed it to restore the circulation.

"I'm so sorry!" he said.

She sighed. "It is nothing."

Justine watched Chaillot make another graceful pass, but this time it was not the octoroon beauty drawing a critical eye. What shocked her more than seeing her husband with his mistress of color was Blancard himself. It had been only three weeks since she had seen him last, yet the man seemed to have aged ten years. She hadn't noticed until he danced close enough to reveal details, a pinched face with sunken eyes and an unnatural tightness around the lips. Certainly the alcoholic bloat endured, but it was overshadowed by something different, a plagued visage Justine had seen before. Hilaire Blancard had the look of death on him, the same look she had seen on the faces of countless fever victims.

It terrified her as she half-remembered something, but what? Hadn't Toinette promised . . . oh, what had she said that wretched day when she took Blancard's picture to that crazy old *voudouienne?* Justine watched closely as Blancard waltzed by again, closer than ever, and Toinette's warning came flooding back.

"*It's too late, mon cher. The wheels have already begun to turn. Even now word will be spreading through the Negro grapevine that someone is looking to put a curse on Hilaire Blancard. Within the hour, Marie Laveau herself will know about it.*"

"Marie Laveau!" Justine gasped.

She was halfway down the crowded stairs before Duncan could pursue her. Watching from across the room, Christophe trailed discreetly, catching up in the street. Justine leaned weakly against the carriage, breath ragged and heavy, heart racing. Both men misread her terror, and Christophe hastily apologized. His urge to crow over their little triumph had been undone by Blancard's most unexpected arrival.

"I'm so sorry you saw them, Justine. If I had had any idea they would be coming . . ."

"No matter, dear Christophe. So what if our little adventure was more than we bargained for? I'm not sorry. Are you, Duncan?"

"I wanted to kill him," he said, teeth still clenched.

"I know," Justine said. "I saw the look in your eye. I've seen rage like that only once before. It's not something you forget, especially when it's directed toward . . ."

She immediately regretted the slip. She was not yet ready to reveal anything more of the sickness in her marriage and sought quickly to change the subject. But not before the men traded wary looks.

"But never mind about all that. It's carnival and now, gentlemen, it is my turn to select a *divertissement.*" She hesitated only slightly before adding, "I can't wait to show my new outfit to Madam Pearl!"

Christophe sighed with relief as the evening was saved. He called to the drowsing coachman. "Your favorite destination, L'Eveillé! To the Faubourg Marigny to find Red Bill Wilson!"

If the Rue d'Orléans had been busy, Gallatin Street was positively teeming. The crush of traffic was due not to carriages but a mass of humanity overflowing from the taverns and bordellos to spill wildly into the street. Even with Red Bill Wilson and a couple of his cronies brandishing weapons and shouting murderous warnings from the carriage, L'Eveillé could barely navigate the throngs.

"It seems half the city is in the streets tonight," observed Justine.

"Because Mardi Gras is only a week away," said Christophe. He chuckled. "And before you suggest it, my dear Justine, you are coming nowhere near the District on Carnival day. What happens here is something I forbid you to see. Even *I* am shocked!"

"As you say." Justine recognized that brotherly tone and accepted it. If it was something Christophe found repugnant, she certainly need know no more. As it was, despite her insouciant posturing, she was having difficulty dealing with everything from Red Bill's stench to the crush of harlots and hooligans heaving the carriage like a vile sea of human flotsam. She had thought her first visit would inure her sensibilities, but she was smitten once again by the tragic desperation of it all. How could so many people fall so far from grace? Of course she had only to recall Madam Pearl's story to understand and the recollection made her shudder. Blanche Genois's social position had been every bit as lofty and rarefied as her own, and if she could suffer that terrible tumble, no one was exempt.

"Are you cold?" Duncan asked, misreading the shudder.

"No," Justine assured him. "Just an unpleasant reminiscence."

Duncan accepted the explanation without question, although he naturally suspected Hilaire Blancard was involved. Try as he might, he could not wrest the man's image from his memory.

"Here we are!" Red Bill cried, his announcement accompanied by a gross belch. Justine found it oddly appropriate.

Once again, Wilson and his cronies moved as a forceful wedge, carefully protecting their three charges from the madness. Because it was carnival, Christophe wisely slipped the miscreants an especially hefty fee with the promise that there was more to be had. He also had the foresight to warn Red Bill that any untoward acts from his men would kill his personal golden goose. All too hungry for the seemingly bottomless Arnaud purse, the man understood and assured Christophe he would be safe. Red Bill Wilson might have been amoral but he was no fool.

Pearl's elegant bagnio was bustling like every place else, but she quickly found time for the new arrivals. She received them as before, regally perched on the tufted settee, surrounded by men like a queen amidst loyal courtiers. She beamed when she saw Justine, greeting her as though she were a long-lost daughter. Vastly amused by the outrageous costume, Pearl roared with laughter when she learned Madame Blancard had crashed the quadroon balls, but warned against overstepping her boundaries.

"If you had been exposed . . . well, *ma chéri*, I shudder to think of the consequences."

Justine smiled. "I find that comment most interesting, coming from you of all people."

Pearl took her hand. "I may have survived my scandalous behavior, dear Justine, but at a terrible price. It's one I don't wish to see anyone else pay. Least of a sweet soul like yourself."

"I appreciate your concern," Justine said, still smiling. She grew fonder of the old woman with each visit. "And now I will ask a favor of you."

The wizened eyes widened. *"Moi?* What could I possibly have that you might want?" Justine leaned close, whispering so that the men could not hear. Startled by the outrageous request, Pearl snapped open a plumed fan and concealed further conversation from prying eyes. "My hearing is not what it used to be. Surely you didn't ask for . . ."

"A night in your swan bed," Justine finished. "I most certainly did. And the expense is not a consideration."

Pearl studied the tranquil face, looking for chinks in the serene armor. When she found none, she said, "It would be my gift of course, but surely you do not intend to enjoy the bed alone."

"I do not."

Madam Pearl studied Duncan's blurred image through the feathery tendrils of the fan. She squeezed Justine's hand. "You're fixing your fate as surely as I fixed mine, my dear."

"So be it."

"But what prompted you to make such a decision?"

"I believe it was made for me," Justine confessed. "By too many voices to be ignored. Twelfth Night when I first met Duncan. At the marketplace. Here. Tonight when we stood in my garden and I saw the love in his eyes, and at the *Salle d'Orléans* tonight when that love turned to rage, to hatred even." She squeezed Pearl's hand in return. "To see that rage and know it will never be directed at me is beyond my most desperate hopes. I . . ."

When she fell silent, Pearl asked, very gently, "Are you trying to tell me something about your husband?"

"Quite the opposite, Madam Pearl. I . . . I think I'm trying *not* to tell you something."

"Then I shall say it for you. I've already told you I've seen much in my life. We need not belabor that point. I've seen men like your husband. It's not simply that he gives you no pleasure in the boudoir."

"Please, Madam Pearl . . ."

"It's that he gives you pain!" When Justine winced and looked away, Pearl urged a response. "Tell me, girl!"

In a very small voice, *"Oui."*

"That evil bastard!" The vitriol in the old woman's voice was more shocking than her crude language. "Men like that are . . . but, no! *C'est impossible!*" She shook her head as though to free it from nightmares, prompting an ugly frown to cross Justine's face.

"What are you talking about? You look as if you've seen a ghost."

"An apt description," Pearl conceded. "I've just remembered one. Your husband!"

The stories tumbled back through the madam's lengthy memory, a hideous cascade of unspeakable acts perpetrated by men more animal than human. Prostitution had forever been a magnet for beasts preying on women, men seeking helpless targets for their basest desires. Such men became quickly known in the secret circles they frequented, and their notoriety oozed steadily like pus from a festering wound. Pearl had heard of Hilaire Blancard, but until now she had not juxtaposed Justine's surname with a memory she preferred to suppress. He was—he had to be—the man who had beat whores some fifteen years ago.

"His evil misdoings were well known to me, to everyone in the life," she told Justine, voice riven with sympathy. "But you know the story. Dear God, child! You've *lived* it!"

Justine took a deep breath as another piece of the hideous puzzle fell into place. "Yes, I have."

"But you must get away from him!"

"Up until recently, I hadn't realized that I needed to flee," Justine said without a trace of irony. "But now . . . well, the swan bed is a step in the right direction. *N'est-ce pas?*"

"Oh, yes! And I will tell you something else! When I was forced into flight, I had nowhere to turn. Women like us are helpless."

"As helpless unbound as when we are bound," Justine offered boldly.

The worldly Madam Pearl nonetheless recoiled at the image of the elegant beauty before her tethered for a man's wicked whims. Such perversion, she well knew, did not confine itself to the ignorant and destitute. Indeed, its more elaborate realizations often required a cleverness and innovation beyond the ken of the average man. She had always believed man's malevolent imagination was at its *apogée* when carnal matters were involved, and Hilaire Blancard was living proof.

"What I wish to tell you is this, Justine. For what it's worth, I will always be here for you. This retreat, as I told you before, is reached through a human cesspool, but it's a retreat nonetheless. And it's yours if you should ever require it."

Neither Duncan nor Christophe knew what prompted the exuberance with which Justine hugged the old woman. Nor did they understand why she hurried away, vanishing into Madam Pearl's private quarters, or the twinkle in Pearl's ancient eyes as she dispatched a maid in the same direction.

"Is Madame Blancard all right?" asked Duncan.

"Quite," replied Pearl. "Now you two sit and chat with me a while. We'll have some champagne. Tonight is a very special occasion indeed!"

While Christophe was distracted by Pearl's vivacity, laughing at her risqué stories and forgetting about the unpleasant conclusion of the untimely visit to the quadroon ball, Duncan thought of nothing but Justine. He was maddened by her disappearance, one that grew so long as to be unbearable. Just when his patience was evaporating, the maid returned and whispered in his ear. He all but leapt to his feet, hurriedly trailing the young colored girl into Pearl's quarters. Christophe, equally curious, started to rise but Pearl grabbed his knee with surprising strength.

"With respect, Christophe, it is not you Justine has summoned."

"*Quel dommage,*" he murmured, settling against the lush settee. He sighed, breath buoyed by the bitter lament of unrequited love. Pearl, all too familiar with such loss, felt the man's pain and soothed it the only way she knew how.

"Clarice has been asking for you, *cher* Christophe." She ordered his champagne refilled. "With some fine wine and a fine woman . . ."

Christophe chuckled. "I know the scenario only too well, Pearl old girl. I've been rehearsing it far too many years."

Duncan squinted in the darkness, startled when the maidservant discreetly closed the door and left him alone. At first he couldn't discern anything in the darkness, but when his eyes adjusted, he made for the glow of a lone candelabra between heavy *portières*. A bizarre silhouette curved ahead, a shape that metamorphosed into the head of a swan as he approached. It appeared to be a figurehead, graceful neck swelling into a prow before flaring again into a graceful mahogany boat piled high with pillows. The flickering candlelight played tricks on Duncan's eyes. He suspected movement and when he moved closer still saw a vision that stole his breath away.

Justine lay naked beneath a translucent coverlet drawn to her throat. The candlelight bathed her sweetly, a pale *houri* nestled against the opulence of silks and satins. Her hair was unbound, a black tangle splayed across a single golden pillow beneath her head. Her lips were touched with scarlet, cheeks flushed roseate by natural desire.

"Justine . . ." he breathed.

"Say nothing," she whispered, raising an arm to beckon languidly.

The coverlet slipped away, baring her nodding breasts. "Only come to me."

The thin sound of buttons and Duncan's clothes falling to the floor pounded in Justine's ears for what they made manifest. She welcomed the man with all her heart, yet she was terrified by what she sought to embrace. Both Toinette and Pearl had promised her there was a tender side to men, one she had clearly never encountered, and she wanted it desperately. Still, when she saw Duncan naked, she shrank from the strength of his arousal. And when he slipped into bed and sought to take her in his arms, she was seized by last minute panic. She gasped a half-hearted retreat.

"It's not too late, Duncan," she whispered in a suffocated voice. "Not too late to end this before it's begun."

"Now it is you who must not speak," he said.

Justine's misgivings were steadily eroded as Duncan enveloped her and gently drew away the coverlet. She gasped and recoiled, just once, when his hardness erased the emptiness between them and pressed against her thigh. Duncan sensed her hesitation and, desperate to conquer it, withdrew only to touch again with a gentleness that was all but heartbreaking. To her own amazement, Justine was thrilled by his hesitance, and boldly abandoned her fears by taking his hand and pressing it to her skin, here, there. When his hands at last closed over her naked flesh, they blazed a trail of fire.

Justine sank deeper into the mass of cushions, losing herself in their voluptuous softness even as the man was lost in her. Her flesh grew humid with his breath, her nipples bloomed between his lips, stiffening sweetly and tempting him to explore further.

She breathed his name.

His hand sculpted the swell of her breasts, soft belly and thighs but faltered until Justine again encouraged him. Duncan sighed with blissful surprise as his hand was deftly directed lower still until it brushed against her pubic down. She murmured something very soft, in French, that he did not understand as she reached to touch his arching sex. Her natural response was to grip hard, eliciting a moan of raw lust. Justine was glad the golden candleglow did not reveal the crimson blush flooding from her forehead to her breasts.

Now, secure that her demons were vanquished, Duncan came fully alive. Justine gasped, deliriously paralyzed as his hand dared venture farther between her thighs, rousing her steadily, irrevocably. Far from resisting the invasion, she fought for it, pleaded with him and cried out when, at long last, he slowly sheathed himself with one long, glorious thrust in the very quick of her. As he was buried, hardness warmed by exquisite heat, Duncan knew he was forever lost to this strange woman he loved, but he embraced the knowledge with a long dormant passion. Justine was awakening him even as he awakened her, caught by a force requiring two to spawn.

The power in Duncan's loins was suddenly diffused as she drained him with a frightening ferocity. To his astonishment, she seemed to soar with him, arching her back suddenly and releasing a series of low, guttural whimpers that both thrilled and frightened him. He'd never known anything so completely, utterly finished, and such loss made him cry out and reach for her, as though he could reinstate the glorious lost moment. Justine was no less moved.

Duncan wanted to speak, but as his lips parted she touched them into silence. "Let me, first," she whispered, "while I can." His eyebrows rose, heart racing. "I . . . I no longer feel afraid. I've done all that I can to curse my destiny and yet, far from being frightened, I feel exhilarated. It is your love that gives me this strength, and although I want desperately to accept it, I already fear its loss."

"But why, my love?"

"Because I do not understand why you . . . love me."

"That isn't what you were going to say," he said gently.

"No. I was going to say 'saved' me."

"A strange choice of words." But he knew, of course. The implicit allusion was doubtless to her husband.

"Perhaps because I am a strange woman, *ma cheri.*" She kissed him swiftly. Then, "But why do you say that?"

"If I, as you say, 'saved' you, I was unaware of it, but I am glad because I have also saved myself."

"Would you do it again?"

"Of course," Duncan said. Her sudden need to be reassured was discomfiting but he supposed it was necessary. Women of her station were scarcely bred to commit fornication, and their actions after the fact were destined to be cautious. Not the least of her concerns was fear of eternal damnation by her cloying Catholic faith.

"What if you changed your mind, Duncan?"

"I won't," he promised.

She was not yet convinced. "But what if you did?"

He gathered her tighter in his arms. "If I no longer saved you, my love, I would be lost again myself. That is anathema to me. Can you not understand that?"

"It's just that I've never known such joy before, and I'm terrified that it will be taken away as suddenly as it was given. I was sold to a husband who loves no one and punished me for the love I tried to offer.

And I am doomed by a faith that decrees pleasure must be paid for with pain."

So there it is, Duncan thought. At last. At long last, there is Justine Blancard in her own words!

His first impulse was to ask what Blancard had done, but he didn't believe his heart could bear what she might reveal in this vulnerable moment. Instead he wisely reassured her.

"I told you earlier tonight that I would find a way out of this. I meant that with all my heart. Promise you believe me."

She nodded and, for the first time, smiled. "I promise."

They lay quietly for a few moments, for the first time hearing violins oozing softly through the walls. They drifted with it, and their own thoughts, until a gust of wind tore at the windows, ripping open a shutter. Duncan sprang from bed to close it, but Justine bade him otherwise as moonlight flooded the room.

"Leave it and gutter the candles instead." She was astonished by the way his caress lingered after he'd moved away. "There! Now look how the bed is flooded with silver."

"It is indeed," he said, losing himself in her as he again took to the swan bed.

"The gold of candles traded for the silver of the moon," she said. "A fair exchange, I think." She sighed and rested her hand on his chest, studying the newborn shadow and changing it at will. "I'm not sure I ever saw moonlight until now." She touched the fur below his throat. "See how it casts my shadow there!"

"Sometimes I think *you* are the poet," he smiled.

"*Mais non.* I should never think of anything so magnificent as your poem to me. It is my most treasured possession."

"And my greatest creation," Duncan added.

"Ah, but you're wrong," she insisted. "Deeply wrong."

Duncan frowned, puzzled as he often was by this mercurial creature. "What do you mean?"

"Your most remarkable accomplishment lies right here beside you, *mon amour.*"

"And what might that be?" he smiled.

What Justine said shocked him, but Duncan could not deny that he was amused and his masculinity wildly flattered.

"You have done the impossible, sir. You have made a whore of me!"

CHAPTER 19

Clad only in linen drawers, merino vest, and jeweled scarlet shoes, Duncan was an amusing sight as he paced the bedroom floor. Although Randolph stifled a chuckle, Junon's patience was steadily eroding.

"Please stand still and raise your arms, Mr. Duncan," the valet admonished. "Otherwise I'll never get this tunic over your head."

"Listen to him," Randolph said. "Unless you want to greet her in your underwear!"

Duncan sighed. "I'm sorry. I guess I'm just too full of excitement." He looked at Randolph and beamed. "I still cannot believe she's coming here!"

"I don't know why you continue to act surprised. We're all entitled to a change of heart, are we not?"

"And thank God for that!" Duncan said. "I know you promised and you've never broken a promise to me, but . . . well, inviting Justine to dinner here! And Christophe, too!"

"And to the ball afterward!" Randolph crowed. "Don't forget the ball!"

"Dressed like this, how can I?"

Duncan smiled as the ankle-length white silk tunic was slipped over his shoulders and carefully smoothed. Junon then added a purple cape and secured it with an enormous bejeweled epaulet. With its elaborate gold embroidery, the cape was eclipsed only by the imperial diadem Junon adjusted on Duncan's head. Bernard Clovis had done an excellent job recreating the emperor Justinian's headpiece, a close-fitting cap dripping with jewels and a *faux* pearl necklace trailing the nape of Duncan's neck.

When Duncan stood in all his Byzantine glory, Randolph executed a grand bow. "You look splendid, your imperial highness. I cannot wait to meet your empress."

Duncan grew serious for a moment. "I want you to like her, Randolph. Very much."

"If she's half the lady you claim, she will be irresistible," Randolph smiled. "This Justine seems to have bewitched you, little brother."

"She has indeed! I tell you, I think of nothing else. Morning, noon, and night, she sings to me, a beatific angel perched on my shoulder."

"Always the poet, eh?" Randolph winked at Junon.

"Which reminds me," Duncan said. "I wrote a new poem for her."

"So that's what has been keeping you up so late," Randolph said. "Sometimes I hear you in the night, pacing. Then quiet. Then pacing again."

"This one expresses my love even more than the other. Just thinking of her sends my imagination soaring. Let Dante have his Beatrice. Marlowe, his Helen of Troy. I have my Justine."

Randolph shook his head. He had never seen anyone so smitten, and he was not a little unnerved because his brother seemed to be reeling out of control in a potentially volatile situation. Duncan might love the woman to all extremes and write endless paeans praising her grace and beauty, but the undeniable, irrefutable fact remained that Madame Blancard was a married woman. Randolph was sure there was nothing to change that, nothing that could ever allow Duncan more than a distant platonic love and a few stolen moments shared in the presence of others. And even that would be vanquished when Hilaire Blancard changed his mind as he had so often done in the past. It was inevitable, of course, only a matter of time before Blancard tired of his fresh young mistress and turned his attentions back toward his wife. When that happened, Randolph feared deeply for his brother and the terrible consequences. He knew only too well what it was like to lose the only one he really loved, to have it snatched away when he was so young, so ill-prepared to fill that agonizing void. The fact that Duncan had embraced the abnegation inherent in this peculiar liaison would not, Randolph worried, ease the shattering aftermath of pain.

Yet Randolph could not, would not, protest further. He knew his brother well and was wise enough to put himself in Duncan's position. If he had a second chance at happiness with Molly Lewis, he would not hesitate to pursue it. Perhaps that is our legacy, he thought wryly. We brothers are men doomed to a barren destiny with women.

"I cannot wait to read it," he said finally. He smiled as Duncan, purple mask in place, paused to preen before the mirror. "May I see it now?"

Duncan's heart teemed with affection. "It is already in the lady's possession, dear brother. In truth, however, it is for her eyes only." His voice hovered but briefly, then soared with rapturous memory. "Although I wish you could have seen her face when she read it." Randolph nodded, startled when Duncan abruptly changed the subject. "And you, Randolph. Are you not changing as well?"

"My costume is a surprise. You will not see it until later."

"Oh." Duncan thanked Junon before taking Randolph's arm and walking him downstairs. "You know what the rumors are, don't you? By now everyone knows there is to be a parade."

"Tell me more," Randolph urged. He knew several of the krewe members had purposely leaked tales about their secret plans and he was eager to know how they had metamorphosed through repetition. As he listened to the wild speculation, he was thrilled. It was better than he expected and, best of all, nowhere near the truth.

"An Arabian nights fantasy," Duncan reported. "King Arthur and the knights of the Round Table. Caesar and Cleopatra."

"No!"

"And speaking of Helen of Troy, I also heard a wooden horse filled with Greek soldiers in golden armor will disgorge its cargo in the middle of Canal Street." Randolph was positively gleeful. "But considering what you showed me the other morning, none of those tales seem right."

"Exactly," Randolph said. "So this will be an even bigger surprise. What is it?" Duncan had suddenly squeezed his brother's arm.

"Did you hear a carriage?"

"The house next door, I think. Good heavens, boy. You're shaking. What you need is a whiskey!"

"Perhaps you're right."

As they walked past the dining room, he glanced at the china, silver, and crystal gleaming atop the table. A servant was arranging freshly picked camellias in a crystal bow, and Duncan was touched. Randolph had spared neither expense nor detail to make this night memorable. Although an intimate supper for four, it was easily the most elaborate his brother had ever offered.

"No!" he said suddenly. He broke from Randolph and rushed to the door. "That coach was *not* next door. She's here, Randolph! She's here!"

"Calm down, Duncan. You're acting like a smitten schoolboy."

Duncan beamed and embraced him. "And why not, big brother? That's precisely how I feel!"

He stepped aside as the ever vigilant Junon, acting now as butler, swung the door wide and went to assist the arriving guests. What he saw startled him as much as the others.

Steadying herself on Junon's hand as she alit from the carriage was Justinian's empress Theodora. She was even more lavishly costumed than Duncan, purple robes elaborately embellished with gold braid and a jeweled collar piece covering her shoulders. Her diadem was a glittering masterpiece of *faux* jewels sewn into a black velvet cap, the whole affair drizzling streams of pearls from head to breasts. Such glamour nearly obscured the priceless angel brooch she had worn the first night they met. Justine gathered her robes and dropped a deep curtsy.

"Your highness," she said with mock gravity.

Bursting with excitement, and not a little pride at such a beautiful creature for his fanciful consort, Duncan bowed and took her hand. As he led her toward the wide porch where Randolph waited, he was so thrilled he could barely speak. Justine exuded elegant *sangfroid* as she dropped a curtsy for Randolph as well.

"Madame Blancard," he smiled. "Welcome to our home."

"I'm honored, Mr. Saunders," she said, voice husky and richly accented. "And so pleased to meet you at last. Duncan speaks of you endlessly, and with such pride."

Randolph succumbed instantly, utterly disarmed as Justine took his arm and turned her full gaze upon him. What her charm did not accomplish was completed by her beauty. Like his brother, Randolph felt as though he could swim in the *chatoyant* eyes, tending toward violet by the swarm of purple engulfing her.

"I might say the same of you," he managed finally. His eye was caught by more glitter as Christophe followed her to the porch, resplendent as a court jester in maroon and gold velvets. "Ah. Monsieur Arnaud. Welcome." Both Christophe and Justine were amused at Randolph's efforts to pronounce that most common and difficult of French words, *"monsieur,"* but appreciated the effort. Duncan had not exaggerated when he'd told them his brother's attitude toward Creoles had dramatically changed.

During dinner, Duncan watched, beguiled, as Justine cemented her conquest of his brother. A study in exquisite complaisance, she lavished praise on the Creole menu prepared in her honor, picking gracefully through oysters on the half shell, *soupe á la tortue vert,* pigeon sautéed with mushrooms, and broiled pompano in sauce *á la Maitre d'Hotel* with carrots, cauliflower and julienne potatoes. At the same time, she stitched an engaging conversational tapestry of myriad topics, eventually leading to a story about the Byzantine court that thoroughly captivated Randolph. Duncan knew the tale and relished her retelling.

"Before the emperor appeared, the floor of the throne room was strewn with laurel and roses, crushed underfoot to release a sweet perfume. His so-called throne of Solomon contained mechanical twittering birds and roaring lions, but most amazing of all an ability to rise to the ceiling while visiting dignitaries prostrated themselves. When they stood again, the throne had buoyed the emperor to a dizzying and of course appropriately intimidating height above them." She smiled radiantly. "It was a mutual love of the Byzantine that brought your brother and myself together."

The remark was uttered guilelessly yet carried with it a thunderbolt of insinuation.

"Fascinating!" Randolph said, a little too quickly.

He rushed to steer the conversation away from indelicate waters. Indeed, lurking just below the surface was the obvious question: Why would a married woman, especially one of such rarefied status, risk compromising her honor? As much as Randolph was charmed by her, he could not comprehend how she could behave so recklessly. There remained much about the exotic Creole mystique, especially manifold in this woman, that eluded him, but it was not something he wished to explore just now, not on Mardi Gras itself.

"And what a marvelous story!" he added. "I shall keep that in mind as a theme for next year's Comus ball."

"And what is the theme this year?" asked Justine.

"Milton's Paradise Lost," he replied. "We've prepared four rather extravagant *tableaux* I hope you'll find entertaining."

"And what are they?" Justine pursued.

Randolph pursed his lips while considering his answer, eventually deciding he'd said enough. "I fear I'm sworn to secrecy, madame."

"No matter," Justine smiled. "I look forward to being surprised."

While dinner concluded with *pouding a la Reine* in wine sauce, *petit fours,* raisins and cheese, accompanied by black coffee, Randolph asked Justine how she came to be so well-versed on so many topics.

"You sound surprised," she said.

"With all due respect," he explained, "the Virginia ladies I have known rarely evince interest in anything . . . well, of an intellectual nature."

"Perhaps you have not met the right ladies," Justine offered. "Or more likely they were never encouraged to pursue anything more tax-ing than ball gowns or dinner menus. Such worlds are tragically lim-ited and limiting."

"Perhaps," he conceded, uncomfortable with a thought that had never occurred before. The unpleasant moment was compounded with memories of his mother, a woman whom Justine had so succinctly de-scribed.

"I was never content to stop learning when my formal education ended," Justine continued. "Some people read to improve themselves, others to keep informed. Others still to find escape. I fall primarily into the latter category." She demurely considered a *petit four* while adding, "In a situation such as mine, there is much time for reading. Unfortu-nately perhaps, I discovered an insatiable hunger for knowledge of all sorts." She nodded toward Christophe, who had been oddly quiet all evening. "Monsieur Arnaud is my partner in literary crime. He often brings me books and shies from no unsavory topics. Just last fall he gave me a book by Edgar Allan Poe that gave me nightmares. All about plague, as if we needed to read about *that* in New Orleans." She popped the tiny cake in her mouth, swallowed daintily and said, "Why I haven't been so frightened since there was all that talk of vampires at *Point du Lac* plantation!"

"Sheer nonsense, of course," Christophe said, breaking a long si-lence.

"*Vraiment, mon ami.*" Embarrassed that she had unwittingly lapsed into French, Justine hastily added, "So we shall speak of it no further. Certainly Mardi Gras is much too festive an occasion to dwell on some-thing as macabre as vampires."

"Then please tell me something about Theodora," Randolph sug-gested. "All evening I've been meaning to ask about the inspiration for that superb costume."

"A most complex lady," replied Justine. "And my favorite in all of his-tory."

"High praise from someone with your knowledge," said Duncan, not hiding the sheen of pride in his voice.

Justine gave him a brief smile before turning her attention back to Randolph. "Theodora's father was a bear keeper at the Hippodrome in Constantinople," she explained. She paused, carefully weighing her words. "She became an actress and a *demimondaine* of considerable no-toriety, a voluptuary so outrageous that people publicly shunned her rather than be accused of keeping her company."

"*Mon Dieu!*" gasped Christophe.

Randolph too was amazed. Justine was, after all, discussing prostitution. Coming from any other woman, both subject and choice of words would be considered highly improper, but because Justine spoke so casually, in a tone more appropriate for discussing the opera, all was oddly inoffensive.

"She was also highly intelligent and courageous. By some accounts she captivated Justinian upon first sight, but since she was of lower rank, law forbade any marriage. Naturally, her only recourse was to become his mistress, and once that was accomplished, she pressured him to change the law. She had learned early on to refuse to accept things as unchangeable, and it is that trait I envy most of all."

Her glance at Duncan was neither subtle nor coy, laid bare for the others as well.

"When Justinian assumed the throne, she became empress." She laughed softly. "Not bad for an animal trainer's daughter."

"Was she a good ruler?" Randolph asked.

"She was a consummate autocrat but not without compassion. She converted an old palace to a home for destitute women and established hospitals throughout Constantinople. At the same time, she was ruthless with her opposition and simply made them disappear." She smiled at Duncan who clung to her every word. "Many historians claim she was stronger than the great Justinian, indeed the *raison d'etre* for his greatness, that she stood down rebellions when he was ready to abandon the throne."

Duncan said, "That was when she announced, 'I hold with the old saying that royalty makes a fine winding-sheet.' "

"Correct. But enough about Byzantium," Justine insisted. She glanced at a baroque clock perched atop a mantelpiece. "It's boring for anyone who doesn't share our passion. And we must delay Mr. Saunders no longer. Did you not say you must leave early to take your place in the parade?"

"So thoughtful of you to remind me, Madame Blancard," Randolph said, rising reluctantly. Despite his misgivings about Duncan's future with this woman, he found her decidedly difficult to leave. "But please answer one more query. What is it about Theodora that you admire most?"

Without hesitation, Justine smiled beguilingly and replied, "Absolutely everything, sir!"

When L'Eveillé deposited his anxious passengers on St. Charles, lines of hopeful spectators, many costumed and masked, had begun lining both sides of the avenue. By nine o'clock, anticipation was feverish, and the restless crowd craned a collective neck uptown.

"Look!"

The throngs pitched and swayed as a strange light was sighted. Then another and another still, until finally one width of the divided avenue was ablaze with lights. As they grew closer, figures emerged slowly and a cheer exploded from the crowd as they identified Negroes carrying blazing *flambeaux*. The dozens of flaming torchlights seemed to set fire to the sky and lent a magical golden glow to the great moss-hung oaks embracing the avenue.

"Look! Look!"

The procession of torch-bearers illuminated the approach of Comus, on a throne perched high atop the first float. Swagged with gloriously colored bunting, it was drawn by six lavishly caparisoned horses, feathers dancing regally as if they knew they were on display. The Lord of Misrule, Comus himself, looming twenty feet in the air, was a magnificent, appropriately distant masked figure. He drew screams of laughter and wild approval from his adoring subjects, waving his scepter royally above their heads before vanishing in a blaze of more glittering *flambeaux*.

"It's like nothing I've ever seen before," Justine said, whispering through her mask.

"It's like nothing New Orleans has seen before," Christophe added, only slightly resentful that the Americans had staged this marvel. He was ecstatic simply to see something so grand. "But look there! It's not over yet!"

Indeed it wasn't. Trailing Comus at a respectable distance was the blaze of more torches and a second float. The crowd gasped and pointed as the Great Palace of Lucifer hove into view, a mountain of gold rocks surmounted by pyramids and minarets sparkling like diamonds.

"How on earth . . . ?!" cried Justine.

"And there he is!" Duncan shouted to be heard above the crowd, but his salute was the same as hundreds of others. "The devil himself!"

Overseeing his evil domain from a height greater even than Comus was Satan, a tall masker with a great black cape flaring wide to reveal a muscular body beneath red tights and tunic. His cloven hooves, horns, and tail glistened with some sort of silvery *bijoux*, and his painted leer drew frightened squeals from countless children. A loud, maniacal laugh added to the menacing illusion.

"Our city's parents will be dealing with plenty of nightmares tonight," Justine laughed sympathetically.

"And those fellows will scarcely help!" added Duncan.

Behind Satan's float came his armies, dozens of devils trailing beneath the glow of still more torches. Indeed the avenue now looked as though it were on fire as the satanic troops marched on and on, brandishing tridents, waving pointed tails and twirling with their great capes until they resembled whirling dervishes. It was a grandly maleficent illusion, a blur of scarlet burned golden beneath the wildly dancing *flambeaux*.

"Look there!" Duncan cried, pointing and waving frantically. "There's Randolph!"

"But how do you know?" Christophe asked.

"Easy!" Duncan laughed. "Only my poor bowlegged brother could be that poor bowlegged devil!"

As if Comus' street parade had not been dazzling enough, the spectacular ball that followed would keep the city talking for years. It was by far the most glamorous of the full thousand balls that had thrilled the city since Twelfth Night. Held at the Gaiety Theater, modestly touting itself as "the most magnificent theater in the United States," it drew three thousand spectators who gaped and gasped at the four glittering *tableaux* Randolph had secretly confided to Justine before he left for the parade.

Even though she knew what to expect, she was nonetheless awed by "Tartarus," "Expulsion from the Garden of Eden," "Conference of Satan and Beelzebub," in which Randolph's bowlegs were once more on display, and the magnificent grand finale, "Pandemonium." Thunderous applause, including enthusiastic cheers from the small Creole minority, filled the great hall and all present agreed the Mistick Krewe of Comus had launched Mardi Gras 1857 into a new era. It was the rare mask not concealing a smile as the dancing began in earnest.

"A most auspicious beginning, wouldn't you say?" Justine asked as she and Duncan whirled around the vast dance floor.

"For us as well as the city," he said.

"What do you mean?"

"Didn't you feel it tonight at supper?" he asked, holding her tighter. "Don't you feel it now, this fire consuming us?"

"Yes . . . yes!" Justine managed, breath drained as if by a succubus. She knew exactly what he meant. "But what are we to do about it, my love?"

"We must first tell Christophe we are leaving. And Randolph."

Justine did not think to ask where they were going, nor did she care. And no one took note as the emperor Justinian and his empress Theodora left the thousands of revelers for a much-desired moment of solitude. After much difficulty securing a hack, they headed for the Garden District, away from the madness of carnival and into long-awaited erotic oblivion at Randolph's house. If Junon was shocked when the couple disappeared into Duncan's bedroom, he discreetly kept his feelings private.

Once alone, Duncan reached to lower the wick of the gaslight, but Justine boldly pushed his hand away. "I want to see you better this time."

Duncan smiled. "Vixen!"

"That I am," she sighed, eagerly enveloped by his arms. "Harlot too, perhaps, but I care not. If ever there was a sin I wantonly, willfully embrace, it is this!"

Duncan found her heresy arousing and told her as much. That emboldened her all the more, enough to take his hand and put it on her breast. Duncan's fingers molded against her flesh, as though they belonged there, and Justine sighed rapturously as heat coursed freely between them. They stood silent, transfixed for an eternal moment, until, as if by magic, Justine's imperial diadem and purple robe evaporated. Only the white silk tunic remained, and Duncan gasped when he explored further. Underneath she was totally naked.

"My God, woman!"

"Do I shock you, *ma cheri?*"

"A little," he confessed.

She smiled. "Good." Then, but without apology, "Myself as well."

Justine lifted her arms, angel's wings rising, as a signal for Duncan to remove the tunic. It too disappeared and she kissed him before slipping naked into his bed. She watched with interest as he disrobed, transforming himself from Byzantine emperor to lusty young lover. She no longer looked away when she saw his sex, hard now and risen for her. Instead she reached for his flesh and drew him quickly between her thighs. He gasped at her indelicate urgings, unspoken as she locked legs about his waist and held him impossibly tight.

"Ah, yes!"

Their lovemaking was no less consuming than it had been the first time. For Justine, it was perhaps even more exciting as the man sated his ravenous appetite, hurling her to dizzying heights when she hovered uncertainly, a comet poised to plunge. Then, while she whimpered and clung frantically to broad shoulders obliterating all from sight, she plummeted rapturously into a mysterious drift. Inside, she lost her balance, ebbing, drifting again, then shimmering like a lotus in a Turkish lagoon.

For Duncan's part, his energies were steadily decimated, exquisitely sabotaged as he lost himself in the woman. He was vanquished, subjugated, and spent as he began his own mysterious drift. Their route toward liberation was frantic and circuitous, finally coming full circle when neither could further delay the delicious inevitable. They cried each other's names as they melted together, flesh merged in a fashion both wished could last forever. At last they lay still, locked together for an undetermined length of time, and when Duncan sought to withdraw, Justine whimpered again and fought to keep him in place.

"If only!" she whispered. "If only I could keep you there. Always!"

Thrilled by the indelicate wish, Duncan was aroused anew and took her again. The second time he knew she was not quite with him and willed his lust to linger until she gasped again with the precipitous ascent and plunge. Justine was so exhausted it was with difficulty that she found her voice.

"I don't wish to shock you, *ma cheri*, but if I could die at this moment I would not hesitate."

"Nor would I," he whispered with a gentle kiss. Then, "And yet, with equal fervor I wish us freedom from this terrible prison, this jail to which your husband holds the key."

"Duncan!" They had never spoken of it, never addressed any hopes or plans for a future of more than stolen moments. "What are you saying? You know there can be no escape."

"I don't believe that," he said evenly.

"But I was born in *La Nouvelle-Orléans!*" she insisted, so unnerved that she unthinkingly lapsed into French. "Everyone knows me and knows Blancard as well. They would . . ."

"Then it's quite simple. We will leave the city."

"Impossible!"

"Nothing is impossible," he pronounced. "It's as simple as going to the levee right now and buying passage on any of a number of ships. I remember the first time I strolled the waterfront with Christophe. The destinations are endless." He kissed her again. "And so are our possibilities for a future together. Mexico. New York. Jamaica, perhaps."

But Justine heard no more, and to her own surprise, she welcomed it wholeheartedly. It was completely new, the concept of escape, a seductive addendum to those other new discoveries of choice and defiance. She was astonished that such liberation had simply never occurred to her, damned as it was by religion and doomed by an unwavering fear of her husband. Yet she embraced it as though it was an ancient desire. Perhaps, she thought, it had been within her always. Perhaps it needed only Duncan to coax it free.

"Yes!" she cried, throwing her arms around him and happily suffocating him with kisses. "Oh, yes!"

"Have you a preference?"

"Somewhere neither of us have ever been!" she cried happily, mind racing desperately. "Oh, Duncan, Duncan! Let's go! Let's go to the Caribbean, to a place where they speak neither French nor English! Let's go in the morning, on the dawn of Ash Wednesday! We'll truly make it a fresh beginning!"

"Agreed," he said, holding her so tight his touch approached pain. Justine felt nothing, only the mounting exhilaration of freedom looming no further away than an Indiaman bound for the open sea. "You must go home for the necessary traveling papers. Do I dare accompany you without Christophe?"

Justine quickly shook her head. "No."

"But the streets will be chaos," he protested. "It may take you hours to get home. Besides, don't you hear that thunder?"

"It doesn't frighten me, Duncan. And I prefer to go alone." This last was said so firmly that he did not challenge her again. "This is something I entered alone, my love. I prefer to exit the same way."

"As you wish."

Her mind raced with the technicalities of this grand escape. "Only tell me where to meet you and at what time."

"At dawn. On the levee where I gave you the poem that long-ago day."

"I will be there without fail, beloved."

Blancard drained his glass and extended it to Chaillot for refilling. "*Encore, ma petit!*" he grunted. He tossed down the second shot and repeated the gesture. "*Encore!*"

The whiskey blossoms on his face, lately rawer and more abundant than ever, repulsed her deeply, as did the stench of whiskey. Even in formal dress his dishevelment was appalling. Blancard had never come to her unshaven or with a stained shirt bosom as he had now, and Chaillot could only speculate at the abuse heaped upon poor Figaro when he urged his master to bathe. She dared not suggest anything was wrong, and instead smiled gamely and wondered how long this new drinking bout would last. She well knew Blancard's enormous capacity for liquor, as she knew his mood might turn suddenly ugly if his alcoholic gluttony went uncurbed. She was immediately on the alert when he set aside the empty glass and patted his lap.

"Here," he said with a lopsided smile. "Come sit here and let me contemplate your beauty. Let me assure myself yet again that there are none to compare with you in all the city."

"You praise me too much, Michie Hilaire," Chaillot protested softly.

Her sensation of dread deepened as she slipped onto his lap. Per Blancard's instructions, she was naked beneath the filmy negligee, always an invitation to trouble. She knew what was coming, fear confirmed as he fumbled roughly with the bows of her white *peignoir* and, when they would not yield, tore them apart. Her full breasts swung free, immediate targets for his ravenous mouth.

"Michie, please," she said, repulsed by such coarseness. "Might we not retire to the boudoir and . . . ?"

"Make love?" he said, humiliating her with laughter. "In spite of your ample charms, mademoiselle, I assure you the boudoir is of no interest to me just now. *Mais non, mon petite.* We're going to a very small, very exclusive supper where you are going to help me win a considerable amount of money."

"I don't understand."

He pushed her away so abruptly she very nearly fell to the floor. "You're not supposed to understand!" he snapped. He reached for the leaden decanter and sloshed half a glass full. "You people are not supposed to understand or think or do anything other than what you're told."

The insult stung, as he intended. "We people, michie?" Chaillot coaxed gingerly, knowing she was sailing into dangerous waters. "What do you mean?"

"Get dressed," he said, ignoring her as he glanced at his watch. "We are due at Monsieur Meilleure's home within the hour. And tell Iris to take special care with your toilette. The blue gown will do, the one you wore to the *Salle d'Orléans* last week. Then as now, you must look especially ravishing."

"I always try to make you proud," she said, desperate to please him. The storm clouds were deepening and she frantically sought safe harbor. She gave the bell pull a quick tug and moved toward the bedroom. "*N'est ce-pas?*"

"I suppose. But tonight your appearance is worth a great deal of money to me."

"Oh?" she smiled, uneasily.

"Tonight will be the costliest display of colored flesh in the city's history. Not even under the great dome at the St. Louis Hotel has there ever been anything to compare with this."

Chaillot's blood turned cold, an instinctual reaction that surged painfully as Blancard swaggered after her. He made no secret of his perverse desire to watch her dress and had even destroyed the exquisitely painted screen she sought for modesty. It had not gone unnoticed by Chaillot that, little by little, the man found more ways to demean her, was ever exploring new avenues of humiliation, especially of a sexual nature. She was not even permitted to turn her back as she dressed, a bitter lesson paid for with a night of rough ravishment. She was shamed anew when Iris removed the *peignoir* and she stood as naked as any wretched slave on the auction block.

"Wait!" he grunted as Iris approached with the silk undergarments Blancard had ordered from Paris. "Let me look again." Chaillot's mortification was complete when the man walked around her, inspecting the curve of calf, the soft swell of belly, and especially the abundance of bosom.

"Ah, yes!" he crowed. "*This* is what will win me the ten thousand dollars! When those poor bastards see what I have stashed in the Rue Rampart, they will have no choice but to reach deep into their pockets!"

It was too much! "What on earth are you talking about?" Chaillot hissed.

"How dare you!" he snarled.

Without thinking, Chaillot had attempted to cover her nakedness, but the arm across her breasts was slapped away, as was the hand between her thighs. Iris wisely retreated to a far corner of the room, fearing she might be next. She had long heard the painful whimpering emanating from this bedroom and, like Catin the cook, swallowed her suspicions.

"Such actions displease me, Chaillot," he growled, circling her like a predator. "I don't know whether I am a poor teacher or you are a bad student, but one thing is certain. You had best be comfortable with your nakedness because tonight *I will not be the only one admiring it!*"

Chaillot screamed as the final piece of the heinous puzzle fell into place.

"No, Michie Hilaire!" she cried, voice trembling uncontrollably. "You dare not ask me to . . ."

"I ask nothing," he reprimanded sharply. "*I order you!* Yes, that's right. I *order* you to take your place along with the girls belonging to Henri Meilleure, Dominique Duplessy, Albert Barbé, and Alexis Chalaron. We will settle once and for all which girl, in her natural state, is the most beautiful."

The protest died in Chaillot's throat. What the man demanded was unconscionable, a perversity beyond comprehension. She had been bred with the sensibilities of the most delicate Creole belle, and yet this man, this animal, proposed to strip her naked before a crowd of strangers so he might win a wager. Fury stirred inside Chaillot, a rage that steadily eroded her beauty into something supremely hideous. She was physically changing, and when the terrified Iris saw the metamorphosis she hastily fled. Blancard was unseeing, catapulted into darker oblivion by the potent power of whiskey and female nakedness. He drank deep as he paced the little room.

"How peculiar life is," he mused, happily wallowing in the victory not yet won. "All this time I saw you as nothing more than a frivolous extravagance, but now it seems that I am to get a substantial return on my investment!"

Chaillot edged backward until she felt the cold of a marble-topped table against her bare derriere. Her fingers closed around the heavy crystal decanter where Blancard had left it and with all her might she swung it into the air and aimed it for the back of Blancard's head. It tore through the air with a lethal silence and would have ripped open his skull had he not caught her ferocious reflection in the dressing table mirror. For someone half drunk, he ducked and spun with amazing dexterity. The decanter crashed loudly against the far wall, hurled with an intensity Blancard begrudgingly admired. He had no doubt she would have killed him.

Chaillot winced with pain as Blancard seized her wrist, twisting until she crumpled, naked and helpless, to the floor. Trapped, she found herself staring at the toes of his highly varnished boots, almost hypnotized by their sheen until his frozen, murderous tones menaced her back to reality.

"A question for you, my darling Chaillot," he grunted, tightening his grip and relishing the anguish escaping her lips. "Do you know the penalty for raising a hand against a white man?" Silence. "*Answer me!*"

Very low, quavering. "Yes."

"Do you know that I can send you to the calaboose and have your clothes whipped from your flesh?"

Softer still. "Yes."

"Good. Now then. One way or the other your naked flesh is to be bared tonight. The choice, dear one, is yours!" Chaillot could not find her voice, earning her another painful wrench on the wrist. The liquor had infused him with a ferocious strength Chaillot was helpless to resist. "Answer me!" he boomed.

Chaillot's breath caught in her throat. She coughed hard and shook her head, hair tumbling free of the chignon Iris had fashioned earlier. It cascaded down her back, giving Blancard something else to seize as he released her wrist. Fingers snarled in Chaillot's long hair, he yanked her head back hard, turning her face to his. Chaillot was not a deeply religious woman, but was convent-educated and knew pure evil when she saw it. At that moment, in the contorted, bloated features of the man she had chosen as her lover, Chaillot Baptiste saw the face of Satan himself. Oddly, she did not cower but was instead imbued with a mysterious strength that buoyed her voice through the malignant cloud threatening to choke her.

"Neither!" she spat. "Not now! Not ever!"

Blancard's face ran dark with craven fury, besotted mind struggling to comprehend Chaillot's response. *Impossible!* he thought. It was impossible and unthinkable that the bitch would resist him in any way, much less speak to him with such defiance. She would be punished, of course. But it was a special night indeed. She must be handled carefully, dealt an unusual punishment for her insubordination.

"Don't!"

When he yanked her up by her hair, the pain was such that Chaillot could not stifle the scream. She was half-pushed, half-dragged to the bed where she was hurled against the towering headboard. The impact against her skull very nearly knocked her unconscious, but Blancard knew exactly what he was doing. He had been working his heinous magic for too many years to calculate anything less than perfect evil. No, he thought. She must be aware of every phase of the punishment I have planned. She must remember everything, draw upon that memory if she ever again thinks to defy me. Blancard considered the evil extremes, phallus swelling hard and fast as he settled upon a choice.

This time she will be marked!

Blancard leaned into her face, breath hot and rancid with whiskey. His wet lips were contorted into a maleficent smile, drool spinning onto her creamy breasts as he growled a warning that would have sent lesser women spiraling into a swoon.

"I had hoped tonight would be memorable, my dear Chaillot. And so it shall be, but not for the reasons I thought."

Chaillot was silent, pale nakedness crushed against the mahogany headboard like a bruised magnolia. There was, she knew now, no retreat, no escape from his madness, and she trembled in the face of pure horror.

"Until now, I have never left you with any physical signs to remind you of disobedience or insolence, but that is about to change. You have pushed me too far and must be punished, must be made to remember who and what you are." He sneered, smacking his lips, a malevolent monster savoring raw meat. Chaillot's gorge rose. "It's a peculiar thing about scars, Chaillot. They have the ability to remind us of things whether we want to be reminded or not. They sing a strange song about our past, as inescapable as the sirens luring sailors to death on the rocks. They refuse to be ignored, just as *I* refuse to be ignored!"

White hot pain shot through Chaillot's breast as he seized a nipple and cruelly twisted.

"Do you understand me, girl?"

Chaillot had no idea where the response came from. The words materialized and issued forth almost before she realized it. "Is it just me, Hilaire?" she asked with maddening calm. "Or is it all women you hate?"

"Wha . . . what?" She had caught him off guard and for a moment he lost control of his purpose. He retreated, studying her as if she were a stranger. He hadn't heard correctly. Or had he? "What did you say?"

"I've met your wife," she continued. "Madame Blancard told me of the pain you've inflicted upon her. She told me she knows what it's like to be held in thrall. No! Worse than that! She said what you did was worse than beating a slave, that there's at least a shred of dignity about a man disciplining his disobedient chattel."

Thunder grew deep inside Blancard's head, a painful, numbing rumble that swelled until it threatened to explode. He was not hearing this! He was not! His precious, adored Justine and this Negro slut together? He was not hearing this!

"You're lying!"

"I met her at Toinette Clovis' shop," Chaillot said, not knowing where the dangerous confession might lead. "She told me everything!"

"She told you nothing!"

"Everything!"

"Nothing!"

His hand shot out, open palm catching Chaillot's cheek with such force her head slammed against the headboard. She had barely recovered when a second blow followed, striking from the other side like the winds of a hurricane. It spun her head in the opposite direction and wrenched her neck with agonizing pain.

"I will hear no more!" he thundered. "How dare you speak my dear wife's name?"

Chaillot's voice rose slowly, quavering with pure, sweet defiance. She knew she was heaving fuel onto the flames of his perverse hatred, but could not stop. It had gone too far. Her tolerance had reached its *apogée* and now returned to earth, like a wayward far-flung moon spinning home. Her loathing was nearly palpable and left a metallic bitterness in her mouth. Her breath was foul with it.

"I am not your property, monsieur, not your slave. Your plaything perhaps, but no more. I am a free woman and I will not be treated like an animal."

"Indeed!" Blancard roared, outrage tempered by laughter as he considered her pathetic pronouncement. This pitiful creature cowering before him was a comic figure indeed. How could he ever have thought she could win a fortune for him? Why, if his friends ever saw this naked *thing* they would respond not with money but cackles of ridicule. He laughed and leaned closer, voice dripping with derision as he gleefully prepared to deliver the ultimate indignity.

"What you *are*, Chaillot . . ."

"*Don't!*"

". . . is a nigger whore!"

"No! *No!*"

"Nothing more, nothing less!"

Calculated and vile, as Blancard knew it would be, the pronouncement was far more painful than any blow to her bare flesh. It stung because it was an ancient reality, as proven and irreversible as the eternal flow of the great river rushing around them, binding black and white together, paternally benevolent one moment, cruel and destructive the next. As Chaillot struggled to comprehend, her mother's old warning shimmered and hardened in the poisoned air, so hurtful it wrenched from her a primordial cry as timeless as Africa itself.

". . . nothing more than prostitutes," Colette had cautioned, "beautiful, skillfully bred animals, niggers masquerading behind white masks."

"No!" she screamed, again and again. "No!"

Blancard seized her by the throat, arousal surging anew when he saw the bruises already blossoming on her face. "As a nigger, you will do the bidding of your white master."

Drawing from a reserve of strength unknown to her until now, Chaillot spoke with a dignity so pure, so fine, that Blancard almost withdrew.

"I would," she said clearly, "rather die!"

Her proud declaration vanquished all hope of escape and earned her a jaw-shattering blow to the chin. White pain exploded behind her eyes, plunging her into an abyss of black oblivion. She heard Blancard's last words as though from a great distance, from another room perhaps, or another world.

"You just may get your wish, wretched wench!"

PART FIVE

Ash Wednesday

The stars, / That nature hung in heaven, and filled their lamps /
With everlasting oil, to give due light /
To the misled and lonely traveller.

—John Milton, *Comus*

And therefore I have sailed the seas and come
to the holy city of Byzantium.

—W. B. Yeats, *The Scholars*

CHAPTER 20

Chaillot felt as though her head was crushed beneath heavy weights, pulsing painfully as she lingered in that hazy world of half-sleep, half-wakening. She wondered if she was dreaming the bells. After Blancard struck her, the bells seemed as remote and insubstantial as his threats, but as she lay still and listened, words materialized, sentences were formed. Both were buoyed to her on rushes of air stirred by the incessant bells.

"Bells," she breathed, emerging slowly and with difficulty from unconsciousness. Although her mind was fogged, her soul still possessed by terror, Chaillot knew instinctively not to move, frozen in the fetal position where he had left her. "Bells and voices."

Wildly fought by fevered revelers, Ash Wednesday had triumphed at last, arrival proclaimed by the pealing, clanging bells of the city's churches. In a desperate effort to encourage reformation and curb crime, special services were being held everywhere. No bells were more dolefully insistent than those of St. Louis Cathedral, whose deep tolling stirred the breasts of all but the most heathen. Its great doors were flung wide to splay an inviting path of golden lanternshine into the midnight darkness of Jackson Square. It was quickly filled as the faithful thronged, costumed and masked, drunk and sober, all seeking to proclaim penitence through foreheads smeared with ashes.

Occasionally the bells were smothered by bold thunderclaps as a storm swept over the delta, deafening crashes accompanied by a constant dance of light over the Gulf of Mexico. Chilled winds lashed the crowded square, but the penitent would not be disinterred, steeling themselves against the inevitable rains, praying they would be provided sanctuary before the storm crashed upon them all.

"Bells and thunder," Chaillot whispered. "And voices."

It took her a few groggy moments to recognize Blancard's voice, longer to identify an unfamiliar second party. Marie Tonton! What on earth was she doing there and why was Blancard's voice growing increasingly heated? With the door to the bedroom ajar, it was impossible not to eavesdrop.

"I found them behind the portrait of her mother," Marie Tonton explained. "I didn't know what they were, but since they were hidden I knew you would want to see them."

Chaillot heard a fluttering of paper followed by the crash of a fist against a tabletop. "Damn her!" he shouted. "What unspeakable betrayal!"

"Did I do right, Michie Hilaire?" the slave pressed gently.

Distracted, Blancard spoke in the tone of someone only half listening to a boring story. "What? Oh, yes. Yes, Marie Tonton. In fact, this is the best you've ever done for me."

"Is it good enough for you to give me what you've promised all these years I been spying for you?"

"Yes, I suppose it is," he muttered. A long pause. "Since I won't be needing you after tonight, I'll draw up your papers tomorrow. You'll soon be a free woman, Marie Tonton."

Chaillot cringed as she heard the slave's squeal of joy. Freedom, was it? What on earth could that thoroughly disagreeable woman have done to earn such a prize? No doubt it was something affecting Justine. This was far from the first time Marie Tonton had rushed here to tattle on her sweet mistress, but as Chaillot listened closely, she realized it would be the last.

"For now you'd best go to the cathedral and thank God for your good fortune. But first, a final order. Get Figaro and the rest of the servants and take them with you. Services will no doubt run quite late tonight, and I want you to stay until the sacristan puts out the lights. I will be home within the hour and I want no one in the house when I arrive. And if your mistress is there, say only that you are going to tonight's special mass. Not another word to her. Do you understand me, Marie Tonton?" Blancard's tone was low, burdened by a hatred and rage that penetrated the walls and turned Chaillot's skin to gooseflesh. She retreated deeper beneath the covers.

"Oh, yes, michie!"

Marie Tonton fairly sang the words before rushing into the approaching storm, eager to get home and flaunt her news before the less fortunate slaves. Blancard only half heard the sound of Iris closing the door behind the woman, shutting out the howling winds. He had one thought only as he paced the room, trying to sort through the anger threatening to consume him. For the first time in his life, he actually wished he had not drunk so much, wished he had a perfectly clear head for what he must do next. What an eventful night it was turning out to be. My God, but women were a deceitful, endlessly troublesome lot!

Damn them all!

"Iris!" he barked. "Bring me coffee. And hurry!"

Iris had been so frightened by the muffled screams from the bedroom that she very nearly followed Marie Tonton into the storm. She had heard strange noises before, but nothing like this, and it was certainly strange for Missie Chaillot not to request her for such a long period of time. Iris knew something was wrong, but she was one of those poor black souls powerless to do anything about it. In the face of sure calamity, all she could do was fetch coffee for the white man!

While she listened to Blancard's rhythmic pacing, Chaillot allowed herself a little stretch. It was painful, but she realized no bones were broken. She had passed out early on, but not without faintly realizing Blancard was raining blows upon her with calculated fury. The deep ache in her most private place assured Chaillot she had been violently ravished, but she was otherwise intact. The worst seemed to be her left eye, swollen nearly shut and excruciatingly tender to the touch. She whimpered and tried not to think how frightening the injury must look. A sudden pain in her mouth alerted her to more damage, but she didn't want to consider what madness had caused her to bite her own tongue.

Chaillot didn't know how long she lay there, listening to the thud of Blancard's boots on the floor and the clink of coffee cup against saucer. Like the unceasing bells, his sounds were occasionally drowned by the crash of thunder and the scream of wind rattling the shutters. But one thing he said emerged with terrifying clarity, only because it was repeated like a murderous mantra.

"She will pay for this. She will pay with her life. She will pay for this. She will pay with her life."

Chaillot's soul trembled as the words assaulted her over and over. She was powerless even to scream, drawing herself into an even tighter ball and shivering beneath the covers as the storm moved full upon them. That was how Blancard found her when he returned and took her into his arms, quivering, shivering, a mass of whimpering madness. At his touch, Chaillot choked back bitter vomit.

"You've had a bad dream, *mon petite chou,*" he crooned gently, "but now it's over. All over. You know I would never do anything to hurt you, don't you, my angel?" He expected no answer and got none as he stroked Chaillot's tangled hair and made a feeble effort at unsnarling it. "Of course you do."

For Chaillot, time again lapsed and shimmered into unreality as the monster cradled her and promised her the world. He would be back, he said, after spending some time at home. How much time? Oh, he didn't know just now but Chaillot need not worry herself over that. And didn't she realize he was only teasing about that wager? He could never share her beauty with anyone. Never! Why, the notion was preposterous!

As for what had happened between them, well, it would be their little secret. She would have to stay at home for a few days until her eye healed, but he'd bring her something pretty to make the hurt go away. What about some more sapphires? Yes, that was it. Sapphires had always been her favorites, *n'est-ce pas?*

"Always remember I love you," Blancard whispered, brushing her bruised flesh with his lips. "And remember something else. Are you listening, dearest Chaillot?"

She nodded, too weak to speak. The dull pain in her body paled against the sharp fear penetrating her heart when she heard his parting words.

"If you ever tell anyone about tonight, I will kill you."

After a muddled eternity, Blancard finally released her and left the room. Again Chaillot froze, temples pounding as she waited for the sounds signaling his departure. Although she was at the rear of the house, fear made her hearing acute and her heart leapt when she heard the front door open to admit the roar of the storm. The moment it closed, she found the courage to sit up and heard Iris' approaching footsteps. The poor girl screamed when she saw her crumpled, wild-haired mistress.

"*Mon Dieu,* Missie!" she cried. "What has Michie Hilaire done to you?"

"What he's wanted to do all along, I suspect," Chaillot said weakly. "Bring me some brandy, Iris."

"Don't you want a doctor?"

"No!" she cried. "Just now I need something to numb the pain. Hurry, girl. We haven't much time before you have to dress me."

"Dress you?" Iris was incredulous. "Where you going?"

"I said bring me brandy, girl. Now move!"

Left alone, Chaillot crept from the bed and struggled to the dressing table where she forced herself to stare into the mirror.

"Dear God!" she muttered. "No wonder the girl screamed! If I had enough strength left, I would do the same."

She turned up the gaslight and leaned closer to the mirror, utterly horrified by her reflection. What looked back was not the beauteous Chaillot Baptiste but a battered stranger. Her left eye was a slit in a mound of puffy, discolored flesh, and in the center of her forehead was a streak of dried blood where Blancard's ring had nicked the flesh. She reached for a towel, thought better of it and stepped back.

"No," she seethed. "I want her to see me as he left me. I want *maman* to know the truth about Hilaire Blancard!" Then, "Iris! Damn your hide! Where is that brandy?"

Although several shots of Blancard's finest cognac eased the torment in her head, Chaillot's entire body ached as Iris dressed her. She endured the pain just long enough to don the simplest of frocks and turned her back so Iris could drape a black cape over her shoulders. She turned up the hood and clutched it at her chin, concealing as much of her face as possible.

"You can't go into that storm, Missie!" Iris pleaded, close to tears as a thunderclap rattled the windows and rocked the house to its very foundations. She loved her pretty young mistress and was genuinely concerned for her well-being.

"I have no choice," Chaillot said. "You saw what he did to me, Iris. When he comes back, he might kill me."

"But where will you go?"

"It's best I not tell you. He'll ask you, of course, and I don't want you to know."

"I'm afraid, Missie!" the girl wailed. "Catin is afraid too!"

"How thoughtless of me!" Chaillot cried. "You'll both come with me. That's even better. Let him come home to an empty house. Hurry, Iris! Put out the fires and we'll go now. We'll go to *maman!*"

As midnight settled in, the winter storm's full fury slammed into the city. The streets filled rapidly with water, turning the rain-glossed banquettes into islands slick with muddy bootprints. Glutted gutters erupted from the galleries and balconies overhead, unleashing streams of water quickly shredded by the screaming wind. Chaillot and the two Negro girls clung desperately to each other as they struggled the short distance to the house in the Rue St. Louis, and when Colette herself answered the door, she confronted a pathetically bedraggled trio.

"If you're looking for the Ragpicker's Ball," she joked, "I'm afraid carnival is over."

Chaillot pushed the other girls ahead of her and swung the door shut against the howling winds. "Go to the kitchen and get dry," she grunted, tongue thick with brandy.

"Chaillot, what . . . ?" began Colette.

Chaillot said nothing as she stepped into the light and pushed back the hood of her cloak. Colette gasped as the lampglow fell on her daughter's discolored cheeks, throwing a sharp shadow over the eye now swollen shut. She took a step closer, inspecting Chaillot's face as though it were a grotesque Mardi Gras mask. When she saw it was not, her scream brought Gautier running.

"*Mon Dieu!*" he cried. "What happened to you?"

"Not *what*," she amended tiredly. "*Who.*"

"Then in the name of God, who?"

A shudder coursed through Chaillot's body, a vile trembling that reminded the man of a serpent coiling beneath the long cape. Gautier actually backed away as she spat the name, expelling it like a fatal disease her body wished to shed.

"Hilaire Blancard."

"*Mais non!*" cried Colette. "This cannot be!" She rushed to embrace her daughter but Chaillot quickly waved her away.

"Don't touch me, *maman*. There is not a place on my body that does not ache."

"A doctor!" Gautier said. "I'll go for a doctor!"

"You'll find no one, dear Marius," Chaillot insisted. "Not now. Not while carnival still grips the city. But no matter. I want no doctor. All I seek is a warm spot by the fire and a glass of cognac."

Instead of reminding her daughter she was not accustomed to strong drink, Colette hurried after the brandy while Chaillot made her way slowly toward the fireplace. Gautier longed to embrace her, to hold her as he had so often when she was a child, to pet her and tell her everything would be all right, but he was afraid to touch her lest he cause further pain. It seemed so long ago now, those golden days of innocence. Its fleeting fragility was driven home by the sight of this pitiful creature easing herself painfully onto the settee. I can no longer protect her, Gautier thought sadly, feeling as though his heart would break. This child that Simon and I so wished was our own has been hurt, and I can do nothing but stand helplessly aside and feel her pain. How I wish I could take that pain upon myself!

"Dear God!"

Colette had returned with the brandy and took her place beside Gautier. In the bright glow of the fire, they saw how badly hurt Chaillot really was. Colette too ached for the girl, agony fueled by hatred for Blancard and bitter memories of those terrible years with Bernard

Lestain. She knew only too well the pain her daughter felt, and she understood why Chaillot had lied when she had questioned her about Blancard's treatment.

Some things a woman cannot admit even to her mother, she thought grimly. Especially when she has not admitted them to herself.

"How long has this been going on?" Colette asked gently.

Chaillot regretted taking a deep breath when it garnered a new ache in her ribs. The confession was equally painful, albeit in a different way. "About a month ago, after Marius and I went to the lake. Blancard was furious when Monsieur Meilleure told him he'd seen us together."

"He beat you for that innocent outing?" Gautier asked through clenched teeth.

"He didn't beat me," Chaillot said. "Not exactly."

"What then?" Colette pressed.

Chaillot sipped more brandy, hungrier than ever for the numbness that deepened with each swallow. How like men to keep such a wonderful secret to themselves! She was desperate for a deep breath but feared more pain in her ribs. Instead she simply moaned the truth. "He handcuffed me."

Colette and Gautier together. "He *what?*"

"He actually presented them to me wrapped as an expensive gift." Chaillot grimaced. "And then . . ." She paused awkwardly, unable to face the others when her face blazed from the terrible memory. "After . . . afterward, he gave me a diamond and sapphire necklace, as though that justified his perverse behavior." She sipped again. "But what I most remember was the warning he gave me."

"Warning?" asked Colette.

"He said if I ever tried to get away from him that he and his men would hunt me down. To the ends of the earth if necessary." Another sip. The brandy was making her drowsy at last. "Tonight he made an even worse threat."

"What could be worse than that?" asked Colette.

"He said if I told anyone what happened, he would kill me." She laughed, a bitter sound that chilled the room. "Then he said I only had a bad dream and that I must always remember that he loved me."

"The man is insane," Gautier said.

"That much is evident," added Chaillot.

Colette said nothing. She went to a window and peered into the dark, sheeting rain. She felt the cold driving itself against the glass and penetrating her soul. She blinked away tears forming in the corners of her eyes and spoke from the heart.

"I've known all along, haven't I, Marius?"

"Don't do this to yourself, Colette," he warned. "It's not fair."

"Fair or not fair, it's the truth," Colette lamented. "Did I or did I not tell you that Chaillot was lying about Blancard? Answer me, Marius!"

"You did," he conceded after a painful pause.

"And did I not also say there was something terrible between my daughter and that monster?"

"You did," he echoed.

Colette looked hard at Chaillot. Like Gautier she was grieving for something forever lost. "This arrangement with Blancard, Chaillot. It was wrong and of my making. I should have known all along . . ."

"*Non!*" Chaillot fairly screamed the word, silencing her mother and startling the man. She looked at them, face pleading, voice plaintive but steady in its conviction. "There will be no more blame, no more laying of guilt. Nor will we speak again of *plaçage* after tonight. I was wrong to despise you for taking me to the *Salle d'Orléans, maman.* I told myself the choice was yours, but that is not so. Marius helped me understand the truth that day at the lake." She held out her hands. "Take them, *maman.* They are the only part of me I can bear to be touched."

"Oh, my poor darling!" Colette cried. "My poor Chaillot!" She dropped to her knees and pressed Chaillot's hands against her cheeks. Chaillot had never loved so much as that moment when her hands grew wet from her mother's tears. "What have I done?"

"You have done what any other loving mother would have done," Chaillot assured her gently. "You explained the lot of the *sang-melées* quite well and I understood the path I chose. If there was bitterness, *maman,* it was not because of you. It was because of my lot. It was myself I hated, not you."

"But why did you hate yourself?" Colette asked softly, looking up at last. "You had everything."

"Everything and nothing," Chaillot said.

"What do you mean?" asked Gautier.

"I was so close to being white that I could taste it," Chaillot explained. "Yet because of *plaçage* it remained something forever out of reach." Another sad laugh. "I was like poor little Combas. Do you remember her, Marius? My pretend playmate?" He nodded as did Colette. "No one ever knew that I could change her color. Some days she was black, others white. Some days I was black, others white. My favorite game was pretending I was a grand Creole lady and she was my black slave. How I hated her then!"

"Chaillot, don't . . ." Colette pleaded.

"But none of it matters anymore. As long as I remain here, I will always be what Blancard called me tonight. Would you like to know what that was, *maman?*"

"Oh, please, *ma bébé*. Don't do this to yourself."

"Oh, but I must!" Chaillot insisted, face twisted with a potent pride. "I must not only say the words, I must commit them to memory. I must conjure them every morning when I arise and again when I go to sleep. They must be with me always, my motto for what I am."

"Chaillot!" Gautier groaned. "For the love of God, don't!"

"A nigger whore!" Chaillot screamed. "Do you hear me, *maman? A nigger whore!*"

Colette whimpered while Gautier turned away, unable to face the loathsome epithet. Even though it was not he who had spoken it, he suffered the collective guilt of all whites who felt compassion for the plight of the *gens de coleur libre*. Those people might be educated, refined, cultured, and rich, but in Louisiana they could never earn the dignity or legal rights of the lowliest stevedore from the Irish Channel. Their fine and deserved pride could be lacerated by that single, hideous word Chaillot now hurled with a heat stinging Gautier like fire.

"How strange that the best advice I have ever been given should come from that monster," she continued finally. "He's absolutely right, you know. As long as I remain in *La Nouvelle-Orléans*, that is all I will be, but if I were in New York . . . oh, don't look at me that way, *maman*. I've spoken of this before, but as you can plainly see I now have no choice. And say nothing to me of seeking ways to extricate myself from this arrangement. We all know the laws. It would be difficult enough if I had the gentlest protector in the world. With a man like Blancard it will be fatal. No, *maman*. I have no choice but flight, and the sooner the better."

Colette's eyes pleaded with Gautier. "Talk to her, Marius. Tell her why she must stay here with us. Tell her she would only be fooling herself if she attempted to be something she is not."

"She is what she thinks she is," Gautier said evenly. "I believe in taking any and all steps necessary to survive in a world where injustice dictates you be punished for something not of your choice. She did not ask to be born a *sang-melée* any more than I asked for my strange lot in life." He spoke ferociously while something dark rose on his pale face and retreated. "We are outcasts, Chaillot and I, and if we do not find this world to our liking, then we are obliged to move on."

Colette listened with compassion but she still fought for his support. This was her only child who spoke of leaving, and she could not bear the loss. It had been little over three years since the death of her beloved Narcisse and she was not yet prepared for another great loss. When she looked in their daughter's sapphirine eyes, she could see dear Narcisse, and as long as she had that escape she could endure the near tangible melancholy threatening to suffocate her. No, she thought. I cannot bear to let Chaillot leave!

"But dear Marius!" she cried desperately. "We cannot let her go!" Colette protested wildly, irrationally. Her arguments were sadly vacuous to the others and, when she forced herself to listen, they were transparent to her as well. Still she fought on. "Surely you don't agree with this madness!"

"I agree with anything that will free our beloved Chaillot from such torment. I love you deeply, Colette, but I must speak from the heart. I believe Chaillot deserves this chance and I will do everything in my power to secure it for her."

"You would help her go to New York?"

"I would indeed." His smile warmed Chaillot who realized then how much she had always loved him. "I will take her myself if necessary."

"But . . ."

"You know what her fate will be if she stays with that devil Blancard. And you've heard his threats. One look at Chaillot's swollen eye should tell you he will no doubt carry them out."

Colette's face streamed tears. In her soul she conceded they were right. She knew flight was Chaillot's only hope for survival, just as she knew it was her duty to help her only child in this most terrifying moment of need. She shook her head with an unbearable sadness, feeling suddenly much older than her years.

"Forgive such selfishness, my darling Chaillot. I will not stand in your way."

"Oh, *maman!*"

Heedless of the pain, Chaillot threw her arms around her mother and crushed their cheeks together. They held each other a long time while Gautier shared their tears. Their grief, elation, compassion, and love all were his as well. These women were his family. Still, he felt they needed to be alone and slipped quietly from the room. They were not aware of his departure for some time, and though they loved him they were grateful for his discreet consideration.

Colette poured herself a whiskey and nestled beside Chaillot on the settee. Obviously the brandy had worked its numbing charms on Chaillot because she did not recoil in pain when her mother draped a protective arm around her. Her tongue was growing thicker as she and Colette planned her escape.

"Where is Blancard now?" Colette asked.

"At home I suppose," Chaillot said, wiping her nose with her mother's handkerchief. "At least that's where he said he was going when he . . . oh, no! *Mon Dieu!* How could I forget?!"

"What is it, dearest?" asked Colette.

"Madame Blancard of course!" Chaillot's eyes flashed fear. "He will kill her!"

"What are you saying?!"

Chaillot's mouth gaped in horror when she remembered what she had overheard Blancard tell Marie Tonton. She didn't know what the slave had discovered and delivered to him, but it had triggered a rage prompting him to order all the servants from the house and forbid Marie Tonton to say anything of her actions to her mistress.

"He's gone home to kill her, *maman!* I heard him say so! I thought he was talking about me, but it's not me after all! He's going to kill his wife!"

When Chaillot's voice dissolved into a frantic gasp, Colette knelt and took her hands. "Calm down and explain yourself."

Through ragged breaths, Chaillot repeated what she had heard of the interchange between Blancard and Marie Tonton. The horror was contagious as Colette listened carefully, piecing together the heinous puzzle that was Hilaire Blancard. Perhaps Madame Blancard had been a victim of his ruthless cruelty all these years. Perhaps Josette Beaulieu, as well. That last suspicion was especially terrifying because it occurred to Colette that perhaps the poor girl had not died in childbirth after all. Especially now that the evil reality of Blancard's character was emerging. Hadn't there been rumors about Josette? Colette couldn't remember. Besides, there was always talk when an arrangement fell apart, speculation that was rarely confirmed, and she could scarcely be expected to keep up with such gossip.

"And there's something else," Chaillot cried. "Something I've never told a living soul."

"Hold me tighter," Colette said. "You're trembling like a leaf."

The pain in her ribs numbed by the brandy, Chaillot took a deep breath and continued. "Do you remember the time I met Madame Blancard in *La Mode?*"

"I could never forget it," Colette answered.

"When we talked alone, she told me terrible things, and one thing in particular I will never forget as long as I live. She told me, *maman*, that she knew what it was like to be held in bondage, and from what she confessed I have no doubt that she speaks the truth."

"He beat her then?" Colette asked, seeking confirmation of what she feared all along.

"He did not actually beat her," Chaillot said, "but in that truth is the greatest lie of all."

"I don't understand."

"There are ways to damage women without actually striking them. You know that as well as I. There are fiendish ways of humiliation and abuse and debasement that involve no marking of the flesh, no use of the whip. That is where Blancard excels. *Mon Dieu, maman!* The man makes love as though he is seeking revenge!"

"*Non!*"

"*Mais oui, maman!* He marks us *within!*" she groaned, tears forming anew and streaking the bruised cheeks. She touched the swollen flesh beneath her eye. "And that is far worse than something like this."

"But I don't understand, Chaillot," Colette said as the girl's confession grew muddled with sobs. "If that's the case, why did he do this to you?"

Chaillot choked back a sob and forced herself to continue. "It was like what you told me about Monsieur Lestain, *maman*. When he forced you to do things in public."

"Dear God!"

"*C'est vrai.*"

"I don't want to know," Colette protested.

"But you must, *maman!* There must be no more lies between us. You must know everything if we are to put this terrible thing behind us and continue with our lives." Chaillot swallowed hard. The evil Blancard had proposed was ponderous enough in her head, but to be verbalized before her mother only increased the agony. "He and some other men made wagers to be settled by . . . by stripping their women naked and . . . comparing us."

"Dear God!" Colette cried again. It was all she could summon as a wave of nausea swept over her and mercifully passed.

"When I defied him, he went beserk and began beating me. I passed out . . . I don't even know everything he did. In any case, it doesn't matter now. But one more of Madame Blancard's confidences does."

"What?" Colette asked weakly, unsure how much more she could endure.

"Josette Beaulieu," Chaillot expelled in a long, tired breath.

Colette was instantly on the alert, heart pounding. "Did Blancard kill her?"

Chaillot nodded. "But again, he worked without leaving marks. The girl was apparently scared to death."

"But how could Madame Blancard know?"

"Toinette Clovis learned the truth from Marie Laveau!"

"What has that old *voudouienne* to do with all this?"

"I was too frightened to ask," Chaillot confessed. "And when Madame Blancard said no more, the matter was closed." She sobbed, losing control again. "Oh, *maman!* He will kill her. I know he will kill her. What are we to do?"

Colette's head swam hopelessly from all the madness, but one thing was certain and the reality disgusted Colette because she was so deeply compassionate. Regardless of what might transpire between Hilaire Blancard and his luckless wife, she and her daughter had no place interfering with it. The reason was simple: The Blancards were white and the Baptistes were not. It was the oldest unwritten law in Louisiana.

"Nothing, *ma chére* Chaillot," she managed at length. "We can do nothing at all."

CHAPTER 21

Constant lightning over the city rent the winter night with blinding spider webs. The storm scattered all but the most drunken revelers and even emptied Jackson Square of the Lenten faithful. Those who could not crowd into the cathedral sought refuge in nearby taverns or cowered beneath galleried banquettes offering only minimal protection from the sheeting rain. The crowded streets had miraculously emptied, and by the time Justine's hackney turned from the Rue des Ursulines into the Rue Dauphine, she had seen no one for blocks. The crescendo that was Mardi Gras had been washed away in a noisy deluge.

"It's as though God is cleansing the city of its sins," she muttered to herself.

As the hackney drew up before the Blancard home, an especially fierce lightning bolt crackled so close the hair on Justine's neck tingled. Outside the coach window, the dark was washed out by bright unnatural daylight. The horse whinnied and reared, jerking the coach away from the carriage block. The driver barely managed to control the terrified animal long enough for Justine to gather her Byzantine robes and scurry to the front door.

"*Merci, monsieur!*" she called into the driving rain.

The hackman's only response was to snap the reins and send the hapless horse tearing into the wet night. Justine didn't blame the animal for seeking some place warm and dry. She knew exactly how it felt as she entered the house and started up the stairs. She was so tired she was halfway up the stairs before she remembered she had left the front door unlocked.

"Marie Tonton! I'm home!"

Except for the crashing thunder, the house was oddly still, something Justine didn't realize until her foot triggered the telltale creak of the eleventh step. She paused, waiting until the thunder stopped, and heard a stillness so intense her ears hummed. The phenomenon was not strange in such storms, but something else was. The house was empty. She confirmed it when she called again for Marie Tonton and got no response.

"Marie Tonton!" Then, "Figaro! Agathe! Where is everyone?" The answer dawned on her as she reached the top of the stairs. "Of course. They'll be at the Ash Wednesday mass."

Justine pushed her door open. The room was dark, but enough gaslight spilled in from the hall to lead her to the lamp on the dressing table. She struck a match and lit the lamp, hand inexplicably shaking as she turned up the wick. As the light rose before the mirror, Justine jumped as her shadow suddenly scaled the wall. She had forgotten she was still dressed as the empress Theodora.

"For shame!" she chided herself, laughing softly. "Empresses are not afraid of their own shadow!"

Thoughts of Theodora spawned thoughts of her Justinian, and Justine couldn't resist a slow spin around the room. Her long robes rustled in the heavy stillness as the storm noise at last subsided, and she hummed softly to herself.

Dear Duncan, she thought. This time tomorrow night, where will we be?

As Justine continued her solitary waltz around the room, her mind raced with the incredible events of the day. She had made her very first visit to the Garden District, been warmly received by Randolph Saunders and, most exciting of all, been offered escape by Duncan. Less than two months ago, she had not even known this man who was to become her saviour, this man who had taught her the true meaning of love and stirred a passion within her she never knew existed. He knew her, it seemed, better than she knew herself.

It all seemed so unbelievable, as insubstantial as carnival itself, as unreal as the Byzantine costume swirling gracefully about her.

Justine giggled immodestly as she envisioned making love to Duncan at sea, aboard a ship taking them to a mysterious destination where gentle tradewinds whispered and summer never ended, where Blancard would never find her. The conjured image thrilled her and, suddenly weak in the knees, she ended her impromptu dance and sat at the dressing table. She turned the lamp higher still and studied herself in the mirror, toying with the angel brooch at her bosom and remembering how secure Duncan's arms had felt about her as they waltzed at the Comus Ball.

"Oh, Duncan," she sighed to the night. "When I think of these long, wasted years I could weep."

Justine unpinned the brooch and tucked it safely away. The diadem came next, set at the end of the dressing table where she carefully draped the long strands of *faux bijoux*. She removed an earring and was reaching for another when she thought she heard something. She chuckled at the cry of a wayward reveler, taking again to the streets now that the rains were ceasing.

Justine picked up a hand mirror and considered her theatrical makeup. What an extraordinary difference it made, as though she were looking at a stranger. She was not the only one captivated by her image. Ravenous eyes consumed the ersatz empress as she contemplated her reflection. Then something moved behind her, and she gasped when a second face emerged from the shadows to loom over her shoulder. It was deadly pale, unctuous with sweat, features fixed in a crooked smile.

The terrible name escaped her lips, obliterated as the mirror slipped from her hand and shattered on the floor.

"Hilaire!" Justine's hand flew to her throat, quickly followed by her heart. "You startled me! Why on earth were you lurking in the dark?"

"Watching you, of course."

"Oh?"

"You must be more careful, my sweet," he warned, emerging slowly from the shadows where he had been patiently waiting. "That broken mirror carries seven years of bad luck."

"You're sweet to worry," she smiled, noting with satisfaction and not a little surprise that he wasn't drunk. Still she was puzzled and disturbed by his presence. "Did you enjoy Fat Tuesday?"

"Not nearly as much as I plan to enjoy Ash Wednesday," he smiled.

What a strange thing to say about this grim, most serious of days, she thought. But then, why not? It was to be a time of jubilee for her as well.

"Are you going to tonight's special mass then?"

He made no reply as Justine watched his approach, his face a complete enigma. She didn't know what to think when he rested his hands lightly on her shoulders and leaned to brush her cheek with his lips. Something was wrong, terribly wrong. She was overwhelmed with a sense of painful foreboding, mind inexplicably flashing to something she had seen as a child. Strolling the wide banquettes with her mother, she saw a woman crushed by a carriage in the Rue Canal. Watching the runaway coach approach the luckless woman, Justine's heart was pierced by a sharp pain and she grew so weak in the knees she grabbed *maman*'s hand for support.

That unique pain had now returned, poisoning the room with awesome presentiment.

"I have no particular Lenten sacrifice to make," he said smoothly. "And you, my dear wife? What will you be giving up for Lent?"

"I . . . I hadn't given it much thought," she said.

"No? Do you mean to say you have anything special to relinquish, no special sin for which you must seek atonement?"

Dear God! she thought, soul shrieking silently to heaven. *He knows!*

"What a strange thing to ask," she said, flesh turning cold where Blancard's hands took a firmer grip before retreating. His touch was so provocative it lingered after it was gone, the seductive caress of pure, unadulterated evil.

"Well then. Perhaps if you have nothing to share with God, you will instead share it with me."

Justine watched in horror as he reached inside his waistcoat and retrieved two pieces of paper. He carefully unfolded them, placing them on the dressing table and awaiting her reaction, a cat toying with its prey.

"Well, Madame Blancard?"

Justine began quivering, seized by a violent shaking as fear cascaded over her like great sheets of rain. The pain in her heart intensified as she was overwhelmed by raw terror from which there was no flight. She could not even find her voice to make a plea.

She could only tremble and stare at Duncan's two poems.

"Marie Tonton has never been the world's best housekeeper," Blancard announced with a malevolent laugh, "but she uncovered this trash nonetheless. She was correct in assuming I would want to see it." When Justine remained mute, he picked up the poems and scanned. "You seem unfamiliar with these works, madam. Perhaps I should refresh your memory." The erotic passages he chose sent flames to Justine's cheeks.

" 'The sun's soul paled against the heat of her thighs . . . her breasts, bold and inviting as honeysweet melons . . . fired his loins with bittersweet, unanswerable desire.' "

The damning poems fluttered to the dressing table. For Justine, they were forever vilified by her husband's touch.

"It would seem you are quite the inspiration for this anonymous poet," he continued. "And who might the gentleman be?"

"Duncan Saunders," Justine answered in a surprisingly steady voice. No use lying, she thought. There was no end to the evil Blancard could employ to force the truth.

"He has great talent," Blancard said. "But I'm afraid his career as a poet, indeed as a human being, is about to be cut short."

Justine had expected him to expend his full wrath on her. Until now it had never occurred to her that he would go after Duncan as well.

"Once I'm finished with you, I'll pay a call on the gentleman first thing in the morning. That's why I'm taking such care to sober myself, my dear. I must be in complete control of my faculties when I meet the man beneath the Dueling Oaks."

"Hilaire, don't!" she pleaded. The room was suddenly stifling with humidity. "This business is not of his doing. The fault is mine. Punish me if you must, but leave him alone."

"A pretty picture indeed," he snarled. "The whore pleading to the cuckolded husband."

"Please don't . . ."

Blancard exploded. "Do you really dare to make me the laughing-stock of New Orleans?" He leapt like a wild animal, grabbing her shoulders again, thick breath hot against her neck. "Do you think you and this wretched poet can cuckold me without expecting to pay retribution? Answer me, bitch!"

Justine's lips trembled violently as she struggled to speak, but it was useless. She was literally frozen with fear, a paralysis that deepened as Blancard made the most macabre confession of his life. She glanced at his reflection and saw that his perpetually bloated features were hideously contorted and erupting with sweat. Something was taking over the man, crawling beneath his skin and into his brain and transforming him into an unrecognizable entity.

Justine cried out and shrank from him but there was no sanctuary as Blancard's rage blew full force, rampaging through the room. With one sweep of his hand, he cleared Justine's dressing table, shattering the army of perfume bottles and drenching the room in a chaos of different scents. The vanity itself was overturned, along with a washstand and fine silk *bergére*. He seized the cords of the portieres screening Justine's dressing room, yanking them free with a single fierce tug. He then stopped, glaring at her, fists closed so tight upon the velvet cords his knuckles were ashen.

Dear God! Justine thought. It was Paris again, their terrible honeymoon, come back to life!

The hall was her only escape from this malefic force, but her path was blocked by Blancard's bulk when he moved with surprising agility. She was now the sole target of his anger.

Blancard tore off his jacket and tossed it aside. He lunged for her, spinning her violently so he might grab the front of her glorious robes. They were rent and cast aside, leaving Justine clad only in her chemise. She threw her arms protectively across her bosom, too late to defend herself as Blancard's hand caught the side of her face and sent her reeling. She toppled backward, hurtled against the heavy mahogany footboard with such force the wind was knocked from her. She lay gasping as Blancard shredded her clothes and underclothes, stripping her naked before binding her wrists and ankles with the velvet curtain cords.

"For the love of heaven, Hilaire!" she gasped. "Don't . . ."

The words died in her throat when Blancard menaced her jaw with a fist. "Don't make me, Justine. Not yet!"

She wished she could faint, prayed that he would knock her unconscious and that she would remember nothing more of the inevitable pain to come, but Blancard had no intention of granting her such merciful reprieve. He was a man possessed, one revealing his true self for the first time in his life. For this, he wanted Justine fully cognizant, and to set his perverse stage, he threw her on the bed, propping her so she could see him clearly. She felt something hard beneath the pillows, horrified when he retrieved the malacca cane he had stashed there earlier.

"I never wanted to mark you," he began, touching the cane to her shoulder before drawing it slowly over her breasts, menacing her left nipple with a few light jabs. "I never wanted to mark Chaillot either, but like you she disobeyed me." The cane slid lower, forcing apart Justine's thighs when she made a pathetic attempt to keep them closed. "No, no, my dear. We both know how readily you can open these gates to paradise."

Dear God! she prayed.

"When I'm disobeyed, you know, someone must be punished."

The tip of the cane swept lightly through the dark down between Justine's thighs, nudging the tender flesh, and she nearly fainted when she considered the evils Blancard might work before this night of horror was played out. The possibility that he might kill her was scarcely new, but for the first time she believed it might actually happen.

"The first to disobey me were the whores," he said. "Or was it the slaves? It's been so long I can't remember, but I do remember that none of them were left without a memory of my whip or my bonds."

The cane trailed down to the tips of Justine's toes before fetching her a sharp smack against the soles of her feet. She screamed in agony, never imagining the flesh there was so sensitive.

"All was handled with great finesse, of course. Well most of it anyway. There was one girl . . . I forget her name . . . who foolishly resisted me. Fought like a tigress when I only wanted to give us both pleasure. You may have noticed a small scar at the back of my scalp, Justine. That's where she broke a bottle over my head." He frowned. "She never should have done that. It cost her dearly." He frowned, then smiled at the memory. "I always wondered if some fisherman found that pretty painted body floating downriver."

So, Justine thought as unspeakable fear stirred her bowels, the man was indeed a murderer!

Blancard laughed, a hideous sound that soured the bedroom. "I believe there was another, but I cannot be certain. You know, my memory is not what it used to be."

Justine's mind careened wildly from one thing to another, unable to focus on the hideous truth threatening her. Nothing was real, not even the pain of the bonds cutting her naked flesh. Justine remembered when she had selected those velvet cords in a Paris shop. Who could have ever imagined those exquisite gold threads would travel the seas to be damned to such inglorious ends? All of it, none of it, made sense.

She lay still, numbed.

"Then there was poor Josette," Blancard continued. Justine's ears pricked up at the mention of his dead mistress. "She defied me too, caught in an effort to rid herself of our baby. I solved both dilemmas with a gang of drunken Irishmen eager to take their pleasure with a *femme de coleur* as beautiful as she."

"Mother of God!" Justine whimpered.

Again she prayed she would faint from the horror, but something beyond her control fought to keep her alert. She watched as Blancard's left cheek began to twitch, further contorting his features. The ruddiness was draining, replaced by a gray unnatural pallor. His sweat was more profuse than ever, flaring Justine's nostrils with its deepening, fetid stench. Wave after wave of nausea swarmed over her.

"I don't know anymore if such punishment is . . . right . . . or not," he muttered slowly. "I used to think it was, but . . . now . . . I'm not so sure."

The mattress sagged deep with Blancard's weight as he sat on the edge of the bed and tugged off his boots. The pain in Justine's breast soared when he unbuttoned his waistcoat and slipped it off. The fine silk shirt and undervest came next, and Justine was appalled at the deterioration of the man's bloated, sagging physique. The combination of age and alcoholic debauchery had taken a hideous toll, leaching the man of life. Blancard's fuzzy white belly was immense, overhanging his trousers like a fleshy pillow. Even in her terror, Justine thought of Duncan's hard, flat stomach, the arrows of dark red fur directing her to forbidden places. Oh, dear God! Duncan!

Feeling her eyes on him, Blancard turned to Justine and shrugged. His voice was high, unnatural, utterly resigned. "When I am finished here tonight, I don't know what will be left. There was a time when I might have cared, but no longer. That option was stolen from me and I now surrender to something that knows no bounds." His voice quivered like a spiderweb, strained and broke. "Per . . . perhaps I should apologize, Justine. Because I don't know what I'm going to do with you."

Blancard stood and fumbled with his trouser buttons.

"I must take my obvious pleasure of course, but when that's done . . . well, there will be other, more forbidden ecstasies. Those which you have never witnessed, those for which I am celebrated." The trousers dropped and Justine recoiled from the sight of his arousal, grossly apparent even through his drawers.

"I will say only this, my sweet," he grunted, lightly brushing her cheek with his filthy fingertips. "To put things in the language of your beloved opera, what I have done to you before was merely an overture, a prelude if you will, to a crescendo unlike anything you could ever imagine." Blancard's voice blistered and cracked with hatred, poisoning the room like fever.

"I fear Ash Wednesday's coming dawn will be your last."

Justine's mind was numbed by the death sentence. The room swarmed with her mute screams as she was gagged by another velvet cord. She was swallowed by a dull roar that swelled until its slow retreat into silence was punctuated by a faint creak, one that turned Justine's flesh clammy. A froth of cold sweat erupted on her forehead, in her armpits and at the small of her back. She heard it again, the familiar creak. It was unmistakable, the sound created only by a foot on the steps just outside.

The eleventh stair!

Fumbling with the buttons of his drawers, consumed with malignant intent, Blancard, head howling with demons, heard nothing but his own ragged breathing. Justine remained frozen with fear, only vaguely hearing his last words.

"It's suddenly clear to me, *mon cher* Justine," he grunted, the guttural voice unfamiliar. "Before I am finished with you tonight, you will beg me to kill you."

The masked, hooded figure swept into the room with the speed and silence of a shadow. Blancard scarcely felt the cold metal against the base of his skull before another unfamiliar voice tipped the balance of perverse power.

"One false move, monsieur, and your brains will be all over this fine carpet."

"What . . . who . . . ?" Blancard sputtered.

"And keep silent!" Blancard's right wrist was seized and shoved high against his back. Grunts of pain were met with derisive laughter that increased when he pleaded for mercy.

"If you're after money . . . unghh!" He winced in agony as his arm was wrenched higher still.

"I told you to keep silent, you filthy bastard! For someone who has made a career of pain, you don't suffer it well. Blancard grunted but did not speak, stilled by a fear that mushroomed when the derringer was shoved harder against his neck.

"You're such a despicable sort it's quite tempting to shoot you without an explanation, but that would be much too easy. I want to be able to tell dear Chaillot how you squirmed and suffered before you drew your last breath."

Chaillot! Blancard thought. How could she be involved in this? Didn't I leave her whimpering and helpless at home? Was it possible she told someone the truth? By God, I'll kill her! When I'm finished with Justine I will damned well kill her! But first I will draw her blood. First I'll whip that white nigger skin until it's torn to shreds. Oh, Chaillot! My poor, sweet Chaillot! How could you betray the one who loves you most? You miserable bitch!

Blancard gritted his teeth, ignoring all threats as he plotted his terrible revenge. He was so far descended into his abyss of madness that he didn't realize he no longer held the reins of power. He muttered, low and incoherent, drawn sharply back to reality when a bone-jarring blow to the collarbone brought him to his knees.

"Have mercy!" he cried.

"Did you show mercy to Chaillot, you swine? Or to your wife?"

Blancard's plea brought more laughter and another blow, this to the side of his head. Justine winced when blood erupted from his ear, gushing down his neck and chest. She whimpered, stirred by unnamed emotions as she comprehended that she was about to witness the execution of her husband. The assassin studied her through his mask.

"I'd advise you to look away, madame. The terrible moment of redemption is at hand!"

Justine's voice sprang loud and clear, verging on sweetness, as though delivered by angels.

"*Mais, non, monsieur.* I am moved to see this for myself."

"So be it." Pause. The beat of three human hearts. "For Chaillot!"

Blancard opened his mouth in a final plea. Nothing emerged, only a peculiar gasp, more animal than human, as the explosion turned his head white hot. His jaw sagged unnaturally to one side, and he gaped at Justine for an agonizing moment, expression pure bewilderment as the bullet buried itself in his brain.

"For Madame Blancard!"

Justine screamed at the derringer's second report, soul seared and cleansed as a sickening thud proclaimed her emancipation. Blancard pitched violently forward and crumpled to the floor. The intruder bent over the body, washed in atonement as he watched the man's life ebb quickly away. There were no final words, only a pathetic gurgle as Blancard choked on his own blood. The stranger nodded, satisfied, before turning his attention to the terrified woman. Her eyes were riveted to the gun smoking in his hand.

"Mother of God!" she cried. "Please . . . please . . . help me!"

The man discreetly covered her nakedness while loosening her bonds. "My apologies for the indelicacy of the moment, madame."

But shame was the last thing on Justine's mind. "Do I know you, monsieur?"

"Perhaps you remember me," he said enigmatically. "Perhaps not. In any case, you are liberated at last."

He tossed aside the last cord and politely turned his back as Justine donned a dressing gown. That done she knelt beside Blancard's body where she sought more than confirmation of his death. The stranger watched, puzzled, as she touched her husband's cheek, almost tenderly, as though unable to comprehend what had happened. But he understood when he heard the final whisper.

"*C'est fini*, Hilaire," she sighed. "For both of us."

Justine closed her eyes, made the sign of the cross, and stood. She then approached the intruder, pale but without fear.

"I cannot yet comprehend what has happened here, monsieur, but I know I owe you more than thanks. I owe you my life." She studied the powerful figure, baffled as to the man's identity. "Can you not tell me who you are or how you came to be here?"

"I had planned to do my deed in disguise," he explained, "but now I see no harm in sharing my identity." He tossed back the hood and lifted his mask. The face was vaguely familiar, but it was the mass of pale curls that Justine readily identified. Creoles this blond were rare indeed.

"Monsieur . . . Gautier, is it not?"

"*C'est moi!*"

"But how . . . why . . . ?"

"Perhaps fear deafened you, madame. I acted for Chaillot Baptiste as well as yourself."

"Poor Chaillot! Is she . . . ?"

"Not dead," he said. "But that monster beat her so badly her pain is such that no one can touch her."

"Dear God!"

"He would have eventually killed her, madame," Gautier said evenly. "As he would have killed you." They stared at the body for a moment, each lost in terrible reverie. "The man had to be stopped at all costs, and clearly there was no time to invoke the code of honor."

"Clearly," Justine echoed, never once considering that she had witnessed murder. "It ended as the duel should have ended, and as far as I'm concerned . . ."

Gautier interrupted when he noticed the crimson pool oozing fast from Blancard's head. "There's no more time for talk, madame. I must get the body out of here before there's too much blood to hide."

"The body!" she cried, as though noticing it for the first time. "The body!"

"My horse is downstairs," he said quickly. "It will be easy enough for me to wrap the body in something and . . ."

"The carpet," Justine suggested coolly. "It's soaked with blood. Wrap him in the carpet and take both with you."

"An excellent idea!"

Luckily the Rue Dauphine was still deserted as Gautier and Justine made their way into the night. He was surprised at the way the woman helped in getting the bloated body downstairs and across the rear of his horse. He did not pause, swinging hurriedly into the saddle and hissing farewell.

"We shall see each other no more, Madame Blancard. As son as Chaillot heals, I will take her away from New Orleans where we can both start anew. As for you, quickly put the bedroom back in order. Rest assured foul play will be blamed when this body is discovered. After all, what's one more naked corpse thrown in the Rue Gallatin?" She nodded, stepping back as he jerked the reins and dug his knees into his horse's sides. "Hyah, Xanadu!"

As Gautier sped away with his macabre cargo, Justine recalled Christophe making an almost identical remark about the Rue Gallatin. It had been oddly prophetic.

Justine watched Gautier until he disappeared into the night, as if she needed to see Blancard's body vanish in order to close an agonizing chapter in her life. Although clad only in the thin peignoir, she was oblivious to the chill. Indeed she might not have noticed it at all if a dark figure hadn't emerged from the shadows and gently chided her.

"Best get inside before you catch cold, *maitresse.*"

Justine spun, heart leaping, to face the coachman. "Dear 'Polyte!" she cried, using her pet nickname for the old man. "You gave me a fright!"

"Don't worry, *maitresse,*" Hippolyte said gently. He opened the door and ushered his mistress into the warmth of the house. "Things are going to be different now."

There was no point in pretending, Justine thought. He knows. The question was how much.

"How long have you been standing there, 'Polyte?"

"Long enough," he said. Then, "Long enough to know one of the most evil men on God's earth got just what he deserved."

If there is anyone who had a history of Blancard's indiscretions, Justine thought, it would be this poor man who had been driving him to the city's tenderloins for years. She squeezed his arm affectionately.

"You're a fine man, Hippolyte. Fine enough to earn your freedom."

The slave's shock was almost tangible. "You wouldn't be fooling old Hippolyte, would you, *maitresse?* Michie Hilaire, he was always promising us freedom."

"I assure you I am serious, 'Polyte." She added with meaning, "Quite serious."

Tears stung the Negro's eyes when he comprehended the unthinkable. "*Merci, maitresse.* You've always been a fine lady and kind too, but I never thought the day of jubilee would come for me."

"It's come for both of us," Justine said softly, patting his wrinkled cheek. "Now off to bed. I'll be needing you to take me to the market before dawn."

Hippolyte thought it peculiar that his mistress would want to go shopping the morning after carnival, but he knew enough to hold his tongue on this most extraordinary night. "Me and the horse will be ready, *maitresse.* And if anyone asks, I'll just say I dropped Michie Hilaire off in the Rue Gallatin about an hour ago. After all, I've done it a thousand times."

"You're a good soul, 'Polyte. And wise. *Bon soir.*"

But the old man grabbed her hands and kissed them, staining them with grateful tears before walking slowly and with great dignity down the hall. Justine savored the joyous moment before hurrying back upstairs. His mood was contagious and, despite all that had happened, she actually hummed as she went to work. She purposely concentrated on transporting herself into a rarefied realm where no dangerous realities could touch her. For now, she would not—*could not*—fathom what had happened in this room. She knew only that, somehow, her husband was forever gone, and she refused to delve beyond that.

Although Justine had never so much as dusted a tabletop, she managed to straighten the room and clean up the broken perfume bottles with astonishing speed, tossing them in the trash heap before the rest of the servants returned from mass. She thought her last ordeals were past until Marie Tonton came upstairs and burst into the room just as she was getting into bed.

"Where's Michie Hilaire?" she demanded, tone more imperious than ever.

"I don't know," Justine said tiredly. How difficult it was for her to contain her rage at this awful woman who had triggered tonight's horror. "Besides, I'm sure you would know more about that than I."

"I got to see him!"

"Well, obviously he's not here. I suggest you look in that little cottage in the Rue Rampart. You're familiar with it, of course."

"He's not there!" she spat. "He said he was coming here after I gave him those papers you hid behind the pictures."

Justine shrugged, finding it remarkably easy to feign indifference. "I have no idea what you're talking about," she said, drawing comfort from the knowledge that Duncan's poems were tucked safely in her nightgown. She could feel them against her bare flesh. "And I think that *voudou* is making you crazy."

"*Voudou* got nothing to do with this!"

Justine ignored the protest and dismissed the woman. "As you well know, Marie Tonton, I have not seen my husband in days. He was not here when I arrived home an hour ago, and I know nothing of his present whereabouts. Now turn out the lights and leave me alone."

"No!" Marie Tonton shouted, thoroughly confused. She had come home certain she would find her mistress weeping behind locked doors, in a state of hysteria, the target of Blancard's rage. Instead, she had found a composed Justine and an absentee Blancard. "He promised me my freedom!"

"Then that's between the two of you," Justine said icily. Stay calm, she thought. Nothing must seem out of the ordinary. "Now for the last time, leave me alone."

Justine didn't know where she summoned such controlled coercion but she was deeply grateful when Marie Tonton obeyed. When she first saw the evil woman, she felt something unraveling inside and feared she would be unable to maintain the charade any longer. She needed a few hours alone to compose herself, to reach into that well of inner strength she knew would be replenished to overflowing the moment she saw Duncan.

"Duncan," she whispered to the dark. "Will the dawn ever come?"

The midnight thunderstorm ushered in a freshness hugging New Orleans like the Mississippi itself. Duncan drank deep from it as he paced the dark levee, mingling the river's fecund breath with his own and finding it as always a potent, mysterious restorative. It was a peculiar lull engulfing him, indeed the entire city. The insanity of Mardi Gras had finally past, all but a few diehard merrymakers gone home, the cathedral bells hushed, the great square deserted. The usually thrumming French Market was doing scant business, and even the riverfront was subdued. Entire crews were rendered comatose by the final long night of revelry, still too drunk to challenge the might of the fierce riverine arm wrapping the city.

Although New Orleans lay wholly east of the Mississippi, that grandiose curve dictated that the sun rise across the river. Duncan unhappily wondered if that black watery sweep was turning brown, if dawn was settling in without Justine. He turned around, searching the nearly deserted marketplace for a sign of her. A plangent heart pained him when he saw gold glowing on the cross atop the Cathedral's central spire. The sight inspired a hasty prayer, for strength to endure these final moments. He had no doubt that Justine would come, but the waiting! It was not to be borne as the ineluctable dawn, refulgent with rose and deep amber, sent the stars winking in retreat and moved full upon the city.

Where was she?!

Duncan heard music. With the deceptive play of wind and water, it was difficult to identify the source, but as he turned again toward the river, he saw a steamboat returning after an all-night revel. Although few of its tired passengers appreciated the effort, a band of Negro musicians played gamely on, plaintive strains deepening Duncan's anxiety. As the ship approached, he remembered the tickets in his pocket for passage on the *Troubadour*, an Indiaman steaming in two hours for the Dutch island of Saint Maarten.

Would she never come?

When Duncan thought he could endure not a single moment more, he heard the clanking harness of an approaching carriage. He didn't need to be told the occupant of the coach, pain lifting from his heart before he even saw her. If there were such things as preternatural bonds between two human beings, he and Justine haply possessed them.

As the coach secured an obscure niche in the maze of marketplace stalls, Duncan wondered why it stationed itself at such a distance. At this juncture he and Justine had nothing to hide. Indeed, they would soon be aboard the *Troubadour*, bidding farewell to the city that had brought them together yet threatened to forever tear them apart if they remained. He longed to call her name and rush to the carriage but restrained himself when old Hippolyte helped her out.

Justine was coming to him, yes, but not as they had planned. He sensed a change, as potent and irreversible as the current of the great river, and stood transfixed as the cloaked figure approached. All he could see was a pale hand clutching the folds of the hood together, obscuring her identity. She parted the hood only slightly when she passed, drawing just close enough to be heard.

"Follow me at a discreet distance," she whispered. "I risk everything by coming to you now."

"But what . . . ?"

"Do as I say!" she hissed.

Duncan was bewildered by the circuitous path Justine pursued, winding through the labyrinth of ships, cargoes, and warehouses, pausing at last in a shadowy alley raw with ripening bananas. Duncan followed, sweating terribly, apprehension high on his brow. Something was wrong, terribly wrong.

"Our time is brief, beloved," Justine said, tone desperate as she slipped into his arms. Her face, unnaturally pale in the growing dawn, alarmed him further. "Blancard is dead!" A finger against Duncan's lips delayed the inevitable avalanche of questions. "No, I did not do the deed myself, but if it had been in my power I would have acted without hesitation."

"But what . . . ?"

"He was going to kill me, Duncan. He was going to murder me in my own room and would have succeeded but for a most unexpected saviour. The particulars aren't important just now. All that matters is that I'm free, my darling. *We're free!* Free to do anything we choose!"

Duncan's mind burned for details but Justine's urgency quelled his curiosity. He remembered passage on the *Troubadour.* "What are we to do now?"

"Nothing. Wait. Pray. Hope. Oh, dear God! Help me sort my way through this! I'm so . . . !"

Duncan feared Justine had fainted as she swayed against him. He enveloped her in his cloak, wrapping her tight as if he might shut out the world. She leaned hard against his chest and drew power from his protective embrace, her mind a harpy screaming that she had no time to waste. Her recovery was swift, a woman reborn, eager to wield new-found strength. She spoke decisively.

"You will go home and pretend you know nothing. Tell no one what has happened, not your dear brother, not even Christophe. They will know in time of course. I must be home when the authorities come with the news. In the aftermath of carnival madness, who knows when they will identify the body." She grimaced. "Blancard was dumped naked into the gutters of the Rue Gallatin."

Duncan snorted. "No one could be more deserving of such an igno-minious fate."

Justine said nothing. She was too busy struggling to resurrect reality from the insanity swirling around them. "Once the matter is settled, this 'grieving widow' will leave New Orleans for an indefinite stay abroad." She tilted her head so that the hood fell away and she looked him full in the eyes. "Somewhere along the way, God willing, I will be joined by my lover."

Duncan smiled and showed her the tickets for the *Troubadour*. "It seems then that our trip is merely delayed."

"Yes," she whispered. "And for all the right reasons. Don't you see, Duncan?! It was divine providence! God has finally blessed us on this glorious morning. It's so . . . perfect!"

"Waiting for you will be the hardest thing imaginable," Duncan said. "But I do so willingly and with all my soul."

"As do I," Justine promised. "Oh, Duncan! In time we will take all the trips in the world. To Paris. Greece. Egypt. And Constantinople! How I yearn to share it with you! In spring, when peach trees bloom along the Bosphorus."

Duncan inhaled the familiar rosewater as he brushed lips against her forehead. It was a strangely chaste kiss, appropriate for the dawn of Ash Wednesday, but he drew an oddly sensual solace from her fervent vow of reunion.

"Constantinople," he whispered, heart swelling. "In the spring."

"I must go before anyone recognizes me." Justine clung tight, her trembling a nervous reminder of the importance of silence. "Say noth-ing, my darling. And pray for me!"

"I shall pray for us both!"

"*Adieu!*" And she was gone.

Duncan lingered in the alley before discreetly trailing the small hooded figure winding through the fleeing shadows of stargazers and moonrakers. She vanished at last, leaving that supernal bond to tug again at his soul, a reminder that she had taken part of him with her.

When Justine reached the carriage, that same bond clutched at her heart and turned her toward the river. She did not need to see him to know he was there but sought his image nonetheless. Ah, yes, she thought. There he was, a solitary figure on the levee, arm raised in silent farewell. His words rushed back to warm her soul, steeling her against the rough realities waiting in the Rue Dauphine.

"Constantinople. In the spring."

EPILOGUE

She slipped from bed some time after midnight, after the storm had passed and the insistent bells ceased tolling. She drew on a merino cloak, careful not to rouse the scaly creature dozing at the foot of her bed.

In the darkness of her backyard, she knelt to scoop the wet earth, sifting carefully until she found the wad of cloth. It was withdrawn, wiped free of mud, and laid reverently in her lap. She felt what was inside before she saw it. Light and insubstantial. Almost nothing.

"A good sign," she muttered, satisfied.

She unknotted the peculiar package with sure fingers, deftly unfolding the cloth to reveal fragments of a thoroughly deteriorated daguerreotype. She inspected them in the glare of full moonlight. They were scant more than wet ashes, and when she raised them toward the moon, a wayward gust caught the shreds and scattered them to oblivion.

"It's done then," said Marie Laveau, bones creaking as she rose and shuffled back to the house. "Rest in hell, Monsieur Blancard."

AFTERWORD

I owe an immeasurable debt to those who have earlier written about mid-nineteenth century New Orleans. Among those who have inspired by anecdote, innuendo, or historical fact are: Herbert Asbury, *The French Quarter*; Henry C. Castellanos, *New Orleans As It Was*; Susanne Everett, *The History of Slavery*; Mary Gehman, *The Free People of Color in New Orleans*; Ann Rice, *The Feast of All Saints*; Lyle Saxon, Edward Dreyer, and Robert Tallant, *Gumbo Ya-Ya: Folk Tales of Louisiana*; and Robert Tallant, *Voodoo In New Orleans*.

Although *Twelfth Night* is clearly a work of fiction, I have made every effort to be accurate in my depiction of the lives and times of my characters. I have taken limited liberties with street numbers and other minor details. I have chosen to call the French Quarter the *carré de la ville*, rather than the more familiar *Vieux Carré*, widely regarded as a twentieth-century term.

—Michael Llewellyn, New Orleans, 1996